Entrepreneur Adrian Turner has just invested millions of dollars in a new product — when a horrifying accident occurs during its high-profile promotion. But was it really an accident? It's up to Jaye Z. Montgomery to find out in Deborah Whittaker's *"Dead Cat Bounce"* . . .

P.I. Freddie O'Neal hasn't seen her cousin Billy in twenty-five years. When Billy asks her for a favor, she agrees to help him — and finds herself face-to-face with a killer in Catherine Dain's *"Billy the Goat"* . . .

A wedding rehearsal dinner and a gruesome murder are keeping private eye and caterer B.T. Jefferson busy. As she alternates between rolling puff pastry and questioning suspects, B.T. reveals a deadly cover-up in Ruthe Furie's *"A Matter of Taste"* . . .

In Jan Grape's *"Funny How Deceiving Looks Can Be,"* Jenny Gordon and C.J. Gunn discover that when it comes to murder, what you see isn't what you get . . .

LETHAL LADIES II

MORE MYSTERIES FROM THE
BERKLEY PUBLISHING GROUP . . .

CHINA BAYLES MYSTERIES: She left the big city to run an herb shop in Pecan Springs, Texas. But murder can happen anywhere . . . "A wonderful character!" —*Mostly Murder*

by Susan Wittig Albert

THYME OF DEATH	WITCHES' BANE
HANGMAN'S ROOT	ROSEMARY REMEMBERED
RUEFUL DEATH	LOVE LIES BLEEDING

KATE JASPER MYSTERIES: Even in sunny California, there are cold-blooded killers . . . "This series is a treasure!" —Carolyn G. Hart

by Jaqueline Girdner

ADJUSTED TO DEATH	
THE LAST RESORT	MURDER MOST MELLOW
TEA-TOTALLY DEAD	FAT-FREE AND FATAL
MOST LIKELY TO DIE	A STIFF CRITIQUE
DEATH HITS THE FAN	A CRY FOR SELF-HELP

BONNIE INDERMILL MYSTERIES: Temp work can be murder, but solving crime is a full-time job . . . "One of detective fiction's most appealing protagonists!" —*Publishers Weekly*

by Carole Berry

THE DEATH OF A DIFFICULT WOMAN	GOOD NIGHT, SWEET PRINCE
THE LETTER OF THE LAW	THE DEATH OF A DANCING FOOL
THE YEAR OF THE MONKEY	DEATH OF A DIMPLED DARLING

MARGO SIMON MYSTERIES: She's a reporter for San Diego's public radio station. But her penchant for crime solving means she has to dig up the most private of secrets . . .

by Janice Steinberg

DEATH OF A POSTMODERNIST	DEATH CROSSES THE BORDER
DEATH-FIRES DANCE	THE DEAD MAN AND THE SEA

EMMA RHODES MYSTERIES: She's a "Private Resolver," a person the rich and famous can turn to when a problem needs to be resolved quickly and quietly. All it takes is $20,000 and two weeks for Emma to prove her worth . . . "Fast . . . clever . . . charming." —*Publishers Weekly*

by Cynthia Smith

NOBLESSE OBLIGE	IMPOLITE SOCIETY
MISLEADING LADIES	

LETHAL

LADIES II

EDITED BY

CHRISTINE MATTHEWS

&

ROBERT J. RANDISI

BERKLEY PRIME CRIME, NEW YORK

LETHAL LADIES II

A Berkley Prime Crime Book / published by arrangement with
Christine Matthews and Robert J. Randisi

PRINTING HISTORY
Berkley Prime Crime edition / April 1998

The Penguin Putnam Inc. World Wide Web site address is
http://www.penguinputnam.com

ISBN: 0-425-16268-0

Berkley Prime Crime Books are published
by The Berkley Publishing Group,
a member of Penguin Putnam Inc.,
200 Madison Avenue, New York, NY 10016.
The name BERKLEY PRIME CRIME and the BERKLEY PRIME CRIME
design are trademarks belonging to Berkley Publishing Corporation.

PRINTED IN THE UNITED STATES OF AMERICA

10 9 8 7 6 5 4 3 2 1

Contents

Lethal Ladies II

(Ed. note: Part of the enjoyment for me in editing anthologies is not only reading all of the wonderful short stories, but working with equally wonderful co-editors. In the past when I edited the two *Deadly Allies* anthologies with Marilyn Wallace and Sue Dunlap, and the original *Lethal Ladies* with Barbara Collins, we combined our voices into one "editorial" voice for the introductions. Christine Matthews, however, has such a fresh, new outlook on the genre, I decided to let her speak out on her own.)

RJR

Introduction

Until six years ago I hadn't read many mysteries and certainly no private-eye fiction. For fifteen years I kept myself busy writing short stories in the horror/dark fantasy genres . . . and then I met Bob Randisi. He challenged me to create a private eye for his anthology *Deadly Allies* II. Never one to admit there is anything I cannot do, I said "yes" and then ran home to research this private-eye person. What I found out surprised as well as delighted me. I found the female investigator of the twentieth century to be complicated, because she is so very real. Somewhere inside of her is a bit of every woman I have ever known. She was not at all the contrived, artificial person I had been led to believe she was.

When Bob challenged me again by asking me to co-edit this second volume in the *Lethal Ladies* series, I accepted gladly. The opportunity would give me the chance to read and edit short stories (a great passion of mine) as well as work with some of the wonderful mystery writers I have become acquainted with over the past few years. I have to laugh when a discussion turns into a debate as to whether women writers are "hot" or will be "in" this year or the next. Good writing is what it's all about and you are holding an anthology crammed with intelligent, well-crafted stories by established writers as well as new voices, screaming to be heard.

Stephen Vincent Benét once described a short story as "Something that can be read in an hour and remembered for a lifetime." I know that after you've read *Lethal Ladies* II you'll take away enough memorable characters to last you that lifetime.

Christine Matthews
St. Louis, Missouri
May 1997

Shelley Singer is the author of two P.I. series, the first featuring Jake Samson and Rosie Vicente, and the second starring Barrett Lake. This story features none of those characters, and perhaps launches a new series (Shelley?). (The title is self-explanatory.) Her most recent book was the Barrett Lake novel Interview With Mattie. *Shelley lives in the San Francisco Bay area.*

ME, LOUIS, AND THE SKINHEAD

by Shelley Singer

I WAS SITTING at a window table, eating Roland's deep dark gumbo and facing up St. Ann toward the dead end at the entrance to Armstrong Park. A big lighted arch, a million bulbs, like a combination rainbow and theater marquee, spelling "Armstrong." A few of the bulbs were dead, just like Louis.

So was the street. A cab coming in off Rampart now and again. Occasional foot traffic heading down toward the action a few blocks away.

The night was so hot the window glass felt warm. I was the only woman in the place, and, at the moment, the only customer.

I'd found the little restaurant my second day in the French Quarter and made it my home away from home, a place to escape from the general frenzy. A quiet place to go when I got tired of tripping over drunken college boys whose primitive idea of humor seemed to consist of mooning other tourists down on Bourbon Street.

1

Besides the gumbo, which would have been enough, the place had a good tape collection of someone I'd always loved. The great Satchmo himself, maybe in honor of the view from the window.

The sound system was playing "When You're Smiling." Armstrong had just put down the trumpet and was grating out the lyrics. After the whole world had smiled with him, he picked up the trumpet again. The song brought back a decade I could hardly remember, a dark nightclub in San Francisco, and the taste of old-fashioneds sipped through the smoke of unfiltered cigarettes.

No more old-fashioneds. Certainly no more cigarettes. Just gumbo, and wine, and listening to Louis, and thumbing through a stack of brochures, trying to decide what tourist attractions to visit the next day. Bunch of stuff about swamp tours. The advertising said they use these flat-bottomed boats, ferries, all seat and window, so you don't miss even the smallest alligator nosing through the brown murk.

Well, there are boats and there are boats. I could skip the alligators and blow every last dollar at the Cajun Queen riverboat casino. That floats, too.

I asked Louis what he thought. No help there. None of the dead bulbs blinked.

I knew I wanted to visit one of the above-ground cemeteries. When I'd first arrived in town and asked around, a tourist not looking to get mugged, a few people had warned me about Armstrong Park, but everyone had warned me about the cemeteries. Addicts, they said. Guys with guns sitting on top of the picturesque tombs and picking off sightseers for the few bucks in their wallets. Seven of them last year, a cabbie said. I thought I'd go anyway.

My wineglass was nearly empty again. California chardonnay. From Sonoma, close to home. Home where my former sweetie sat waiting patiently—she always was patient—for the lawyers to say who got what. The house, the cars. The cat. The CDs. The framed copy of our domestic partners registration.

Rachel, my partner at the agency, had gone through her own actual legal divorce that year and she was sympathetic. She'd insisted I take some vacation time, despite the work-load. Get away, Judy, she said. Get some perspective, have some fun. I objected. I really wanted to work on that case where they'd found the plumbing contractor in the septic tank. But she couldn't be convinced. I wasn't thinking too well, she said. Not watching my step. She said better off gone for a couple of weeks than gone for good.

I guess.

I looked over at the waiter. The fuzzy regrowth on his shaved head was looking thicker every day. He was dressed in his usual outfit: Doc Marten boots, black jeans, two earrings in each ear, a black leather vest over his restaurant T-shirt. Bet he never gets the smell of sweat out of that leather. Place didn't seem to be gay; I figured his costume had some other significance. Skinhead drag.

He was still wearing the bandage he'd had on that first night, a two-inch gauze square on the bicep of his long, muscular right arm.

He came to my table.

"Want another glass of wine, ma'am?"

"Yes. Thanks, Billy." Not much of a name for a grown man, but he wasn't much older than eighteen or so. Maybe he'd mature into a Bill or a Will.

One more drink and then I'd finish my gumbo and take a walk down the street to hear some jazz. A good trumpet.

Eleven o'clock, shank of the evening, but the place was pretty empty. The owner, his name really was Roland, was watching some old movie on the TV back in the kitchen. I could just see his curly orange hair over the low partition. And I could just hear the voices on the TV— George Raft? James Cagney? One of those old guys—saying something about Alcatraz.

Another reminder of home. The Rock.

Maybe went I went back to San Francisco I'd take one of those tours to the island. You never do that kind of thing in your own town. I've ridden on a cable car maybe twice, with visiting relatives.

The waiter brought my wine and carried a cup of coffee to the table across the small room where two women had just sat down with a six-year-old girl who should have been in bed. Probably, like me, tourists from a different time zone.

An elderly couple came in and sat down near me. They asked Billy for a dessert menu.

Two men in shorts hurried by outside, laughing. A few minutes later a man and woman strolled past, dressed in matching Hawaiian shirts and carrying matching cameras.

People in New Orleans, natives and tourists, seemed so happy and friendly. I was just wondering why I'd never made it to the city before—before Louis Armstrong was a park—when a pair of walks with big-time attitude appeared at the end of the block, swaggering in our direction.

Like my waiter, they had boots and not much hair. One wore Doc Martens, jeans rolled up to show off the boots, and a black T-shirt. The other one was more into the military look: combat boots, fatigue pants with a black T-shirt, and a bomber jacket that must have smelled worse than Billy's vest.

As they got closer, I could see they were also wearing cold, mean expressions. One of them laughed at something the other said. The laugh set off alarms in three sets of instincts at once—P.I., woman, and dyke. Or maybe not instincts. Maybe just different layers of the same learned response.

So I wasn't really thrilled when they pushed through the door and came into the restaurant.

The waiter looked even less thrilled.

He didn't say anything, but he moved fast, putting an empty table between himself and his clones. The whites of his eyes showed all around the blue irises and his mouth hung loose.

The tape had moved on to another song. "Basin Street Blues." Where the elite meet.

The one in jeans spoke in a tone of voice he might have learned from George Raft if he'd ever heard of him. "Come on outside, Billy. We need to talk to you."

Billy didn't answer and he didn't move.

The one in fatigues pulled a pistol out from under the flak jacket. A grimy little .32. I'd have expected at least an AK-47. Small-time punk.

"Now, Billy."

"Help me!" Billy cried out to no one in particular. I tried to figure out how I could do that. I wasn't carrying and I'm not as young as I used to be. Then Roland came rushing out of the kitchen.

The little guy was waving a butcher knife. "Hey, you, get—"

The revolver went off, Roland went down, bleeding from his thigh. Probably not the artery, though. Not pumping out. The knife lay on the floor beside him.

"You're a bad guy!" the little girl yelled, lurching toward the man with the gun, her dark eyes angry, her small fists clenched. The two women grabbed the child and wrapped themselves around her indignant little person.

The elderly couple sat paralyzed in their chairs.

"I was thinking," fatigue pants said to jeans. "That food

smells awful good. I ain't had a meal since we left home. And Billy, he don't want to go outside." He laughed. He'd thought of a new way to have fun, you could just tell. The women, the little girl, the old people . . . I felt cold, and that's not easy in New Orleans in summer.

"I'll get you some food," Billy said. Then he echoed the thought that was pounding in my head: "Don't hurt anybody."

Roland was lying there, holding his leg, crying silently, his chubby cheeks wet with tears.

Fatigues waved the gun at Billy. "No. Forget that. You lay down on your yellow belly and shut up. Everybody else, too. On the floor."

"I'll get you something to eat," I volunteered, trying to keep the others out of direct contact, wishing I had something to put in the food. Maybe there was rat poison in the kitchen.

"No. This one here, she should do it." Fatigues moved closer to the two women, where they lay on the floor with their arms around the child, and poked one of them in the hip with his booted foot. Not the blond woman. The black one.

"Hey," jeans objected. "I don't want her touching my food."

"This is the South, man. We got a slave."

"Not my food, man."

Fatigues shook his head in resignation and made eye contact again with me. "Okay, then. You go ahead."

I stood up and headed for the kitchen, getting as good a look as I could at Roland on the way past him. The bleeding had slowed way down, and he had his hand pressed hard against the wound. He nodded at me, to show he was okay. But his red hair and his neat mustache were dark with sweat.

"Stay alert," I muttered. That was all I had time to say.

A huge old black iron pot of gumbo squatted on the stove. I quick looked in the cabinets under the sink. No rat poison. No Drano. I ladled out a couple of big bowls, too good for the likes of them for sure, and found a metal tray to put them on, a piece of art, a reproduction of the forties. A rosy-cheeked, turbaned girl smiling at a bottle of Coke.

Fatigues had taken off his jacket and sat down at the other window table, right next to mine. He was holding the gun down by his side.

The guy in jeans was standing over Billy. He had a weapon out now, too, a buck knife.

"How'd you find me?" Billy said.

"Aryan Command, we don't let traitors get away. You shoulda known that."

"Wow," I said, batting my eyelashes. Funny how that's gotten less effective in recent years. "Are you members of the Aryan Command?"

"Heard of us, huh?" The one with the knife grinned at me.

As a matter of fact, I had. The cops in Chicago had caught three of their local chapter's members dribbling gasoline between the pews in a black church. One of them had a silver Star of David in his pocket. The police didn't think the star went too well with the swastika he had tattooed on his hand, so they asked him about it. He confessed he'd been planning to leave it at the scene of the fire.

That way, the Aryan Command figured, the blacks would blame the Jews and the Nazis could just sit back and watch the fun.

Major race war, no-fault, multilateral genocide.

Half a dozen other cities had active groups, too, all working on their own plans to set the cities on fire. There was a bunch in L.A. I knew about. Very big, very connected with neo-Nazis in Europe.

And very infiltrated by law enforcement and by investigators working for various private clients.

I put the bowls of gumbo down on the table.

"You go ahead, Matt," the skinhead with the knife told his buddy. "I'll wait'll you're done." Matt began eating, noisily, the gun in one hand, the spoon in the other.

I saw pretty quickly why Matt's friend was so willing to wait. He wasn't being altruistic or even considerate. No, he just wanted to play more than he wanted to eat. He stood over Billy and put his boot in the small of the kid's back.

"Been having a good time down here, huh, Billy? Your slut girlfriend in New Orleans, too?" He pronounced it "Noo Orleens."

Down here. Well, that didn't tell me much about where they were from. New Orleans was "down here" to almost everyone in the U.S.

"She's not my girlfriend, Jordan."

Jordan began to laugh, a wheezing, phony guffaw.

"That's pathetic, man. You got dumped? You're a real loser, you know that?" Still laughing, he aimed a hard kick at Billy's ribs.

Billy cried out and Jordan kicked him in the head. He groaned.

Louis Armstrong was singing "Sweet Sue." Jordan looked over at me, a satisfied look on his potato face. "Get me a beer."

I did as I was told, and brought one for Matt, too. Maybe they'd get drunk and pass out.

When I came back, Jordan was kneeling at Billy's side, his hand on the bandage on his arm.

"Look at this, Matt—think he's trying to hide something?" He ripped the bandage off. The boy had a swastika tattoo.

"There you go. Wear it proud. Hey, I got an idea, Billy.

Hey, Matt, what do you think about this?" The other skinhead stopped, his spoon poised, a grin on his face, and waited for the punch line.

"Maybe his girlfriend dumped him for a Jew. Maybe we can fix that. Come on, Billy, roll over. I'll make you a Jew."

They both laughed. Then Matt went back to his gumbo and Jordan went back to aiming carefully placed kicks at the cringing body of Billy. One must have scored some kind of direct hit. The kid screamed.

"I didn't do nothing, man! I never told the cops nothing."

"They were waiting. They were expecting us. You were backing out, man. You stopped coming around. You wouldn't do the church." Chicago. They must be from Chicago. "You wouldn't smash the windows. You wouldn't—do—nothing!" Three solid kicks.

Billy was lying still, rigid, breathing hard, waiting for the next one.

I smiled at Matt. It wasn't easy. "You want more beer?"

"Yeah. Get me another bowl of this soup, too." He reached across the table, slid his partner's bowl over in front of himself, and began spooning it into his mouth.

More gumbo, more beer. Maybe they'd float out the door.

Or maybe they'd just get tired of the game. But then they might kill Billy in front of these people, or take him away and do it quietly somewhere else. If he really had betrayed their group, snitched to the cops about their plans, he didn't deserve to die.

Louis Armstrong was saying hello to Dolly. So glad to have you back where you belong. Not appropriate, Louis, I thought. Not at all. Catch up with the action, here.

The elderly man spoke.

"You're welcome to your friend." He nodded toward Billy. "Why don't you just take him and let the rest of us go?"

Jordan strode over to where the gray-haired man lay,
beside his wife. The kid knelt down and put the point of his
knife against the man's hand, pressing lightly, his nose
practically touching the other guy's face.

"You're a useless old man." He spoke softly. "Shut up or
lose some blood now."

I get both my Nazi friends some more beer.

Matt had finished his second bowl of gumbo and his third
beer.

Why, I wondered, didn't one of them have to go to the
bathroom?

Jordan sat up and glanced at Billy, who wasn't moving.
Then he slid back over to the two women with the
dark-haired child.

He was looking at the child. "This little girl. She looks
like mixed blood."

"She's not," the white woman said. "She's my niece.
She's Italian." The woman's voice shook.

Jordan laughed, a manly guffaw that meant, I supposed,
he was enjoying her fear. He stood up. "I could use some of
that soup now. And another beer. What do you say, Matt?"

Matt got up from his plate at the table and walked to
where Roland lay clutching his wounded leg. He kicked the
butcher's knife well out of the wounded man's reach. It
skittered close to the elderly woman. Then Matt glared at
Roland and leaned against the wall, pointing his gun at him.

"Pow," he said.

I made myself laugh.

I brought him another beer, while Jordan sucked up his
"soup."

I sat down across from Jordan.

He squinted at me, his blue eyes flat. "I didn't ask you to
sit down."

This time I skipped the eyelash-batting. "I wanted to talk to you. Not often I get a chance to talk to a hero."

He wasn't buying it completely, but he went from flat to puzzled, as if he were wondering why he felt suspicious.

He'd put his knife down. When he reached for his soup spoon, I noticed a small tattoo on his hand. A double flash of lightning. A skinhead trademark. It looked like a swastika someone had pulled apart.

"Yeah? What do you want to talk about, lady?"

"I wish you guys had been around earlier. Maybe you'd have done something about some of the people I saw before when I was sitting here, looking out. People who walked by. Disgusting."

"Yeah? Like what?"

"Black drag queen. Propositioning a white man. And a black man with a white woman."

"You saw all that? Here? In like what, an hour?"

"Sure did." How gullible was he?

"You see any of that again, you let me know?"

Pretty gullible.

"I will. Why don't I just sit here and look for them. While you eat."

He studied my face. I tried to look like a Nazi. I must have finally succeeded.

"Yeah. Go ahead."

"What are you talking about over there?" Matt demanded. Jordan told him.

Matt got a crazy, wild-eyed look on his face. "I want the queer. Use his spike heels on his face."

"Me," Jordan argued, "I want the one with the white woman. I hate that."

They were actually responding to what I'd said, chatting about their hate preferences. They believed me. That was good. I wanted them to believe me. Wanted to be their buddy.

Because right now these guys had the edge: all the weapons, all the meanness. I needed to turn that edge around somehow and slash them with it.

Now Matt was pointing his gun at Billy. "Pow!"

He walked around to Billy's head.

"I thought Jordan told you to roll over, traitor. On your back."

Billy groaned and rolled over. His pants were soaked with urine. Matt laughed at him.

"We come here to kill you, Bill. I want you to see the gun pointing at you." He looked around the room. "You know, Jordan, we got an awful lot of witnesses here . . ."

I'd been hoping that wouldn't penetrate his worm-sized brain.

"That don't matter," Jordan said. "Kill 'em all." His manly guffaw cracked and trailed off in a high whinny. Like a demented horse. He was really getting excited now. "Set fire to the place." His eyes glowed. "Tie 'em up and—whoosh!"

The elderly woman began to cry. So did the little girl. I brought both the skinheads another beer, thinking these guys must have bladders the size of basketballs. If I could just get rid of one of them for a minute . . .

Matt stroked the barrel of his gun.

Jordan stood up. "Gotta use the head, man."

Matt nodded, grinning down at Billy, who was shaking and crying. "I'll wait for you. Then me."

The tape had moved on to another song. Louis was rasping, "I'll be glad when you're dead, you rascal you." Yes, I thought. That was more like it.

As Jordan went for the men's room, I went for the diversion I'd been working on. This was it, now or never, no choice, no other chance, and no point in even thinking about failing. I raised a hand, tensed, and focused out the window on an imaginary person somewhere between me and the Armstrong Arch.

"Matt," I called out, pointing down the street. "There he is." I didn't elaborate about the "he." I figured Matt would imagine what he wanted to imagine. His little eyes lit up and he came rushing over to the window to peer out, his back to me, the gun slack in his hand. I grabbed the table vase. I was just about to clobber good old Matt when all hell broke loose behind me.

Jordan had finished too quickly.

He came slamming out of the john. I dropped my hand, trying to conceal the vase at my side, jabbering at Matt about the nonexistent victim on the street: "Gee, I thought I saw him go in—wait a second—"

But Jordan must have seen the vase. He yelled, "Hey, she's—"

Crash! Something had stopped him. I didn't wait to see what it was. As Matt turned I caught him on the jaw with the vase and gave a good chop to his gun-hand wrist at the same time. The gun fell; so did Matt. I heard more noise behind me, grunts and crashes and then a long scream that tailed off into groans and sobs.

I grabbed the gun and swung around, ready to shoot Jordan. But I didn't have to.

Roland had a tight grip on Jordan's ankle, so I figured he'd been the one who pulled him down. But at this point, the ankle-grip was probably as extraneous as the gun I was holding.

When Jordan went down, he must have lost his knife. The blond woman had picked it up and pinned his hand to the floor with it.

I knew that's what had happened, because she was still holding onto the hilt.

Jordan was screaming again. The child was screaming.

The blond woman was laughing, but she sounded more hysterical than happy.

A few feet away from that scene, the elderly man and woman sat hugging each other. At some point in the confusion, he had picked up Roland's butcher knife. He was holding it tightly and glaring at the skinhead, who was writhing on the floor, pinned like an ugly butterfly.

Matt started to get up.

I kicked him. "Someone call the cops."

Billy, the waiter, the battered bone of contention, tried to get up. Not a chance. He screamed in harmony with Jordan, and lay back down again. Something broken, I guessed.

The elderly man kissed his wife, patted her arm, and stood up, trembling. He tried to brush something off his white shirt—gumbo, maybe. Or blood from the fracas. It didn't come off. He went to the phone and called the police.

"Don't let up on that knife," I warned the blond woman, "and don't pull it out. We don't know what's been cut and what we'd be unplugging. The guy could bleed to death. Let the medics do it."

She stared at me and started to argue.

"Honest. I'm a private investigator." Yeah, that would make me an expert on medicine.

But she thought it did. She gagged and held on to the knife, turning her head away.

I could already hear the sirens heading toward us when Billy called me over to him.

"My bandage. Where's my bandage?" He had his hand covering the swastika on his arm.

I spotted it lying in a corner under a chair, retrieved it, and put it back on him.

"Thanks. I really did rat to the police, you know. I hate those guys. I can't believe they found me down here."

I was thinking they might send someone else to look for

him. He needed to grow hair, clean up his act, buy a normal wardrobe.

And he sure needed to get rid of the swastika. He couldn't wear a bandage for the rest of his life. What if it fell off in the wrong neighborhood? Or the right one?

"You can get tattoos taken off, you know," I told him.

"Yeah, but I don't have any money. I was saving up for it. All my tips."

Billy wasn't a bad waiter, but that could take a while.

Armstrong's trumpet was finishing up a "St. Louis Blues" as deep and tasty as Roland's gumbo.

"If I were you," I told the kid, "I'd get a credit card."

By the time the police and the EMTs got there, the Armstrong tape had worked itself all the way back to the beginning.

The whole world was smiling again.

Maybe so. But when I sat down at my window table with one of the cops to tell him what had happened, I was facing the Armstrong Arch again, up at the end of the street. And I got the feeling a couple more bulbs had gone out.

Since her first appearance in the ground-breaking Indemnity Only *(Delacorte, 1982) V.I. Warshawski has appeared in a total of eight novels and, recently, a collection of short stories called* Windy City Blues *(Delacorte). This story appeared in Sara's own excellent anthology,* Women on the Case *(Delacorte, 1996) and she was kind enough to agree to allow us to reprint it here.*

As mentioned before in his book Sara has edited anthologies of her own, Women on the Case *and* A Woman's Eye *(1992), probably two of the finest anthologies of women's stories in the field.*

PUBLICITY STUNTS
A V. I. WARSHAWSKI STORY

by Sara Paretsky

I

"I NEED A bodyguard. I was told you were good." Lisa Macauley crossed her legs and leaned back in my client chair as if expecting me to slobber in gratitude.

"If you were told I was a good bodyguard, someone didn't know my operation: I never do protection."

"I'm prepared to pay you well."

"You can offer me a million dollars a day and I still won't take the job. Protection is a special skill. You need lots of people to do it right. I have a one-person operation. I'm not going to abandon my other clients to look after you."

"I'm not asking you to give up your precious clients

17

forever, just for a few days next week while I'm doing publicity here in Chicago."

Judging by her expression, Macauley thought she was a household word, but I'd been on the run the two days since she'd made the appointment and hadn't had time to do any research on her. Whatever she publicized made her rich: wealth oozed all the way from her dark cloud of carefully cut curls through the sable protecting her from February's chill winds and on down to her Stephane Kelian three-inch platforms.

When I didn't say anything she added, "For my new book, of course."

"That sounds like a job for your publisher. Or your handlers."

I had vague memories of going to see Andre Dawson when he was doing some kind of baseball promotion at Marshall Field. He'd been on a dais, under lights, with several heavies keeping the adoring fans away from him. No matter what Macauley wrote she surely wasn't any more at risk than a sports hero.

She made an impatient gesture. "They always send some useless person from their publicity department. They refuse to believe my life is in danger. Of course, this is the last book I'll do with Gaudy: my new contract with Della Destra Press calls for a personal bodyguard whenever I'm on the road. But right now, while I'm promoting the new one, I need protection."

I ignored her contract woes. "Your life is in danger? What have you written that's so controversial? An attack on Mother Teresa?"

"I write crime novels. Don't you read?"

"Not crime fiction: I get enough of the real stuff walking out my door in the morning."

Macauley gave a self-conscious little laugh. "I thought

mine might appeal to a woman detective like yourself. That's why I chose you to begin with. My heroine is a woman talk-show host who gets involved in cases through members of her listening audience. The issues she takes on are extremely controversial: abortion, rape, the Greens. In one of them she protects a man whose university appointment is attacked by the feminists on campus. She's nearly murdered when she uncovers the brainwashing operation the feminists are running on campus."

"I can't believe that would put you in danger—feminist-bashing is about as controversial as apple pie these days. Sounds like your hero is a female Claud Barnett."

Barnett broadcast his attacks on the atheistic, family-destroying feminists and liberals five days a week from Chicago's WKLN radio tower. The term he'd coined for progressive women—femmunists—had become a much-loved buzzword on the radical right. Claud had become so popular that his show was syndicated in almost every state, and rerun at night and on weekends in his hometown.

Macauley didn't like being thought derivative, even of reality. She bristled as she explained that her detective, Nan Carruthers, had a totally unique personality and slant on public affairs.

"But because she goes against all the popular positions that feminists have persuaded the media to support I get an unbelievable amount of hate mail."

"And now someone's threatening your life?" I tried to sound more interested than hopeful.

Her blue eyes flashing in triumph, Macauley pulled a letter from her handbag and handed it to me. It was the product of a computer, printed on some kind of cheap white stock. In all caps it proclaimed, YOU'LL BE SORRY, BITCH, BUT BY THEN IT WILL BE TOO LATE.

"If this is a serious threat, you're already too late," I

snapped. "You should have taken it to the forensics lab before you fondled it. Unless you sent it yourself as a publicity stunt?"

Genuine crimson stained her cheeks. "How dare you? My last three books have been national best sellers—I don't need this kind of cheap publicity."

I handed the letter back. "You show it to the police?"

"They wouldn't take it seriously. They told me they could get the state's attorney to open a file, but what good would that do me?"

"Scotland Yard can identify individual laser printers based on samples of output, but most U.S. police departments don't have those resources. Did you keep the envelope?"

She took out a grimy specimen. With a magnifying glass I could make out the zip code in the postmark: Chicago, the Gold Coast. That meant only one of about a hundred thousand residents, or the half-million tourists who pass through the neighborhood every day, could have mailed it. I tossed it back.

"You realize this isn't a death threat—it's just a threat, and pretty vague at that. What is it you'll be sorry for?"

"If I knew that, I wouldn't be hiring a detective," she snapped.

"Have you had other threats?" It was an effort to keep my voice patient.

"I had two other letters like this one, but I didn't bring them—I didn't think they'd help you any. I've started having phone calls where they just wait, or laugh in a weird way or something. Sometimes I get the feeling someone's following me."

"Any hunches who might be doing it?" I was just going through the motions—I didn't think she was at any real risk, but she seemed the kind who couldn't believe she wasn't at the forefront of everyone else's mind.

"I *told* you." She leaned forward in her intensity. "Ever since *Take Back the Night*, my fourth book, which gives a whole different look at rape crisis centers, I've been on the top of every femmunist hit list in the country."

I laughed, trying to picture some of my friends out taking potshots at every person in America who hated feminists. "It sounds like a nuisance, but I don't believe your life is in as much danger as, say, the average abortion provider. But if you want a bodyguard while you're on Claud Barnett's show, I can recommend a couple of places. Just remember, though, that even the Secret Service couldn't protect JFK from a determined sniper."

"I suppose if I'd been some whiny feminist you'd take this more seriously. It's because of my politics you won't take the job."

"If you were a whiny feminist I'd probably tell you not to cry over this because there's a lot worse on its way. But since you're a whiny authoritarian there's not much I can do for you. I'll give you some advice for free, though: If you cry about it on the air you'll only invite a whole lot more of this kind of attention."

I didn't think contemporary clothes lent themselves to flouncing out of rooms, but Ms. Macauley certainly flounced out of mine. I wrote a brief summary of our meeting in my appointments log, then put her out of mind until the next night. I was having dinner with a friend who devours crime fiction. Sal Barthele was astounded that I hadn't heard of Lisa Macauley.

"You ever read anything besides the sports pages and the financial section, Warshawski? That girl is hot. They say her contract with Della Estra is worth twelve million, and all the guys with shiny armbands and goose steps buy her books by the cord. I hear she's dedicating the next one to the brave folks at Operation Rescue."

After that I didn't think of Macauley at all: a case for a small suburban school district whose pension money had been turned into derivatives was taking all my energy. But a week later the writer returned forcibly to mind.

"You're in trouble now, Warshawski," Murray Ryerson said when I picked up the phone late Thursday night.

"Hi, Murray: good to hear from you, too." Murray is an investigative reporter for the *Herald-Star*, a one-time lover, sometimes rival, occasional pain-in-the-butt, and even, now and then, a good friend.

"Why'd you tangle with Lisa Macauley? She's Chicago's most important artiste, behind Oprah."

"She come yammering to you with some tale of injustice? She wanted a bodyguard and I told her I didn't do that kind of work."

"Oh, Warshawski, you must have sounded ornery when you turned her down. She is not a happy camper: she got Claud Barnett all excited about how you won't work for anyone who doesn't agree with your politics. He dug up your involvement with the old abortion underground and has been blasting away at you the last two days as the worst kind of murdering femmunist. A wonderful woman came to you, trembling and scared for her life, and you turned her away just because she's against abortion. He says you investigate the politics of all your potential clients and won't take anyone who's given money to a Christian or a Republican cause and he's urging people to boycott you."

"Kind of people who listen to Claud need an investigator to find their brains. He isn't likely to hurt me."

Murray dropped his bantering tone. "He carries more weight than you, or maybe even I, want to think. You may have to do some damage control."

I felt my stomach muscles tighten: I live close to the edge of financial ruin much of the time. If I lost three or four key accounts I'd be dead.

"You think I should apply for a broadcast license and blast back? Or just have my picture taken coming out of the headquarters of the Republican National Committee?"

"You need a nineties kind of operation, Warshawski—a staff, including a publicist. You need to have someone going around town with stories about all the tough cases you've cracked in the last few years, showing how wonderful you are. On account of I like hot-tempered Italian gals, I might run a piece myself if you'd buy me dinner."

"What's a nineties operation—where your self-promotion matters a whole lot more than what kind of job you do? Come to think of it, do you have an agent, Murray?"

The long pause at the other end told its own tale: Murray had definitely joined the nineties. I looked in the mirror after he hung up, searching for scales or some other visible sign of turning into a dinosaur. In the absence of that I'd hang on to my little one-woman shop as long as possible.

I turned to the *Herald-Star*'s entertainment guide, looking to see when WKLN ("The voice of the Klan," we'd dubbed them in my days with the public defender) was rebroadcasting Barnett. I was in luck: he came on again at eleven-thirty, so that night workers would have something to froth about on their commute home.

After a few minutes from his high-end sponsors, his rich, folksy baritone rolled through my speakers like molasses from a giant barrel. "Yeah, folks, the femmunists are at it again. The Iron Curtain's gone down in Russia so they want to put it up here in America. You think like they think or—*phht!*—off you go to the Gulag.

"We've got one of those femmunists right here in Chicago. Private investigator. You know, in the old stories they used to call them private dicks. Kind of makes you wonder what this gal is missing in her life that she turned to that kind of work. Started out as a baby-killer back in the days when she was at the Red University on the South Side of Chicago and grew up to be a dick. Well, it takes all kinds, they say, but do we need this kind?

"We got an important writer here in Chicago. I know a lot of you read the books this courageous woman writes. And because she's willing to take a stand she gets death threats. So she goes to this femmunist dick, this hermaphrodite dick, who won't help her out. 'Cause Lisa Macauley has the guts to tell women the truth about rape and abortion, and this dick, this V.I. Warshawski, can't take it.

"By the way, you ought to check out Lisa's new book. *Slaybells Ring*. A great story which takes her fast-talking radio host Nan Carruthers into the world of the ACLU and the bashing of Christmas. We carry it right here in our bookstore. If you call in now, Sheri will ship it right out to you. Or just go out to your nearest warehouse: they're bound to stock it. Maybe if this Warshawski read it she'd have a change of heart, but a gal like her, you gotta wonder if she has a heart to begin with."

He went on for thirty minutes by the clock, making an easy segue from me to the First Lady. If I was a devil, she was the Princess of Darkness. When he finished I stared out the window for a time. I felt ill from the bile Barnett had poured out in his molassied voice, but I was furious with Lisa Macauley. She had set me up, pure and simple. Come to see me with a spurious problem, just so she and Barnett could start trashing me on the air. But why?

II

Murray was right: Barnett carried more weight than I wanted to believe. He kept on at me for days, not always as the centerpiece, but often sending a few snide barbs my way. The gossip columns of all three daily papers mentioned it and the story got picked up by the wires. Between Barnett and the papers, Macauley got a load of free publicity: her sales skyrocketed. Which made me wonder again if she'd typed up that threatening note herself.

At the same time, my name getting sprinkled with mud did start having an effect on my own business: two new clients backed out midstream, and one of my old regulars phoned to say his company didn't have any work for me right now. No, they weren't going to cancel my contract, but they thought, in his picturesque corpo-speak, "we'd go into a holding pattern for the time being."

I called my lawyer to see what my options were; he advised me to let snarling dogs bite until they got it out of their system. "You don't have the money to take on Claud Barnett, Vic, and even if you won a slander suit against him you'd lose while the case dragged on."

On Sunday I meekly called Murray and asked if he'd be willing to repeat the deal he'd offered me earlier. After a two-hundred-dollar dinner at the Filigree he ran a nice story on me in the *Star*'s "Chicago Beat." section, recounting some of my great past successes. This succeeded in diverting some of Barnett's attention from me to Murray—my so-called stooge. Of course he wasn't going to slander Murray on the air—he could tell lies about a mere mortal like me, but not about someone with a big media operation to pay his legal fees.

I found myself trying to plan the total humiliation of both Barnett and Macauley. Let it go, I would tell myself, as I turned in the bed in the middle of the night: this is what he wants, to control my head. Turn it off. But I couldn't follow this most excellent advice.

I even did a little investigation into Macauley's life. I called a friend of mine at Channel 13 where Macauley had once worked to get the station's take on her. A native of Wisconsin, she'd moved to Chicago hoping to break into broadcast news. After skulking on the sidelines of the industry for five or six years she'd written her first Nan Carruthers book. Ironically enough, the women's movement, creating new roles for women in fiction as well as life, had fueled Macauley's literary success. When her second novel became a best seller, she divorced the man she married when they were both University of Wisconsin journalism students and started positioning herself as a celebrity. She was famous in book circles for her insistence on her personal security: opinion was divided as to whether it had started as a publicity stunt, or if she really did garner a lot of hate male.

I found a lot of people who didn't like her—some because of her relentless self-promotion, some because of her politics, and some because they resented her success. As Sal had told me, Macauley was minting money now. Not only Claud, but the *Wall Street Journal*, the *National Review*, and all the other conservative rags hailed her as a welcome antidote to writers like Marcia Muller or Amanda Cross.

But despite my digging I couldn't find any real dirt on Macauley. Nothing I could use to embarrass her into silence. To make matters worse, someone at Channel 13 told her I'd been poking around asking questions about her. Whether by chance or design, she swept into Corona's one night when I was there with Sal. Sal and I were both enthusiastic fans of Belle Fontaine, the jazz singer who was Corona's Wednesday night regular headliner.

Lisa arrived near the end of the first set. She'd apparently found an agency willing to guard her body—she was the center of a boisterous crowd that included a couple of big men with bulges near their armpits. She flung her sable across a chair at a table near ours.

At first I assumed her arrival was just an unhappy coincidence. She didn't seem to notice me, but called loudly for champagne, asking for the most expensive brand on the menu. A couple at a neighboring table angrily shushed her. This prompted Lisa to start yelling out toasts to some of the people at her table: her *fabulous* publicist, her *awesome* attorney, and her *extraordinary* bodyguards, "Rover" and "Prince." The sullen-faced men didn't join in the raucous cheers at their nicknames, but they didn't erupt, either.

We couldn't hear the end of "Tell Me Lies" above Lisa's clamor, but Belle took a break at that point. Sal ordered another drink and started to fill me in on family news: Her lover had just landed a role in a sitcom that would take her out to the West Coast for the winter and Sal was debating hiring a manager for her own bar, the Golden Glow, so she could join Becca. She was just describing—in humorous detail—Becca's first meeting with the producer, when Lisa spoke loudly enough for everyone in the room to hear.

"I'm so glad you boys were willing to help me out. I can't believe how chicken some of the detectives in this town are. Easy to be big and bold in an abortion clinic, but they run and hide from someone their own size." She turned deliberately in her chair, faked an elaborate surprise at the sight of me, and continued at the same bellowing pitch, "Oh, V.I. Warshawski! I hope you don't take it personally."

"I don't expect eau de cologne from the sewer," I called back heartily.

The couple who'd tried to quiet Lisa down during the singing laughed at this. The star twitched, then got to her feet, champagne glass in hand, and came over to me.

"I hear you've been stalking me, Warshawski. I could sue you for harassment."

I smiled. "Sugar, I've been trying to find out why a big successful gal like you had to invent some hate mail just to have an excuse to slander me. You want to take me to court I'll be real, *real* happy to sort out your lies in public."

"In court or anywhere else I'll make you look as stupid as you do right now." Lisa tossed her champagne into my face; a camera strobe flashed just as the drink hit me.

Fury blinded me more than the champagne. I knocked over a chair as I leapt up to throttle her, but Sal got an arm around my waist and pulled me down. Behind Macauley, Prince and Rover got to their feet, ready to move: Lisa had clearly staged the whole event to give them an excuse for beating me up.

Queenie, who owns the Corona, was at my side with some towels. "Jake! I want these people out of here now. And I think some cute person's been taking pictures. Make sure she leaves the film with you, hear? Ms. Macauley, you owe me three hundred dollars for that Dom Pérignon you threw around."

Prince and Rover thought they were going to take on Queenie's bouncer, but Jake had broken up bigger fights than they could muster. He managed to lift them both and slam their heads together, then to snatch the *fabulous* publicist's bag as she was trying to spring out the door. Jake took out her camera, pulled the film, and handed the bag back to her with a smile and an insulting bow. The attorney, prompted by Jake, handed over three bills, and the whole party left to loud applause from the audience.

Queenie and Sal grew up together, which may be why I got Gold Coast treatment that night, but not even her private reserve Veuve Clicquot could take the bad taste from my mouth. If I'd beaten up Macauley I'd have looked like the brute she and Barnett were labeling me; but taking a faceful of champagne sitting down left me looking—and feeling—helpless.

"You're not going to do anything stupid, are you, Vic?" Sal said as she dropped me off around two in the morning. "'Cause if you are I'm baby-sitting you, girlfriend."

"No. I'm not going to do anything rash, if that's what you mean. But I'm going to nail that prize bitch, one way or another."

Twenty-four hours later Lisa Macauley was dead. One day after that I was in jail.

III

All I knew about Lisa's murder was what I'd read in the papers before the cops came for me: her personal trainer had discovered her body when he arrived Friday morning for their usual workout. She had been beaten to death in what looked like a bloody battle, which is why the state's attorney finally let me go—they couldn't find the marks on me they were looking for. And they couldn't find any evidence in my home or office.

They kept insisting, though, that I had gone to her apartment late Thursday night. They asked me about it all night long on Friday without telling me why they were so sure. When Freeman Carter, my lawyer, finally sprang me Saturday afternoon he forced them to tell him: the doorman was claiming he admitted me to Lisa's apartment just before midnight on Thursday.

Freeman taxed me with it on the ride home. "The way she was carrying on, it would have been like you to demand a face-to-face with her, Vic. Don't hold out on me—I can't defend you if you were there and won't tell me about it."

"I wasn't there," I said flatly. "I am not prone to blackouts or hallucinations: there is no way I could have gone there and forgotten it. I was blamelessly watching the University of Kansas men pound Duke on national television. I even have a witness: My golden retriever shared a pizza with me. Her testimony: She threw up cheese sauce in front of my bed Friday morning."

Freeman ignored that. "Sal told me about the dust-up at Corona's. Anyway, Stacey Cleveland, Macauley's publicist, had already bared all to the police. You're the only person they can locate who had reason to be killing mad with her."

"Then they're not looking, are they? Someone either pretended to be me, or else bribed the doorman to tell the cops I was there. Get me the doorman's name and I'll sort out which it was."

"I can't do that, Vic: you're in enough trouble suborning the state's key witness."

"You're supposed to be on my side," I snapped. "You want to go into court with evidence or not?"

"I'll talk to the doorman, Vic: you go take a bath—jail doesn't smell very good on you."

I followed Freeman's advice only because I was too tired to do anything else. After that I slept the clock around, waking just before noon on Sunday. The phone had been ringing when I walked in on Saturday. It was Murray, wanting my exclusive story. I put him off and switched the phone to my answering service. In the morning I had forty-seven messages from various reporters. When I started outside to get the Sunday papers I found a camera crew parked in front of the building. I retreated, fetched my coat and an overnight bag, and went out the back way. My car was parked right in front of the camera van, so I walked the three miles to my new office.

When the Pulteney Building went under the wrecking ball last April I'd moved my business to a warehouse on the edge of Wicker Park, at the corner of Milwaukee Avenue and North. Fringe galleries and nightspots complete with liquor stores and palm readers for air here, and there are a lot of vacant lots, but it was ten minutes—by car, bus, or L—from the heart of the financial district where most of my business lies. A sculpting friend had moved her studio into a revamped warehouse; the day after visiting her I signed a five-year lease across the hall. I had twice my old space at two-thirds the rent. Since I'd had to refurnish—from Dumpsters and auctions—I'd put in a daybed behind a partition: I could camp out here for a few days until media interest in me cooled.

I bought the Sunday papers from one of the liquor stores on my walk. The *Sun-Times* concentrated on Macauley's career, including a touching history of her childhood in Rhinelander, Wisconsin. She'd been the only child of older parents. Her father, Joseph, had died last year at the age of eighty, but her mother, Louise, still lived in the house where Lisa had grown up. The paper showed a frame bungalow with a porch swing and a minute garden, as well as a tearful Louise Macauley in front of Lisa's doll collection ("I've kept the room the way it looked when she left for college," the caption read).

Her mother never wanted her going off to the University of Wisconsin. "Even though we raised her with the right values, and sent her to church schools, the university is a terrible place. She wouldn't agree, though, and now look what's happened."

The *Tribune* had a discreet sidebar on Lisa's recent contretemps with me. In the *Hearld-Star* Murray published the name of the doorman who had admitted "someone claiming to be V.I. Warshawski" to Macauley's building. It was Reggie Whitman. He'd been the doorman since the building went up in 1978, was a grandfather, a church deacon, coached a basketball team at the Henry Horner Homes, and was generally so virtuous that truth radiated from him like a beacon.

Murray also had talked with Lisa's ex-husband, Brian Gerstein, an assistant producer for one of the local network news stations. He was appropriately grief-stricken at his ex-wife's murder. The picture supplied by Gerstein's publicist showed a man in his mid-thirties with a TV smile but anxious eyes.

I called Beth Blacksin, the reporter at Channel 13 who'd filled me in on what little I'd learned about Lisa Macauley before her death.

"Vic! Where are you? We've got a camera crew lurking outside your front door hoping to talk to you!"

"I know, babycakes. And talk to me you shall, as soon as I find out who set me up to take the fall for Lisa Macauley's death. So give me some information now and it shall return to you like those famous loaves of bread."

Beth wanted to dicker but the last two weeks had case-hardened my temper. She finally agreed to talk with the promise of a reward in the indefinite future.

Brian Gerstein had once worked at Channel 13, just as he had for every other news station in town. "He's a loser, Vic: I'm not surprised Lisa dumped him when she started to get successful. He's the kind of guy who would sit around dripping into his coffee because you were out-earning him, moaning, trying to get you to feel sorry for him. People hire him because he's a good tape editor, but then they give him the shove because he gets the whole newsroom terminally depressed."

"You told me last week they met up at UW when they were students there in the eighties. Where did they go next?"

Beth had to consult her files, but she came back on the line in a few minutes with more details. Gerstein came from Long Island. He met Lisa when they were both Wisconsin juniors, campaigning for Reagan's first election in 1980. They'd married five years later, just before moving to Chicago. Politics and TV kept them together for seven years after that.

Gary rented an apartment in Rogers Park on the far north side of the city. "And that's typical of him," Beth added as she gave me his address. "He won't own a home since they split up: he can't afford it, his life was ruined and he doesn't feel like housekeeping—I've heard a dozen different whiny reasons from him. Not that everyone has to own, but you don't have to rent a run-down apartment in gangbanger territory when you work for the networks, either."

"So he could have been peevish enough to kill Lisa?"

"You're assuming he swathed himself in skirts and furs and told Reggie Whitman he was V.I. Warshawski? It would take more—more gumption than he's got to engineer something like that. It's not a bad theory, though: maybe we'll float it on the four o'clock news. Give us something different to talk about than all the other guys. Stay in touch, Vic. I'm willing to believe you're innocent, but it'd make a better story if you'd killed her."

"Thanks, Blacksin." I laughed as I hung up: her enthusiasm was without malice.

I took the L up to Rogers Park, the slow Sunday milk run.

Despite Beth's harangue, it's an interesting part of town. Some blocks you do see dopers hanging out, some streets have depressing amounts of garbage in the yards, but most of the area harks back to the Chicago of my childhood: tidy brick two-flats, hordes of immigrants in the parks speaking every known language and along with them, delis and coffee shops for every nationality.

Gerstein lived on one of the quiet side streets. He was home, as I'd hoped: staking out an apartment without a car would have been miserable work on a cold February day. He even let me in without too much fuss. I told him I was a detective, and showed him my license, but he didn't seem to recognize my name—he must not have been editing the programs dealing with his ex-wife's murder. Or he'd been so stricken he'd edited them without registering anything.

He certainly exuded misery as he escorted me up the stairs. Whether it was grief or guilt for Lisa, or just the chronic depression Beth attributed to him, he moved as though on the verge of falling over. He was a little taller than I, but slim. Swathed in a coat and shawls he might have looked like a woman to the nightman.

Gerstein's building was clean and well maintained, but his own apartment was sparely furnished, as though he expected to move on at any second. The only pictures on the walls were a couple of framed photographs—one of himself and Lisa with Ronald Reagan, and the other with a man I didn't recognize. He had no drapes or plants or anything else to bring a bit of color to the room, and when he invited me to sit he pulled a metal folding chair from a closet for me.

"I always relied on Lisa to fix things up," he said. "She had so much vivacity and such good taste. Without her I can't seem to figure out how to do it."

"I thought you'd been divorced for years." I tossed my coat onto the card table in the middle of the room.

"Yes, but I've only been living here nine months. She let me keep our old condo, but last summer I couldn't make the payments. She said she'd come around to help me fix this up, only she's so busy . . ." His voice trailed off.

I wondered how he ever sold himself to his various employers—I found myself wanting to shake him out like a pillow and plump him up. "So you and Lisa stayed in touch?"

"Oh, sort of. She was too busy to call much, but she'd talk to me sometimes when I phoned."

"So you didn't have any hard feelings about your divorce?"

"Oh, I did. I never wanted to split up—it was all her idea. I kept hoping, but now, you know, it's too late."

"I suppose a woman as successful as Lisa met a lot of men."

"Yes, yes, she certainly did." His voice was filled with admiration, not hate.

I was beginning to agree with Beth, that Gerstein couldn't possibly have killed Lisa. What really puzzled me was what had ever attracted her to him in the first place, but the person who could figure out the hows and whys of attraction would put Ann Landers out of business overnight.

I went through the motions with him—did he get a share in her royalties?—yes, on the first book, because she'd written that while they were still together. When she wanted a divorce his lawyer told him he could probably get a judgment entitling him to fifty percent of all her proceeds, even in the future, but he loved Lisa, he wanted her to come back to him; he wasn't interested in being vindictive. Did he inherit under Lisa's will? He didn't think so, I'd have to ask her attorney. Did he knew who her residuary legatee was? Some conservative foundations they both admired.

I got up to go. "Who do you think killed your wife, ex-wife?"

"I thought they'd arrested someone that dick Claud Barnett says was harassing her."

"You know Barnett? Personally, I mean?" All I wanted was to divert him from thinking about me—even in his depression he might have remembered hearing my name on the air—but he surprised me.

"Yeah. That is, Lisa does. Did. We went to a conservative media convention together right after we moved here. Barnett was the keynote speaker. She got all excited, said she'd known him growing up but his name was something different then. After that she saw him every now and then. She got him to take his picture with us a couple of years later, at another convention in Sun Valley."

He jerked his head toward the wall where the photographs hung. I went over to look at them. I knew the Gipper's famous smile pretty well by heart so I concentrated on Barnett. I was vaguely aware of his face: he was considered so influential in the nation's swing rightward that his picture kept popping up in news magazines. A man of about fifty, he was lean and well groomed, and usually smiling with affable superiority.

In Sun Valley he must have eaten something that disagreed with him. He had an arm around Lisa and her husband, stiffly, as if someone had propped plywood limbs against his trunk. Lisa was smiling gaily, happy to be with the media darling. Brian was holding himself upright and looking close to jovial. But Claud gave you the idea that thumbscrews had been hammered under his plywood nails to get him into the photo.

"What name had Lisa known him by as a child?" I asked.

"Oh, she was mistaken about that. Once she got to see him up close she realized it was only a superficial resemblance. But Barnett took a shine to her—most people did, she was so vivacious—and gave her a lot of support in her career. He was the first big booster of her Nan Carruthers novels."

"He doesn't look very happy to be with her here, does he? Can I borrow it? It's a very good one of Lisa, and I'd like to use it in my inquiries."

Brian said in a dreary voice that he thought Lisa's publicist would have much better ones, but he was easy to persuade—or bully, to call my approach by its real name. I left with the photo carefully draped in a dish towel, and a written promise to return it as soon as possible.

I trotted to the Jarvis L stop, using the public phone there to call airlines. I found one that not only sent kiddie planes from O'Hare to Rhinelander, Wisconsin, but had a flight leaving in two hours. The state's attorney had told me not to leave the jurisdiction. Just in case they'd put a stop on me at the airport, I booked a flight under my mother's maiden name and embarked on the tedious L journey back to the Loop and out to the airport.

IV

Lisa's new book, *Slaybells Ring*, was stacked high at the airport bookstores. The black enamel cover with an embossed spray of bells in silver drew the eye. At the third stand I passed I finally gave in and bought a copy.

The flight was a long puddle-jumper, making stops in Milwaukee and Wausau on its way north. By the time we reached Rhinelander I was approaching the denouement, where the head of the American Civil Liberties Union was shown to be opposing the display of a Christmas crèche at City Hall because he secretly owned a company that was trying to put the crèche's manufacturer out of business. Nan Carruthers, owing to her wide and loyal band of radio fans, got the information from an employee the ACLU baddie had fired after thirty years of loyal service when the employee was found listening to Nan's show on his lunch break. The book had a three-hanky ending at midnight mass, where Nan joined the employee—now triumphantly reinstated (thanks to the enforcement of the Civil Rights Act of 1964 by the EEOC and the ACLU, but Lisa Macauley hadn't thought that worth mentioning)—along with his wife and their nine children in kneeling in front of the public crèche.

I finished the book around one in the morning in the Rhinelander Holiday Inn. The best-written part treated a subplot between Nan and the man who gave her career its first important boost—the pastor of the heroine's childhood church who had become a successful televangelist. When Nan was a child he had photographed her and other children in his Sunday school class engaged in forced sex with one another and with him. Since he held an awful fear of eternal damnation over their heads they never told their parents. But when Nan started her broadcast career she persuaded him to plug her program on his Thursday night "Circle of the Saved," using covert blackmail threats to get him to do so. At the end, as she looks at the baby Jesus in the manger, she wonders what Mary would have done—forgiven the pastor, or exposed him? Certainly not collaborated with him to further her own career. The book ended on that troubled note. I went to sleep with more respect for Macauley's craft than I had expected.

In the morning I found Mrs. Joseph Macauley's address in the local phone book and went off to see her. Although now in her mid-seventies she carried herself well. She didn't greet me warmly, but she accepted without demur my identification of myself as a detective trying to find Lisa's murderer. Chicago apparently was so convinced that I was the guilty party, they hadn't bothered to send anyone up to interview her.

"I am tired of all those Chicago reporters bothering me, but if you're a detective I guess I can answer your questions. What'd you want to know? I can tell you all about Lisa's childhood, but we didn't see so much of her once she moved off to Madison. We weren't too happy about some of the friends she was making. Not that we have anything against Jews personally, but we didn't want our only child marrying one and getting involved in all those dirty financial deals. Of course we were happy he was working for Ronald Reagan, but we weren't sorry they split up, even though our church frowns on divorce."

I let her talk unguided for a time before pulling out the picture of Claud Barnett. "This is someone Lisa knew as a child. Do you recognize him?"

Mrs. Macauley took the photo from me. "Do you think I'm not in possession of my faculties? That's Claud Barnett. He certainly never lived around here."

She snorted and started to hand the picture back, then took it to study more closely. "She knew I never liked to see her in pants, so she generally wore a skirt when she came up here. But she looks real cute in that outfit, real cute. You know, I guess I can see where she might have confused him with Carl Bader. Although Carl was dark-haired and didn't have a mustache, there is a little something around the forehead."

"And who was Carl Bader?"

"Oh, that's ancient history. He left town and we never heard anything more about it."

All I could get her to say about him was that he'd been connected to their church and she never did believe half the gossip some of the members engaged in. "That Mrs. Hoffer always overindulged her children, let them say anything and get away with it. We brought Lisa up to show proper respect for people in authority. Cleaned her mouth out with soap and whipped her so hard she didn't sit for a week the one time she tried taking part in some of that trashy talk."

More she wouldn't say, so I took the picture with me to the library and looked up old copies of the local newspaper. In *Slaybells Ring*, Nan Carruthers was eight when the pastor molested her, so I checked 1965 through 1967 for stories about Bader and anyone named Hoffer. All I found was a little blurb saying Bader had left the United Pentecostal Church of God in Holiness in 1967 to join a television ministry in Atlanta, and that he'd gone so suddenly that the church didn't have time to throw him a going-away party.

I spent a weary afternoon trying to find Mrs. Hoffer. There were twenty-seven Hoffers in the Rhinelander phone book; six were members of the United Pentecostal Church. The church secretary was pleasant and helpful, but it wasn't until late in the day that Mrs. Matthew Hoffer told me the woman I wanted, Mrs. Barnabas Hoffer, had quit the church over the episode about her daughter.

"Caused a lot of hard feeling in the church. Some people believed the children, and they quit. Others figured it was just mischief, children who like to make themselves look interesting. That Lisa Macauley was one. I'm sorry she got herself killed down in Chicago, but in a way I'm not surprised—seemed like she was always sort of *daring* you to smack her, the stories she made up and the way she put herself forward. Not that Louise Macauley spared the rod, mind you, but sometimes I think you can beat a child too much for its own good. Anyway, once people saw little Lisa, joining in with Katie Hoffer in accusing the pastor, no one took it seriously. No one except Gertrude—Katie's mom, I

mean. She still bears a grudge against all of us who stood by
Pastor Bader."

And finally, at nine o'clock, I was sitting on an overstuffed horsehair settee in Gertrude Hoffer's living room,
looking at a cracked color photo of two unhappy children. I
had to take Mrs. Hoffer's word that they were Katie and
Lisa—their faces were indistinct, and at this point in the
picture's age so were their actions.

"I found it when I was doing his laundry. Paster Bader
wasn't married, so all us church ladies took it in turn to look
after his domestic wants. Usually he was right there to put
his own clothes away, but this one time he was out and I was
arranging his underwear for him and found this whole stack
of pictures. I couldn't believe it at first, and then when I
came on Katie's face—well—I snatched it up and ran out
of there.

"At first I thought it was some evilness the children
dreamed up on their own, and that he had photographed
them to show us, show the parents what they got up to. That
was what he told my husband when Mr. Hoffer went to talk
to him about it. It took me a long time to see that a child
wouldn't figure out something like that on her own, but I
never could get any of the other parents to pay me any mind.
And that Louise Macauley, she just started baking pies for
Paster Bader every night of the week, whipped poor little
Lisa for telling me what he made her and Katie get up to. It's
a judgment on her, it really is, her daughter getting herself
killed like that."

V

It was hard for me to find someone in the Chicago Police
Department willing to try to connect Claud Barnett with

Carl Bader. Once they'd done that, though, the story unraveled pretty fast. Lisa had recognized him in Sun Valley and put the bite on him—not for money, but for career advancement, just as her heroine did her own old pastor in *Slaybells Ring*. No one would ever be able to find out for sure, but the emotional torment she put Nan Carruthers through must have paralleled Lisa's own misery. She was a success, she'd forced her old tormentor to make her a success, but it must have galled her—as it did her heroine—to pretend to admire him, to sit in on his show, and to see a film of torment overlay his face.

When Barnett read *Slaybells*, he probably began to worry that Lisa wouldn't be able to keep his secret to herself much longer. The police did find evidence of the threatening letters in his private study. The state argued that Barnett sent Lisa the threatening letters, then persuaded her to hire me to protect her. At that point Barnett didn't have anything special against me, but I was a woman. He figured if he could start enough public conflict between a woman detective and Lisa, he'd be able to fool the nightman, Reggi Whitman, into believing he was sending a woman up to Lisa's apartment on the fatal night. It was only later that he'd learned about my progressive politics—that was just icing on his cake, to be able to denounce me on his show.

Of course, not all this came out right away—some of it didn't emerge until the trial. That's when I also learned that Whitman, besides being practically a saint, had badly failing vision. On a cold night anyone could have passed himself off as me.

Between Murray and Beth Blacksin I got a lot of public vindication, and Sal and Queenie took me to dinner with Belle Fontaine to celebrate on the day the guilty verdict came in. We were all disappointed that they only slapped him with a second-degree murder. But what left me gasping for air was a public opinion poll that came out the next afternoon. Even though other examples of his child-molesting behavior had come to light during the trial, his listeners believed he was innocent of all charges.

"The femmunists made it all up trying to discredit him," one woman explained that afternoon on the air. "And they got the *New York Times* to print their lies."

Not even Queenie's reserve Veuve Clicquot could wipe that bitter taste out of my mouth.

This is Deborah Whittaker's first P.I. story, and despite the title, there is no cat in it. The title does have significance, however, and we believe that one day Deborah Whittaker and her CyberFemme P.I. Jazz Montgomery will have equal significance in this genre.

DEAD CAT BOUNCE
A JAZZ MONTGOMERY STORY

by Deborah Whittaker

"Sometimes even a death stock will rebound before it fades away completely. Hell, even a dead cat will bounce if you drop it from high enough."

> Adrian Turner
> President and Founder
> Adrian Turner Ventures

We stood on the grass squinting up at the building's glassy surface. Above us the climber's reflection appeared as a second struggling figure, laboring face to face against the original as they made their way toward the ninth-floor roof. Their progress was slow, the lifting and settling of hands and feet, maneuvering upward inches at a time. Overhead, thin clouds splayed across the sky, driven slowly by the slight wind. A shiny yellow emergency vehicle lingered at the edge of the parking lot, its rescue squad lounging against the van, good-naturedly drinking coffee and waiting to be sent home.

Not every eye was on the climber. Mitchell had been working his way to the top for almost an hour, long enough for onlookers to grow bored and turn toward other diversions in the carnival atmosphere. Ten or fifteen people stood in line at the beer keg; two dozen or more kicked back in little clusters near the refreshment stand, munching hot dogs and soy burgers as they came off the sizzling grill. The ambiance was classic Silicon Valley: a high-profile product announcement by SkyeTech Software, disguised as an elaborate Friday afternoon beer bust on the corporate grounds.

I was enjoying the suspense of Mitchell's climb, but also taking in the atmosphere, feeling light on my feet and just plain happy for an excuse to be outside in the warmth of early spring. My presence was required, as an employee of Adrian Turner Ventures, SkyeTech's primary investor. But since I didn't have any special duties to perform, I'd pushed Adrian's professional dress code to the limit and was mostly sopping up sunshine.

"When I was a kid, this place was a pear orchard. Or maybe it was apricot."

I half-turned, to see my boss standing beside me. As always, Adrian Turner stood out in the crowd. Today his tall-dark-and-handsome good looks were set off by a sleek charcoal double-breasted suit. Of course, in the mostly jeans and T-shirt software crowd, anyone in a suit was high contrast. I saw him suppress a sigh as he took in the tasteful (I thought) purple suspenders holding up my black leather miniskirt. The sudden arch of his eyebrows made me glad I had taken the time to rinse the chartreuse streak out of my hair. I put a hand to my ear before he could count the earrings, and pitched my voice to an inquisitive tone.

"What's the deal with this urban mountaineering?" I asked him.

Adrian lifted his shoulders and allowed himself to be distracted. "You know Mitchell Greenway. If he's not risking his neck, he doesn't know he's alive."

I shrugged back at him. "Sure, Mitchell's the original adrenaline junkie. But I didn't know *anyone* could climb a glass building."

"It's not common," he conceded. "That's why it's good publicity. Dan Goodwin climbed the Sears Tower about fifteen years ago." He made a gesture toward the building. "Take a look at Mitchell's hands and feet."

I watched as the climber positioned his left hand overhead, secured it, then used his right hand to loosen the right foot. Anchoring him to the building were four cherry-colored discs. The wind teased the white scarf around his neck into a fluttering ribbon.

"Those red bowls?"

"Suction cups. Not exactly state-of-the-art climbing technology. Same as Goodwin's, though. Think of them as oversized plumber's helpers."

The thought gave me goose bumps and I automatically resettled my feet more firmly on the ground. I didn't bother to ask where he'd learned all this. Adrian is to information as a Dustbuster is to dust. As the brains and guts behind ATV, more often than not he spins the dust into gold. Five years ago he hired me away from the computer fraud division of the Santa Clara County's D.A.'s office. I have a private investigator's license I can pull out when I think it will do me some good, but my current business card reads, "Jaye Z. Montgomery, Research Associate." Look, Ma— I'm a venture capitalist!

Adrian swept back an ivory cuff and peered at his watch. "If Mitchell draws this out much longer, we'll lose the news media before the formal announcement." He let his eyes scan the scene. I could practically hear his thoughts worrying the bottom line. *Is this working? Is it cost effective? What's the return?* He had reason to be concerned. ATV's six-million-dollar investment was riding on the success of SkyeTech's new product line. Behind us, a camera operator from KTSV was recording Mitchell's climb. With any luck, we'd land a plump sound bite on the evening news, exposure that would more than pay for today's extravaganza.

"Can you believe this? Count on Mitchell to make a fool of himself." Colin Rice lowered his voice confidentially as he came up to stand beside us. Even though his words were negative, his face was scrunched into a professional smile.

Rice was Mitchell Greenway's partner and the co-founder of SkyeTech. But where Mitchell was hiking boots, VW buses, and Berkeley UNIX, Colin Rice was Armani, Volvos, and a Stanford MBA. Together, they were odd-couple brilliant. When I'd investigated them as part of ATV's pre-investment due diligence, I'd concluded that the hints of discord were the usual oil and water squabbles between entrepreneur and technoid. Annoying, but not fatal. I hadn't noted in my report that I'd liked Mitchell better than Colin.

I turned toward the woman Colin had been possessively towing behind him. She was blond and fragile in a way that suggested illness or stress. Belatedly, he introduced her as his wife, Sandy, and after a few social niceties, they moved on, Colin dragging her like a dinghy in his wake. Almost immediately we were joined by Martin Stephanos, SkyeTech's chief financial officer. When he and Adrian began a friendly argument about the viability of certain high-tech stocks, I turned away to check out the scene.

I wandered toward the games pavilion, drawn by the cacophony of electronic beeps and synthesized yowls. The open-air canopy was filled with PC stations, where a dozen children were playing one of the new games. On either side of the entrance stood six-foot replicas of the packaging for Here Kitty, Kitty!, a computer game aimed at the emerging market of pre-adolescent girls. The artwork on the box was of brilliant, primary-colored cats stuck in trees, caught on roof tops and clinging to the ledges of towering skyscrapers.

I joined a small crowd behind a red-haired ten-year-old who was using a joystick to maneuver her cartoon counterpart through the game. The object was to use the available equipment—fire trucks, ladders, parachutes, etc.—to rescue the stranded kittens. While I watched, the girl rescued two kittens, gathering points and electronic applause, but then tripped on a tree branch as she reached for the third cat. Cartoon kitten and cartoon child tumbled toward the bottom of the screen and certain disaster. Just before cartoon impact, a kinder, gentler marketing approach morphed the characters into winged kitty angels who fluttered gently up and off-stage. Game Over. My hands were itching for a chance to play, but the kid had the joystick in a death grip. I watched the girl muscle her way through two more of her feline lives before I gave up and moved away.

Stepping from shade into bright sunlight, I nearly tripped over the thick black video cables snaking across the lawn, but managed to right myself before I landed on the grass. When I had stopped teetering, I shaded my eyes and looked up to where the camera was still pointing. Mitchell's vertical crabwalk had brought him to the sixth floor, but the rhythm of his ascent had faltered. His right arm slammed the red cup against the glass, but the cup was finding no purchase on the slick surface. Even from that distance we could see the coiled tension in his arm as he thrust the cup again and again against the thick glass. Suddenly, the purchase of a second rubber piton failed, and Mitchell's foot slipped, leaving his leg dangling. He hung quietly for a moment, staring at his own reflection.

Then his body burst into panicked energy, opposite arm and leg flailing. As if in response, the 12-foot window tile he was climbing to shifted, shimmied, and loosened itself from the rest of the building. It tilted toward the ground, its mirrored surface giving the illusion that the sky itself had cracked along its seams. The window tipped out of its casing, and in a slow-motion somersault, tumbled end over end as it fell, still holding Mitchell by two of the ruby suction cups.

The sound that Mitchell's body made hitting the ground was swallowed up by the explosion of plate glass disintegrating into shards of light. Pebbles of safety glass blew thirty feet into the air and then hailed down around the felled climber. The crowd retreated, shrieking and shielding their faces from the debris. Then we stood for a moment in stunned silence, staring as if we expected Mitchell to rise up and throw us one of his daredevil smiles. But there was no angelic morphing. When the ladders, fire trucks and police cars arrived, it was only to cart away a broken corpse.

Three days later I was sitting in my cubicle facing my monitor when Adrian quietly walked up behind me and leaned against the door. I could see his reflection in the screen, though I couldn't read his expression. But I knew from his tone that he was agitated.

"Have you been following SkyeTech this morning?"

I nodded glumly, swiveling to face him. It was a rhetorical question. The Valley lives and breathes by its hourly NASDAQ service. This morning's news was all bad.

SkyeTech was falling.

"Down eleven points since the market opened," Adrian said. On paper at least, a fifty percent loss on ATV's investment.

"It gets worse. I got a call from Colin Rice this morning.

He thinks Mitchell may have sabotaged the source code for the line."

My response came out in a yelp. "Why would Mitchell cut his own throat like that?" Under the circumstances, it was a bad choice of words, but Adrian didn't seem to notice.

"He thinks Mitchell was making some sort of power play. They were always at odds over something."

It was a familiar problem. To make it big in the Valley takes both vision and hard-headed realism. After an intensely focused beginning, start-up companies often go through power struggles between their idealistic and more pragmatic factions. It had been inevitable that Colin and Mitchell would clash.

Seconds passed before Adrian continued. "SkyeTech's new products should make the stock bounce back. Their gross margins look good and their management team is solid, even without Mitchell's talent. But if they lose much time to market on the next delivery . . ."

Time streaks through the Valley at the speed of electrons, measured by digital clocks ticking so fast you only hear a hum. Chips that cost $50 million to build are obsolete in eighteen months. Last year's cutting-edge technology is today's doorstop. Adrian spread his hands in front of him, palms up, saying nothing and everything about how much we had riding on SkyeTech's success.

"What can we do?"

Then he smiled, and a lock of dark hair curled across his forehead as he leaned toward me. "*I* am going to make some calls, check out the reaction on the street. *You* are going to SkyeTech to nose around."

"But I've already done all the background research—I've even pulled the original files and reviewed them. There's nothing there that could have predicted this." I was hoping I was telling the truth. Could I have missed something?

"I'm sure the time won't be wasted. Look at Mitchell's computers and file systems. Colin's agreed to give you the run of the place. If Mitchell intentionally sabotaged the product, he'll have left some traces." His smile deepened. "Do some of your magic, Jazz," he said. "Be a hero."

There it was. Adrian was counting on my overinflated sense of competence as a technocrat. Well, hey . . . all those midnight hours in the comp sci lab have got to be good for something.

"I'll report back this afternoon."

Before I left the office I took another look at the information I'd gathered as part of our due diligence on the SkyeTech investment. I'd done public records searches, credit reports, corporate affiliation searches through the state capitol, and conducted interviews with every relevant subject I could dig up. I also secured every net source I could find, trying to weasel out whatever dirt the software community might be holding. What I had found was mostly goose eggs.

Colin Rice and Mitchell Greenway had met when they both worked for a large game company in San Mateo, twenty miles up the bay. They'd both hated working for someone else when they were convinced they could do it better on their own. When management trounced their ideas for the nth time, they'd quit their jobs, put together a business plan, and hacked together just enough code to impress investment houses like ATV. SkyeTech Software, Inc. was born.

Mitchell Greenway had been thirty-one at the time of his death, young, but not outrageously so for the founder of a software company. I'd found no public record of malfeasance, no outstanding liens or foreclosures, no other record of outstanding misconduct. He was single, and had the unusual reputation as a technoid connoisseur of blondes.

But the worst anyone could say about him was that he didn't always fasten his seat belt.

Colin Rice, thirty-seven, was the businessman of the partnership. He was a little older, a little smoother, and a little more willing to play the corporate game. He and Sandy had been married since college and had two small children. Like Mitchell, Colin was driven to succeed, but he was sure to be buckled up for the ride.

On the way out, I stopped in the rest room and stood for a moment in front of the full-length mirror. I straightened a crease in my linen skirt, glad I was already dressed for a client visit. My vintage 1960's fuchsia A-line dress might not have been what Adrian had in mind, but it was well within the limits he had laid down as the law of professional attire. Besides, I thought, grinning at myself, it looks great with my black thigh boots and my zippered motorcycle jacket. Satisfied, I clomped down the stairs to my car.

By early afternoon I was parking in the SkyeTech visitors lot. I shivered as I glanced up at the building, but the only trace of Friday's tragedy was a residual sparkle in the lawn next to the walkway.

The SkyeTech "campus" consisted of a single floor of the nine-story building, which in San Jose pretty much passes as a skyscraper. The receptionist gave me a sticky visitor's pass to slap on my chest and left me to find Colin's office. To get there, I made my way past the mahogany row of executive offices, throwing a wave to Martin Stephanos who sat behind his wide desk raking a calculator with frantic fingers. He didn't wave back.

Colin Rice had lost his slick smile along with the energy it took to maintain the façade. He rose to greet me, then slumped back in his chair.

"I'm sorry about Mitchell," I started, but he waved me off, nodding.

"We'll survive that," he said, then stopped himself. "I didn't mean that the way it sounded. I'll miss Mitchell once I get over being angry with him." His frown deepened. "He's completely screwed us over."

"So Adrian tells me. What's the problem?"

"It's the graphics libraries for the new product line. All the new games use them, but the source files are corrupted. Like someone went in with an eggbeater. Some are missing completely and the version control program has been tampered with."

"But the game is packaged and ready to ship, right?"

"Sure, we've got the binaries, the compiled files. But heaven help us if there's a malfunction and we need to build replacements. And forget about using any of the existing work to create new games." His tone became more frantic as he spoke.

"What about your off-site backups?" I knew our contract with SkyeTech required them to keep copies in a holding company vault.

"We checked them an hour ago. They're useless without the encryption key. Mitchell must have changed it months ago without letting anyone know. Every backup tape we have is worthless."

"Any idea why he did it? Or even if it *was* Mitchell?"

"Oh, it was Mitchell, all right. And I've a pretty good idea why. A year ago he withheld a release until I hired the crew he wanted. There was nothing I could do but cave. He probably wanted another concession of some sort—but his timing is a disaster, to say the least."

It's not a secret, but it's something we don't talk much about in the industry. Computer code is fragile. The damage a single person can do in an unprotected environment is enormous. Forget about two-weeks' notice: when a disgruntled employee leaves the company, he's hustled to the door like a potential terrorist.

We talked for a while about some things I might do to help, but he had no concrete suggestions. I gathered he was weighing some alternatives, but he didn't share them with me. As we were finishing, there was a timid knock on the door. It opened slightly before he could reply and Sandy Rice hesitantly peered inside.

"Oh, you're busy." She was retreating by the time I stood up and moved toward the door.

"That's okay. I was just leaving."

She gave me an apologetic smile that was as pale as her complexion. Then the lines of her face drooped in an echo of Colin's. "I was just dropping off some insurance forms. For vaccinations this time. I feel like I spend my whole life either at preschool or in the pediatrician's office."

Having neither spouse nor offspring, I wasn't sure how to respond. I gave her what I hoped was an encouraging smile and left them to their domestic arrangements.

Colin had given me the run of the building, and encouraged me to ask as many questions as I needed. But in fact, only a handful of employees were working in the village of cubicles that made up the floor's interior. Those I saw spoke in hushed voices, their shoes barely making any sound as they scuffled along the industrial carpeting.

Mitchell had a walled office on the west side of the building's sixth floor. Three computers crowded his large L-shaped desk: a PC, a Mac, and a top-of-the-line Silicon Graphics workstation. An empty chrome hatrack was angled awkwardly against the wall and a six-foot blow-up stegosaurus loomed in one corner. I stopped in the doorway, taking in the juvenile atmosphere. The painted surfaces were covered with posters and shelves full of wind-up toys. Valentines from last month's holiday plastered the left wall, the biggest a bold crimson heart with the inscription, "Love always, BB."

As I moved further inside, I let myself be pulled toward the pale light filtering into the office from the west side. The coated glass panel filled the wall, giving the illusion that there was no separation between the room and the empty sky beyond. Looking out, I could see all across the Valley to the foothills of Los Gatos and the gray haze of pollution collected in the pass.

The only indication of the pane's thickness was the steel frame that bordered it, running about six inches around the perimeter. It seemed a fragile holder for such a monolithic piece of glass. My arms lifted reflexively, and I pressed my palms against the middle of the panel, looking for give. The chilled surface stayed firm, but I heard a slight rasping sound when I put my elbows behind it. With my head down, I found myself looking directly at the pathway and bushes below and became aware for the first time of the distance to the ground. Vertigo struck me, disrupting my sense of balance. I started to tip forward, righted myself with an effort, and stepped away from the window, shaking my head. From the open door, a woman's voice came to me.

"It must be an eerie sensation, falling."

Still dizzy I swiveled, slowly, to see who had spoken. She was dressed in a denim skirt and baggy sweater, her sunlit hair tied in a ponytail low on the back of her neck. I recognized her as someone I'd met in connection with SkyeTech's IPO, but I couldn't pull up her name.

"Colin said you needed some help." She crossed the room and put out her hand. "I'm Anna Simoni."

I placed her then and remembered that we had a connection even further back than SkyeTech. I used to see her nights when I would sneak into the Stanford computer science lab to freeload hours on their machines. Even in those days Anna had a reputation as a talented hacker. Since then, she'd parlayed a savvy for product strategy into V.P. of marketing at SkyeTech. By convincing Colin and Mitchell to both create and publish their own product, she'd pushed them beyond the status of a development house and into a potential megastar. I took her hand and regarded her with interest.

"It was this window, you know." Anna raised a hand and pointed with one finger. "They had a crane out here by dawn on Saturday. You can still see the putty they used to seal the new pane."

I looked where she was pointing. Along the inside of the frame, viscous transparent beads had dried to the color of pale amber. Remembering the feel of the cool glass, I stared down at my hands.

Following my gaze, she said, "It wouldn't pop out so easily today, when they've just sealed it. But it gets less secure after the gel has aged. It's a classic exercise for architecture students. 'How to build with glass walls.'" She stared out the window. "Mitchell and I were close. We used to stand here together inventing lives for the people we saw down below." She paused for only a second. "Lately the stories were angry and sad."

I waited for her to continue, but she only stood staring. "Is that why he took such risks?" I asked.

She shrugged. "Who knows?" She waved a hand to indicate the view of metropolitan San Jose and beyond. "It's not as if we have lives of our own. We put in such long hours. We sit with our heads in our computers and communicate via E-mail. Everyone knows someone who's opted out."

"Suicide? You think Mitchell's fall was intentional?" I didn't try to hide my surprise.

Without answering, she wrapped her arms around herself and rocked from side to side, a movement that made her head shake slightly. But she didn't say No.

Instead she uncurled her arms and headed for the workstation on Mitchell's desk. She seated herself and began tapping the keys purposefully as I slid behind to watch over her shoulder.

"These are the program directories where we store the source code. On the surface everything looks fine, but you can see from this"—she tapped a fingernail against a column on the screen—"that everything was last updated on the same date, late last Thursday. I'm guessing Mitchell had been working on the changes in a shadow directory for some time, and finally moved everything into place that day."

"Why? What was he trying to accomplish?"

Her face took on a puzzled expression. "That's the difficult part. Mitchell was reckless, but he wasn't into power games. Except with Colin, of course. And that was just for the sport of it." She made a sound that was half laugh, half sigh. "Poor Colin makes an easy target."

She dropped her head into one hand and smoothed the hair back with her palm. When she looked up, she said, "Still, doesn't this *accident* seem like an untidy coincidence? Just when the files were corrupted? Just before a board meeting next week? With Mitchell's melancholy state of mind?"

I was beginning to ask myself similar questions. Could Mitchell have planned a spectacular exit, leaving behind the ruin of all he'd worked for the past three years?

I changed the subject. "Will you be able to restore the files?"

"Of course. I mean, *I* can, given some time. I don't know

if anyone else could." Simoni's arrogance was something else I'd belatedly remembered.

She turned back to the computer and used the mouse to pull up a full-screen video window. I found myself inspecting a freeze frame of the building from the outside, a climber already established on the sixth floor.

"This was on the eleven o'clock news last night. Someone captured it with a VCR and posted it on the net today." When she tapped the mouse again, the climber on the screen began a disjointed crawl up the building's surface.

"I downloaded it at only ten frames per second. That's why the video looks spastic. It's only displaying one frame for every three you'd have seen on last night's broadcast."

I couldn't pull my eyes away from the image. I watched Mitchell stare at the windowpane, mesmerized by his own reflection. I saw again his desperate flailing and the terrible descent. I recoiled at the spectacular smashup just before the clip ran out. Seeing the action through the familiar interface of the computer hadn't given me any emotional distance. My shoulders were tensed and my knees were shaking. I was glad to take the chance to leave.

As I was about to step out the door, I glanced into an open cardboard box off to one side. It was filled with yellow cable, chrome pulleys, and four red rubber suction cups that looked like they belonged on toilet plungers, each with a metal clamp, dead center.

I felt a chill run up my spine, but I didn't know of any reason why they shouldn't simply have tossed the climbing equipment into Mitchell's office. The police hadn't declared the area a crime scene and, except for Anna's suspicions, there was no indication of suicide.

At least Anna's questions had given me something new to look into, and an excuse to put off calling Adrian with bad news. I picked up the box and lugged it down to my car.

As I took the elevator downstairs, I still couldn't get the video image out of my mind. Over and over I saw Mitchell beat his arm against the glass, then tumble to the ground still attached to the mirrored pane. I couldn't stop asking myself, *What was he thinking as he watched himself fall?*

Radical Mountain is a twenty-four-hour sporting goods shop and climbing wall tucked into the corner of a strip mall on Stevens Creek Boulevard. Their clientele tends to be the late-night crowd, mostly software engineers bugged out from long hours hacking code. When I arrived in the midafternoon, the only other patrons were a couple of high-schoolers taking a lesson on the wall.

The clerk had the narrow, stringy muscles of someone who pushes them to the extreme, not lifting weights in an air-conditioned gym, but doing real work, such as lifting his body up the face of a cliff. He reacted instantly to the red rubber objects I plopped on the counter.

"Whoa! Dan Goodwin specials! Did somebody actually use these things?"

I was surprised he hadn't heard about the accident, and I told him so.

"Cowboy stuff. Yeah, I heard about it. A stunt."

"What do you mean?" I asked.

"Serious climbers don't pull stunts. I mean, you might go for some extreme urban shit, but not for publicity." He put his elbows on the counter and leaned toward me conspiratorially. "See, real urban climbers don't want to take the chance of being stopped before they start. It's better to ask for forgiveness than permission, right?"

"So you recognize this equipment?"

"Dan Goodwin's the only guy I know who seriously climbed using suction cups. Straight up the Sears Tower in

1981. Wearing a Spiderman costume. Fifteen hundred feet. Totally gonzo."

He picked up one of the cups. "See this? Way too much play around this metal clamp in the middle."

I hunched up over the counter and looked as he held the clamp. "Why? What's wrong with it?"

"Well, for starters, they're either really old or really badly maintained. Doesn't take much to corrode rubber like that. And there's way too much air around the fitting. Not enough suction. Guy'd be a fool to climb with equipment like this." He leaned back and straightened his shoulders. "Either a fool or another total gonzo. Know what I mean?"

Having seen the failure for myself, I didn't argue with him. "What about loosening a window enough to make it pop out of a glass building? Could that happen?"

His response straddled the line between a guffaw and a snort. "Haw! Doesn't take much to pop those puppies out. You know about the Bernoulli effect?"

Harkening back to a high-school physics class, I asked, "You mean the effect that keeps planes in the air, right?"

"Same thing happens vertically. Wind flowing past the building creates a negative air pressure on the outside. Sooner or later—kerpow! Buildings like that are scary to walk under. I wouldn't even want to *think* about climbing one."

Only in the Valley, I thought, could you get a lesson in aerodynamics from a guy whose nametag said "Biff."

I thanked him for his time and gathered up the equipment wondering if I was any further ahead. What I'd been told certainly seemed to confirm Mitchell's death wish. Something else was bothering me, too, ricocheting around the back of my head like an old Ping-Pong game, but never quite making it into my consciousness. I decided to pursue one last detail before I checked back with Adrian to report my defeat.

Heading toward the offices of KTSV, I cruised across town on the Guadalupe Expressway and parked in the underground garage on First Street. As I hopped out and turned the key in the handle to lock up, I felt someone reach across and grab my hand. I whirled into what I hoped was a defensive posture, elbows bent and hands out in front of me. Sandy Rice stared back at me with big eyes, then swiveled her head around to see what monster was lurking behind her.

"Jeez Louise!" I smacked my hand across the front of my jacket to keep my heart from exploding out of my chest. "What are you doing here? Don't you know better than to startle someone in a dark parking lot?"

Her lips trembled, but she didn't make any sound.

"Get in," I told her, and turned the key again to unlock the passenger door.

When she was seated, staring at the floorboards, she finally spoke. "I left Colin's office when you did and followed you," she said. "I almost died when I saw you going into the mountaineering shop. I guess you know everything now."

She gave me another one of the wide-eyed stares and a hesitant smile. She wasn't making any sense, but she was triggering my curiosity.

"Tell me."

She grasped at my hand again, her fingers bony against my wrist. "You have to believe it was an accident. I never meant for him to be killed."

Subtlety is not my usual forte. So it cost me something to contain my reaction. I managed to hold it down to a stiff nod of encouragement, and waited for her to go on.

Sandy took back her hand and pressed the heel against

her forehead. "I never thought he'd actually make the climb, not with damaged equipment. I only meant to show him that he couldn't take such risks with our future at stake." Her voice dropped to a whisper. "With *me* at stake."

I studied her for a moment through a different glass. Slender, blond, attractive when she had some color in her cheeks. Married to an execubot, and trapped at home most days with two small children: Caesar's wife with toddlers. Had she rebelled?

I took a guess. "You're BB?"

The sound she made was almost a laugh. "It was a joke. It stood for Blond Bombshell."

"And Colin? Were you going to leave him?"

"Yes. If I could have. Colin's so strong, and I'm . . ." She was weeping now, curling her arms around herself, leaning her head toward the dash. "Mitchell told me he had a plan that would make Colin let me go. He said that by next week he'd have the upper hand."

So that's why Mitchell needed a hold over Colin, I realized. But he died before he could use it.

"I thought loosening the fittings would stop him. It only took me a few minutes with a screwdriver and some Vaseline to damage them enough to jeopardize the suction." She stopped, head still hanging. "I should have hacked them into little pieces."

By the time she finished, I wasn't really listening. A process running in the back of my head had finally produced its output. The questions were starting to answer themselves.

"Listen, Sandy, you'd better go. I've got an errand to run, and then I'm going back to SkyeTech. Can you meet me there in an hour?"

"You're not going to bring the police?" There was genuine horror in her eyes.

I promised I wasn't, and she left, throwing glances at me over her shoulder as she moved toward her own car.

Upstairs at KTSV, I used a small, white lie in the form of a promise, to get access to the tape I wanted to see.

"So Adrian will be here Sunday morning at nine-thirty for makeup, right? The show airs live for thirty minutes, and Adrian will be the only guest." Emily, the producer of *Silicon Valley Sunday*, turned to me with a burst of enthusiasm. "I can't believe I finally landed Adrian Turner."

"Me too," I told her.

In the little viewing booth, we sat huddled over a small monitor while Emily cued up the thirty-minute segment. She fast-forwarded past the anchors' happy talk, and then slow-mowed through Mitchell's fall.

"Euuuwww. Gruesome! I can't believe we got the whole thing on tape. I mean, all the way down. Yech!"

For another twenty minutes I directed her as she moved forward and backward, a frame at a time, until I'd seen what I'd come for. I waited while she made me a copy of the tape, then called Adrian from my cell phone. He took the news without comment, and agreed to meet me at SkyeTech. I thought I'd wait to mention his new plans for Sunday.

In the little conference room at SkyeTech, I stood at the head of the table with the television and VCR on a stand to my right, the remote control in my hand. I'd had no trouble convincing everyone to join me, especially when I told them Adrian had called the meeting. Seated around the table were Anna Simoni, Colin Rice, Adrian Turner, Sandra Rice and Martin Stephanos. I waited until I had their full attention before giving them the bad news.

"I'm afraid Adrian and I have brought you here under false pretenses," I told them. "Nothing I have found today will help us recover from Mitchell's sabotage of the source code."

Rice and Stephanos immediately began protesting. Anna Simoni looked smug, as if it wasn't news to her. I held up my hand for silence.

"Instead, I have a videotape of Friday's accident. Once you've seen it, I think you'll agree that we have a bigger issue at stake. This tape will clearly show that Mitchell's fall was no accident. And what's caught on this tape will reveal Mitchell's murderer."

This time the protest was louder and came from both sides of the table. Colin rose as though headed for the door.

Adrian's voice took on a tone of command. "Sit down, Colin."

Colin hesitated, then returned to his chair, the muscles of his neck and shoulders bunched with tension.

I used the remote to turn on the machine and start the tape, playing the entire fall at regular speed. There were gasps around the table, and Sandy put her hands to her eyes.

"Let me show you only the crucial frames." I rewound the tape to just before the first failure of Mitchell's rubber pitons, then stepped it forward one frame at a time until the window separated itself from the building's façade and leaned its weight toward the ground. Stephanos was squinting at the television screen, his face jutted forward. Anna Simoni stiffened in her chair, but said nothing. Colin Rice was sitting back with an expression of wonderment and relief.

"There's nothing there. You can't see anything."

"Actually, you can see quite a lot, Colin." I looked up, not at Colin, but toward Adrian, who nodded with an expression of grim satisfaction. "What was it you were expecting to see?"

Colin turned his face to mine, but he had seen the look Adrian and I had exchanged. "Nothing. Why are you asking me? Why should there have been anything to see?" His voice was an octave higher than usual and his jaw kept working after he stopped talking.

"What I wanted you to notice was this," I told Colin. As I stepped the video forward, frame by frame, we watched again as the window tipped forward. But this time we saw the window separate from its frame well before most of Mitchell's blows struck home. What hadn't been obvious at ten frames per second was much clearer at thirty.

Adrian's voice was calm, but his words were pointed. "When did you know, Colin? And how hard was it to keep the knowledge to yourself?"

Colin squirmed in his seat and didn't answer. Adrian nodded to me, and I spilled it, still speaking directly to Colin.

"They say it's impossible not to know that your spouse is having an affair. I think you knew. And you also knew that Anna Simoni felt abandoned when Mitchell took up with Sandy. After Mitchell's accident you guessed that Anna had taken her revenge. But you couldn't say anything without risking your only chance of resurrecting the corrupted files."

Anna stood up, and then thought better of the impulse. "I want a lawyer," she said, and sat back down.

The next day, when the news hit the street, SkyeTech stock took a dive that was unrelieved by even a dead-cat bounce, and was then quietly withdrawn from trading. Without Mitchell's creative vision and Anna's marketing skills it seems unlikely that Colin and the remaining employees will be able to soften the landing. Too late, one of Anna Simoni's programmers discovered a complete, immaculate backup on one of Colin's home computers.

Anna's silence didn't help her much. I heard later from a source in the SJPD that her fingerprints had been found on the chrome hatrack in Mitchell's office. Upside down, in a position consistent with her having used the feet of the hatrack to push out the west wall-window. We'll probably never know whether her act was premeditated or only an impulse as she stood inside Mitchell's office watching him stare in at her.

ATV lost nearly all of its investment in SkyeTech, but Adrian never suggested that, like Colin, I should have withheld what I learned that day. His reaction to the loss was characteristic: his mood turned black for a week, then rebounded over the excitement of a new opportunity in the next hot market. His segment on *Silicon Valley Sunday* was the highest rated of the year. As penance for tricking him into it, I haven't worn leather to the office in a week.

As for me, I learned a valuable lesson about the fallibility of using human nature to predict return on investment. In the end, it wasn't Mitchell's wild recklessness I should have worried about, or even the dark side of the conservative businessman. I thought living in the world of circuitry and logic made us immune to the rages of the human heart. After Anna's revenge, I realized that flesh and blood makes us all subject to the same shattering pain, and we are all reflections of each other.

The original title of this story was "Buddha's Belly" and if you like that one better don't blame the author because she didn't change it, we did. Margaret Lucke's story "Identity Crisis" was one of the highlights of the original Lethal Ladies *anthology, and we were delighted when she and Jess Randolph agreed to come back for LL2. Jess appeared in the novel* A Relative Stranger.

DREAMING OF DRAGONS
A JESS RANDOLPH STORY

by Margaret Lucke

"PROMISE ME YOU won't go to the police," Celine said.

I set my chopsticks on my plate and looked at her. "Have you committed a crime?"

"Of course not, Jess." She sipped her jasmine tea. Her nails were perfect rosy ovals against the blue china cup. "All I want you to do is return a lost necklace to its rightful owner."

"Who is that?" I asked.

With a deep sigh she sank back in her chair. "I don't know," she said. "I wish I did."

I'd been surprised when Celine Pratt phoned that morning and asked me to lunch. We both served on the board of the San Francisco Initiative for the Arts, but otherwise we had little in common. I worked as a private investigator; Celine was a senior executive of a Fortune 500 company. She lived at the crest of Pacific Heights with her banker husband, Garrick, and two teenage kids. I lived in a Haight-Ashbury flat with a mixed-breed pup and my painting easel. Having met Garrick, I figured I had the better deal.

But I couldn't resist her invitation. It was a bleak February Friday and the case report I was trying to write was driving me crazy. I suggested Shen Nung in Chinatown. Not only was it convenient to her office and mine, it served excellent fiery Mongolian beef.

I grasped another peppery morsel with my chopsticks, imagining that the other diners were tut-tutting over my clumsy technique. This was the week of the Chinese New Year celebration, so the restaurant was crowded. Celine and I were among the few non-Chinese customers. She'd played it safe, ordering the timidly seasoned cashew chicken and eating it with a fork.

"I'm glad to help," I told her. "But the police might be your best bet. If the owner's reported the loss, they can return the necklace right away."

"No police," Celine insisted as she shook something from a black plastic bag. "Feast your eyes on this."

She held it up—a disk of grass-green jade, as wide as my fist, hanging from a heavy gold chain. Carved on the stone in sharp relief was a prancing dragon.

Taking the necklace, I stroked the creature's sinuous curves. "What a handsome fellow."

"Isn't he? I thought you could check with the store whose name's on the bag. The medallion's so distinctive—they might remember who bought it."

She smoothed the bag out on the table. MING'S HOUSE OF TREASURES was printed in gold on the black plastic. The Grant Avenue address was just a block away.

"If this isn't yours, Celine, where did you get it?"

"I . . . found it."

"Lying on the sidewalk? In a hollowed-out book? Buried in a container of cottage cheese?"

"Does it matter where, as long as it gets returned?"

I had a flash. "This has to with one of your kids, doesn't it?"

"Really, Jess, I don't think . . ." She fell silent and looked away.

"Celine," I said, "you're hiring me to help you. I can do that better and faster if you'll tell me what you're hiding."

She poured more tea for both of us. I picked up my cup, inhaling the flowery scent as I waited for her to speak.

Finally she did. "You're right. Ricky gave me the necklace for my birthday yesterday. There's no way he could afford something like this, not even if he saved his allowance all year. And he didn't, I assure you."

"Where does he say he got it?"

"He refuses to tell. I cajoled and prodded, even threatened to ground him. All I could get out of him was the plastic bag. I'm afraid he—Jess, he's only fourteen, he's a good kid. If we can just find where the necklace came from and return it . . ."

"You think Ricky stole it."

"No, of course not . . . oh, I don't know what to think. Jennifer never gives me a minute of trouble, but Ricky . . . he started high school in September. He's had a rough time adjusting."

"Where does he go?"

"Oceanview Academy. Jennifer's a senior there, she gets straight A's." Celine's expression mixed bewilderment and pride.

"Good place." It was one of the city's most exclusive private high schools.

"Yes. It's excellent scholastically. And the student body's very diverse, every culture and ethnic group in the city is represented. Garrick and I wanted a school that will prepare the kids for the real world."

Right, I thought. A real world where every family has a six-figure annual income.

Celine took a bite, then continued. "Ricky's not paying attention to his schoolwork any more. He's fallen in with this gang that—"

"They've got gangs at Oceanside?"

"I don't mean a drug-dealing, drive-by-shooting kind of gang. Just a group of kids who seem . . . reckless, I guess. They get into scrapes, tempt each other with silly dares, and then they're surprised when they get into trouble. They don't seem to consider that actions have consequences."

"You think these kids dared Ricky to steal the necklace?"

"No, but . . . it occurred to me he could be protecting Peter or Mark."

"Who are . . . ?"

"His new best friends. Peter Chan and Mark Santoro."

I took my sketchbook from my satchel and jotted down the names.

Celine put out a hand to stop me. "Jess, I told you, I don't want the kids involved—"

"They're the only lead you have, Celine, if the store doesn't work out. Don't worry, I won't get them in trouble." Unless they deserve it, I added silently.

With the necklace in my satchel, I walked north on Grant into a bitter wind, jostling around the horde of pedestrians, the postcard racks, the tables covered with souvenir T-shirts and cloisonné trinkets. The rainy afternoon was brightened by red-and-gold banners fluttering from lampposts, wishing everyone GUNG HAY FAT CHOY—Happy and Prosperous New Year.

When I reached Ming's House of Treasures I was welcomed by a smiling wooden Buddha, four feet high, that stood by the door. A sign was posted beside him: RUB MY

HEAD FOR WISDOM OR MY BELLY FOR LUCK. His belly, I noticed, was much shinier than his head.

I massaged Buddha's brow. Better to be wise than lucky, I decided. I felt wiser just for having reached that sensible conclusion.

But inside the shop I had second thoughts. I stepped back out and rubbed the fat tummy, just to be on the safe side.

"Splendid jade," Mr. Ming announced as he examined the dragon through his loupe. "Best quality."

If that's so, I wondered, why is he frowning?

Ming's House of Treasures was a long, narrow shop. Down both sides, display cases overflowed with jade pendants, ropes of pearls, baubles of coral and amber and rich blue lapis lazuli. I saw a dozen things I'd have bought in an instant if I'd had a few hundred dollars to spare. But nothing as appealing as the prancing dragon.

Mr. Ming was a middle-aged man in a stiff-looking suit, as thin as the wooden Buddha was plump. He put down the loupe and eyed me sternly across the glass counter. "May I ask where you obtained this exquisite piece?"

I deflected his question, saying, "The plastic bag suggests it came from here. But you don't have anything on display quite like it."

The door chime sounded. I turned to see a pair of men touch Buddha's belly as they strode in. They headed straight to the rear of the shop, nodding brusquely at Mr. Ming before they disappeared through a curtained doorway. He nodded back, then gave his attention to me.

"I would be honored to sell such a treasure," he said. "But someone has deceived you using my bag. This necklace was never in my inventory."

"Any idea what it's worth?"

"I would say it is priceless. It is an antique piece, one of a kind, hand-carved by a true artist. See how intricate the work is. The dragon's claws, the twist of its tail—they are perfect."

I admired it lavishly but failed to bring a smile to his worried face. "I'm sorry you can't help me find its owner," I told him.

His fingers curled around the dragon. "I did not say that. Do you know the Initiative for the Arts? Go there and talk to Alice Murata. She may be able to assist your search."

"Okay, I know Alice. Thanks." A good suggestion. As the executive director, she would have been researching the subject in connection with the Initiative's newly opened New Year exhibit of Chinese painting and crafts.

I reached to take the necklace, but Mr. Ming clutched it tight. Then, clearly reluctant, he handed it to me. I started to put it in the plastic bag.

"No, wait," he said. "This deserves something finer."

Snatching the bag from the counter, he ducked behind the curtain. I thought, Must be an office back there, or a storeroom. A moment later he returned with a velvet drawstring pouch. "Carry it in this."

Priceless. One of a kind. Suddenly I felt very uncomfortable walking around carrying a treasure. As I left Ming's shop I gave Buddha a couple of extra pats.

Back in my office, I placed a sheet of computer paper on my desk and laid out the necklace on the white background. I snapped several shots with my Polaroid camera, then locked the dragon securely in the office safe.

Alice Murata gasped when I spread the Polaroid prints across her scarred wooden desk.

"Lady Moon's Dragon!"

"You do know this necklace, then," I said.

"Oh yes." She shoved her wire-rim glasses up the bridge

of her nose. "This medallion was made by a master carver in the eighteenth century. It was commissioned by the Ch'ien-lung Emperor for one of his favorite mistresses. The emperor loved jade. He was a great patron of artists who worked with the stone."

I looked around Alice's office, trying to come up with a logical reason for Ricky Pratt to have Lady Moon's precious ornament in his possession. The room was little more than a closet, furnished with the secondhand furniture and castoff file cabinets typical of small nonprofit organizations. Alice had brightened the space with paintings from the art classes the Initiative sponsored for inner-city kids.

A great teacher, Alice had warmed up for a lesson. "Confucius said jade is like wisdom, strong and dependable. And the dragon means success and wealth. So—"

A young man with a pencil-stroke mustache appeared at the office door. "Alice, could you—oh, sorry to interrupt."

She beckoned him in. "Hi, Thomas, come meet Jess Randolph. She's on our board. Jess, this is Thomas Chan, one of the brightest interns in our Oceanside Academy program. He's a senior there."

Thomas was tall and attractive, dressed in tight jeans and a T-shirt with the Initiative's logo. "What's this?" he asked, brushing a shock of black hair out of his eyes as he bent to look at the photos.

"Jess brought these to show us," Alice said.

Thomas gathered the pictures off the desk and fumbled through them with a look of dismay.

"Hey, what's going on?" he blurted. "Where'd you get these?"

"I took them," I said. "A client asked me to find the necklace's rightful owner."

"Where'd you see it? What about the other stuff?"

"Calm down, Thomas," Alice said. "I'm sure Jess has an explanation."

"I don't," I said, looking from one to the other. "But I'd sure like to find one."

Alice removed her glasses and tapped them on her desk as she spoke. "Lady Moon's necklace was stolen from us last week, along with a dozen other irreplaceable jade pieces. A collector who came here from Hong Kong loaned us almost a hundred jade items for our New Year exhibit. We returned his generosity by allowing some awful security breach to happen, I don't know how."

"I hadn't heard about this," I said. "You didn't notify the board? What about the cops?"

"I asked them to keep it very quiet. I didn't want to make us more of a target or frighten away donors. These pictures are the first clue that's turned up."

I picked up my satchel. "I'm going to talk to my client. I don't know anything about the other pieces, but I'll make sure you get back Lady Moon's Dragon."

As I walked out her office door I heard Thomas ask, "What are you doing?"

Alice's voice replied, "I'm calling the police."

I rang the doorbell of Celine Pratt's Victorian home, then turned to admire the view. It was just past dusk. Through the rain I could see lights winking on, bright ones along the waterfront below me, mere pinpricks on the distant Marin hills. In between was the black expanse of the bay.

Garrick Pratt, still in his business suit but with loosened tie, opened the door. He was an imposing man, with slicked-back graying hair and sharp features that gathered into a frown when he saw me. He didn't say, "No solicitors," but I could have sworn I heard him think it.

I introduced myself, reminding him that we'd met at the last Initiative fundraising dinner. "Is Celine home?"

"She's busy in the kitchen. Dinner's almost ready." He made no move to invite me in.

"I need to see her. It's important."

After a moment Garrick relented. "I'll get her," he said, and headed toward the back of the house.

I stepped into the foyer. Noise drew me to the entrance of the living room. The furniture in there was shoved back to the walls. Newspapers were spread on the Oriental rug. Three boys in oversized T-shirts were sprawled on the floor, fussing over a large papier-mâché contraption. They were surrounded by chicken wire, bamboo sticks, paint and glue and yards of glittery silver fabric. They glanced up at me. Realizing I was a grownup and therefore of no interest, they turned back to their work.

Garrick Pratt returned from the kitchen. "How's it going, guys?"

For replies, he got two shrugs and an "Okay, I guess."

"That looks pretty impressive," I said to them. "What is it?"

"Dragon head." The boy who responded was wearing a baseball cap, bill to the back, over his blond hair.

Garrick looked peeved. "Ricky, how often do I have to tell you, don't mumble. Stand up, kids, remember your manners." The boys struggled to their feet. "Jess Randolph, this is my son, Garrick Pratt, Junior. Ricky, give her a good firm handshake, the way I've told you."

Casting a dark look at his father, Ricky extended his hand. I gave him a high five and he grinned. Garrick, highly unamused, introduced Mark Santoro and Peter Chan. Mark, tall and dark, was the only one with any bulk to his chest and shoulders. Peter looked like a younger version of Thomas, the Initiative intern.

A pretty young woman, yellow hair cascading down her back, came in and slipped her arm around Garrick's waist. "Hi, Daddy."

"Hey there, sweetheart." He beamed as he said, "Jess, this is my daughter, Jennifer."

Jennifer gave me a pleased-to-meet-you smile and a proper handshake. "Excuse all the mess," she said. "We're getting ready for the Chinese New Year parade tomorrow. Our school has a float every year. I'm going to ride on it. These guys will be the dragon leading the way."

Celine appeared, greeting me with a friendly smile and a worried crease between her brows. "Jess! I didn't expect to see you again so soon. Come on back," she said, steering me into the hall. "Can you stay for dinner? I'm fixing lots. Mark and Peter are staying so they can get the silly dragon built. Peter's brother is coming over too."

A heady scent of garlic and basil hit my nose as we entered the kitchen. "It smells wonderful. But I just came to let you know I've found the owner of the necklace."

"Already?" Celine lifted the lid of a kettle on the stove and gave the contents a stir. "Wow, you do good work. I mean, I knew you would, but—who is it?"

"Before I tell you, I'd like to talk with Ricky."

"Ricky? Now?" Moving to the butcher-block island in the center of the room, she picked up a sharp knife and began sawing on a loaf of crusty bread. "It's bad news, isn't it?"

"When you gave me the necklace, you told me no crime had been committed."

"Not exactly. You asked if I had committed a crime, and I said no. Which is true."

"But you knew the necklace was stolen property."

"All I knew was, Ricky had no business having something like that in his possession. How terrible is the trouble he's gotten himself into?" She stabbed the blade into the bread and looked at me pleadingly. "He's just a kid, Jess. His whole future's ahead of him. We can't let one little incident ruin things for him."

"That's why I want to talk with him. Find out what happened."

"What makes you think he'll answer your questions? He refuses to say 'boo' about this to Garrick and me."

"I'm not his parents," I pointed out.

She sighed. "No doubt that's a point in your favor. I'll get Ricky and find you someplace quiet to talk."

Okay, Buddha, I thought as Ricky Pratt stood squirming in front of me, now's the time for that strong, dependable wisdom to kick in.

We were in Garrick's den, a rosewood-and-leather room that smelled of pipe tobacco. I leaned against the desk.

"Ricky, I'm here because your mom asked for my help today."

Wrong opening. Under the back-to-front baseball cap, the boy's face tightened into stubborn lines.

I tried again. "Actually, I'm the one who needs help. Your help. I'm a detective and—"

"You mean like a cop?"

"I mean like a private eye. I'm investigating a jewel theft."

He gave me a sly look. "Is there a reward?"

"Maybe." I was tempted to tell him he'd be rewarded with a clear conscience, but that was the kind of pious claptrap from grownups that turned kids off. "If you help catch the thief, I imagine some kind of reward can be arranged."

Ricky flopped into a leather easy chair. "This is about the necklace I gave Mom, huh? She doesn't like it."

"She loves it. Who wouldn't? It's gorgeous. But she's concerned about where you got it."

"It's mine. Someone gave it to me." The defiant lift of his chin was contradicted by his tentative tone. "I picked the necklace 'cause it was the coolest one."

"The coolest one? Did the person who gave it to you have other jade pieces?"

"Yeah, a whole bunch of stuff. Me and Mark and Peter each got something. Mark took this lion-dog figure. It's pretty cool too. Peter got stuck with earrings."

"So who was giving away all this cool stuff?"

"I can't tell. That's part of the deal."

"I see. What was the rest of the deal?"

He stared down at his jumbo-sized athletic shoes. Ricky reminded me of a puppy who hadn't yet grown up enough to fit his feet. I said nothing, just waited for him to speak.

"I'm not supposed to tell that either," he said finally, his voice cracking. He was clearly uncomfortable with his secret.

"In other words, whoever gave you the dragon was buying your silence."

"I guess."

"Which suggests he shouldn't have had the jade in the first place. He stole it, and you and your friends found out."

Ricky didn't lift his head. I took his lack of protest as confirmation that I was right.

I asked, "Did he tell you that accepting stolen goods makes you a criminal, too? An accessory to the theft."

That brought his head up. "Not till it was too late. I never would have taken the stupid necklace if I knew I was gonna get arrested. I didn't steal anything, honest. I just didn't want . . . anyone to get in trouble."

"I don't either," I said. "How about this? If you can't say

who gave it to you, can you tell me how you knew he had it?"

"We found it at school. Peter and Mark and me. I was looking for a book and—"

Celine chose that moment to poke her head in. "Aren't you done? Dinner's ready." She stood in the doorway with her arms folded across her chest—a clear signal that the interview was over.

Fast as a shot, Ricky pushed past her and out of the room.

Celine said, "It's all okay, isn't it? Ricky didn't steal anything?"

"No, but someone did." As she escorted me down the hall, I told her about the jade missing from the Initiative gallery.

Opening the front door she said, "Well, you accomplished what I asked you to do. You found the dragon's owner. That should end it."

I stepped outside, pulling my jacket tight against the chill. The drizzle was making halos around the streetlights.

Hearing a sound, I glanced to my left. In the shadowed corner of the porch, two people were locked in a passionate embrace. I could see the gleam of Jennifer's yellow hair. As my gaze fell on them, she became conscious of my presence and pushed her boyfriend away. He turned toward us—it was Thomas Chan.

They both flashed me smiles before slipping into the house. Jennifer's was embarrassed. Thomas's looked menacing.

As I approached the three-flat building I call home, I spotted a dark figure lurking in the unlit entryway.

I stopped on the sidewalk, muscles tensing. My key ring was in my hand, and I worked the keys between my fingers so that points would protrude. When I made a fist, they'd be ready to scratch a face or claw out eyes.

"Jess? That you?" The figure had a deep male voice. "It's Dalton Humphreys."

Great. I'd almost unleashed my destructive power against a cop. Letting my keys dangle, I mounted the front steps. Scruff was scratching and whining behind the door.

"My God, Dal, I was afraid you were a mugger lying in wait."

His smile made his handsome mahogany face even more attractive. "Sorry to disappoint you. I'm merely a humble public servant. Your tax dollars at work."

I unlocked the door and Scruff jetted out. He skidded to a stop in front of Humphreys and gave a low growl. Humphreys scratched the dog between his ears.

"Good watchdog," he told me. "Made a lot of noise. He didn't like me being out here one bit."

"He was just annoyed that you didn't come in and fix him supper. Let's get out of the rain."

Scruff led us upstairs to my flat and straight into the kitchen. As I cleaned out his bowl and scooped a can of dog food into it, I asked, "Can I give you something to eat, Dal?"

"He ran a hand over his frizz of black hair. "If that's what you're offering, I'll have mine fried."

"I have people food too." I put together a platter of cheese and crackers, a glass of wine for me, and coffee for him since he was on duty.

"Had a call this afternoon from Alice Murata at the Initiative for the Arts," Humphreys said as he settled onto my sofa. "She said you brought her some interesting photos. My first question is, Where did you get them?"

"That's easy. I took them myself."

"Question two is, Where did you obtain the object you photographed, and where is the object now?"

"That's two and three," I pointed out. "The answer to the third is, in my office safe."

"And the answer to the second one?"

I sliced off some jalapeño jack, put it on a cracker and let the combination of heat and mildness tickle my tongue. What was the wise response? I had suspicions about who'd stolen the jade. But I was missing pieces of the puzzle, and I'd promised Celine to try to keep Ricky out of trouble.

I said, "Lady Moon's Dragon came to me in a plastic bag from Ming's House of Treasures. But it may belong to a benefactor who lent it to the Institute. If so, I'll be happy to return it."

"And the other items?" Humphreys asked. "When the dragon walked away from the Initiative gallery, it took a dozen friends with it."

"The dragon's all I have."

Scruff, the lying beggar, nudged Humphreys's knee and gave him an "I'm starving" look. The cop rewarded him with a chunk of Swiss cheese. A man who's kind to dogs deserves the truth, I decided. So I told him the story—or at least a highly edited, no-names-mentioned version of it.

"My client's son merely stumbled onto the place where the dragon was hidden," I concluded. "When he gave the necklace to his mom, I think it was a subtle way of asking for help. Sorry I can't give you more, Dal. Check with Mr. Ming. He steered me to the Initiative, so he must know something."

"I already had a chat with him," Humphreys said. "We kind of keep an eye on his place. The jewelry store's legit, but he's got this back room where he keeps a game running."

"A game? What do you mean?"

"It's a gambling establishment. We've been working a long time, trying to put together enough evidence to shut it down and indict all the right people, but they're a slippery bunch. My hunch is the jade theft and the gambling ring are connected."

"Then why would Ming point me to Alice Murata?"

"You scared him when you showed up with the dragon. A little honorable gambling, where's the harm in that? he says. But stealing jade's bad luck. He's worried about the robbers as much as the cops. He gets some unsavory characters visiting his back room."

"What happens next?" I asked.

Humphreys put down his coffee cup. "Next you and I go for a ride."

"Now? Where to?"

"Your office. You're holding a key piece of evidence in a case of felony theft. I'm sure you're eager to turn it over to the proper authorities."

I'd been right in the first place, I thought as I drifted off to sleep late that night. Celine's wisest course would have been to go straight to the police.

I was dreaming of dragons when the phone rang. Picking it up, I sleepily mumbled hello.

Silence on the line.

I was wider awake now. "Hello?"

"Keep out of our business," a voice said. "You and the cops and the kids. You don't and there'll be a parade of trouble."

"Who is this?"

But the line went dead. I hung up. A few minutes later, I punched in the code that dials up the number of the last incoming call.

I wasn't surprised to reach a message machine: "Thanks for calling Ming's House of Treasures . . ."

I'll talk to Ming again tomorrow, I decided, as soon as I

get back from taking Scruff to the beach for our ritual Saturday romp.

The drizzle the next morning didn't stop Scruff from having a soggy, sandy, wonderful time. Even I felt refreshed by the salt-tinged wind and the rhythm of the ocean waves. Driving home, I turned on the radio, hoping for some mellow jazz. Instead I caught a news bulletin: ". . . New Year's celebration marred by a brutal murder. The victim, Walter Ming, was shot to death . . ."

Grant Avenue was bustling with tourists, New Year revelers and Saturday shoppers. I made slow progress as I pushed through the throng. A pair of lion dancers were weaving from shop to shop amidst bursts of firecrackers. Stopping in front of me, they bowed the lion's gaudy head and snapped its sharp teeth. A toddler close by screamed with fear and delight.

As I reached the block where Ming's House of Treasures was located, the crowd's mood shifted. Here people were hushed, apprehensive. A black-and-white was angled across one lane of the narrow street. Uniformed officers and a blockade of sawhorses kept the curious at bay.

I elbowed my way toward Ming's store, muttering "Excuse me" every few steps and trying not to step on any more feet than necessary.

Yellow crime-scene tape was draped across the shop. Someone, either a wit or a philosopher, had wound it like a sash around the wooden Buddha's belly.

I could make out people milling around in the gloom of the interior—more cops, no doubt, and crime lab technicians. I caught sight of Dalton Humphreys as he passed across the doorway.

"Dal!" I yelled, waving to grab his attention.

He stepped out onto the sidewalk, scanning the crowd

with a puzzled look. When he spotted me he came over and escorted me through the barrier. "Glad to see you," he said. "We need to have a little chat."

"What happened?"

"One of the gamblers showed up a while ago, ready to join the game. Place was locked up tight, even though it was supposed to open up at ten. He peered in, saw Ming's body lying on the floor."

"Any idea who the shooter is?"

"No. But one thing's damn odd."

"What's that?"

"You show up yesterday talking to Ming about this dragon necklace. Hours later he's dead. Anything you haven't told me, Jess, you sure as hell better tell me now."

"Someone called me from here last night, Dal."

As I described the telephone threat, I heard a *rat-a-tat-tat* of firecrackers at the end of the block. The lion dancers emerged from a corner building. The crowd, frustrated by the lack of action at the murder scene, surged in that direction to see the livelier show.

Dal shook his head. "*Gung hay fat choy* indeed," he said. "Bad enough it's going to rain on the parade tonight. But there's nothing like a murder to really start the year with a bang."

The parade. *A parade of troubles,* the caller had said. I suddenly realized he'd meant it literally.

"Quick, Dal, where's a phone?" I dashed off down the street in search of one before he could answer.

"I can't, Jess," Celine said.

I pressed the receiver tighter against my ear. I'd found a pay phone in a coffee shop. Between the clatter of dishes and the chatter of diners' voices, it was almost impossible for me to hear.

"Celine, you have to pull the kids out of the parade. It's important, a man's been killed—"

"But they've worked so hard. The boys were up all night getting their dragon ready."

"They're in danger, Celine. Don't let them out of the house."

"It's too late, Jess. That's what I'm trying to tell you. They're already downtown at the staging area. There's thousands of people there. I don't know how to find them."

I stared through the windshield of a flatbed truck as the wipers swept away a last spatter of rain. Despite the weather, the sidewalks along the parade route were jammed. I could see people gazing down from high-rise office windows.

In front of the truck, a dragon's silver scales sparkled in the orange glow of the streetlights. The creature danced on six legs—legs belonging to Peter Chan, Mark Santoro and Ricky Pratt.

Ahead of them, the Oceanside Academy band was strutting along Kearny Street, playing "When Irish Eyes Are Smiling." An odd choice, I thought, but in San Francisco the Chinese New Year, like almost everything else, was a multicultural celebration. On the truck bed, the students had constructed an elaborate globe to symbolize their float's theme: Everybody's World.

The truck lurched forward. The wipers screeched across the now-dry glass.

"Rain's finally stopped." Thomas Chan was at the wheel of the truck, a loaner from his uncle's heavy-equipment firm. "That's lucky." He turned the wipers off.

"Lucky," I echoed. I'd been reading about the Chinese New Year, how much its celebration was associated with good luck. The color red, the dragon. The ritual of sweeping the house, brushing bad luck out the door with the dust. I thought about the Buddha's polished bald head and its even shinier belly. Maybe that's what wisdom was—having enough knowledge and judgment to make sense of luck.

Thomas looked over at me, his fingers drumming nervously on the steering wheel. He had seemed both relieved and upset when I finally located the Oceanside group in the staging area. The other kids had not welcomed me. They refused to drop out of the procession, and the telephone threat had been so vague that the teachers in charge couldn't understand my sense of urgency. The best I could do was persuade them to let me ride along.

Humphreys had been more sympathetic, but he was wrapped up in Ming's homicide investigation. The police would be out in force along the parade route, he reminded me. He promised to pass along word that something—who knew what?—might happen.

I gazed back at Thomas, feeling depressed. He was so young, so full of promise. Yet I was sure he was a thief—and maybe a murderer.

I said, "You must have felt really lucky when all that gorgeous jade showed up at the Arts Initiative, ripe for the plucking."

"What do you mean?"

"You know what I mean. By now the cops do too. I can tell you want to talk about it. Being up-front might help things go easier for you."

His shoulders slumped and his face crumpled. He looked younger than ever. "I never should have done it. But what choice was there? We needed so much money."

"Money you owed to the gambling ring at Ming's shop," I said.

"I . . . yeah. Mrs. Murata gave me the job of setting up

the jade exhibit. A hundred pieces. I thought, Who'd miss a few?"

"So you took the jade and sold it to Mr. Ming."

"No, Ming didn't run the gambling. He just provided the space. We gave some of the jade to my brother and his buddies after they found the stuff in Jennifer's locker. The rest went to the guy who operates the game. He said he could take it back to China, get a huge price for it on the black market. And that would wipe out the debt."

I did my own gambling with the next question. "Why did you kill Mr. Ming?"

"I didn't kill him! You can't accuse me of that. It's your fault he died."

"*My* fault?"

"Yeah. Everything was fine until you showed up with the dragon. That made him scared. When we went to see him last night, he said he was going to talk to the cops."

I took another gamble. "Thomas, you keep saying 'we.' It wasn't your own debt you were paying, was it? It was Jennifer who owed the money."

He bit his lip and stared straight ahead. Even so, I could see the glisten of tears in his eyes.

"I had to help her out," he said in a choked voice. "I'm the one who got her started at Ming's. For me it was just recreation, you know? But Jennifer took the game so seriously. And then—she got unlucky. Things got worse and worse. Last night—believe me, I tried to stop her."

The puzzle pieces came together. "You called me after she killed Ming, didn't you?" I said. "To warn someone she might try to silence the boys."

He lowered his head to the steering wheel, and the truck jerked to a stop. I heard shrieks from the kids in the back.

"Oh, God," Thomas said. "Don't tell her parents. They'll kill her if they find out."

● ● ●

I got out of the truck cab, went to the rear of the bed and
hoisted myself aboard. At least thirty students, costumed to
represent worldwide cultures, were crammed onto the float,
leaning over the edges, waving and yelling to the crowd.

Which one was Jennifer?

The Oceanside band launched into a brass-and-percussion
rendition of "Frere Jacques." Behind the float a girls' xylophone ensemble was ringing out "I Left My Heart in San
Francisco." A troupe of performers nearby was wowing the
onlookers by tossing and twirling flame-tipped batons.

There she was—standing at the front of the truck bed, her
arms folded into the wide sleeve of a blue silk kimono. The
streetlights glinted off her yellow hair.

The silver dragon, with the three boys underneath,
zigzagged from one side of the street to the other, pausing to
let children pat its head or pull its red satin tongue.

I edged around the tall globe, getting looks of shock and
puzzlement from the students.

A tumultuous cheer rose from the sidewalks. Glancing
back, I saw a mammoth dragon, the traditional finale to the
parade, turn the corner into Kearny Street. I knew there
were a hundred people inside the fabulous beast.

A fusillade of firecrackers greeted the dragon, echoing off
the high-rise buildings like the crash of thunder.

With the noise to cover her, Jennifer withdrew a gun from
her sleeve and aimed across the roof of the truck cab.

I grabbed her hand, pushing down hard as she fired and
fired again. Two bullets pinged against the pavement.

She twisted around, pointed the gun into my face and
pulled the trigger.

The gun clicked. It was empty. Or jammed. Or—

Whatever had happened, I thanked Buddha's belly as I
tackled Jennifer and we tumbled off the truck into the street.

Two cops yanked us up almost before we landed. The truck rolled forward. The xylophone band, the baton twirlers, the monumental dragon, all marched by us without missing a beat.

Celine's face was blotchy from crying. She sat on her living-room sofa, hugging Ricky to her side.

"I guess I'm supposed to thank you, Jess," she said. "But somehow I just can't."

I fidgeted uncomfortably in a wing chair. "I understand," I said.

Garrick was pacing in front of the bay window with its incredible view. Sunshine, the first in days, sparkled on the bay. The Marin hills, shades of soft blue-green, looked like a Chinese landscape painting.

Celine dabbed at her eyes with a handkerchief. "I can't believe it. My perfect daughter. First gambling, then stealing, then . . . murder. And I didn't even know."

That was the point, I thought—to keep you from knowing. Each time Jennifer escalated her actions, it was to prevent you from learning about the bad thing she'd done before. To keep from having to face your anger, disappointment, and scorn.

"We'll get her off," Garrick announced. "Don't worry. I've already lined up the lawyers." He socked his fist against his opposite hand. "We should have never sent her to that bleeding-heart school, let her get sucked in with that damn Chinese . . ."

"Garrick," Celine warned.

"They're in love," Ricky muttered into his mother's shoulder.

"Love! I'll tell you about love, young man. I—"

Seeing Ricky's stricken eyes, I interrupted his father's tirade. "I have to leave. I just came to bring Ricky this." I handed the boy a small wooden Buddha I'd bought that afternoon in Chinatown.

He caressed the fat stomach with his thumb. "What is it?"

"Something to help you get through the rough times. If you rub his head, he'll bring you wisdom, so you can handle whatever happens."

"Hey, cool." He thanked me with a shy smile.

I debated telling him about Buddha's belly. After all, it had saved us both from his sister's gun. But I decided against it. I didn't want the boy betting his future on luck.

Phyllis Knight's Lil Ritchie books, Switching the Odds *and* Shattered Rhythms *(St. Martin's Press, 1993 and 1995) have been published to critical acclaim, and the former was nominated for a Shamus Award for Best First P.I. Novel. In this story she illustrates how P.I.'s can get themselves involved in other people's business* without *being hired to do so.*

WHERE SHE WENT
A LIL RITCHIE STORY

by Phyllis Knight

IT WAS ONE of those days of early spring, when the only thoughts in your head have to do with lush blooming things—lilacs, tulips, jonquils, Virginia bluebells. Where I live, in Charlottesville, it's a garish time, a tacky time, the contrasting hues jumbled together as if tossed by dice, or the color-blind hand of fate. But you love it, and in spite of dire warnings nearly every year about that last late freeze, the one hell-bent on destroying every blossom between south Jersey and Alabama, there's one thing you can count on. Spring always comes.

For most of us, that is. Up ahead I could see a string of vehicles that had pulled off the road, or half-off, the best most could manage, given the narrowness of the shoulder. I'd noticed others at the same spot on the drive north that morning, but hadn't taken the time to find out why. But this time curiosity won out over my craving for the cold Beck's waiting in the fridge. I slowed, glanced in the rearview to

make sure nobody was riding my tail, then pulled in behind
the last car.

I let down the window and sat there for a couple of
minutes, feeling the sun on my arm, taking in the scent of
the freshly plowed field across the road. There's nothing
like the smell of dirt in the spring; that's why kids like to dig
in it, and why two-thirds of the people I know spend long,
back-breaking hours working in their gardens, digging
weeds, trying to come up with new and better ways to
outsmart the deer, groundhogs, and rabbits who want a taste
of that first tender shoot of the asparagus just as badly as
you do, yourself.

But meanwhile, two more vehicles had pulled up behind
me; a GMC two-toned pickup and a red Toyota. A man of
about seventy-five, with the permanent red-burned skin of
fair-completed people who worked outside in all kinds of
weather, turned off the pickup's motor. The air was quiet
again. He took his time getting out, placing one foot down
gingerly, testing his weight on it, before sliding the rest of
the way out of his seat. Then he stood there, letting things
settle, the way you do when your feet hurt, or your knee's
acting up. I waited until he'd taken a few tentative steps
before catching up with him.

"What's going on up there?" I asked, falling into step. "I
noticed cars here this morning, but I was running late."

His eyes were a clear blue, one side of his mouth slightly
stained with the brown telltale signs of tobacco juice. He
was wearing overalls, the kind every city person thinks
country people, especially Southerners, wear all the time.
Well, let me be the first to tell you: they don't. This was an
old-timer, a farmer, a dying breed.

He took in what I was wearing—jeans, a tan denim shirt
with the sleeves rolled up, a pair of hiking boots—and then

tipped his cap at me anyway. "Afternoon, ma'am," he said. "This is the first time you been here, then?"

I nodded. "Yes, sir, it is."

He motioned to me with a callused hand. "Then you better come on with me," he said. "The first time's the worst."

We took a few steps in silence, and I was starting to believe he was one of these non-talking men my family's full of, when he gestured toward the field I'd been admiring. "That's my place over there," he said. "And when she was last seen, she was getting into a green truck right over yonder, right where these folks are standing."

I should have guessed. Two months earlier a young woman driving from D.C. to Lynchburg had disappeared without a trace. Well, almost no trace; several witnesses had seen someone fitting her description get into a small green pickup driven by a medium-sized, bearded man. Since her emergency lights were flashing, it hadn't appeared out of the ordinary; she needed help, and the man was taking care of things. A Good Samaritan, perhaps, or a mechanic.

But when she failed to show up at her cousin's house the alarm was sounded, and the next day her vehicle was found, the flashers no longer flashing, the battery long since run down. Her picture had been on the news several times a day ever since, and billboards with her photo and a police sketch of the man were erected alongside the highway, with a number to call. Someone had to have seen something.

A week later, and some ten miles away, two teenage boys fishing along the Rivanna came across a blue hand-knit wool sweater caught in some briars. Since the boys were regular watchers of *Unsolved Mysteries*, they knew enough to leave the sweater where it was and call the 800 number the police had given out. Within a matter of hours the State Police had a verification; the woman's mother had identified the sweater as the one her daughter was wearing the day she left home. The other witnesses were called back in, and were in agreement; the young woman getting into the green truck had been wearing such a sweater. She had looked so neat, one person said. So pretty, even at a glance.

By now the farmer and I had reached the place. Flowers had been attached to the guardrail; wreaths, mostly. One in the shape of a huge heart, another perfectly round and pink. Other small flowers were taped or tied to the metal. Someone had woven jonquils into a six-foot strand of running cedar. The largest wreath was the hardest to look at; in its center was a large photo of a smiling young woman. She was pretty, with dancing, intelligent eyes. There was something genuine about this woman, something special; you knew this was someone to contend with, someone who would marry, have children, find meaningful work, make her mark. She'd make others happy, a girl like that.

I felt shaken, in spite of myself. I'm a private investigator, so occasional violence is a given, like it or not. It's part of the baggage I carry. But there's something about a certain kind of innocence that gets to you, that wakes you up in the middle of the night. And seeing her photograph—standing in the exact spot where she met with disaster—had an unsettling effect.

I wasn't alone in this. I looked around at the people who stood sentry: two couples in their sixties, three women who were dressed for bridge, two teenagers, another old man, a well-dressed woman in her twenties. Some were praying out loud, some quietly staring off into the distance, others wiping silent tears away.

I didn't stand there too long. I walked back to the car, got in, found an old pack of dried-out cigarettes in the glove compartment, lit one up. It tasted stale, and was, but I smoked it down, and lit another. When the farmer came back he looked in.

"I told you the first time was the worst," he said. "I come every day, sometimes twice, but it ain't easy *any* time. Bless her poor little heart, I don't know whether to wish her alive or dead by now."

I sighed, and shook my head. I knew what he meant. What was worse, I wondered: a sudden violent death, or a lingering, protracted period of torture? Not that we always get to choose. She hadn't been looking at her death that day; she'd been on her way to a family outing. She'd probably been humming a little song, or singing along with the radio; perhaps her stomach was growling, and she was looking forward to her cousin's special potato salad. But then something happened.

The farmer and I talked for a few minutes more. He told me his name, Jack Fincham. I gave him my card, which he handed back to me, with apologies. "You're gonna have to tell me what this says, if you don't mind," he said. "I cain't see a thing that small without my readin' glasses." So I read it to him: Lil Ritchie, Private Investigations, giving my office address in downtown Charlottesville, and my work number.

"Is that so?" he said afterward, pocketing the card. "My goodness, don't that beat all? My wife likes to read those detective stories by the dozen; buys 'em by the bagful. She'd sure like to talk to you."

Well, one thing led to another, and before I drove away I'd foolishly promised to come back out to the farm for Sunday dinner. I tried insisting he check this out with his wife first, to no avail. "She loves meetin' new people," he said. "She's one good cook, too, so you better bring your empty stomach along."

The rest of the week I took care of odds and ends that had

piled up. I was between jobs, but I didn't mind. I had money in the bank, time on my hands, and like I said, it was spring. I drove to my favorite greenhouse just south of town, bought some petunias and pansies, some rosemary, oregano and basil, and spent a couple of days digging around in the dirt like everyone else.

Which set me to thinking. I walked over to the public library and read every article I could find on the missing woman. Her name was Isabel Martin, and I found myself saying her name to myself, over and over again. Isabel Martin. She was no stranger, no statistic; she was Isabel Martin, who had people who loved her and wanted her back.

After I finished the newspaper articles, I walked down to the cop shop on Market Street. Lieutenant Jackson and I had a grudging respect for each other that stopped somewhat short of friendship, but lately the lines were beginning to blur. She and I had now cooperated on two investigations, and, at the very least, knew how to use each other to best advantage.

When I told her why I'd come, she sighed, long and hard, fixing me with her pitying look. "Ritchie, this is way over your head. Everybody from the State boys to the FBI are working on this one, and if this woman is to be found, they'll find her. You'd just be in the way."

"Look," I said. "They've had two full months, and still no trace. You have to assume the worst, I know, but still . . ." I trailed off.

"I know what you mean," she said, after a moment. "You got to wonder, that's for sure. You think, 'What if she was mine?'"

She'd hit it on the head, all right. But still no dice. For once, not even Lieutenant E.G. Jackson—famous locally for being the highest-ranking African-American officer on the Charlottesville police, male *or* female—could help me.

The feds played it close to the vest, and to them, all yokels looked alike.

On Sunday I wasted most of the morning searching for something inoffensive to wear out to the Finchams. Finally I settled on a loose, colorful Guatemalan shirt and a pair of white pants. I'd also worried about what to take. My usual bottle or two of wine wouldn't do; country people don't sit around and sip wine after church. Finally, I picked up a nice bouquet of gladiolas and hit the road.

The Finchams lived in one of those white frame farm-houses once peculiar to the region. More wide and tall than deep, nearly half the thickness coming from the generously made front porch, these houses were cool in the summer months and cozy in the winter. I knew this from having been raised in one. The Fincham house was set up on a knoll in full view of the guardrail, where a good dozen people now stood. Clad in flowered dresses and hot-looking dark suits, they had obviously come directly from church. They stood quietly, in a posture of prayer, before the image of Isabel Martin. I stared at them, transfixed.

I heard a screen door close, and turned around. Mr. Fincham stood there, in a starched white shirt and dress pants, his jacket and tie discarded. He gave me a shy smile, then said something to someone still inside. Mrs. Fincham came out, still dressed in her church outfit, with a spanking-clean apron on top. She had lovely, healthy-looking white hair pulled into a graceful bun. She smiled, offered me her hand, and without a lot of fuss, ushered me into her home.

The house was spotless, the meal extraordinary: fried chicken with all the trimmings, done the old-fashioned way. After we finished eating, Mrs. Fincham suggested we take our iced tea out to the front porch, so we could catch a breeze. That's what she said, anyway, although I could tell she was as obsessed with the shrine across the road as her husband.

When Mr. Fincham went in to answer the phone, I took the opportunity for a little girl-talk. "What do you think really happened over there?" I asked, gesturing toward the highway.

She looked at me, looked away. "Well," she said slowly, "there's the one theory you hear all the time about murderers roaming the interstates, killing and then moving on."

I nodded, having a certain amount of belief in this particular theory myself; hundreds of thousands of people disappear every year, and many are never seen again. "So do you think that's what happened to Isabel Martin?" I asked.

She sighed. "Not really."

"So what else could have happened? If it was anyone local, somebody would have recognized that truck by now."

She shrugged. "That's what they say."

"Okay, then tell me this: where else would you look? You know, if you were in charge."

She laughed. "Honey, you know a lot more about this kind of thing than I do. I just like to read mystery stories."

I wasn't buying it. "Don't tell me nobody around here has some out-of-control nephew; one who's developed a mean streak along with his crack habit. That stuff is everywhere now, even here in the country."

She nodded. "It's a sad thing. Parents eaten up with guilt. Good people asking themselves what they did wrong in raising their kids."

"Yes, but how far does family loyalty go?" I asked. "If a father suspected his son, and knew he had a green truck, would he come forward or not?"

"Most would, I guess. But there's all kinds of people in this world."

I became aware of Mr. Fincham's presence behind the

screen door at about the same time I sensed his wife's discomfort. "Come on out, Jack," Mrs. Fincham said, without raising her voice, or turning her head. "I need you here. This girl's too smart for me to handle alone."

I must have looked puzzled, because she then gave me a quick, reassuring pat on the arm. Her husband settled himself into a wooden rocker, and cleared his throat. "Me and my wife have been talkin' about this ever since you and I met the other day," he said. "We'd like to hire you to find this poor young girl." He pointed across the road. "We cain't stand it no more. Somebody's gotta do something, and it might as well be us."

I sat there, stunned. "But, Mr. Fincham—Mrs. Fincham— the police are giving this case top priority. All the stops are out. They're using the media, there are 800 numbers, everything."

Mrs. Fincham nodded impatiently. "Yes they are, and they won't find a durned thing out, the way they're goin', either. There's too much talk, not enough doin', you ask me." She threw her husband a glance. "Jack, now *you* say somethin'," she said. "Make yourself useful. Tell her."

I looked from one to the other. "Tell me what?"

He cleared his throat. "There's a feller lives over there close to the mountains, partway between Geer and Dyke. You know that area?"

I nodded. "A little."

"He's kin to some people I know. I been hearin' things, bad things, about this boy. There's been places broken into, and more'n one person I talked to thinks this boy's been doin' it, and a whole lot more, besides. Likes to go around in those army suits, shoots deer out of season. He just plain don't care about nothin'."

"Mr. Fincham, that doesn't mean he's a kidnapper, or a killer either."

"There's more," he said. "This boy's gotten away with too

much already, so he's gettin' full of hisself. A woman lives near Geer got pistol-whipped in the face the other week; woke up when her place was bein' robbed. Like to've scared her into another heart attack."

"I heard about that on the news," I said. "But as unfortunate as it was, and as much as I feel for the woman, the reporter said she wasn't able to identify her attacker."

Mrs. Fincham grabbed my arm, held on tight. "Ain't you never been plain afraid? Deep-down, bone-afraid? 'Cause if you have, I won't have to explain it to you. I happen to *know* she knows exactly who done it to her; she told somebody who told me. It was that same boy. Name's Stevie Dees."

I thought about that some, sighed. "I still don't understand how this implicates him in the disappearance of Isabel Martin," I said.

"There's somethin' else," Mr. Fincham said. "This boy been seen more'n once driving new vehicles, just for a day or two, never no longer'n that. A fellow I been talkin' to thinks he's part of a ring of car thieves; maybe they steal 'em up in Washington, bring 'em down here and he paints 'em over in his repair shop. He's got one right there at his house, did I tell you that?"

Mrs. Fincham grabbed my arm again. "Two days before this young girl got snatched outa her vehicle, this Dees boy was seen drivin' a green truck. Just like the one they said this girl got into."

I frowned. "Why wasn't this reported to the police?" I asked.

She shook her head. "Girl, how many policemen do you know? Some of 'em are as dumb as dirt. Half the high-school cutups I know got jobs as deputy sheriffs, and some even made it all the way to the State Police. I don't know about you, but I'd just as soon take my chances with a buncha rowdies as the State Police. And anybody turns in this boy without plenty of proof is gonna have a pile of trouble on their hands. That's why we thought we'd do something a little bit quieter; come to you first."

I sat there for a few minutes, thinking. "What do you want me to do?" I asked. "I'm not saying I'll do it, but you may as well tell me anyway."

This time Mr. Fincham spoke. "We want you to walk a parcel of land for us. That's all there is to it. If this girl ain't on it, dead or alive, then that'll be that. But I got a sneakin' feelin' about it. It's keeping me from gettin' a good night's sleep. Neither one of us's hardly slept for two months."

When I got back to my place, there was a message on my machine; Lieutenant Jackson, asking me to call her at home.

She got right to it. "Two things happened since I saw you the other day. I been thinking about the conversation we had, for one thing," she said. "And then, on top of that, one pissant too many got in my face. And I don't care for that, never have."

"Funny you should get interested right at this moment in time," I said. "I just had a conversation with a couple of old folks that was a real eye-opener."

She didn't say anything right away. "You like softball?" she asked. "I'm playing with some friends of mine over in Azalea Park later this afternoon. You could drop by, and we could have us a little talk. See if we could work somethin' out."

I tried and failed to get any more out of her. By four-thirty I was sitting in my car, watching the two teams scrap it out. Jackson worked first base a hell of a lot better than the Red Sox in the '86 World Series; nothing could get by her. She did her job the same way.

She waited until the equipment was packed up, and most of the others had left the park. Then she walked over to the car, ducked way down to look me in the eye, and said, "You wanna go for a little ride?"

"Who's driving?"

"I am," she said. "I made a vow not to ever get in a car of yours. I don't care much for your taste in sardine cans."

I let it go. It was pure Jacksonese, and it flowed right over my head, like a peaceful river. I locked up and slid into the passenger side of her huge Mercury. She continued out Old Lynchburg Road until it connected with 29 South, then opened it up. I sat there a while, watching the scenery rush by. "So it's true, what they say about old hot-rodders turning into cops," I said.

She grinned. "Not really. I'm just on the lookout for violators; this way I'll be going their speed, and they'll be easier to see." I didn't bother to mention that her jurisdiction had ended about ten miles back.

We eventually ended up at Walnut Creek Park, where a few fishermen's boats still dotted the water. She turned off the motor. "Now why don't you tell me what you just found out. Then I'll tell you some of what I know."

I told her everything, for once, leaving nothing out. When I finished, she shook her head. "Sorry son of a bitch," she said. "I think the part about the chop shop's likely to be true, too; law enforcement's been on the lookout for somebody doin' that kind of work, but you know how long it takes to get anything done when people won't cooperate with each other." I wondered, but didn't ask, if she meant the public, or the "pissant" officer who had ticked her off.

"One other thing's missing that we need to find out," I said, "and that's how this Dees feels about women. I mean, other than beating up old ladies."

She nodded. "Let me go back, check the computers, see if I can find anything out on that."

"So does this mean you're gonna help me out with this?

We're actually going to work together? I can't believe it." I really couldn't. Lieutenant Jackson was a straight shooter, a by-the-book kind of officer; fair, but hard—on herself, as well as on others. Someone must have really stepped on her toes, and I was willing to bet they'd live to regret it.

An hour later the phone rang. "Dees is about what you'd expect," she said. "Been married twice, but for no longer than a few months, either marriage. County police called six times for domestic disputes, no charges filed. You know the type."

Sorry to say, I did. "So if I do decide to walk this piece of property, can you make things a little easier, get me some help?"

"I can do better than that," she said. "I've got someone all set to draw you a map and everything. I can also try to make sure the suspect isn't at home, so don't worry too much about that. I also found out that this land has been in the man's family for a long time. He grew up huntin' on it, knows it like the back of his hand. If I was going to stash a body, I'd do it somewhere I felt safe, wouldn't you?"

"I wouldn't stash a body anywhere," I said. "I'd have to kill somebody first, and I find that a weentsy bit distasteful, don't you?"

She chuckled. "Most of the time I do."

I didn't ask. "I don't exactly understand how this is gonna work, with search warrants, judges, all that," I said.

"You just let me take care of the details," she said. "Tuesday okay?"

"Yeah. Jesus."

"Prayin' won't hurt," she said, and hung up the phone.

On Monday a map was delivered to my front door by Jackson herself. It was the first time she had been in my house; an invisible line had been crossed in our relationship. I made some coffee and we went over the lay of the land like a couple of soldiers on drill. She didn't offer me the name of the mapmaker, and I didn't ask.

"And just where will you be tomorrow, while I'm all alone in the woods?" I asked, for the hundredth time.

"I'll be sitting by the river, fishin', less than a mile away, waitin' for you to signal on the walkie-talkie. No kidding, if you see anything even slightly suspicious, I'll be there like a shot."

"Bad choice of words," I grumbled, but the truth was, I was hooked. Baited and hooked, maybe, but hooked.

I didn't sleep much that night. When it was light enough outside to see my watch without turning on a lamp, I got up, dressed, drank a little coffee, and headed out to the contact spot. Jackson was already there. "You don't look so good," she said, by way of greeting.

"If all I had to do was fish, I'd feel a whole hell of a lot better," I said. "Let's get it over with."

Ten minutes later I was tromping along in the woods, armed with my Walther, a walkie-talkie, a small flashlight, and a carefully drawn map. According to the map, the piece of land was roughly divided into three sections—hilly scrubland, which should eventually give way to an old-growth juniper forest; the third, and largest section, contained a meandering creek, and, at least at one time, a spring.

I spent the better part of the morning sweating, stumbling, and cursing, as I attempted to maintain my footing through one vine-infested thicket after another. To my inexperienced eye, it didn't appear as if anyone had set foot on the land in the last generation or so. I thought of the poor Civil War soldiers on both sides, who were decimated as much by the conditions of life in the Virginia woods as by each other. But I did as thorough and as scientific a search as I could, moving about in ever-widening circles. Nothing.

I wolfed down two sandwiches at eleven-thirty, and drank half of my canteen's worth of water. I felt as if I'd put in a hard week at boot camp. I got to my feet, already beginning to stiffen from the morning's exertions, and within minutes, found myself in a lovely juniper forest. The trees were large—big-city Christmas-tree-size—which made the walking a good deal easier. Again using my map, I traversed this section in less than half the time I'd wasted in the thickets. When I spotted the creek-bed, I sat down to rest again. I raised Jackson on the walkie-talkie. "How's it going?" she asked brightly. Too brightly. "I caught two fish."

"There's nothing happening here," I said. "I think this theory might have been a dud. I haven't found as much as an old tin can to make me think anyone's been here."

Through the static I could hear Jackson's weary tone of voice. "You callin' it quits on me, then?"

"I didn't say that," I told her. "I just said I'm not expecting much, and I don't think you should either."

"You let me worry about that," she said.

I shrugged. "Okay," I said, and rang off. I usually didn't quit what I started, anyway.

The creek was beautiful; lady's slipper, mosses, and ferns grew abundantly along its banks, and chinkapins and huckleberry bushes thrived nearby as well. I walked past smallish sassafras trees, pink and white dogwoods, and redbuds in full bloom. For the first time since waking up I began to feel calm, and in sync with myself.

Ten minutes later I came upon the spring. It was hard to miss; someone had nailed three boards together, making a kind of lid to discourage frogs and snakes and keep out leaves. Kneeling down to remove the lid, I came upon some of the clearest-looking water I had seen since childhood. It bubbled up out of the ground like a gift, a little miracle, which, given the times, I suppose it was. Someone had taken the time to line the bottom and sides with smooth round stones, which served as a natural filter. I stuck my hand in; the water was from deep down, icy cold. I looked around, and saw a tin cup hanging from a sassafras branch. To drink or not to drink, I thought—on the one hand it would be utterly foolish, knowing what I did about pollution, but on the other, here I was, alone in the woods, face to face with cold water from a natural spring. I rinsed out the cup, dipped in, drank. Refilled it, drank again. The water was delicious, sweet. Afterwards, I carefully replaced the lid and put the cup back where I had found it.

If I hadn't been close to the ground, I might have missed it. The footprint was made by a Birkenstock sandal, considerably smaller than my own size ten-and-a-half shoe. I knelt down, staring at the ground with one eye closed, at eye-level, and was able to detect another print; not as clear, but definitely there. I scoured the ground for others, but it had been weeks since a really good rain had fallen; there wasn't enough moisture in the ground to hold bare soil in place. As it was, the clear print was only visible because of the dampness around the spring.

My heart started pounding. Okay, I thought, let's slow down, let's eliminate. Let's see who this print does *not* belong to. Stevie Dees was out; that much I was sure of. Redneck men just did not wear sandals—especially expensive ones. It seemed just as unlikely that Dees's mother would've been wearing them; it was partly a country thing, partly a class thing, but move away from ex-Hippie and Yuppie areas, and your Birkenstock population trickles, then stops.

I concentrated on the photographs I had seen of Isabel Martin, a good-looking young woman last seen wearing a blue hand-knit woolen sweater. I had watched her parents on TV; educated, articulate, comfortably middle-class. City people. I had no trouble imagining such a young woman wearing a pair of Birkies; at this time of the year, most likely with a pair of socks. I stared at the prints some more, then made a quick decision. I'd check this out first, and call Jackson afterward.

True, I didn't exactly have a clear trail of bread crumbs to follow, but I could still tell the general direction the person had been heading. I walked carefully, praying I wasn't erasing important evidence with every step I took. If—big *if*—the person wearing the sandals hadn't changed direction, they were headed toward Dees's auto shop and house. I double-checked the map again to be sure, thought briefly of raising Jackson on the walkie-talkie. But I didn't.

I'd gone another thirty feet when I thought I heard something; a scraping sound, maybe, or banging. The wind had picked up, so I couldn't be sure. I looked way up, and saw branches from two oaks rubbing and creaking against each other in the breeze. That was probably it, I thought, continuing. But a minute later I heard the sound again. It was scraping, no doubt about it.

Now the Dees place was just barely visible through the thick vegetation. I didn't like it. The fact that the newly leafed-out trees kept me from seeing the homestead in more detail also meant that it would be harder to ascertain whether I was still alone in the woods. That thought sent a direct message to my sweat glands, then to the adrenals. Knees shaking, heart pumping, I crouched low, and with my knees cracking in protest, followed the sound.

Abruptly, it stopped. I stopped with it; waited. When it started again I realized it was coming from somewhere close by. I sank to my knees, listened, then lay down, one ear pressed to the ground. Incredulous, I turned my head, straining with my other ear. The sound was coming from underneath the ground. Almost directly underneath.

I shivered. Looking frantically around, I grabbed a sturdy-looking stick and poked at the debris left on the forest floor; leaves, pine needles, twigs. But something was wrong; something was off. Just think, I said to myself. What's wrong with this picture? I stood stock-still for what seemed like hours, although, in real time, it was probably closer to thirty seconds. I forced my breathing to slow, swallowed my panic, and let my eyes do the walking. And that's when I knew.

Just to the left of where I was standing, under a large black locust tree, was a thick pile of leaves. Too many, and the wrong ones; maple and oaks. I swept aside part of the pile, and jammed my stick down hard. A resounding, hollow *thump* answered me back. Not the dull sound of wood hitting dirt, but one of wood hitting wood. I did it again, then dropped to my hands and knees and, like a dog digging a hole, swept away the rest of the camouflage. In the blink of an eye I was face to face with a thick wooden lid, not unlike the one protecting the little spring. But this one was held down by metal clamps, and was never intended to protect.

With clumsy fingers I fumbled at the clamps until they snapped free. The scraping sound was louder now, and in my state of heightened awareness, seemed to reverberate off the very treetops around me. The lid was the work of an over-builder, far too heavy. I stood up for better leverage, and pushed. And pushed again. I took a deep breath, steadied myself, and with a heart full of dread and hope, pushed one more time. It was off.

I'll say one thing: I've never done anything harder in my life than to look into that hole. It was dark, so at first I didn't see much. Now that I think back on it, I remember first being aware of a rank smell; something you'd expect if you ventured close to a bear's den after a long hibernation.

Somehow, I must have clicked into automatic pilot, because I remember unhooking the flashlight from my belt and shining it down, down, down, for what seemed like endless time.

A face stared back at me. A human face. A smallish human. It blinked, covered its eyes with a filthy hand. I switched the flashlight off and said something, I forget what; it probably doesn't matter, because I wasn't speaking in any language known to me. Neither of us were. The person in the hole was shaking violently, and the sounds coming from her were that of a dying, frightened animal. You know how it is; somebody runs over a dog, and you jump out of the car, but it's too late; the animal is already on its death journey. Its anguished cry raises the hair along the back of your neck. You try to comfort, but there's no true comfort to be found. All you can do to help is simply to be there. Bearing witness to this departing life.

That's what it was like the first time I saw Isabel Martin. But she was not dead. She was not on her death journey, not anymore. So she wailed, a guttural, racking sound devoid of tears, while I cooed back soothing words to her, like a mourning dove, as gently as I knew how. *It's okay, it's okay, it's okay.* I said it like a prayer. I reached down to help her out, but she cowered from my touch. *It's okay, it's okay,* I chanted. *Here, take my shirt, it's big enough to cover you.* Finally, like a half-starved dog accepting a hand-held piece of meat, she grabbed the shirt and scrambled into it, covering her nakedness. Afterwards, I lay down, braced my feet against some tree roots, and pulled her out by the arms as carefully as I could, wincing as she strained and her thin body brushed against the earthen walls of the hole.

She weighed no more than eighty pounds. If that. Her fingernails were mostly torn off and bleeding, from trying to claw her way out; red clay had soaked into her skin and hair, making her look like some otherworldly apparition left over from Halloween. And, as I said, she was beyond filthy; if it was a basic human instinct to recoil inwardly from her appearance and smell, that instinct was tempered by a huge sadness that hit me like a blow aimed directly at the heart. It prevented me from turning away.

Or from paying attention to anything else. I heard a twig snapping and wheeled around, a few seconds too late. A man stood watching us from a distance of less than twenty feet, a hunting rifle casually cradled in his arms. The barrel pointed down harmlessly, but his eyes told me it wouldn't remain that way for long.

I was still holding Isabel Martin. Letting out a high-pitched shriek, she began to thrash and kick wildly, like a swimmer going down for the last time. She may have been all skin and bones, but they were sharp little bones, and I knew I'd have to set her down.

Dees noticed my dilemma and started to smile. "I betcha you'd like to put that little tiger down, wouldn't you, now?" His voice was surprisingly gentle, and full of the country inflections I had known as a child. Under more favorable circumstances it might have sounded soothing to me, but right now it filled me with dread. Dees was a local man who knew the woods, knew how to hunt, how to kill.

I tried to control my voice. "Just let me set her down by that tree, okay?" I said, gesturing with my head. "Then we can talk."

"Talk, huh?" Now Dees was definitely amused. "I've been told I ain't much of a talker on the best of days, but you can let go of her if you want. It don't matter to me."

I carried her to the foot of a large oak and set her down gently, like a newborn. "Stay still," I whispered.

"Hey!" Dees yelled. "You keep your mouth shut over there. You're s'posed to be talkin' to *me*."

I stepped away from the tree carefully. For now, Isabel Martin was out of the line of fire, but if I didn't think of something fast, it wouldn't do her the slightest amount of good. My Walther was sheathed in its holster, next to the walkie-talkie and the flashlight, but while I was making a grab for it . . . well, I couldn't afford to think about that.

"I'll betcha you wish you'd practiced your fast draw a little bit more," he said. "Why don't you just take that belt off and get done with it? You know I cain't let you walk around with that thing on."

What could I do? I took off the belt and laid it down. When I looked up, Dees was standing only a few feet away. I did what my mother would have done. I started talking. "I take it you're Stevie Dees."

He shook his head; frowned. "Now, how the livin' hell would you know that?"

"It doesn't matter," I said. "What *does*, is that I'm not the only one who knows. There's a police unit just down the road, and I've already given them the signal."

He spat on the ground, showing his indifference. "Yeah, what with?"

I nodded toward the walkie-talkie. "I did it when I laid it down," I lied. "So you might as well stop what you're doing before you've got murder charges on your hands. And you know what that means in this state."

"Yeah, we like our so-called criminals and our chicken cooked the same way—fried." He laughed at his own bitter joke. "No kidding, if I worried about that, I wouldn't'ta done a single one of 'em." He fixed me with an appraising look. "Now get on over there by the girl."

I stalled, sweat streaming down my face. "What others? You said 'a single one of 'em.'"

He gestured with the rifle. "You're standin' on top of the

second one right now," he said. "The one before that one over there."

I looked down, stupidly; looked back up at him. "But why?"

"Maybe I'm just doing the girls a little favor. It's a shitty world. Now get on over there."

I stood rooted to the spot, unable to command my feet to move. I watched as Dees started toward me, my senses taking in every detail; cracking twigs under his feet on the forest floor, the dappled sunlight filtered through the trees, the feel of the breeze on my face, the roaring of my own pulse. In seconds, or minutes, it would all be over. This life.

Dees stopped. There was no more than six feet between us, even less if I counted the rifle, whose barrel now pointed toward my middle. "C'mon, move it," he said.

I turned around and looked right into the eyes of Isabel Martin, who half-lay, half-sat in a heap upon the ground within a few feet from her vile dungeon. All that was left of her was a little bone and muscle, some skin, and a heart that for some reason continued to beat; Dees had robbed her of all the rest.

I spun around so quickly that it caught him off guard. I kicked him in the knee and he went down, on top of the rifle. I dove for the Walther, as if I were sliding into third, but it had been a while since I'd played softball; my hand wrapped around the walkie-talkie instead. But in the next breath I was somehow clutching the Walther, still in its holster. I rolled over and quickly raised the gun, the walkie-talkie, the flashlight, and prepared to fire my weapons.

Dees lunged toward me, but for some reason he didn't get far. He fell down hard, struggled back up, took another step, and landed squarely on his face this time, blood spurting from his broken nose. Instantly, it dawned on me: Virginia creeper. He'd become entangled in his own forest. And suddenly I was up, moving rapidly toward him. He saw me coming and tried to scramble up once more, to his detriment.

I aimed at the ground next to his face and squeezed the trigger. The sound seemed to echo off the trees. I fired off another shot close to his head, and he screeched like a terrified child. I stepped closer. "Turn over and look at me," I said. He hesitated for a moment, so I shot again. When he finally faced me, his expression was vulnerable, innocent, confused. I didn't care. "Now crawl into your own hole," I said. "You're almost there anyway."

When he was all the way in, I dragged the cover back over the opening and then walked over to Isabel Martin. I squatted down in front of her and tried to make eye contact. "You want to do something to him before the cops get here? Because we've only got a couple of minutes, if that." She stared blankly off into the distance. I tried again. "I'm not trying to get you to kill him," I said. "But it might help you later if you could remember that you got him back a little. Now's your chance." I waited. "Okay," I said. "Last chance. The cavalry's coming."

Lieutenant Jackson was already on her way. She'd also raised the State Police, the FBI, two ambulances, and a whole slew of county deputies. When I told her where she could find Dees she looked at me strangely, then went over and said something to the others. Within the hour, a considerably shaken Dees was talking; Isabel Martin was the third young woman he'd duped into one of his stolen vehicles. But she would be the last.

After a while Jackson came over and carefully lowered her bulk to the ground beside me. We sat there until I felt like getting up; then she drove me back to my car. I went home and called the Finchams, poured myself a stiff single-malt, then watched the whole circus on the evening news: Dees being led away in handcuffs; his mother throwing herself onto the hood of the squad car, sobbing, while three deputies tried various methods of lifting her off; and last of all, a quick shot of Isabel Martin, staring out at nothing. And only then did I dare to wonder how the woman being strapped to the gurney would ever come back from where she'd been.

S. J. Rozan's novel Concourse *(St. Martin's Press, 1995)*
won the Shamus Award for Best P.I. Novel of that year. It was
only her second novel in the series. She has come a long way
in a short time, and will go much further in this genre. If
you'd like to see just how far, read the newest Lydia Chin-Bill
Smith novel, Mandarin Plaid *(St. Martin's Press, 1996).*

This story first appeared in The Fourth Womansleuth
Anthology, *from Crossing Press, in 1991.*

PROSPERITY RESTAURANT
A LYDIA CHIN STORY

by S. J. Rozan

T HE MAN I'D killed was still haunting me when the new
case began. It was two months later, hot steamy
summer. The damp Chinatown air was crowded with
odors battling like warlords: black bean sauce, vegetables
frying in oil, the low-tide reek of fish in boxes of cracked ice
on the sidewalk, and the smells of car exhaust and softening
asphalt that never go away in summer in New York.

It was a glaring sunny day, and the sidewalks were
crowded, half-and-half tourists and Chinese. I threaded my
way along Mott Street, past sidewalk vendors selling
peaches cheap and the OTB selling luck legally. The jobs
I'd worked in the last two months had all been middle-of-
the-case lawyer jobs, the kind where the P.I. tails the guy or
traces the paper and then reports to the lawyer, collects the
fee, and the lawyer settles out of court and the P.I. never
even finds out what it was all about.

In my mood, they'd suited me fine; and this one, I assumed, would be the same.

The door to Peter Lee's second-floor law office was just past Pale Orchid Imports at the corner of Mott and Pell. Before I went up I stuck my head into the shop to greet Peter's distant uncle, Lee Liang, who owns the shop and the building.

"Ling Wan-ju, how cool and lovely you look!" Smiling, the old man looked up from a packing crate whose contents he was checking. He was speaking Chinese, and he used my Chinese name. It's not what I go by, but I didn't correct him. "How do you manage it in this terrible heat?"

"I don't work as hard as you do, uncle."

"Here, sit. Will you have something to drink? How is your mother, and how are your brothers?"

"My mother is fine, and my brothers are prospering, thank you, uncle. I can't stay; I have an appointment upstairs with Peter." His dark eyes sparkled, and I blushed. "Peter's hiring me for a case."

"If Peter thinks of work when he looks at you, Ling Wan-ju, then Peter is a fool. But," he offered philosophically, "I have other nephews."

"Your uncle thinks you're a fool," I told Peter as I settled stickily into the vinyl chair across the desk from him.

"Uncle Liang? Did he say why?" Peter asked distractedly, shuffling papers. A venerable air conditioner wheezed in the grimy window behind him, trying to convince us that anything working that hard must be making a difference.

"I think because you won't marry me."

He looked up, owl-eyed behind his thick glasses. "Why, Lydia. You never asked me."

"Don't worry, I'm not about to."

Now that Peter's eyes were on me, he didn't move them. "How are you doing?" he asked.

"I'm doing fine," I said impatiently. "How should I be doing?"

Peter shrugged. "Okay," he said. "You don't want to talk about it."

"Oh, for God's sake, Peter. It was two months ago. He shot at me. He had a hostage. It was the only thing I could have done and I'm glad I did it." I didn't add, And he was nineteen. I didn't add, And his shot was wild. I didn't add anything about the shadows in the sleepless nights since then, shadows I search for something to make me believe that shooting a nineteen-year-old kid through the heart really *was* the only thing I could have done.

What I added, to Peter, was, "Why am I here?"

He settled the papers and leaned forward, resting his weight on his chunky forearms. "Chun-Wei Hsu," he said, "can't find his roommate."

"Who's Chun-Wei Hsu?"

"He's our client."

I shook my head. "He's your client. You're my client. For how long can't he find his roommate?"

Peter frowned at me; then he went on. "Since yesterday."

"Who's the roommate?"

"His cousin. A recent arrival named Li-Han Weng."

"What does he think happened to him?"

"He doesn't know. Li-Han Weng arrived here two weeks ago from Fukien. He's been waiting for his brother, Li-Po, who was supposed to come separately. The brother never arrived and now Li-Han's disappeared."

"One day doesn't make 'disappeared.'"

"Under Li-Han's circumstances, it might."

"What are they?"

"You know Jimmy Tung?"

"Not personally. He owns the Golden Blossom? And Prosperity Restaurant?"

"Here. And two others in Flushing, and one in Brooklyn. A noodle factory in Queens, and a restaurant supply house on the Bowery. He seems to have sponsored the Weng brothers."

"Sponsored." Light dawned. "They're illegals? And Jimmy Tung paid the smuggling fee?"

Peter nodded. "For Li-Han, anyway, and for Chun-Wei Hsu. Chun-Wei says Tung claims he hasn't been contacted about Li-Po's arrival. Li-Han went to work in the factory the day after he landed here."

I got Peter's point. "So you'd expect Li-Han would be trying to be a very good boy so that Jimmy Tung doesn't change his mind about his brother."

"Right. And that doesn't include running off. But . . ."

"But what?" I rearranged myself, pushed my hair back off my face.

"Chun-Wei says he thinks Li-Po did arrive. Chun-Wei works in the kitchen at one of Jimmy Tung's restaurants in Queens. A waiter there told a story about meeting his cousin at the airport off a flight from Taiwan a day or two ago. There was a man who was sick and had to be helped off that flight. The waiter thought there'd be an ambulance and everything, he looked so bad, but two men took him off in a car. Chun-Wei says the waiter's description of the sick man sounded like Li-Po, to him."

"Did he tell this to Li-Han?"

"No, he didn't get the chance."

I thought. "Peter, who are the smugglers?"

"I don't know. Chun-Wei doesn't know. The Wengs had a contact in Fukien and they did what he said. He got them as far as Taiwan, where they separated." He shrugged. "Lydia, Chun-Wei Hsu came to me, but he's really scared.

He's afraid for his cousin; he's also afraid he'll lose his job, get found out, get shipped back, screw things up for everyone else from his village who wants to come here. I promised him we'd keep him out of trouble."

I was silent for a minute. "I don't like people making promises for me, Peter."

He spread his hands helplessly. "He was ready to bolt out of here the minute he came in. It was the only way he'd let me help him. If you don't want to take it . . ."

"Oh, of course I'll take it! And of course I'll try to keep him out of it. But I don't like people promising I'll do something I may not be able to do."

Peter looked down at the desk, then back at me. "Chun-Wei says Li-Han was worried; apparently the reason he and Li-Po didn't come together is that Li-Po was sick when Li-Han left Taiwan."

Peter and I listened to the air conditioner try.

"They're from Fukien," I finally said. "Then they're not related to Jimmy Tung."

"Not as far as I know."

I chewed my lower lip. "The going rate for entry to this country," I thought out loud, "is twenty grand. Why would you pay that for someone you're not related to?"

Peter grinned a tired grin. "When I see some of the people who come through here," he said, "I sometimes wonder why you'd pay that for people you *are* related to."

So with that and a few others facts filed away, I left. It was early, but I was hungry, and Prosperity Restaurant makes really good pepper shrimp.

The restaurant's old Formica tables were about half full, mostly with tourists. In about twenty minutes when the garment sweatshops broke for lunch, that would suddenly change. The clack of chopsticks would replace the jingle of forks against plates, and the high-pitched, abrupt voices of the women workers calling to each other and to the waiters would replace the tourist chatter. When the workers' half-hour was up it would change back just as fast.

I ordered pickled cabbage soup and pepper shrimp. It's good to eat hot food on a hot day; it makes you sweat. Anyhow, that's what my mother says. I poured sweet, fragrant tea into a thick cup and asked the waiter to point out Jimmy Tung. He said Mr. Tung was not in the restaurant.

In fact, as I dipped the china spoon into the salty soup I noticed there was no one I knew in the restaurant. My brother Elliot's father-in-law worked at Prosperity Restaurant until a year ago, but he and the other organizers had been fired after a failed attempt to unionize. Now all the red-jacketed waiters bustling back and forth around me had unfamiliar faces.

And Fukienese accents.

After lunch I went for a walk. Prosperity Restaurant was on Division Street, a sort of no man's land, but the Golden Blossom—more of a banquet house than a restaurant—was on Mott just off Canal. That made Jimmy Tung's loyalties clear: Mott Street is On Leong tong territory, patrolled by the Ghost Shadows.

Of course, Jimmy Tung might be just an honest business-man who paid his protection money and kept his head down.

On Mott near the corner of Park I found the address Peter had given me for Weng and Hsu. It was an ill-kept five-story tenement, all age-grimed brick and pigeon-spotted lime-stone ledges. I pushed open the unlocked outer door.

Inside the narrow vestibule were sixteen mailboxes, some with doors bulging where they'd been pried and badly repaired. A few had names on them—Tam, Kwon, Chan—

people who could be living here now, or could have lived here before I was born.

I hadn't planned to go inside. I didn't know which apartment Chun-Wei Hsu and his vanished cousin lived in and I probably wouldn't find anything helpful there if I did. I was really just walking and thinking; but as I was thinking, the inner door opened and a man stepped into the vestibule. He gave a little start when he saw me, then a shy smile. He held the door and moved aside so I could pass.

I smiled back and said, a little breathlessly, "Can you help me? I'm looking for my cousin, Li-Han Weng, only I don't know which apartment he lives in."

His smile grew a little uncertain, and he shrugged. I repeated the question in Chinese.

This time his face clouded. "I don't know," he said. He turned and hurried out.

I watched him go, then shut the inner door behind me and headed up the stairs. The hallways were dim and peeling, heavy with the smells of peanut oil and nameless funguses. Three rotting oranges lay in a plastic bag at the top of the second-floor stairs. I picked a door at random on the third floor and knocked.

Behind the door a man's voice rose in complaint and was answered by another. Then footsteps, and the door was opened.

The man who opened it looked tired and short-tempered. Dressed in trousers and white T-shirt, he was barefoot, unshaven, sleep-rumpled. He gave me an impatient grunt which meant the same in English and Chinese.

I chose Chinese. "Excuse me. Does Li-Han Weng live here?"

"No," he snapped. "Wrong place." Like the man I'd met downstairs, he spoke, even in those few words, in the unmistakable cadences of Fukien.

From inside came a muttered obscenity. With a sniggering look at me, the man at the door answered it; then he slammed the door and clicked the lock. Before he did, though, I got a glimpse of a fan turning arthritically on the windowsill, blowing a stale breeze over the recumbent forms on the mattresses which crowded the floor of the otherwise unfurnished room.

Back on Mott Street, I slipped into a pagoda-shaped phone booth and called the Golden Blossom.

The woman who answered spoke in Chinese. I pulled out my best Long Island accent—this only works over the phone—and said in English, "Hi! Um, do you speak English?"

"English, yes," she said with an air of distaste I could hear through the receiver.

I took a deep breath and babbled, "Oh, good! Well, my name's Tracie Lane and it's my parents' thirtieth anniversary—thirty, isn't that amazing?—and we all really *love* Chinese food and I was at a party—a watchamacallit, you know, banquet! at your place a couple of years ago when my friend Janet got married—you know, she's Chinese—anyway, we wanted to set up a thing for Mummy and Daddy—like I think fifty people—anyway, can I talk to Mr.—what's his name?—Mr. Tung?"

There was a silence; then, sharply, "Mr. Tung not here."

"Oh. Oh, but when will he be there? I can call him back. You know, because like *I'm* supposed to make all the arrangements, I don't know how it all got to be *my* job, you know? but anyway, what if I call back like at four, you think he'll be there then?"

More silence; then, slowly, "Yes. Mr. Tung here at four."

"Goody. Okay, I'll call then. Sayonara." I hung up, picturing her wrinkling her nose as she put the receiver carefully in its cradle. I hoped there was someone in the office with her she could complain to about me.

I gave the phone another quarter, called another number. "Immigration and Naturalization Service," a woman answered in tones that implied she was going to do her best to make me sorry I'd called.

"Good afternoon," I said diffidently. "I hope you can help me. My aunt just arrived from Canton and she's having problems with her visa. Is there a supervisor there she can speak to who speaks Cantonese?"

"Just a minute," the woman said huffily. She went away and came back. "You want to speak to Jillian Woo," she said as though I should have known that. "I'll transfer you."

As she was transferring me I hung up, because I didn't want to speak to Jillian Woo.

Then I called Mary Kee. I was surprised to find her in, but then she was always telling me half a cop's job is paperwork. "Lydia! Hey! How are you? How's your mother?" Her voice, as usual, was straightforward, her words a little fast, but clear. When I'm being me, I have a very slight accent in English; Mary has absolutely none.

"She's well, thanks. How's your family? Your new nephew?" Mary Kee is devoted to her sister's sons.

"God, he is so *adorable*! I wish you could see him! I have about a hundred pictures—"

"Well, you can show them to me. I need to talk to you."

She stopped. "I sort of hoped you were calling just to chat."

"At work? You'd kill me if I did."

"Well, that's true, but I wouldn't have this funny feeling I get every time you want something."

"You mean the funny feeling like the sky's about to fall?"

"That's the one."

"Mary, I don't want you to do anything. It's not really even information, what I want. There's just something I need to know."

Mary hesitated. I waited. A male voice shouted a profanity in the background, answered by another. "Okay," Mary finally said. "When?"

"Now? I'll buy you a cappuccino."

"Okay." She seemed to sigh; I chose to ignore it. "Half an hour, at Reggio's."

I walked up from Chinatown to the Village, through dusty streets reflecting heat back out of concrete and granite. The Chinatown street vendors gave way, as I went west along Canal, to electronics outlets and plastics supply houses. North along Wooster they changed again, to small, specialized, pricey boutiques selling handmade lace, cowboy boots, Japanese art supplies.

I crossed Houston, stopped in a little storefront printer I knew where they made business cards While-U-Wait. I didn't wait, just told them what I wanted, and that I'd be back. A little further north there was another change, as the shops yielded to restaurants and coffeehouses. One of these, Reggio's, was where Mary and I usually met, for business or gossip. In Chinatown it would have been instant news if the neighborhood's only resident P.I. were seen having tea with a Fifth Precinct detective, even if they'd known each other since grade school. But north of Canal we were only two Asian women taking a break from a day of doing whatever exotic thing it was that we did.

I got there first. I settled in a wire-frame chair at the only empty outdoor table, ordered an iced Red Zinger, and waited, watching the heat-slowed crowds dawdle along the sidewalks.

Mary arrived just after my tea did, striding along with that don't-mess-with-me cop walk. Wearing jeans, a red T-shirt, and a denim jacket which was heavy for the day but hid the service revolver under her arm, she swivel-hipped her way between the sidewalk tables to get to mine.

"Hi." She plopped into a chair, her long loose braid bouncing behind her. "Jesus, it's hot out. I haven't been out since I got to work this morning." She peered at me through her aviator sunglasses. "You look cool," she objected.

"I'm a master of disguise," I admitted modestly.

"You know," Mary said. "I actually was glad to hear from you. In fact, off the record, I'm glad it was business, sort of." She signaled the waiter.

"How come?"

"Well, because I heard you weren't working for a while after what happened."

I sipped my tea, shrugged. "I wasn't. But I am now."

The waiter suddenly appeared, hovering over us. Mary ordered an iced cappuccino. When he was gone she said, "So are you okay?"

"I'm fine."

She looked me over, my black sleeveless shirt and loose cotton pants. "You're not carrying," she said.

I raised my eyebrows. "Maybe it's in my bag."

"You're too smart for that."

"Okay, so I'm not carrying. As a cop aren't you glad?"

Mary ignored that. "You didn't get it back yet?"

"My permit? I got it back. I just . . . I don't need a gun for this case, anyhow."

"You used to argue with me that the whole point was you never knew when you'd need a gun. You sounded like a cowboy. I hated it."

"So you should like me better this way."

"Only if you're doing what you want to do, Lydia. Not if you're just still spooked."

The blood surged hot to my cheeks. "*Spooked*?" I kept my voice to an angry whisper. "Mary, I killed a man! Something happens to your head when you do that—" I stopped as the waiter materialized with Mary's cappuccino. She peeled a straw and stuck it in the cloud of whipped cream on top.

After a minute of silence she said, soothingly, "I know. I'm sorry. I don't know what I'm trying to tell you, even. I'm sure you're safer not carrying, and as a cop I have to approve. I just . . ." She echoed my unfinished phrase of moments before.

We sipped our drinks in silence as the light on the corner changed and the traffic inched along.

"Okay," Mary said. "Let's talk about what you want that I'm not going to do for you."

I watched a cat slither between the cafe tables. "I'm looking for a missing person," I said.

"Are we looking for him too?"

"No." I shook my head. "He hasn't been gone long enough for you to consider him missing, and besides, he's not officially a person."

"An illegal alien?"

"Uh-huh. And that's the first thing I want, Mary. He's from Fukien, he and his cousin, and his brother was supposed to arrive last week, only we're not sure he ever did."

"Who's we?" she interrupted.

"I'm working for Peter Lee."

Mary gave me a cockeyed, almost wistful grin that spoke volumes.

I grinned back, then said, "So everything on my side is privileged information, although I might be willing to sell some, like where Peter's having dinner, and whether he'd consider dating a cop. Anyway, Mary, listen. Who's smuggling illegals in from Fukien? A lot of them seem to work for Jimmy Tung. Does that mean it's the On Leong, and the Ghost Shadows?" I heard myself drop my voice to say those names, even here, worlds away from Chinatown.

Mary stopped smiling, poked her straw around in her drink. "No," she finally said. "I mean, it's not our department; you need to talk to the INS, really, or the Jade Task Force."

"They wouldn't give me the time of day."

"Probably not." She poked some more. "We've heard rumors. New groups, new gangs. A Taiwanese gang called the White Eagles has been running drugs lately, and possibly illegals, but I couldn't prove that."

"Illegals? Fukienese?"

"We think so, mostly."

"Have they staked out territory? Not in Chinatown, or I'd have run across them."

Mary shook her head. "Flushing. And don't run across them. They're bad people."

"Can you give me a contact?"

"You didn't listen. I said keep away from them." Suddenly she was all cop, cold and commanding.

"Mary, they may have my guys."

"I thought it was one guy."

"And the brother, maybe."

"Well," she said, "if they do, you can't do anything for them."

I finished my tea and tried a new path. "The other thing I'm wondering about," I said, "is Asian John Does."

"In the past twenty-four hours?"

"Well, that would be my guy. But I'm thinking in general, the last couple of months."

"I don't know," Mary said. "I'd have to look."

"Could you?"

"I could, if I knew why."

"I don't know," I said frankly. "It's a hunch. I don't know what it means."

I gave her time.

"All right," she finally said. "Call me later. But Lydia, stay out of trouble, okay?"

"I'll try," I promised her. She looked dubious as she slurped up the last of her cappuccino.

"Did you bring the pictures?" I asked.

Mary grinned and reached into her jacket pocket. "You bet I did." She drew out a Kodak envelope and we spent the time until the check came lost in admiration of Mary's extraordinary nephews.

That was the cops; now for the robbers.

I stopped at the quick-print place, then went window-shopping along Mott Street. It took half an hour, as my shirt slowly plastered itself to my back, before I spotted what I was looking for.

When you want something from a gang member it's always better to approach him when he's alone; but gang members are rarely alone. I also don't know all the Ghost Shadows. They recruit from the high schools and from Hong Kong and there are always new faces. And some of the Ghost Shadows I do know wouldn't talk to me under any circumstances. So I was very pleased to see Henry Kwong shuffling out of the ice cream parlor with a triple-decker cone, and I told him so.

"Pig-nose!" I exclaimed. "What joy!"

Henry's big head jerked around, and his little eyes narrowed almost to nonexistence in the folds of his face. He was big for a Chinese, and fat for anyone, and not happy to hear his gang nickname thrown at him by a civilian.

"Well, Charlie Chan!" he sneered. "Find a man yet?"

"You should learn your ethnic history better, Pig-nose." I smiled. "Charlie Chan was a cop. I'm just a clan cousin who needs a favor."

Henry and I are in fact related: his people come from the village in Kwangtung next to the one my people come from, and our great-grandfathers were brothers.

Henry scowled, looked around uncomfortably. It probably wouldn't do his reputation with the gang much good to be seen talking to me; on the other hand, it might, if he could figure out how. But figuring things out gave Henry a headache. Finally he fell back on, "I don't do business with girls," and turned, relieved, to walk away.

I slipped my arm through his, headed up the block with him. Still smiling, I said, "There's a new gang in town, in Flushing. Taiwanese, called the White Eagles. Maybe you've heard of them?"

Henry shook off my arm, planted himself facing me. His belligerent stance was compromised by the ice cream cone he licked before he spoke, but I don't think he noticed. "Who wants to know?"

"I do, Pig-nose. I want to talk to those guys, so you find them for me."

"Oh yeah? You gonna make me?"

Most of the gang members' toughest dialogue is lifted wholesale from Hong Kong martial arts videos. It's exasperating, but it makes it easy to answer.

"Don't be stupid, Pig-nose. This thing is way out of your league. You'd better play ball with me, because if you don't, I won't be responsible for the consequences." I had no idea what that meant, but it was exactly the kind of talk that would impress Henry. Then, in a Hong Kong video gesture, I spun on my heel and walked away.

I went over to the Buildings Department, on Hudson Street, and did some quick research; then I went home. It was just after three when I turned my key in the four locks on our door, one after the other. "Why carry four keys?" my mother had said, rhetorically. "This way is just as hard on the thief, easier on us."

"Hi, Ma," I called, coming in. "Any calls?" With my mother, of course, I spoke Chinese.

"No," she answered from the sofa, where she was mending an ancient skirt. "Auntie An-Mei is coming to dinner. I'm making watercress soup. She has pictures of her grandson."

"The soup smells great." I bent and kissed her cheek. "Don't count on me for dinner. I'm working."

My mother sniffed. "Working. With thieves and killers. Even Mary Kee's mother feels sorry for me. Who are you working for, the huge white ogre?"

"No, Ma," I answered from my bedroom, where I peeled off my shirt, stepped out of my pants. "Not Bill. Peter Lee. You ought to be happy with this one, Ma. My client's Chinese. His client's Chinese. Everyone's Chinese. Chinese everywhere, thousands of Chinese, stretching over the horizon, as far as the eye can see—"

"Oh, stop, you silly girl!" she grumbled. "When I see a husband for you over the horizon, then I'll be happy."

I deflected the husband talk by picking up the phone. I called Peter.

"News?" he asked.

"Maybe. Do you have a car?"

"No. Do we need one? I could rent one."

"No, it's not worth it. This may not work. If it does, we can take a cab."

"Where?"

"Wherever Jimmy Tung is going."

"What are you doing?"

"Just stirring things up."

"Lydia's Law?"

"What's Lydia's Law?"

"When you don't know what to do, get everybody nervous."

I bit my lip. "God, Peter, is that how I operate?"

"I think so."

"Hmmm. Well, just meet me at that teashop across the street from the Golden Blossom about four-thirty, okay?" Then, because I was a little upset, I said, to get him nervous, "And Peter, guess who owns the building your client lives in?"

"Who?"

"Jimmy Tung."

Then I climbed into the shower. There, in the resurrecting cool of the water, I thought about what I knew, what I suspected, what I was taking wild guesses at. And I planned what I thought would be the rest of my day.

Before I dressed I called Mary. She wasn't in, but she'd left a message for me with the gum-chewing civilian NYPD employee who answered the squad room phone when the place was empty.

"Says here to tell you, yeah, she found what you asked about. It says, 'One, four months ago.' Does that mean anything to you?"

"Yes, thank you. Does it say anything else?"

"'Course not. 'Cause if it did, *I* might find out what's going on around here. You want anything else, or can I get back to work?"

"Is there someplace I can reach Detective Kee?"

"If there is, I don't know about it."

That wasn't as helpful as it might have been. I thought for a few minutes, watching the soft breeze from the fan billow the pale linen curtains my mother had made.

I hauled out the phone book, dialed the Medical Examiner's Office. I got to an assistant ME and introduced myself in clipped tones: "I'm Lydia Chin with *Chung-kuo Shihpao*—that's *The China Times*—and I'm doing a feature on Chinese gang violence. I'm interested in an Asian John Doe you had last March. What can you tell me about that case?"

"Yeah, you know, we're getting a lot of those these days." He had an adenoidal voice and seemed eager to talk; maybe he didn't get much opportunity, where he was. "Not John Does. We always got lots of John Does. But now we're getting all these Orientals. Chinese mostly. What's got into you people? You used to be so quiet, sent your kids to college, never any trouble. And the food, used to be nice, egg rolls, chow mein. Now it's all this hot Szechuan stuff and you're all killing each other. What's the story?"

I thought, And I'll bet the laundry puts too much starch in your underwear, too, these days. Aloud, I said, "That's exactly what I'm trying to find out. What can you tell me?"

"Well, actually, I remember that case. Usually they're identified, y'see, the Chinese, even sometimes only by gang names, but it's something. But this one, no one knew him. Maybe he wasn't Chinese, who knows? It's just the John Does usually are. We kept him around a good long time, finally planted him on Staten Island. But I don't think he'll do you any good, for your story. Now, if you want to talk violence, I had two in here last month, a gang thing, shot five times each—"

"Why won't the John Doe do me any good?"

He stopped his gleeful description, a little annoyed. "Because no one killed him."

"What do you mean? What did he die of?"

"Pneumonia."

As I dressed and did my hair, my mother kept up a running commentary, part gossip, part opinion, part news. She was still talking when I stepped out of my room. She stopped talking suddenly, her mouth open; but she recovered quickly.

"You see, I always say you can make yourself attractive if you make an effort. Why don't you dress like that all the time? You could find a husband, you know, if you put some thought to it. Auntie An-Mei has a nephew—"

"Everyone has a nephew, Ma. The man I'm going to see right now is probably someone's nephew." I glanced in the full-length mirror on the bathroom door. The creamy silk blouse under the lavender suit jacket showed just the right amount of skin—on anyone else it would have been cleavage, but oh well—and the lavender skirt was a half-inch shorter than modesty demanded. I had on gold jewelry and plum lipstick and great big darken-in-the-sun sunglasses. My hair was moussed and brushed like a swirling black storm, and I stood five-foot-three in my two-inch heels.

Altogether, I thought, quite fetching.

I took my briefcase from my closet and loaded it up. "So long, Ma," I said, kissing her. "Give my love to Auntie An-Mei, and don't wait up." I went back down the stairs and out onto the baking streets.

I knocked at the door of the Golden Blossom at four-fifteen. Nothing happened. I knocked again, and then spied a small buzzer on the gilded door frame. I pressed it. A moment later the door was opened by a man in an open-necked white shirt. His face registered surprise; maybe he'd been expecting someone else.

But now he had me.

"I'd like to see Mr. Jimmy Tung, please," I said crisply, in English.

"Not sure he here. I check. You wait here." He started to close the door.

"No, I don't," I said. I shouldered my way smoothly past him. "He's here. Tell him Jillian Woo from the INS is here to see him." I gave him one of my new business cards. He looked at me unsurely and left me alone in the vestibule.

A minute later he was back. "Follow me."

I did follow him, down a hallway that smelled deliciously of slowly roasting pigeon.

At the end of the hallway was a door with a framed crimson scroll embroidered with the ideogram for "prosperity." The door stood half-open; my guide led me to it, pushed it fully open, stood aside to let me pass into the crisp, cool, conditioned air. Behind an elaborate carved desk—too elaborate for the windowless room—a thin, smiling man was sitting. He was in his fifties, I judged, well-preserved, though his black hair was graying at the temples.

He stood and skirted the desk with his right hand extended. I smiled and we shook.

"Miss Woo, is it?" he said, still smiling. "Please, have a seat. I'm Jimmy Tung. What is it I can do for you?"

I took a padded cloth-covered office chair and looked around, giving my sunglasses time to lighten, which they never do completely. The rest of the room, disarrayed, with old-looking stacks of papers and files on the furniture and the floor, did not live up to the desk.

"Mr. Tung." I finally smiled at the thin man, who'd gone back behind his desk and sat looking pleasantly expectant, his fingers lightly bouncing against each other as his hands formed a little tent over the mess on his desk. "It's a pleasure to meet you at last."

He started to say something and I cut him off. "Of course, I know what you're thinking. Why is the INS here? You thought we had an arrangement."

"I—" His face was innocent surprise.

"Not you, of course, and not me. But you must wonder what good your membership in the tong is doing you, if despite it you're forced to entertain an INS agent in the middle of the day in your own restaurant. The tong is supposed to take care of this sort of thing for you."

"Miss Woo—"

"Ms. And we do have an arrangement, Mr. Tung. It's just not exactly what you think."

I paused a minute, fingering the gold chain at my throat, to let him worry. His eyes flashed to the jade dangling where the cleavage should have been. I went on.

"You employ illegal aliens in your restaurants and factory, Mr. Tung. You do this because you can pay them very much less than actual citizens, who believe they have rights, even in Chinatown. There's always been a certain amount of this scummy business in Chinatown, but all you restaurant owners expanded your scope quite a bit after the Hotel and Restaurant Employees' Union almost got their hooks into your places last year."

I shifted in my seat, recrossing my stockinged legs; I didn't stop talking. "But you yourself have actually gone beyond the usual practice, in quite an entrepreneurial stretch. You not only employ illegals, you import them. You house them, too, sleeping in shifts six to a sordid room in stinking buildings you own. So out of the very, very low wages you pay these men, they pay you rent, and they repay the smuggling fee you paid—possibly with interest, am I right?—or you threaten to expose them. To me and my staff. Very enterprising, Mr. Tung."

"Ms. Woo—" Tung started to protest. The phone on his desk rang sharply. He jumped. I looked away, annoyed. Tung gave me an apologetic smile, said, "Excuse me," and picked up the receiver. "Yes," he said in Chinese, then, "Yes, put him through." He smiled at me again, said, "This will

only take a moment." After a short pause he said into the
receiver, "Mr. Han. I hope you have good news for me?" He
listened, and I twirled the jade pendant. "I understand that,
and I understand the price is good. But I don't want them."
More listening; then, with the sound of an interruption, "Mr.
Han, *my* customers *will* notice shoddy merchandise. If you
can't deliver the quality you promised I'll buy my linens
from someone else." Pause. "I don't care what you do with
them. They're nothing I can use and I won't pay for them."
Pause. "No." Pause. "Yes." More pauses. Other words,
which I didn't hear. I'd gotten it. It had come slamming into
me like a missile with an information warhead. I didn't need
Peter to meet me later. I didn't need the White Eagles. I
didn't need to follow Jimmy Tung, didn't need anything
from him except for him to stay on the phone long enough
for me to formulate a whole new plan for the rest of our
conversation.

And bless his larcenous heart, he did.

When he finally hung up, the argument over, he smiled at
me again. He seemed more at ease, a condition I was
determined wouldn't last.

"I'm sorry," he said. "What were we—?"

"Indentured servitude," I said. "Slavery, almost. We were
talking about that. We were talking about why the INS lets
you get away with it. You think it's because certain people
on my staff are paid off by your tong. Some of the people on
my staff think so too, by the way. But that's not it, Mr. Tung.

"What it is, is this: there are certain Chinese who, for
political reasons, the American government prefers to see
out of China. Pro-democracy students and intellectuals and
others. We can't bring them out directly. But we can help
them get to Good Samaritans like you." Tung's face was sort
of collapsing, like a house built over a sinkhole. "Now,
normally we don't interfere. We haven't yet. These men are

actually safer for the time being living in your hovels and working in your salt mines than they would be anywhere else.

"But occasionally you reject someone, a faulty import, a piece of merchandise that isn't up to your low but firm standards. Like your linens, Mr. Tung." I smiled very, very sweetly. "In March you rejected a man who was ill, with pneumonia. He died." In the air-conditioned coolness beads of perspiration sprang up on Tung's upper lip. Bingo, Lydia.

"And now we come to why I'm here, Mr. Tung. You've rejected another faulty import, a man known to you as Li-Po Weng. You bought and paid for another man whom you believe to be his brother, Li-Han, but Li-Po is ill. Now Li-Han has disappeared. I think I know what's happened to him."

"Miss Woo—*Ms*. Woo, I don't really—" Tung began.

"Oh, spare me." I stood, no longer smiling. "You didn't pay for the man who died last March. That must have angered the White Eagles, your import agents, right? They let it pass, and you kept doing business together. But when you wouldn't pay for Li-Po Weng, they snatched Li-Han back. Now you're out the brother you paid for unless you pay for the one you don't want."

I leaned on my fists on the uneven layer of papers on his desk. "But the point is, Mr. Tung, *we* want him. We want both of them. So pay the fee, buddy boy. Get those men here, and get Li-Po a doctor if that's what he needs, because I'm telling you now that the continuing health of your operation depends on the continuing health of the Wengs."

With a broad smile I picked up my briefcase and turned to depart. Tung, white and wide-eyed, said nothing. With my hand on the coolness of the doorknob I looked over my shoulder. "Do it; but don't tell me about it. I haven't been here. If you so much as call my office, I will deny ever having met you." Leaving the door open behind me, I strode down the hallway and out into the ovenlike air of the street.

I was sauntering down Mott grinning to myself when I felt someone jostle me, passing too close. I turned my head to snap at him; as I did an arm snaked around my shoulders from the other side. A voice said, "Act glad to see me or I'll shoot you right here." I beamed up into the hard face next to mine and, still smiling, said, "Who the hell are you?"

From the other side of me a different voice said, "Walk, smile, and shut up."

I did those things, noticing as I was hustled into a waiting Jeep Cherokee the blobby form of Henry Kwong standing in the shadow of a doorway across the street. Pig-nose, you little bastard, I thought. These are White Eagles, and you're a stool pigeon.

One of my handlers, the hard-faced one, got in the front, and the other got in the back with me. There was already a driver, who roared the Jeep hard away from the curb. He rocked that big car in and out of traffic as though it were a Porsche, barreling down Mott, around Chatham Square, and out over the Manhattan Bridge.

"Tell me what the hell is going on!" I demanded, but only once, because the kid beside me pulled out a small revolver with a big silencer on it and said, "No." Then he said, "Take your jacket off." I did, handed it to him. He went through the pockets, finding nothing. He tossed it on the floor, reached over and frisked me. He found more nothing.

"Your ugly cousin said you'd be armed," he told me.

"He makes things up."

"Pull up your skirt," he ordered. I felt myself flush a fierce crimson, but I did it. When he was satisfied there was no pearl-handled .22 strapped to my thigh he grinned, lowered the automatic and slid himself closer to me. I'd lowered my skirt when he lowered the gun, but he put his empty hand on my knee, started to slither up my thigh.

I slapped him, open-handed but hard. He yelped, pulled back, anger reddening his cheeks; then he hauled back and smacked me across the face.

I went with the blow, didn't block it and didn't respond. I couldn't win, here, with the three of them and silenced guns; there was no point in letting them see what I could do and what I couldn't. The sting of his hand made my eyes tear. I yanked myself back against the car door, as far away from him as I could get, and wiped them quickly. I glared at him, fury and contempt equally mixed.

From the front, from the driver, came the command, "Lay off her, Roach. You want that, talk to Ho-kin later."

So I watched out the window from my side and he watched me from his as we sped along the BQE to the Long Island Expressway and then north on a little piece of the Van Wyck. They hadn't made any effort to keep me from seeing where we were going, which I thought was a bad sign.

In Flushing we went a short distance along Main Street, then pulled onto Simpson. The Jeep screeched to a halt in front of the Jade Palace, a strictly take-out Chinese restaurant on the ground floor of a three-story mint-green aluminum-sided building. People on the street looked studiously in every other direction as I was hurried, tripping in the damn high heels, in the street door beside the restaurant and up the wooden stairs. The Jeep screeched off, my lavender jacket on the floor of the back seat.

At the top of the stairs Roach pushed open a door and shoved me inside. I kicked my shoes off as I stumbled in. Roach closed the door behind him and leaned on it. I smiled at him. It was like smiling at the wall. Missed your chance with this one, Lydia, I thought. I shrugged, walked around the room.

It was a kitchen with yellow cabinets, a yellow Formica-topped metal-legged table, and cheap metal chairs. The linoleum floor was sticky under my stockinged feet. "Nice place," I said. "Yours?"

"Keep away from the windows. Sit down, over there."

Moving back toward the table, I pointed to a closed door leading off the kitchen. "Is that where you keep the guys you bring in until someone pays for them?"

He sneered. "There's no one here but you, so stop hoping. Sit down and shut up." He waved the revolver around. I sat down and shut up.

We were like that for a while, maybe ten minutes, before there was a coded knock on the door and Roach let Hard-face in, with another man. Hard-face took a position by the window.

The other man looked at me, unsmiling. His face was lined and his nose was crooked, with a scar where the bend was. He was not old, though older than I: thirty-five, maybe. But his eyes held an ancient, unblinking stare which made me shiver in the heat.

Roach handed the new man my briefcase. He opened it, glanced through the old files and junk I'd stuck in it. Then, unhurried, he went to the refrigerator, took out a can of Miller beer.

In heavily accented English, he said, "You want me. You find me. Happy now?"

"You're—" My voice, to my surprise, was weak; I swallowed, made my heart slow down, and tried again. "You're the White Eagles' dai-lo?"

"Gua Ho-Kin. *You*"—he pointed the beer can at me—"are nosy, stupid bitch. Why you want to see me? Why you go to see Jimmy Tung?"

Thinking furiously, I said, "Jimmy Tung? What does—I'm trying to build up my security business, and I'm looking for clients. Alarm systems, that kind of thing. It's part of what I do. And you, I wanted to see you because I don't like people operating in my territory if I haven't met them."

"Your territory?" Settling in a chair, he seemed faintly surprised and amused.

"Chinatown. It's my home, Mr. Gua. To you it's a prize to be divided up, but I see it a little differently. I have a long-term interest there. You have your operations, as do others, and I know my place, but I also have systems I've developed. If I can help you, or you can help me, I like to know about that." This was complete gobbledygook, but I was hoping his English was weak enough that I could dazzle him with it.

"Tell me," he said with a slow, nasty smile, "why you try to build up security business in name of Jillian Woo. Jillian Woo," he said, taking a handful of my new business cards out of my briefcase and tossing them onto the table, "from INS."

"I—"

"Stop," he said. "Don't lie to me. You lie to me, I cut your face up." Gua reached behind him, fumbled open a drawer, pulled out a big, triangular-bladed knife. It glinted once in the late-day sun. My eyes fixed on that glint, on that blade, and wouldn't let go. I tried to think, but my mind was suddenly spinning free, like wheels on ice, moving at high speed, grabbing onto nothing.

Then a shout from Hard-face, standing by the window. A word I didn't catch; then Gua sprang to his feet, and all three of them ran to the window. Sirens pierced through to my brain, and a woman's voice through a police bullhorn.

Gua shouted an order in Chinese, and Roach spun around to find me, but I was ready. I heaved a chair into the side of his head, dove for the gun as he swayed and fell.

"Gua Ho-kin!" I shouted. Gua stopped dead, arms half-risen from his sides like the wings of a ponderous bird. His cold, ancient eyes were narrowed and fixed on mine. I didn't try to get up off the floor; I held the gun in both hands. It was enormous, unbelievably heavy, hot against my palms. "I'll blow your head off. I know how. I've done it. Don't move and tell him not to move." I said it in Chinese, and was smothered with a sudden wave of fear that my dialect and his were so different that he hadn't understood me. But Gua signaled Hard-face—Roach was motionless on the floor—and the two of them stood still, eyes on me, as I rose.

I hoped they wouldn't see my hands trembling with the effort of holding this heavy, heavy gun. I backed to the window, motioning them away from it. I half-leaned out, yelled, "Come up!" and waited. In seconds I heard the downstairs door being kicked in, and feet pounding the stairs. The room door crashed open and three cops charged in, taking combat positions, guns trained on all of us.

"It's okay," I said calmly, while my heart chattered in my chest. "I'm with you guys." I lifted my hands, held the gun by the grip, offered it to them.

A blue-denim form rose from one knee and said, "That's right, she is." It was Mary. She tucked her gun away, came and took mine. I was glad when it was gone. Mary looked into my eyes; then she hugged me. That was good, warm and reassuring, and I wondered when this 100-degree day had suddenly turned cold right where I was.

"Are you okay?" Mary asked.

I nodded and tried to swallow in my dry throat. "Just scared."

"Well, it serves you right. I told you to keep away from these guys."

"They picked me up," I protested. "They *kidnapped* me."

"All on their own? What a coincidence."

Gua started to snarl something. The cop handcuffing him shut him up with a word.

Mary took me down the stairs. I asked, "How did you know I was here?"

"Peter Lee."

"Peter?" We came out into the late-day sun. I was about to ask how Peter had any idea where I was, but Peter himself came sprinting across the street. He grabbed my shoulders and searched my face.

"Lydia? Are you okay?" He didn't give me a chance to answer, just squeezed me hard against him.

"Go on over to the cars. Wait for me there." Mary turned back into the mint-green house.

"Peter, how did you know where I was?" He had his arm around me as we walked across the street to the police cars. I tiptoed in my bare feet over the hot, pebbly asphalt.

"I followed you."

"You *followed* me?"

"Well, you told me to meet you across from the Golden Blossom. I was on my way there and I saw you with those guys. You didn't look as though you liked them. And you were supposed to meet me but you got in that Jeep. I didn't like it. So I jumped in a cab and followed you."

"The cab driver must have liked that." We sat down together on the thin strip of grass between the sidewalk and the curb. Across the street two uniformed cops were bringing Gua and Roach and Hard-face out of the house in handcuffs. Roach was staggering a little.

"He thought it was great," Peter told me. "He was Jamaican. He kept shaking his head and chuckling and saying, 'Just like the movies, man, just like the movies.' I had to keep telling him not to follow too close." Peter took off his glasses, ran his hand over his face, resettled them.

I kissed him. He blushed, grinned, and looked away.

"How did Mary get here?" I asked.

"After I called 911, I called the Fifth Precinct. I'm not sure why, except I think I thought it was Chinatown crime, it was my fault, I wanted someone there I knew, you know? I was pretty upset by then. I wasn't really thinking."

"First, it's absolutely not your fault. Second, you have great instincts, for a guy with a desk job. Third, Mary thinks you don't know she's alive."

He blushed again. "I didn't think she thought about me enough to think whether I knew she was alive or not."

"Peter, for a lawyer, that's very badly put. *I* think—" I stopped telling him what I thought, because Mary came striding out of the mint-green house, her braid swinging. She crossed the street to her unmarked car, took out its radio mouthpiece and spoke into it. Then she came over to where we were and crouched down next to me.

"Found your boys upstairs," she said. "They're both alive, but one's sick and one's hurt."

"Your boys?" Peter asked a little blankly. "The Wengs?"

Mary nodded. "I called for a bus—an ambulance, I mean. One of them's just been knocked around a little, but the other one—the younger one—I think he was telling me he has TB. But my Chinese isn't so hot, so maybe I didn't get it right."

"No, that's probably right. That would explain it. You don't want that in your kitchen," I said.

"What are you talking about?" Peter asked. "Did you know they were here?"

"I hoped."

As Mary started to say something, a blue BMW turned into Simpson Street, then stopped, then violently backed out around the corner and sped away.

"Jimmy Tung!" I yelled. "Goddammit, that's Jimmy Tung! I was right! Mary, you've got to—! This is all his—"

Tripping over my words, I looked helplessly at Peter, then at Mary. They looked at each other.

"Okay," Mary said. "Calm down. Explain it to me, and if he needs to be taken up, we'll find him."

So, sitting in the long yellow rays of the afternoon sun, I explained it to Mary and Peter. When I was through they both gave me hell for taking chances, charging right in, acting alone on my own wild hunches.

"Hey!" I said. "Hey, you guys! You both saved my life. Thanks. I'm glad. I love you. Now stop. Leave me alone." I stood and walked away, leaving them together on the soft grass. My head was filled with noise, with voices and the smell of rotting oranges and sleeping men crowded together in airless rooms. The ancient cruel eyes of a man not that much older than I was faded into the eyes of a nineteen-year-old kid who wouldn't get older. I didn't know where I was going, barefoot and rumpled in the heat of the evening, but it was time to be by myself for a while.

Catherine Dain's Freddie O'Neal novels have distinguished themselves by being twice nominated for Shamus Awards with Lay It on the Line *and* Lament for a Dead Cowboy. *The most recent novel in the series was* Dead Man's Hand *(Berkley, 1997). Freddie has also appeared in the original audio anthology* For Crime Out Loud. *She is a significant link in the continuing development of the female P.I.*

In this story Freddie finds out what can happen when you try to do a favor for family—especially a cousin you haven't seen in twenty-five years.

BILLY THE GOAT
A FREDDIE O'NEAL MYSTERY

by Catherine Dain

"What Cousin Billy? You mean the Cousin Billy who dragged me around the Idlewild pool with my head under water when I was six years old? That Cousin Billy?"

"You only have one Cousin Billy. The son of my sister, your aunt Freddie, for whom you were named. Yes. That Cousin Billy."

"She doesn't even send me birthday cards, and I wouldn't recognize either of them on the street. And Billy has to be fortysomething. Why would a fortysomething man still use the name Billy?"

"I don't know. You'll have to ask him."

"Why does he want to see me? And why doesn't he just call?"

"I can't answer either of those questions," Ramona snapped.

She was getting testy, probably because I was. Her relationships with her sister, her sister's assorted husbands, and her sister's three adult children weren't any closer than mine. So it wasn't fair of me to push her.

On the other hand, it wasn't fair of Cousin Billy to call her after all these years and ask a favor. Especially when the favor he asked was to arrange a quiet meeting with me. Which meant my mother had to ask me a favor.

Not a good start to the telephone call.

"Okay." I figured I could give in on this one. Find out for myself what was going on with Billy. "Where are we supposed to meet?"

"The Arcade at the Clarion."

"The Arcade? You mean the place next to the ice cream counter where the video games are? The place where the kids are dropped while the adults gamble?"

"That way you can spot each other. He'll be playing Space Invaders, tonight at seven."

"He could be playing anything he likes. He'll be the only person over twelve."

"I think that was the idea. He wasn't certain he could recognize you, either."

"All right. I'll see what he wants."

"Thank you." Her tone was icy. Asking me to help a nephew she hadn't heard from in twenty-five years was tough.

"And I'll call you tomorrow."

She hung up without thanking me again.

The Clarion wasn't one of my favorite places, but I could understand why Billy—or anyone else needing to set up a discreet meeting by way of a third party—might choose it. It was one of the newer hotel-casinos, built a couple of miles south of the downtown gambling center, and airport-handy. There were always at least three conventions on the daily schedule, and the crowd at the tables would welcome the space in a sardine can.

Two people could have a conversation without the possibility of being taped in the din. Only a lip reader would have a shot at picking it up.

I pulled the Jeep into the parking lot about fifteen minutes early. The asphalt covered an area the size of a football field. Even so, the first space I spotted was against the back fence.

The sun hadn't set, and the early evening air was still warm. By late May, the temperature swings run around 40 degrees, dropping slowly from the mid-eighties in the afternoon to the low forties just before dawn. I figured this wouldn't take much time, so I hadn't bothered to bring a jacket.

I walked down a long row of mixed cars, vans, and pickups, mostly with California plates. I wondered where Billy had been living for the past twenty-five years. Not in Reno, I was certain of that.

Scattered lines of people converged on the double doors from the parking lot to the casino, like ants discovering a chocolate bar.

The inside was a sudden explosion of light, color, and sounds. Another football field, with the center open for a couple of stories straight up, the floor jammed with tables and machines all swarming with people.

A glass-encased announcement board welcomed the conventions of the day—orthopedic surgeons, travel writers, and the Arkansas Bar Association.

I stayed on the outskirts of the pit as much as possible, working my way toward the corner escalator that led to the hollowed-out second floor, where the video games and ice-cream counter were located.

The post-World War II gamblers who built the city were probably rattling their dry bones in wonder at the new emphasis on family-friendly entertainment, and the way gambling had morphed from a pastime somewhere between sleazy and sinful to good, clean fun and a healthy source of state revenue to boot.

The video game players were all minors, as usual. A sole adult stood just outside the area, a man about five foot seven, with reddish-brown hair, as twitchy as a pedophile watching for security guards.

Ironically, I would have recognized Billy after all. With that small, tight mouth and pointed chin, he had to share Ramona's gene pool.

The cowboy boots gave him some needed height, but he didn't seem comfortable in them, and they didn't exactly coordinate with his blue suit, white shirt, and burgundy tie. And he was still four inches shorter than I when he walked up and held out his hand.

"My God, Freddie, it's good to see you!"

The hand was a little sweaty. I was glad he hadn't tried to hug me.

"Hey, Billy," I replied. I was trying to reconcile this thin, nervous man with the teenager who had seemed so powerful when he dragged me around the pool.

"We could have met at the bar. I would have recognized you—you look just like your father."

I took my hand back.

"I'd just as soon talk over a beer," I said.

"Fine, fine. How about dinner? We need a little time to catch up."

"I can't handle the line at the buffet, but the area that serves the little pizzas is okay."

"I was thinking about the restaurant across the way." He gestured to the area on the other side of the doughnut hole, where the exception to the rule that casinos serve inexpensive food hid behind a bright seafood menu and a dark door.

Billy had to be doing pretty well. Or be using someone else's credit card. It wasn't a nice thought, but the combination of the twitchiness and the reference to my father brought my guard up.

"Your choice," I said.

We walked the balcony in silence. Billy was working hard at the cowboy boots, but they were pitching him forward, and I was reminded of the way a baby walks, almost falling with every step, half running just to stay upright.

Billy looked both ways quickly before slipping through the door.

A smiling man in a tux who stood somewhere between Billy's height and mine showed us to a corner booth in a room so dim that I couldn't tell if it was full or empty or somewhere in between. He handed us menus and left.

I set mine aside.

"You know what you want?" Billy asked.

"Catch of the Day and a beer," I said. "Now cut the crap and tell me what this is about."

"I thought we might chat a little first."

He looked hopeful, but I didn't help him out. He shook his head and sighed.

"I need you to run an errand for me." The hazel eyes tried to look sincere, but the lids twitched.

"What kind of errand? Why me?"

"I need someone I can trust, and someone who can take care of herself in a tight situation."

"Start from the beginning."

He couldn't focus. He waved at a waiter and ordered for both of us. I didn't bother to react.

"All right," Billy said, but he didn't sound as if he meant it. "I'm a stockbroker. I sell securities at a small, independent firm in Newport Beach—that's in Southern California. We do a lot of private placements for very wealthy people who want investments with an above average return. A few months ago a certain party approached me with an interesting idea—railroad tank cars."

"What's interesting about railroad tank cars?"

"These particular cars would be used to transport oil to Southern California. And they wouldn't be ordinary tank cars. These would be Cadillacs, not Chevys. With shining brass fixtures, and brass plates with the owner's name on the side. For a mere one hundred thousand dollars, a far-sighted investor could own a vehicle making continual trips from the oil-rich territories of Alaska to the automobile-dependent territories of Southern California. A can't-lose proposition."

He pulled a folded brochure from his inside coat pocket and flipped it open to a photograph of a tank car. The brass fixtures glowed, even in the imitation candlelight.

"This isn't a real tank car. This is a model," I said.

"Right. Every investor got a model of a tank car, just like the real one, as a desk ornament. Terrific sales tool."

"So what went wrong?"

Billy sighed. "Nothing was wrong with the idea. I did all the due diligence anyone could ask. The SEC approved the prospectus."

"So what went wrong?" I asked again.

"It seems the person who wrote the prospectus and the persons who created the brochure took the word of the same party who talked to me. That is, we all believed that the tank cars were lined up."

"Whereas?"

"There are no tank cars." Billy cringed as he said it, waiting to be hit.

I shrugged. "You didn't create the scam. You didn't even write the prospectus. Turn the certain party in to the SEC. There may even be a reward."

"That seems like good advice." Billy was twitching again. He must twitch off about eight hundred calories a day. "But the certain party wouldn't like that at all. I need to keep a low profile. Getting in touch with the SEC would mean drawing a little too much attention. I'm not sure who I can trust—except you."

"Why me? You haven't seen me in twenty-five years."

"Hey, Freddie, you're my cousin. Who can you trust if you can't trust your cousin?"

Somebody who doesn't twitch, was what I thought.

"There's something you haven't told me," I said. "Like who this certain party is, the one behind the scam."

"I don't like the word 'scam.' I'd rather call it a misunderstanding." He looked around, making certain no one was within earshot, then lowered his voice anyway. "And I can't tell you the name of the party who put it together. You don't need to know. That isn't the problem here."

"If you say so. But then the problem here has to be one of the guys who bought a tank car on your say-so."

"Right." Billy's eyes were starting to water. He reached up and rubbed them. "For whatever it's worth, there is only one. He is threatening to go to the SEC. And since I can't hand over the party behind the misunderstanding, a complaint means that I lose my license to sell securities, my livelihood."

"Are you the only broker selling these cars?"

"Not quite. Almost. There are three of us."

"But there's a prospectus. This other party's name has to be on it."

"I'm afraid it isn't."

"Oh, Billy." I shook my head. "You're not telling me your name is on the prospectus."

"And the other two brokers," he said. "Not just me. It's like a limited partnership with a silent partner."

"That has to be illegal."

Billy didn't answer. He shifted in his chair and rubbed his eyes again.

The waiter brought my beer, Billy's martini, and a basket of rolls.

"Dinner will be right up," he said cheerfully.

"Looking forward to it," Billy said, with what he surely hoped was a believable smile.

"How did the silent partner talk you three supposedly astute financial types into risking your licenses and livelihoods like this?"

The rolls were sourdough, and warm. I tore one apart and buttered it while Billy decided what he was going to tell me.

"By explaining why it was better that the SEC think it was a deal put together by three Southern California stockbrokers and by pointing out how much more lucrative it was for us. We'd be getting not just the sales commission, but a cut of the partnership profits as well."

"Greed. The silent partner appealed to your greed."

"In a word." Billy nodded, doing his best to hold onto the smile. "And what's wrong with greed? Every man pursuing his own self-interest is what makes the invisible hand of the marketplace work."

"Or not work. If every man pursues his own self-interest at the expense of every other man, and woman, the marketplace is a jungle, and no invisible hand can turn it into a civilization. That takes effort and goodwill."

"Have it your way. I didn't come here to argue with you."

"That's right. You come to ask a favor."

"Jesus. You're not making this easy."

"What do you want me to do, Billy?"

"I just want you to talk to the guy. He's staying at the hotel, with the orthopedic surgeons group. Ask him to forget about the SEC. Tell him I'll give him back the money. Out of my own pocket. Please."

"You also want me to tell him you're sorry? And you'll never do it again?"

"Whatever it takes to get him off my back."

"Why can't you take the elevator to his room and tell him yourself?"

"I tried to tell him. He said he'd hurt me if he saw me again. And the other party might hurt me, too."

Billy shrank in his chair as he said the words. I wondered how big this surgeon was. And how big the silent partner was.

"I'll have to think about it."

"Sure, we'll eat first." He took a deep breath. "And talk about something else. How's your mother?"

"Fine. You ought to go up to the lake and see her while you're in the area. Do you have a car?"

"Yeah. A blue Acura. And the rental agency gave me a map to go with it. Maybe I'll drive up there tomorrow."

"I'm sure she'd like that."

"How are you? You ever get married?"

"No. You?"

"Yeah, twice. One kid, from the first. I guess I should have sent you an announcement or something."

Billy shifted in his chair again.

It turned out to be a long dinner. The more we tried to talk, the less we had to say.

In the back of my mind, I was working out how to tell

him I wouldn't do it. I didn't want to be anywhere near his scam, even to help him out from under a federal investigation.

But things about him—the shape and color of his eyes, the small hands with the long, narrow fingers, the careful way he separated his salmon steak from the tiny center bones—kept reminding me of Ramona. Saying no to him would be like saying no to her, only worse. I'd have to tell her about it afterward. And even though she wasn't close to her sister, she felt some kind of an undefined obligation, one she would expect me to honor.

All conversation had stopped by the time the waiter brought coffee.

Billy looked at me with desperate hope in his eyes, eyes that needed only mascara, liner, and three shades of eyeshadow to match Ramona's.

"How did you find out the tank cars weren't there?" I asked, still not ready to commit.

"The guy—the orthopedic surgeon—found out. The base of operations was supposed to be the railroad yard in Sparks. Since he was coming to Reno for the convention, he thought he'd drive three miles east to check out his investment. But nobody in Sparks had ever heard of the deal, so he called me. I made a few phone calls and discovered he was right. I flew up here yesterday, just to make sure there was no mistake."

"What did the silent partner have to say?"

"Oh, hell, the usual. That I jumped the gun. That the cars weren't supposed to start rolling until September first, and everything would be worked out by then."

"But?"

Billy shook his head. He took a sip of coffee before he answered. "But this is June, and we've started selling cars, and the prospectus—with my name on it—says they're already sitting in the yard. And even if there's some way everything will be different in September, I don't think the surgeon would be willing to wait. And I can't blame him. So I want to give him his money back."

"You have the check?"

"I wish I did." He reached into his jacket.

"Sorry for the delay, sir." The waiter slipped a black leather folder onto the table.

Billy froze, hand in his pocket.

"No problem," he whispered.

The waiter disappeared into the shadows.

"I have a down payment," Billy finished, his voice barely audible. He pulled out his wallet. "Ten now, the other ninety when I can get it together."

His hand was shaking as he held out a sealed envelope. "Please."

I took the envelope. There was no name, or any other mark on it.

"Where do I deliver it?"

"Upstairs. Room 1103. Theo Georgopoulos. And I owe you one, Freddie, I swear, if you ever need anything I can give."

I hoped it wouldn't come to that.

"Are you certain he's in his room?"

"No. But you might as well give it a shot while you're here."

"Okay. Where will you be?"

His eyebrows shot up, and his mouth formed a circle of speechless wonder.

"I have to report back to you," I said. "Let you know what happens. Where will you be?"

"How about the lounge? There's some kind of musical entertainment going on. I'll try for a table at the back."

"Okay. And thanks for dinner."

I left him there. I figured he could settle the bill without me.

Outside the black door, back in the light and noise, I had to pause to reorient myself and find the elevators.

One stopped for me almost immediately. I rode alone to the eleventh floor.

Room 1103 was the second door on the right. Whoever had last gone in or out hadn't bothered to pull it quite shut. I knocked, and it moved.

"Dr. Georgopoulos?"

No answer.

I pushed with my elbow, and the door swung open.

A closet and bathroom blocked the sightline to the bed, beyond them on the left. A solid wall stopped the door on the right.

"Dr. Georgopoulos?"

I stepped cautiously over the threshold and moved just far enough forward to see the rest of the room.

A man was lying on the bed, legs partially hanging over the end.

He was wearing a dark grey suit, white shirt, and striped tie, almost an echo of Billy's outfit, both of them too formal for Reno. And he was here for a convention. Maybe he had decided to come back to his room and take a nap after making some kind of formal presentation. He had unfastened his belt buckle and his pants, getting comfortable. Certainly, he was big enough to intimidate someone as small as Billy. Probably six foot four, if he had been standing.

But he wasn't going to do that again.

His hair had receded to a fringe of black around a high white dome. A bullet hole sat like a third eye in the middle of his forehead.

The wall behind the bed was spattered with blood, as if

the guy had been upright, and the shot had knocked him more or less onto the bed. The blood still looked runny, as if it might be fairly fresh.

I thought I heard a noise from the bathroom. A surge of adrenaline almost sent me flying back out of the room and into the hall, but I took a couple of deep breaths to get the fear and the anger under control, and realized the noise came from the room next door.

I had two choices. I could call hotel security and be stuck for an hour, or I could find Billy and make sure I hadn't been set up. If the guy hadn't been so obviously dead, or if I thought the perp might be hiding in the closet, I would have called security. As it was, I wanted to find Billy.

I slipped back to the door.

A man and woman were walking toward the elevator bank, arguing.

I listened for the elevator doors to open and close, the silence to return.

When I was certain the hall was clear, I left the room and turned away from the elevators. I found the stairs, walked down two flights, and decided I could ride the rest of the way.

I hoped Billy would be in the lounge. I really wanted Billy to be in the lounge.

I wish I could say I was surprised when he wasn't there.

He'd had more than enough time to settle the dinner bill, stop in the men's room, and get to the lounge. I cleared a path through the crowd with my elbows and my boots, apologizing all the way, knowing I was probably too late to catch him in the parking lot if he wanted to escape that way.

Once out of the building, I picked up speed. I trotted to the exit lane, then took it across the middle of the lot, checking the rows both ways for a little man in a blue Acura trying to head for the hills.

I couldn't spot Billy, and I wasn't ready to check the lot car by car, especially when I didn't have a license plate number.

On the off chance that he'd asked me to meet him at the hotel, where he was staying, I went back inside and picked up the house phone near the door.

"Billy Davis's room. William Davis," I corrected.

"Just a minute," the operator answered.

The phone started ringing.

I let it ring until she came back on the line.

"He doesn't seem to be there. Would you like to leave a message?"

"Not just now."

If he had a room, he'd have to go back to it, sooner or later. I just had to find it. I thought again about telling security. I still wanted to talk to Billy first.

I had to check the lounge one more time.

On stage, a man with shoe-polish black hair and a face dripping with flop sweat was belting "What's New, Pussycat," while the band behind him did its collective best to keep playing, and to keep from keeling over with embarrassment.

Billy still wasn't at a table.

I looked around for a sign that would direct me to a restroom. A stall seemed as good a place as any to see what was in the envelope. All I saw were bright, Disneyesque parrots pointing me toward the buffet. I figured restrooms would be close to the buffet line, and I was at least right on that.

The restroom wasn't crowded. The first lucky thing that had happened since I arrived at the casino.

The envelope contained just what Billy told me—his personal check for ten thousand dollars, made out to Theodore Georgopoulous.

For the first time, I wondered if something might have happened to Billy after I left the restaurant, something that kept him from the lounge. I had to check out his room.

Finding his room number would have been a lot easier in pre-electronic days, when rooms had keys instead of programmable cards, and messages were stuck in racks of key boxes behind the registration desk. I could have left him a message and watched where it was placed. But not here.

My only quick idea was the maitre d' at the restaurant. If he wasn't bribable, or if Billy hadn't charged dinner to his room, I'd be reduced to calling security.

I retraced my steps to the escalator, rode to the second floor, then walked around the balcony to the dark restaurant door.

The maitre d' smiled when he saw me.

"Did you forget something?" he asked.

"Not exactly. I wanted to split the dinner bill with my cousin, Billy Davis, and he's being stubborn. Could you possibly retrieve our check from the waiter and let me see it?" I had a twenty folded in my hand.

"Certainly," the maitre d' said, still smiling, once the twenty was his.

He slipped into the dim recesses of the restaurant and came back with Billy's signed receipt. And I had the room number. Room 1115, right down the hall from the corpse.

I thanked the maitre d' and left the restaurant for the second time, heading again for the elevator bank and the eleventh floor.

I barely glanced at 1103 as I passed. The door was still ajar. I hadn't pulled it shut, both because I wanted to leave it as I found it and because I didn't want to put my hands on anything in the vicinity of the dead man.

When I reached the door to Billy's room, I knocked, out of habit, not really expecting an answer.

But I could have sworn I heard a groan.

I knocked again.

"Billy? Are you there?"

Silence.

"Billy, if you're there, open up. Because if I leave, I'm coming back with hotel security. Two of them. One for the room down the hall, and one for you."

I was about to walk away when I heard someone turn the lock.

The woman who opened the door was easily six foot two in her stiletto heels. Long black hair hung straight over her bare shoulders, all the way to her lace-trimmed red corset, the kind with matching underpants, and garters to hold up black fishnet stockings. Her arms were fleshy, and a roll of fat billowed softly over the satin-covered wires.

But the set of her wine-red mouth was hard. I glanced down at her hand, expecting a whip.

She was holding a gun.

"Come in," she said, blinking a heavy fringe of false eyelashes. "You must be Billy's cousin. He's told me so much about you."

"Oh, God. Next you'll tell me he couldn't come to the door himself because he's tied up."

In bare feet, we would have been just about eye-to-eye. I didn't like having to look up to meet her gaze.

She smiled one of those wide-lipped smiles that vampires use to expose their fangs.

"I'm going to step back from the door," she said. "You're going to come in and shut it behind you. If you leave instead, I will end your cousin's life and disappear before you can return with help. Do you understand?"

"Yes, ma'am."

She kept the gun on me as she moved away from the door.

I followed her into a room that was the twin of 1103, except that the man on the bed was Billy, and he was still alive.

He was naked and gagged, and his hands were cuffed behind his back, but he was still alive.

I could tell because he squirmed, and his face turned red. He looked even smaller and more pathetic naked than he had in the suit and boots.

"Sit down." The woman used her gun to point toward a chair on the far side of the room.

I did as told.

She leaned against the wall, regarding me thoughtfully.

"What happens next?" I asked, not wanting to give her too much time to think. "I can't believe you're going to walk out of here and leave us to call the cops."

"No. I hadn't expected you, and I'm afraid I'll have to improvise. In fact, I had specifically told Billy to leave the situation to me. Fortunately, I suspected that he was weak enough to panic. I've had friends keeping tabs on him. And when I saw him meet you, I knew what he was doing. I was about to punish him when you knocked."

"We haven't been introduced. I'm Freddie O'Neal, and you are—?" I broke off the question to wait for her answer.

"You don't need to know my name. You can call me Sada, if you like."

"Sada. Are you by some other name known as a financial whiz?"

"I don't think you need to know that, either."

"Maybe not, but if you are, it would make sense out of why three Southern California stockbrokers chose to risk their licenses in a scam. Had to be something more than greed."

"A scam? Naughty Billy. I've told him not to use that word."

Billy squirmed some more, drawing his knees up to

protect his genitals. He tried to make sounds through the gag.

"He called it a misunderstanding," I said.

Billy nodded rapidly.

"Good Billy," Sada purred.

Billy didn't relax his knees.

Sada looked at me again.

"I had hoped I could control Billy, at least until the money from the investors was safely deposited in an off-shore bank. Unfortunately, I don't think you're quite as amenable to persuasion as your cousin. So this is what we're going to do. You and I will exchange clothes. And poor Billy will shoot you and then himself, after having shot the good doctor down the hall, in a love triangle gone awry." She thought it over and sighed. "This is far too messy for my taste, but I don't see a way out of it. Undress now. Start with your boots."

I bent over toward my right foot. And I pulled the gun out of my boot and shot.

With a small .22 caliber, you have to pray when you shoot. It's the equivalent of throwing a Hail Mary pass in football.

My first shot landed in her right shoulder. Her gun hand wavered.

My second shot grazed her ear.

"Stop." She dropped her gun. Blood ran in one stream down her arm, in another down her neck and across her collarbone. "Stop."

I kept the gun aimed more or less at her chest. My stomach was churning, and I was tempted to walk out and leave both of them. But I didn't.

"Uncuff Billy and let him call security."

"I'll have to get the key."

"Wrong. Just ungag him, then. You can hit O for

Operator, but I want him on the receiver. I don't want you faking the call and somehow alerting a friend instead."

Awkwardly, with her left hand, she loosened Billy's gag, picked up the receiver, hit O, and then held the receiver next to Billy's head.

Hotel security arrived first, then the hotel doctor, followed somewhat later by Detective Matthews and the crime team from the Reno Police Department.

I told the story and Billy confirmed it.

Sada was taken into custody.

The first security guard to arrive tossed a clean towel over Billy, but he spent a lot of time naked and cuffed while people walked in and out of the room. If it wasn't Sada's idea of punishment, it was certainly mine. I'd have to think later whether it was enough.

Billy gave not only his own name and address to the police, but Sada's as well. The silent partner no more.

"How long are you planning to stay in Reno?" Matthews asked him. "We'll need your testimony to make the charge stick."

"I'll stay as long as you need me," Billy said. "After all, I have family here."

I winced.

"Yeah, sure," Matthews nodded. He had raised his eyebrows when I introduced Billy as my cousin, but he was now beyond shock. "I won't blame you if you decide not to stay at the hotel after this. But make certain I have a good local address and phone number, okay?"

That was to me as much as to Billy.

I waited until Matthews had left and Billy was dressed before I brought up the question again.

"Where are you going to stay?" I asked.

"I'll have to think about it." He was still badly shaken. "The detective is right. I don't think I want to stay here."

"Do me a favor and sleep on my couch tonight. I don't want to worry that Sada might make a phone call and get somebody to come after you." I was still pissed at Billy for getting me into this, and I wasn't happy with the idea of spending more time with him, but I didn't want to lie awake wondering if he was going to disappear, whether he wanted to or not.

"Oh, God," he groaned. "She's capable of it."

"Okay. Tonight you sleep on my couch, and we'll figure out the rest of it tomorrow. Maybe you could stay with Ramona for a while. Work on your tan."

"Do you have to tell Aunt Ramona what happened?"

"Billy, there was a murder in a hotel-casino. What happened will be in a police report. TV news vans root out crime scenes the way pigs root truffles. I won't be surprised if Ramona knows before I can call her. She watches the eleven o'clock news."

He thought for a moment.

"She'll know about the murder. She might even find out that the railroad tank car situation wasn't quite on the up-and-up. But I was led astray, and I can explain. It's just—she doesn't have to know about Sada, and about me being naked and cuffed, and all that. Does she?"

Billy was looking up at me with hope in his soft, hazel eyes.

"Maybe, maybe not. I'll have to think about it."

"I'll owe you," he said, starting to twitch. "Remember when I dragged you around the pool? I'll let you drag me around the pool. Any pool in town. What do you say?"

I almost liked the idea. But the thing was, he liked it better. The hope in his soft, hazel eyes was that I would drag him around the pool.

Whatever punishment he wanted, thought he deserved, I wouldn't help him out.

I clapped a hand on his shoulder.

"Hey, Billy, we're family. I forgave you for that a long time ago. And don't worry. Your secret is safe with me."

The hope drained from his eyes, then came back.

"I'll think of something else," he said.

I was uncomfortably aware of the old joke about what the sadist responded when the masochist begged, "Hurt me." But I said it anyway.

"No."

Author of the acclaimed Jenny Cain series, Nancy Pickard is not generally known for writing P.I. fiction. Her first effort in the genre, "Dust Devil," only won her the Shamus Award for Best P.I. Short Story of 1992. Naturally, we felt compelled to challenge her to duplicate that feat, and this is what she came up with, a look at what goes on in the home of a P.I.—maybe. (This is actually Nancy's third P.I. story. Her second appeared in Sara Paretsky's fine anthology Women on the Case. *Is there a change of career direction in the offing?)*

Nancy has won the Agatha, the Anthony, American Mystery, and McCavity Awards in addition to the Shamus. Sara Paretsky calls her "the proud owner of possibly the most eclectic collection of honors in the field . . ."

THE PRIVATE LIFE OF A PRIVATE EYE

by Nancy Pickard

I F SHE HADN'T had to fire the cleaning lady, Lolly Holliday might never have found the first gun.

"What's this?"

Lolly was in her blue jeans, down on her knees in the family room, after coming home from work. She peered under the sofa to see what it was that she had run into with the vacuum sweeper. The rug brush had come up against some obstacle, something hard and unyielding that kept the wand from penetrating into the dark space under the sofa. It had been three years since Lolly had looked under there, a period which exactly coincided with what she had affectionately termed "The Blessed Coming" of the cleaning lady once a week. But finances had grown tight. Lolly's husband, Stewart, had insisted on cutting the woman back to every other week, then to once a month. Finally, Lolly had found herself uttering the words she regretted horribly: "I'm so sorry, but we have to let you go."

The woman had taken it well.

Lolly hadn't.

Now her resentment and irritation at once again having to do heavy housework exploded at the obstacle in her path.

"What the *hell* is this?"

What it looked like in the shadows was a long, thin, rather attractive suitcase. It had a handle, which Lolly grasped in order to pull the mysterious object out from under the sofa. Once exposed in the light, it still looked like luggage, but a piece that would be awfully awkward to carry through airports.

What in heaven's name was it?

Lolly ran her hands over the sleek, slightly nubby surface. Although it had a metallic appearance and the edges were trimmed in silver metal, when she flicked her forefinger against the side of it—*thud*. It had to be Stewart's, of course, but what was it?

By now, Lolly was kind of enjoying the surprise and intrigue of it, the guessing game she was playing in her mind. Was it a surprise for her? But her fifty-fifth birthday was half a year away, and so was Christmas. So, what could something like this hold? What could it be that was very long, thin rather than thick, and which required such substantial packaging?

"I give up."

Lolly flipped the three latches and raised the lid to reveal the contents.

"What is *this*?"

Steward Holliday looked from his wife's angry face to the

open gun case on the floor and then back up again, almost but not quite meeting her blue eyes.

"It's a twenty-five ought-six bolt action rifle."

"I know it's a gun. You don't have to tell me that, Stewart. What I want to know is, what is it doing in this house?"

Stewart raised his eyebrows, as if he were hearing something he had a hard time believing. "The same thing I am, Lolly. Me, your husband, the private investigator, remember? Guns are a part of my business, or do you think I hold off the bad guys by the sheer force of my personality? Charm them into submission, maybe, is that it?"

"Not this gun. This gun is different. It looks brand new. It's packaged like a piece of jewelry. It was under my *couch*. And I know what guns you use for business, so don't give me that. This isn't one of them. This looks expensive, and I thought we were cutting back, and you didn't say a word to me about buying it!" She was breathing fast, like a jogger rounding the last block, and her face was flushed with the heat of her resentment. "How much did it cost, Stewart?"

He put the tip of his tongue against the roof of his mouth and rubbed it there, as if looking for some interior Braille answer, a better one than the one he had to give her.

"Nine hundred dollars."

She made a gagging sound, and stared at him.

"Tax deductible. Think of that."

Lolly glared at him. "Think of this." In rapid succession, she slammed shut the lid of the gun case, then kicked the case so hard that it spun in a circle on the carpet and hit a sofa leg, and then stalked out of the den. A moment later, she was back.

"*Nine hundred dollars?*"

"Why are you so upset about this, Lolly?"

"I *fired* the cleaning lady, Stewart. We couldn't afford her, *remember*? And now I know why, don't I?"

Lolly stalked out again.

Stewart heard the slam of their bedroom door.

When he was sure she wasn't coming back out, he knelt down to examine the case for damage, and was relieved to find she hadn't hurt it. Not that he'd really expected to find a dent—these cases were built to withstand worse treatment than a kick from an angry wife.

Stewart stroked the gun, its stock and barrel, smooth as a cat's back. He hadn't actually paid nine hundred dollars for it, but Lolly didn't need to know that. If she called him a spendthrift, that was better than calling him what he really was. He lowered the lid of the case, latched it, and gently pushed it back under the sofa. Clients didn't always pay in money; sometimes they paid in merchandise, like chickens and eggs to a small-town doctor. Stewart liked comparing himself to a physician; like them, he listened to complaints, investigated symptoms, diagnosed ailments that often suggested their own cure.

It occurred to Stewart that this might be a good night to take his wife out to dinner at a very fine restaurant.

"I thought we were *married*," Lolly whispered furiously over the veal lemonata and angel hair pasta on her plate. "I thought that meant we were partners. I thought partners shared decisions with one another, especially decisions about big purchases, like nine-hundred-dollar guns. How *could* you, Stewart, without consulting me?"

"You would have said no, Lolly."

She put her knife and fork back down on her plate and slumped into the upholstered chair. "Oh, Stewart." She sighed, then gazed across at him, her eyes full of anger and hurt. "Of course I would have said no. *You* should have said no."

"Look, I don't have any other hobbies," he protested. "I

don't play golf, I don't watch television all the time. You ought to be happy that I only collect guns——"

Stewart stopped abruptly, suddenly aware that he had just made a very serious tactical error.

"Collect?" Lolly said, slowly. "Gun . . . s?"

Lolly spent a good part of that night ransacking the house for more guns.

"What's this?" she demanded, as she lifted a pile of spare blankets off a gun that was tucked into a corner of the top shelf of Stewart's closet.

"Pistol," he said tersely. "A twenty-two caliber."

"How much?"

"It was a bargain."

Lolly looked back at the pistol and said wonderingly, "It's even in a holster. Yippeekiyokiyeh."

"Oh, come on, Lolly."

She found three additional pistols in his closet and several in the drawers in his dresser: four Smith & Wessons, three Colts, four more Brownings and an HSC Interarms 9 mm auto-action Mauser, totaling in cost, he admitted, nearly three thousand dollars.

"Are any of these loaded, Stewart?"

"Why, you going to shoot me?"

"Don't tempt me."

"No, of course they're not loaded, do you think I'm crazy?"

Lolly leveled her husband with a look, and repeated, "Don't tempt me."

"Well, you just don't understand," he said heatedly. "I knew you wouldn't, that's why I couldn't ever tell you the truth. Guns are an investment, just like stocks and bonds. They'll increase in value, it's a sure thing."

"Are they registered?"

Taken unpleasantly by surprise by the question, he put everything he had into answering it indignantly, sarcastically. "Of course, they're registered." He thought of a bassett hound he knew, mimicked its reproachful expression, and asked her, "You don't think I'd do anything illegal, do you?"

"No, just—" She shook her head, biting back the words that occurred to her, like, *stupid*, *selfish*, *lying*. "Now we're going to the basement."

He suddenly felt sick as a dog. "Oh, damn. Listen, Lolly, maybe it's a disease, like gambling—"

"Come on, Bat Masterson."

In the basement, she located what she promptly dubbed The Mother Lode. One by one, Lolly pulled open the long drawers of his work cabinet, the drawers where she had always assumed that he kept wrenches, hammers, nuts and bolts.

"What's this one, Stewart?"

"An Ithaca with over and under action."

"Whatever that is. How much?"

"It's, uh, worth five hundred dollars."

"And this one?"

"An automatic with a Redfield three by nine."

"I'm getting such an education. How much?"

"Six hundred and fifty."

In a small drawer, beneath assorted screws and nails, Lolly found a red leather notebook with a gold star on the front and gold lettering that spelled out "Personal Firearms Record." She opened it to find that Stewart had entered the facts about each of his purchases in neat, readable printing. When she finished studying it, while he observed her in silence, she looked up at him again.

"You could have saved us a lot of time if you'd shown me this."

"I'll save you the trouble of asking, Lolly. They're worth about fifteen thousand dollars, total. But believe me, one day they'll be worth twice that, at least."

"Over my dead body."

"Don't tempt me."

"Stewart!" She sounded shocked. "Do you love these guns more than you love me? Never mind, don't answer that. Well, I guess you know you'll have to sell them."

But he shook his head stubbornly, strongly. "No. Absolutely not. I can't. I won't. It's too soon, and we wouldn't get our money back. Really, Lolly, all we have to do is hold on to them long enough, and they'll buy us a retirement condominium in Florida."

She waved an unloaded pistol at him. "It's not about guns, Stewart, and it's not even about money! It's about telling the truth, and it's about being a husband I can trust!"

"I'm going to bed," was his exhausted reply.

Lolly pointed the unloaded pistol squarely at his retreating back, and clicked the trigger.

That night, she slept in the family room, tossing and turning on the couch with the gun beneath it, and feeling like the princess in the fairy tale trying to sleep on top of the pea. *Some princess*, she thought, bitterly, just before she finally slipped into uneasy dreams, *and some damned, deadly pea*.

But even the little bit of sleep she got was enough to clear her mind beautifully by morning. When she awoke, she knew exactly what she must do to save her marriage, and her cleaning lady. There was a way, a risky, brilliant way—if she did say so herself—to get those damn guns out of her house without even having to ask Stewart to get rid of them. It was also a way to get back enough money to rehire her cleaning woman, hell a whole *crew* of cleaning people, if that's what Lolly wanted.

When Stewart walked, warily, into their home the next evening, it became his turn to say in a stunned voice, "What's that?"

His wife grinned, and leaned against their newest purchase.

"Just what it looks look like," she replied, before stating the obvious. "A gun case." Lolly patted the smooth dark wood that enclosed a glass-fronted display in which she had installed his guns, the long and the short of them. "Isn't it gorgeous?" She laughed at the expression on his face. "You look as if you don't know whether to be overjoyed, or suspicious."

Stewart approached cautiously, and admitted, "I don't understand, Lolly. I thought you hated my guns. I thought you wanted me to sell them. What's going on?"

"Oh, honey." She stepped forward and wrapped loving arms around him. "I just figured that if I couldn't beat you, by God, I'd join you. Look, I asked around today, and found out that you're right, guns can be a good investment, amazing though that seems to me. This is just my way of acknowledging that, and of apologizing to you. I'm sorry that I was so narrow-minded you felt you couldn't tell me the truth about your investment decisions. And I'm sorry I put you through hell last night." She snuggled closer, and kissed the side of his neck. "I won't go so far as to say I'm ready to join the NRA, but I'm a believer."

"You're amazing," he said. "I'm sorry, too. I just kind of got obsessed, I guess. But—"

Lolly pulled back to look at him. "But?"

"I hate to say this, but it's not really a good idea to display guns these days. It's the reason—okay, one of the reasons—I hid them. Out in the open like this, they're a temptation to thieves."

His wife looked instantly crestfallen.

His own words were giving Stewart an idea. A risky, but brilliant plan—if he did say so himself—was forming in his mind.

"It's okay," he quickly assured her, pulling her in tight for an embrace. "The important thing is that we're on track again, even if I have to take this case back."

He didn't take it back in time.

"Broad daylight," Lolly said, sounding stunned, when they came home from work two days later to find a pane of glass in their back door broken, the gun case shattered and the guns gone. "I can't believe it."

"Damn it!" Stewart crunched over broken glass to stare at the empty racks, while Lolly ran to the telephone to punch in 911. Too late, he realized what she was doing. "Lolly! No. Wait."

But she was already telling 911 they'd been robbed.

When she hung up, she found that her husband was staring at her with an expression of regret and sorrow, prompting her to say, "I'm sorry you've lost your guns, Stewart, but at least we'll have the insurance money."

"There's no insurance. They weren't my guns."

"There's no . . . what?"

"I stole them, Lolly. They are unregistered guns that have already been used in crimes and which I stole from people I was investigating. I sell them off, whenever I get a chance, through people I know."

"No insurance?" She couldn't seem to focus on the larger issue, but remained preoccupied with the lesser one. Then it hit her: "Oh, my God, Stewart . . . I've already called . . . the police are coming."

If she looked shocked, he looked desperate.

"I'll lose my investigator's license. God knows what else will happen to me. Lolly, you have to tell them it was something else that was stolen. Your china collection, something."

But Lolly lifted her chin and stared right back at him. It crossed her mind that no sane woman would want to continue being married to such a disappointing man. "No, the time for lies is over, Stewart. I will not be an accessory to your shoddy little crimes. It's time for the truth, for once. I'm going to tell them that somebody stole all of your guns."

"Not all of them."

Stewart removed a glove from his suit coat pocket. He walked toward the bookcase to find the empty book with the stolen pistol hidden in it. Behind him, Lolly was asking, "If you didn't purchase those guns, then *where did all of our money go*?"

She never found out.

Lolly was dead, shot and killed by a pistol which her killer had cavalierly dropped on the floor of the den, near the sofa.

Stewart told the investigating detectives that the burglar must have still been in the house while Lolly was calling 911. He told them that while he had stepped out into the backyard to look around, the burglar must have shot and killed Lolly. And then, Stewart said, the burglar must have escaped out the back, while Stewart was coming around toward the front of the house to wait for the police who were answering the 911 call. He also told them there had not actually ever been any guns in the cabinet, and that the burglar got away with nothing . . . except murder.

"So he was still in the house when the two of you got home," the detective repeated, while Stewart sat in a chair in the kitchen, looking pale and shocked. "If she saw him, he thought he had to kill her. But why did he tear your gun cabinet apart, if there weren't any guns in it?"

"Frustration. Anger," Stewart said, and he put his head in his hands. "It's my fault. There were going to be guns in it. I was going to start collecting them, and Lolly bought me that case for an early birthday present." His face appeared grief-stricken as he looked up at the detective. "Wasn't that sweet? Can you imagine many wives doing such a thing for their husbands?"

The detective shook his head; he sure couldn't imagine that.

Stewart went on to say, "And I've been talking about it, around town. You know, bragging about this new collection I was going to start, and how I was going to fill this case with guns. I'm an idiot. I know better. I know when people hear you talking about gun collections, the next thing you know, there's a break-in, and then—goodbye guns. Only, there weren't any. Just an empty case, and poor Lolly on the telephone." He looked as if an idea had just occurred to him. "I'll bet if you trace that gun that killed her, you'll find it was stolen someplace, maybe even killed somebody else."

The detective nodded; he wouldn't be surprised about that.

"You want us to get a search warrant to look around?"

"Hell, no," Stewart said sincerely. "I want you to look everywhere, and the sooner the better. Let me know if I can help. Jesus God, do whatever you need to do."

They did what they needed to do, including searching the basement, where they found his little gold-embossed Firearms Record which he had forgotten about. And including searching the attic, where they found Lolly's old bridal hope chest. It was packed to the brim with the guns that matched the ones listed in the Firearms Record. When they were finished, and Stewart was slouched, utterly defeated, at his kitchen table, the detective asked him, "So you wanted the insurance and your freedom, is that how it was, Stewart?"

"I only wanted the freedom," Stewart said, with his eyes closed. "There wasn't any insurance."

But Lolly thought there was, he knew.

And she'd staged a break-in and hidden his guns, to get it.

And she'd done it before Stewart had a chance to do it first. Her gift of the gun case had given *him* the idea of staging a break-in and stealing them, so that he could continue to sell them for private, profitable reasons of his own.

What a woman!

And what a pair we could have made, he thought, feeling intense regret for the first time since he'd pulled the trigger of his last stolen pistol. *We could have been Bonnie and Clyde*. If only they could have agreed upon which bank to rob.

"The guy was a licensed private investigator for Christ's sake," one of the uniformed cops remarked to the homicide detective. "You'd think he'd have known better than to try to pull a stupid stunt like this, wouldn't you?"

Looking profound, the detective observed, "Well, you have to remember, not every doctor graduates at the top of his class in medical school. Not every lawyer edits a law review. And some private eyes are . . ." He paused, searching for the right word, and when he found it he smiled. "Blind."

Stewart's girlfriend, Melanie, was seriously annoyed at her lover for going to prison and leaving her financially stranded. He'd been picking up her bills for a couple of years, taking the money out of what he earned legally in his job and illegally by selling guns. Now he was broke and gone forever, as far as Melanie was concerned, leaving her all alone with her bassett hound. Plus, he seemed to have developed a ridiculous posthumous crush on his wife. As if he'd given a fig for her while she was alive! Melanie couldn't have cared less, except that now she was going to have to get a real job. But the worst part was that she was going to have to fire her cleaning lady, and *that* really ticked her off.

Since the publication of the first Rainy McGuinn story in the original Lethal Ladies *Donna Murray has published three mystery novels in the Ginger Barnes series, including the most recent* The School of Hard Knocks *(St. Martin's Press, 1997). Could a book about Rainy, a woman with a very unusual phobia, be far behind?*

CHRISTMAS RAIN
A RAINY MCGUINN STORY

by Donna Huston Murray

"**N**URSE!" I CALLED as a tall woman in white walked by. "Please. The man I shot . . . ?"

Judging by her composure and the absence of discernible resentment over being there, she was the veteran of the Christmas Eve emergency crew. She stopped, appraised me, and answered with genuine kindness. "He's still in surgery. We don't know anything yet."

"But he's still . . . ?"

"Yes. They're still working on him."

"Thank you Ms. . . . ?" The name on her tag blurred.

"Thibur," she said helpfully. "But Charlotte will do. Let me see that arm." She carefully lifted the sterile pad I'd been holding against my left upper arm, scowled at the wound underneath, then pressed my right hand against it again.

"A doctor will be with you soon," she assured me, then hurried off on her previous errand.

I slouched back on the uncomfortable chair and let my mind stray back to the beginning.

My appointment with the president of Longshore's Department Store had been for just after closing, six P.M., the Tuesday prior to Thanksgiving. Walking through the store's shadowy displays gave me the creeps, much like a church or a school can after all the people have gone home.

Dennis Longshore himself opened his office door when I knocked. He was a few years older than me, around thirty-one, six feet tall and attractive in a blond, track-star sort of way. He had inherited the town's third largest store two years before.

"Rainy McGuinn," he effused. "Long time no see." He rounded his broad desk and bounced into his swivel chair. "Please." He waved toward a seat, which I took.

My baby brother drowned during a thunderstorm when I was six, and rain has unnerved me ever since. I carry a hypnotherapist's number just in case; but I figure if the cure involves remembering the details of my brother's death, I'd rather live with the anxiety.

"People usually call me Sandy now," I told him. "Please, tell me why you called."

He shifted in his chair and cocked his chin, male posturing to see if I'd stiffen or relax. "Are you aware that Martin Gulliver left under a cloud?"

"Your security chief?"

"Ex-security chief. Drugs, I guess. Started stealing a little here, a little there. We wrote it off as normal attrition at first. But then the frequency increased, losses spiraled. Caught him red-handed myself one night. Sad business. I've known the old guy since I was eight. But drugs change a person. I had to face facts. Marty was a one-man crime wave."

"You prosecute?"

Longshore wagged his head. "The board talked me out of it. I had to be satisfied letting him go.

"Trouble is, the search for his replacement is going

slower than expected; and starting this Friday we're into the Christmas crush. I'm nervous. Who knows who Marty might have told about our setup. If he gets desperate enough, who knows what he might try himself? And what about his staff?"

"So you want an objective pair of eyes around for a while."

"Exactly. You can pass for a shopper, and having you here won't threaten . . . anybody."

That "brainless blonde" albatross again. Getting me employment—again.

"How about if someone recognizes me, somebody who knows I'm a P.I.?"

"You live in town. You've got to shop somewhere. Fake it."

I nodded. I didn't believe an old security chief just shy of retirement would be stupid enough to rob his former employer. But as Dennis said, drugs change people. And it wasn't as if the town had a shortage of shoplifters. In the present economy, our most commercial holiday was bound to put pressure on people who never stole so much as a pack of gum.

"So how about it? Full-time starting tomorrow?" His sensual lips tucked into a smirk before he added, "If that won't interfere with your aerobics schedule too much."

I matched my smile to his. "It'll shoot my aerobics schedule all to hell—thank you very much." I'd been teaching classes at the Y to supplement my income, but the job had bored me from Day One.

"Fine. That's fine. Full-time then until New Year's."

I rose and quoted my rate. We shook hands, and then I asked my question.

"Why me?" If it was a simple business referral, I'd known who to thank. But if word about my work as a private investigator had finally made it around town, I could tell my mother to stop bragging.

"Why do you think?" The local merchandise mogul crossed his arms and regarded me with cool amusement. Denny's eyes never warmed. On our first and only date I learned that he retained a calculative detachment even during seduction.

"Scarp Poletta recommended me?" I guessed.

"The cop? I don't talk to cops."

"Social prejudice or self-preservation?"

Cartoon exclamation points radiated from Denny's eyes. "Cute. Still cute. I can see why I took you to that prom." He scanned my frame. "Would I have better luck now that we're both . . . experienced?"

I shook my head in disbelief. "You better keep your eye on the bottom line."

He glanced toward my rear. "I don't get your drift."

I leaned forward to accentuate my attorney general, pay-attention-bub expression. "I'm suggesting—Dennis—that it would be foolhardy to risk a harassment suit so close to Black Friday. You will probably need all the profit Longshore's makes and then some to pay off that woman who's divorcing you."

Something out of all that heightened the color on his cheeks.

The weeks approaching Christmas kept me and the regular security staff hopping. When little old ladies weren't pilfering perfume and the local thugs weren't pulling a smash and grab, Longshore's sales staff liberated merchandise when our backs were turned.

Timothy Sullivan, for example. Tim was a menswear salesman who grew unacceptably fond of a Rolex watch entrusted to his department. It disappeared from inside a locked display case that showed no sign of being forced.

Sullivan was caught trying to return the $2,500 item to a local jewelry store, swearing he had no receipt because the watch had been a gift from his uncle. Sullivan was so convinced of his own lie that while he was in Dennis's office getting fired, he actually offered to phone his uncle. Longshore's now has Arlene Pamona selling menswear, an improvement in every respect.

And I have a special eye out for Timothy Sullivan.

The smash-and-grabbers cleaned out a tall glass wall case full of Hummel figurines at 12:15 on a Tuesday lunch. Personally, I thought sweet-looking German kids saying "O" were passé, but apparently they still bring good money. The thieves, a couple of local thirty-year-old wastrels, popped the hinge on the five-foot-tall display case door and proceeded to lean it gently against a wall. An actual smash might have damaged the merchandise inside and certainly would have made noise, yet neither consideration spared the door. Flying glass causes cuts and cuts bleed. Leave the cops a little positive proof and you're looking at certain jail time.

Solly's and Harlan's faces were well known in the six-block shopping area in the center of our town. Township cops and privates like me see those two and pay attention. Mostly they'll slip into Gameland to feed quarters into the machines or drop into Lydia's Bar and Grill where the municipal workers go to hide from their bosses. But now and then they'll snatch a purse and snake through the downtown maze to fast freedom. Or they'll hit a specific store display and run. We didn't manage to catch them with the Hummels on them, so we had nothing. But we knew.

Nurse Charlotte came along and lifted my hand off my bandage again. The release of pressure made the wound throb and ooze fresh blood. It was just a graze, as they say in the Westerns, not serious or dangerous, but painful as hell. I flexed my stiff fingers and sat up from my slouched position. "Is he . . . ?" I asked.

"Still in OR. Still hanging on."

I released the breath I'd been holding and slouched back down. While Charlotte replaced my dressing I blocked out the pain and my fears by concentrating on the details of my night.

Georgie Jones had strolled into Longshore's about six-thirty while I was pretending to examine an earring display. To keep him in sight, I rounded the corner of the jewelry case and tried to forget about the Christmas Eve dinner I was missing at my sister-in-law's. Sally hates our side of the family and serves food calculated to break your bridgework or induce a coronary, but Christmas is so much about family tradition that I managed to feel deprived.

Georgie bypassed the jewelry and the calfskin gloves, then with a blatant look in my direction pocketed a box of Godiva chocolates. When I collared him, he practically sighed with relief. While we waited by the door for his official transportation, I said, "Let me guess. The shelters are full and you want turkey and stuffing with your friends. Right?"

"Naw, ye're nuts," he said, exhaling fumes strong enough to straighten my long blond hair.

"Skip Lydia's gravy," I advised as the patrol car stopped out at the curb. "She never did learn gravy." Tomorrow I would call and drop the charge. Probably after lunch.

Georgie gave me a wink as we stepped outside. Then he leaned over and breathed into my ear. "Careful, missy. There's something going down tonight."

I slapped him on the shoulder, figuring he probably meant

Santa Claus, but the sobriety in his eyes corrected that impression.

"What?" I asked.

Georgie Jones, the small-time derelict, shrugged. "Be careful," he said as he climbed into the cop car. The patrolman shut the door, leaving me on the sidewalk shivering inside my sweater and slacks.

I returned to watching the last-minute shoppers fret over prices, buy anyway, and go home proud. People guilty of nothing more than procrastination.

Nevertheless, I suspected each and every one and kept the shoulder bag containing my handcuffs and gun firmly within my grasp. Abandoning all pretense of shopping, I assumed an agitated pace that probably reflected Longshore's frantic clientele.

Despite the prevalence of credit cards, money still found its way into the cash registers, impressing me with just how huge today's final take would be. I couldn't wait for the staff to begin delivering the money to the employees' transaction desk in the room next to Denny's office, usually called the "bank," because it was equipped with a safe. My mental clock became acutely aware of the time span remaining before the special ten P.M. closing.

At nine-thirty a woman strutted past Cosmetics aiming for Denny's office. She carried an oblong package wrapped in silver and green. The rumored vampire wife—Pamela Longshore.

"Wait!" I called, halting her just outside the door.

She spun and skewered me with her eyes.

"Who the hell are you?" she demanded. She was sleek and far too cosmopolitan for our town, decked out in red to contrast with her dark hair. She seemed the sort to bewitch and destroy at will. I heard that Dennis found her on a buying trip to New York.

"Security," I told her, flipping open the ID I kept in my pocket.

"Sandy, it's okay," my current boss said as he appeared in the doorway. "Pamela called. I've been expecting her."

When I stayed put, he remarked—with amusement—that I was very dedicated to my work.

"Down, Rover," Pamela said with tolerant condescension. Her eyes assessed me for signs of competition.

"Does that thing tick?" I asked, indicating the silver and green box.

Dennis Longshore's eyes widened and his mouth dropped. Apparently he was becoming just a wee bit afraid of his estranged wife. Never too late to learn.

"I hardly think . . ." said Pamela. The she noticed her husband's wrinkled brow and capitulated.

"It's just a Christmas present," she told me as if I were mentally deficient. "Oh, hell. Why don't you come in and see."

I still wanted to douse the package in water, but Dennis Longshore had already replaced his discomfort with ire. Toward me. I had to be satisfied following the couple into the office.

Dennis took his usual position behind his broad desk, Pamela stood at one end, and I remained just inside the door.

Then Pamela cast me a final, hateful glance and said, "Oh, hell. I'll open it myself."

The gift was a forest-green cashmere sweater with a V-neck. There were two dozen similar ones on display about a hundred yards away, but I've heard it's the thought that counts.

Dennis embraced his wife stiffly, perhaps because I was there, perhaps because the bomb idea had brought him up short. Before they made the kiss-or-not-to-kiss decision, I used the door. Holidays. What would we do without them?

My feet ached, despite my best pair of cross-trainers, and I simply let them go until a raucous laugh arrested my attention. Directly in my path were Solly and Harlan, wearing party togs—black shirts and gaudy ties, and loafers instead of their usual high-tops. They were drunk.

"Hi, sweetums," said Harlan.

"'Lo there, darlin'," added Solly, wiggling his fingers at me. Harlan wiped some drool off his lips with a black shirtsleeve.

"Merry Christmas," I replied.

That struck both of them funny. They giggled and slapped each other until Harlan had an idea. "Want to join our party?" he asked cleverly.

"Yeah," said Solly. "Our *Christmas* party?"

"Sorry," I said. "I have to finish my shopping."

"Oh, me too," Solly suddenly remembered, giving his pal another brotherly slap as they moved off.

I didn't want to take my eyes off them. Usually they were low-key almost to the point of invisibility. Usually they were sober when they performed their dangerous little tricks. But sometimes they were merely tweaking noses; it seemed all the same to them.

I scanned the immediate area for backup and spotted mousy Timothy Sullivan furtively holding the sleeve of a camel hair sport coat.

For a couple long seconds I divided my attention between the clowns and the ex-menswear salesman.

And then Pamela Longshore strolled past, headed toward Housewares rather than the front door exit. Georgie's warning bristled the back of my neck. *Something's going down tonight.*

From the left Patrick Yang came into sight and I risked a high sign with my hand. A fellow security guard also in civilian attire, Patrick was quick to take my meaning. He inconspicuously attached himself to Solly and Harlan.

That left me with Tim and Dennis's wife to worry about. Although I distrusted Pamela Longshore and judged her capable of masterminding anything you could name, she was probably just toying with her ex-husband's emotions. Tim, on the other hand, looked suspiciously like he wanted to steal at least another Rolex if not the entire day's take.

I tiptoed up behind him. "Hi, Tim. How's it goin'?" I asked.

He jumped half a foot and staggered back a step. "Sandy," he gulped. "What are you doing here?"

"Now, Tim. It isn't nice to steal the words right out of a woman's mouth."

The thin, middle-aged milquetoast drew himself up to his full height and more, in order to peer down his nose at me. "What makes that your business?" he asked. Then he slumped into contrition because he knew perfectly well it was my business.

"I don't have to tell you," he tried.

I just raised an eyebrow and waited.

"Oh, all right. Just don't spread it around—please."

I continued to wait.

He fortified himself with a breath. And then another one. "It's Christmas," he said. "I don't have any family, nobody to buy me . . . anything. So I thought why not buy myself, you know . . . a gift."

He looked at me for help, but I just folded my arms.

"Anyway, I've always wanted this, this jacket, and I looked everywhere else, but I really wanted this one." His eyes pleaded with me.

"So I figured Christmas Eve there wouldn't be many people here who knew, who knew me, and . . ."

". . . and you stopped in to get yourself a jacket."

He blushed and studied the floor.

"Checkout counter's right over there," I told him with a pat on the arm. "New girl's name is Arlene Pamona. Hired after you left. Merry Christmas, Tim."

He lifted the hanger off the rack and held his coveted sport coat to his chest. Without another word he walked straight toward his old post and Arlene Pamona's disinterested smile. The last thing I noticed was Tim reaching for his wallet.

A voice to my right shouted, "Freeze. Nobody move." Trite, but effective.

Two men carrying guns and wearing dark ski masks had come from the "bank," where salespeople had been delivering their register trays for the last half hour. Arlene had remained open only because Timothy and another stray customer lingered in her department.

My senses fine-tuned. I saw everything, heard everything. Pamela Longshore whimpering into her fist twenty yards away, wobbling on those three-inch red heels to join the unfortunate gathering. Timothy's feeble hands raised to the height of his blood-drained face. Solly and Harlan drunkenly stumbling into the wrong place at the wrong time.

"Shut up, assholes, and get down." Harlan and Solly dropped to the floor. While the perps watched them I crouched behind a shirt rack and reached into my purse.

Then Patrick leaped from somewhere out of my sight and chopped the weapon from the stockiest guy's hand. His partner swung and shot Patrick cleanly in the air. I fired into his killer's back.

The stocky guy retrieved his gun, grazed my arm. The impact spun me and I tripped over my victim. By the time I shook the stars out of my eyes and sat up, the shooter was through the revolving door with the money.

Alarm bells clanged. Arlene had finally snapped out of it

and tripped the system, something the two bean-counters in the bank hadn't managed before it was too late. They were found unconscious, their mouths shut with duct tape, their feet and hands also taped.

Next door Dennis hadn't heard a thing until the guns went off. While pandemonium swirled around him, he stood with his hands in his pockets staring at Pamela, who drew herself up, folded her arms and turned away.

I was impatient with their soap-opera scene. Pain makes me uncharitable. However, it does not dull my sense of responsibility. While the rescue squad did some serious work on the "alleged" armed robber I shot, I sat on Arlene's counter and got an outside line on her phone. Information gave me Martin Gulliver's number, and I called the ex-security chief's home.

"Susan?" said the eager voice of an older male.

"No," I said. "Were you expecting her to call?"

"My daughter, yes. Her plane is late. Who is this?"

"Wrong number," I said and then hung up. So now I knew Gulliver's daughter's plane was late, and Martin himself could not have run out Longshore's door carrying a bagful of money. Not much, but something.

"Let's go," said the paramedic, crooking his finger for me to follow the procession headed for the ambulance.

And now I was waiting for the first guy I ever shot to come out of surgery, worrying whether he'd live and trying to figure who hired him and his more fortunate partner.

You see, the first thing I'd done the day before Thanksgiving, my first day at Longshore's, was insist they rent another safe and change the location of the employees' transaction desk. Also, to make spotting the new bank difficult, the sales staff was instructed to vary the path they took to get there.

In other words, the perps probably had inside help.

Scarp Poletta, my cop friend from high school, intercepted me as I was thanking the beardless intern who had worked on my arm. He drew me into a little lounge down the hall.

"Well?" he asked.

"Merry Christmas to you, too."

Poletta pulled a face and flipped a hand toward my arm. "What happened?"

I sighed. "I've been trying to figure that out ever since I got here."

"Bare bones."

I sketched in the facts as I knew them. Then I said, "It feels like an inside job, Scarp. Hired out. But I just can't dope it out."

My old buddy patted my good arm. He was a good-looking guy in an unpressed way, the sort who made faded denim look like home. There had always been a sexual tension between us, but for some reason we both looked elsewhere—in all the wrong places. I can't explain his lousy taste in women, but to me just about anybody felt safer than him.

His beeper went off. "Shit," he said. "Got to go. Call me if you get any bright ideas."

Something in his face made me ask, "Why?"

"Because you're probably right."

"Yeah?"

He stood still long enough to confide, "We've got the other guy, Sandy. A small-time thug named Tom Eaton from Linville. Didn't say word one in interrogation, but when I asked who hired him, his head snapped back as if he'd been slapped." The beeper went off again.

"Merry Christmas, kid," he said, and then he was gone.

I stepped out of the little lounge and leaned against the wall, pouting. There was a pay phone nearby, and after a few minutes I used it to call Denny Longshore's house. He answered as if he was still wide-awake. I wondered if Pamela was with him.

"Can you come over here?" I asked. "They're almost finished operating on the guy I shot, and I want to stay here until he wakes up."

"Is this really necessary? I mean, hell. It's one A.M."

"He had inside help, Denny, and I'd like your input before I question him."

"One A.M. Christmas morning."

"It's my Christmas morning, too, Denny, and my arm just got treated for the bullet wound I received while working for you. Help me out here, will you?"

"All right," he agreed. "But I need half an hour. I'm not dressed."

Charlotte Thibur poked her head around the corner just then, looking as if she'd aged ten years during her shift.

"What?" I asked when she refused to speak.

The tall nurse just wagged her head.

"Oh," I said, and my chest suddenly ached and tears started to come. After a minute, she turned away; but I called after her.

"This, this is a little hard to ask, but can you do me a favor?"

"Sure. Just name it."

I grasped her sleeve gratefully. "I'm going to stick around a little while. Please don't, don't let on that he died. Okay?"

"Okay," she said doubtfully.

"Just play along like he's still in Recovery or something." I showed her the ID from my pocket. She snorted as if it was a joke.

"Busy making some feminist point, are we?"

"Busy finding out who set up that dead patient you've got in there."

She grunted at my ID again. Then she looked me in the eye. "I suppose it'll be a man." An ER nurse would know the statistics.

I thought about Pamela Longshore and said, "Let's find out, okay?"

"It'll be a man," she said. "Want to bet?"

"Hell no," I said. "I'm liberated, not crazy."

Charlotte the ER nurse laughed outright, and the sound eased the ache in my chest, enough so I could almost breathe normally. I still needed a tissue and some TLC. Even some of Sally's Walnut/Cranberry Surprise might have helped just then.

First I phoned Scarp's beeper number to give him an urgent message of my own. Then I spent a few minutes in the quiet of the cubicle collecting myself and preparing my questions for Dennis.

Half an hour later Dennis strolled into the ER lobby businesslike and brisk and much more upright than the usual customer. He had on a blue ski jacket and jeans. The four groggy patients and their companions scattered about the perimeter of the room cast him scornful glances, then returned to themselves. Denny glided into the seat beside me like an eagle landing.

"The guy in Recovery yet?"

"Yeah, he's fine." Lie number one, and on Christmas yet.

"Talk to him?"

"No. He's not awake."

"Listen, Denny. He looked familiar to me. From a warehouse case I had over in Linville." More lies. "Has Pamela ever had any business over there?"

"Pamela? Linville? You're really on her case, aren't you?"

"Nope. Just doing my job."

Dennis looked me in the eye, skeptical about my line of questioning. "I'm sure Pamela never even heard of Linville."

I nodded and offered a mollifying smile, grateful he had confirmed my reasoning. Linville consisted of a railroad station and a jumble of decaying industry about twenty-five miles west, half a mile from the four-lane highway most everybody used. Pamela would never have gone there unless she happened to need a couple of seedy characters from the town's notorious underground industry. But first she would have had to know the place existed.

"How about Martin Gulliver?"

Dennis sighed and raised his eyebrows, his relaxed posture telling me that the ex-security chief was still his favorite culprit. "It's possible Marty has connections in Linville. His work exposed him to lowlife every day. I hate to think it, but he could be behind all this . . ."

Smoothing the skirt of her white uniform, Charlotte stepped out from the second room into the right-hand hall.

"Can I see him yet?" I asked.

"He's just coming out of it," the nurse replied. "In a few minutes."

I nodded.

"Denny," I said with a hand to his knee, "I've got to find the little girl's room before I go in there."

"Sure. Take your time."

I looked around, shrugged and pointed toward a hall opposite the Recovery room Charlotte had just vacated.

When I'd been out of sight about thirty seconds, I peeked back into the ER lounge.

Dennis Longshore was gone. I hustled across the lobby to stand beside Charlotte peering into the Recovery room window—just in time to see Scarp Poletta roll over on the bed and scare the hell out of Denny.

I pushed my way in as Scarp simultaneously cuffed

Dennis and recited his rights. When he finished, I asked what Denny had done.

"Tried to disconnect my tubes," Scarp replied with indignation. "You see that, Ms. Thibur?"

"I most certainly did," she concurred.

Scarp wanted to lead him out, but I stayed his arm a second.

"Why me?" I asked Dennis for the second time.

He eyed me with contempt. "Some fool woman who's afraid of the rain? How good could you be?"

My face flushed so fast, I had to lean against the dummied-up Recovery bed. I didn't even watch Scarp and Dennis leave.

"He needed a scapegoat," I said to myself and to Charlotte.

Her hands finished tidying up the equipment we'd jerry-rigged for the trap. As she turned toward the door and her work, she gloated, "Told you it'd be a man."

Which man had been the question. Although I doubted that Pamela could have found and hired two thugs from such a remote suburb, it was only my perception of human nature that eliminated the other possibles. That's why I called Poletta and enlisted the ER nurse's help.

Given the choice, I didn't believe Timothy Sullivan had the backbone to be anywhere near two thugs with guns, especially if he hired them.

Harlan? Solly? Ditto. They were do-it-yourself artists. More the naughty boys grown into naughty men. Flaky, but smart enough not to use weapons when they played their risky games.

Martin Sullivan had been more likely, except when he picked up his phone right after the heist, he said, "Susan," as if the only thing on his mind was Christmas with his daughter. If he had been involved with the robbery, he would have been expecting a male to call and would never have telegraphed his expectations with anything more revealing than "hello." And, of course, Longshore's bank had been moved since his forced retirement.

Of the insiders known to have sufficient motivation, only Dennis Longshore remained. Scorned husband, spoiled big boy. Hiring thugs to rob the store suited his style. Blaming his security chief for earlier thefts fit, too, especially since he said his board supposedly talked him out of "prosecuting" despite his claim of catching Gulliver red-handed.

Knowing where to start, no doubt the accounting bloodhounds could now find the private stash Dennis intended to conceal, from both his stockholders and his soon-to-be ex-wife.

Too bad his imported thugs exceeded their job description. When Patrick Yang died, Dennis Longshore became guilty of murder.

Except for my testimony at his trial, his fate was outside of my control. For the moment it was just me and his throwaway words. I lingered in the empty Recovery room trying to absorb their ramifications.

"Afraid of the rain." Nobody had said that out loud in so long, I'd forgotten that's what people think.

Luckily I have no nightmare apparitions, no visual picture whatsoever of finding my brother's body. My fear now was my fear then, namely that somehow the jealous little brat I'd been was responsible for Jimmy's death.

Two A.M. by my watch. I would get the hypnotherapist's answering machine.

For now, that would have to do.

Ruthe Furie burst onto the publishing scene with three books featuring P.I. Fran Kirk. If Looks Could Kill *was nominated for a Shamus Award for Best First P.I. Novel of 1995;* A Natural Death *was nominated for a Shamus for Best Paperback P.I. Novel of 1996. The most recent novel was* A Deadly Paté *(all from Avon).*

In this story Ruthe introduces a new character, who is juggling two careers at one time as P.I., and a caterer.

A MATTER OF TASTE

by Ruthe Furie

I WAS WRAPPING the apple parings in yesterday's paper and there was the word: *apple.* Apple? Appleton. George Appleton of Bull Neck, Long Island, to be exact, had been found bludgeoned to death. I went to high school with George, and when he was married to his first wife, Gwen, he was one of my regular clients.

Bull Neck is my hometown, and this was the first I'd heard of George's demise. That's what I get for tuning the world out.

If I had answered my phone or listened to the messages on my answering machine, which I did as soon as the apple parings were garbaged (I love making new verbs.), I would have already heard all the stories, the lurid, the vapid, the turgid.

Stories always run under the surface of this town. But a serious crime disturbs the surface and exposes story and storyteller to a more stringent standard of truth.

I scraped the apple parings aside and read the story. My friend Demi, who works as an aide in the Bull Neck Police Department, had called me too. She was another one of my classmates and she's a valuable resource when I practice one of my professions, namely private investigations.

The reason I had turned off the world had to do with my other profession, catering. The next evening I was putting on an extravaganza of a wedding rehearsal dinner, very fancy, very expensive. I was in the middle of making a puff pastry when I saw the article about George. The dough still had to be rolled and folded again.

I had rewrapped the dough and was preparing to get the real story from Demi when my doorbell buzzed. My offices are on Main Street on the second floor over a dance studio.

I have offices, plural, because my personality split at the same time my marriage did ten years ago. Downstairs in the hallway are two doorbells. One says Belinda Thomas, caterer. The other says B.T. Jefferson, private investigator. (Yes, my maiden name was Thomas, and I married a man named William Jefferson.) The chimes announce a caller for the caterer. The buzz is for B.T.

As I spoke to the person on the intercom, I de-aproned. The voice was female, with an Italian accent. The tone was urgent.

"I want to talk to B.T. Jefferson. It's important." On the closed circuit TV I could see a dark-haired woman, rounded in figure and wearing a raccoon coat that only added to her girth. It registered with me that October was rushing the season for fur. I hadn't even stored my summer clothes yet.

"Come up. I'll buzz you in."

Her feet clopped up the stairs, reminding me of the elephantine dancers at the adult jazz class that chased me from the building and made impossible any cake-baking on Saturday nights.

I turned off the lights on the kitchen side of the room and switched on the desk lamp and a soft light over the visitor's chair. Except for a faint odor of apple, no one would know that I had another life.

"I'm Renata Copolla. Where is Mr. Jefferson?" She was short with expensive shoes. Thick soles and chunky heels, all the style. But they didn't really go with the coat, which wasn't raccoon. It was coyote. Her hair was shoulder-length, a mass of black curls. Pretty in a hard, made-up kind of way.

"I'm B.T. Jefferson. Want a cup of coffee?" I can't help myself. I'm always offering people food and drink.

"I thought it was a man."

"No. Not the last time I looked."

She smiled. "No cream, two sugars. How much do you charge?"

"Fifty an hour. Minimum three hours. Plus expenses."

She rummaged around in her huge leather bag. Tooled leather. By the time I put her coffee down on the table next to her, she had placed three crisp fifties on the desk. "How much is the coffee?"

My turn to smile. "I've got pastries to go with it. It comes with the service." I put a couple of Danish into the zapper.

"The cops are holding my sister. They think she killed her husband, George. It was in the paper."

"George Appleton?" I was wishing I'd had the time to return Demi's call.

Nod.

"What do you want me to do?"

"She didn't do it. You find out who did. These cops know nothing. They know how to arrest kids smoking pot behind the high school. They know how to catch you if you don't stop at the red sign. That's all they know. Can I smoke?"

"If you don't mind using this ashtray." I hauled over the

smoke-eater ashtray designed by my ex, and put it next to her chair. It is the best thing he left me, albeit too heavy to market. I plugged it in and opened the cover. "Smoke away."

She looked at the contraption suspiciously. Her inch-long deep red fingernails held cigarette and lighter motionless. I suppose she eventually recognized the telltale dish for butts with the ridges for the cigarettes, and her habit overcame her distrust of the smoke-eater, which looked a bit like a steam table.

"The cops arrested Maria this morning. Her fingerprints were on the pizza box."

I tried not to betray my ignorance of what had happened to poor George, but she was jumping into the story somewhere in the middle. "Tell me the whole thing. George died yesterday. He was banged on the head. Right?" That was about all there was to the story I'd read in the paper before I'd garbaged it.

She sucked up a lungful. "Maria comes home. She finds him." Another drag. "She calls me. I call the police." Renata looked at me as if she wanted to make sure I understood what she was saying. So I nodded.

"They come and put up that yellow shit tape all over her house and keep her up half the night." Her nonsmoking hand flew around her head as she spoke. "They let her go to bed. They send me home." She raised an eyebrow and then inhaled deeply again.

"She hears the cops all over her house all night. Then this morning they arrest her. She calls me this afternoon. I go see her. I get her a lawyer. Then I come here."

I let out my breath, which I hadn't realized I was holding. "Who told you to come here?"

"The lawyer. Arthur McNulty."

"Ah, yes. He was a friend of George." More like a

drinking buddy, but that passes for friendship in some circles.

"So, when do you start counting the hours?"

"As soon as you leave and I get to work. I keep good records. So tell me about the pizza box."

"Maria doesn't remember that she touched it. She's not thinking good."

"Were she and George getting along?"

"You mean, fighting?"

"Yes."

Renata eyed me, deciding what to reveal no doubt. "Things are not so good. They argue about Frankie."

"Frankie?"

"Maria's son. Frankie Parma."

"The soccer star at the high school?" The boy had been causing quite a stir with his brilliant playing. Somehow, I didn't connect him with George's wife. I felt stupid, which is no way to feel at the start of a job.

Renata nodded and lit another cigarette from the butt. "That's him."

"Do the police know that George and Maria haven't been getting along?"

"No, and you won't tell them. You work for me. Besides, I know who killed him."

"Who?"

"The other wife. That snooty one."

"Gwendolyn Appleton?"

"Her."

Snooty wasn't exactly the word I'd use to describe Gwen. Snotty, maybe. Gwen had been knocked off her pins when George moved out of their expensive place on the hill. When was it? Six, seven years ago?

"Why do you think she did it?"

"Maria says she's always calling him and hollering at him."

Probably because he's late with the alimony payments. "What does she holler at him about?"

"Maria says she's jealous. Maria is younger."

"I'll find out whether she could have done it and let you know."

"No. I want you to get, what do you call it, so that the police arrest her."

"You want me to prove that she did it? Suppose she didn't do it?"

"She did. You prove it."

I handed the money back to her. "I'm not going to prove what you think. I'll investigate and find out the truth."

"Are you her friend?"

"No. But I know her. And if she did it, I would tell you. But I'm not going to try to prove she did it if she didn't."

Renata exhaled a big cloud, which the ashtray pulled in. The Danish sat on its plate. "So okay, you find the truth." She pushed the money back toward me on the desk. "But she did it."

I sighed. "I need your address and phone number." I gave her one of my private-eye cards. They are plain and businesslike. The caterer cards are frillier-looking, with italic type and flowers.

Before she left I took down the routine information. Then she clomped down the stairs. Her car was parked out front, a Mercedes.

I started to dial Demi, but slammed down the phone as I remembered that I had to roll the puff pastry again.

After I had worked the dough, I checked the menu for the Friday night party to see what else needed to be done. The apple filling. That could wait. One more turn on the dough and everything else that could be done ahead would be done. Good.

I needed to start cooking the next morning. The pressure was getting to me. A murder and the social event of the season, wedding rehearsal dinner for the daughter of the richest family in town.

I dialed Demi.

"Hello."

"It's B.T. What's up?"

"You know what's up. The sister's already been there."

"Are you doing surveillance on my place?"

"No, but they're watching the sister and I'm monitoring."

"From home? That's devotion to the job."

"This is the only murder we've had here in five years. Maybe I'll write a book about it."

Demi's a fledgling writer, always looking for material. "Renata wants me to find the killer. She's sure it's Gwen."

When Demi finished laughing, she said, "I've gotta get ready for a date. Let me give you the rundown."

"Who's the lucky guy?" Demi has a rich social life.

"Nobody new."

"Which one of the old ones?"

"Standby."

That was her code name for her high-school sweetheart who was also a cop and was always available. "Are you desperate or getting soft in the head?"

"He does have his charms." She sighed.

Demi's social life was too complicated for me. "Why are they holding Maria?"

"Here's what I have so far. When the officers got to the house at eight-thirty, Maria met them at the door. Her hands were bloody. George was lying on the floor in the front hall.

"The pizza, with pepperoni and anchovies, was un-touched. It was on the dining-room table, which is in the dining room, which is to the left of the entrance hall. The pizza had been delivered from Mama Mia's just after seven-thirty by Billy Watkins.

"The Watkins boy said he delivers pizza every weeknight from about five to eight, and most Wednesdays he delivers one to George."

Anchovies did not sound like George. Pepperoni is stretching it. George didn't even eat pizza when we were in high school.

"Maria told the officers that George was dead when she got home about eight and that she had immediately called her sister. The sister arrived at the house after the officers got there.

"Maria didn't seem to realize that the blood was on her hands, the officer said. And when they pointed it out to her, she began screaming and ran to the sink to wash her hands."

"Anyone going to go see Gwen?"

"One of the uniforms went over there to notify her. But nobody thinks Gwen did it. Why would she do it after all this time?"

"Long-smoldering resentment?"

"Not likely, but it is interesting that the sister is trying to get you to pin the murder on Gwen." I could see a chapter being formed in Demi's book.

"Well, maybe Gwen comes into some money now that George is gone. Maybe that money would go to Maria if Gwen were charged."

"You going to track that down?"

"Of course," I said.

"You want me to tell the guys that you have that covered?"

"Demi!" I shouted.

"Just kidding. Why do you think I talk to you from home? You know the calls are all taped at the precinct."

Demi does have a way of pushing my buttons. She was probably pissed because I ragged her about going out with Standby. I really oughtn't take her for granted. If she didn't give me this information, I would be a long time getting it.

"Do you have the cause of death?"

"With his head bashed in, it was pretty obvious."

"Are they going to look any further? For drugs or anything?"

"Of course, but those other tests take days and weeks. So how come you're not up on this? Where have you been?"

"Working on the wedding rehearsal dinner. Listen, if this investigation drags on, can you help me tomorrow?"

"Mm, let me get back to you on that."

I said a small prayer for enough time and help to do all I had to do.

"So what did the medical examiner find?"

"That everything about the body was consistent with getting bashed on the head until dead."

Demi and I talked until it was time for me to do the last turn on the dough. She didn't have any other information on George except that he ordered pizza every Wednesday when Maria went out with Renata. The boy, Frankie, didn't come home. Maria had told the police she didn't know where he was.

After I finished the last turn of the dough, I called Gwen Appleton. She told me to come up right away and not to forget to bring some of my Danish pastries.

"I need some comfort food," she said.

I didn't say anything, because I didn't think grief was what she was talking about, if I could judge by any of her past remarks about her late ex-husband.

"This is a real shock." That's all she said by way of explanation. But Gwen was not shy. I would get the whole story when I got to her place. Unless, of course, she had killed him.

She was dry-eyed when I got to her house on the shore of Bull Neck Bay. She and George used to give great parties there. I catered most of them. She and George used to argue about the food. His taste ran to plain, while hers was more exotic. One New Year's they almost called the lawyers over the smoked oysters that George had nixed and Gwen had ordered anyway.

But the lawyers were still a couple of years in the future then.

Gwen met me at the door with arms outstretched. Not to hug me, but to grab the pastries. "I've got all kinds of those instant party-coffees and if you want, I'll make some."

"It's too late for caffeine for me. Sometimes lunch is too late."

"I've got decaf cappuccino," she said with a smug smile. "Brewed."

"Yes, yes." This woman could not be a murderer.

She poured the coffee and put out plates for the pastries on the snack bar that just happened to have a great view of the bay. "So what's the deal?"

"I've been hired to find George's killer."

"So did the bimbette tell you I killed him?"

I had heard her refer to her replacement in George's affections before. "No, Maria's sister, Renata Copolla, hired me. She thinks you did it."

Gwen laughed almost as hard as Demi had. "Look, one of those linguinis would lie and the other would swear to it."

"Don't talk like that. You sound so . . ."

"Bitter? Why shouldn't I be bitter? Bimbette needed an American husband because she was here illegally. So she goes after mine. Now she doesn't need George anymore, so he's dead. And I'm worse off financially than ever."

"You and George weren't exactly going around holding hands." That was a mistake.

Her eyes narrowed. "So you think I did it?"

The best defense is a good offense. With all Gwen's culture and civility, she was a street fighter. "Of course not. But you know you're going to be on the suspect list."

"The police were already here. They were very interested in the immigration story."

"What did you tell them?"

She arched one of her perfect brows and took another Danish. "I told them that Renata got here a year before Maria and married the Copolla boy almost as soon as her visa ran out." Triumph lit her eyes.

"Doesn't everybody know that?"

"Apparently the police didn't. Or else they didn't think it was important until I mentioned it."

The Copolla boy is deaf, talks with difficulty, and has been in a wheelchair since childhood. His folks were getting worn down caring for him and Renata was hired to look after him. Well, one thing led to another and before you know it, the parents were delirious with joy that a young person would marry their son and take care of him. It didn't hurt that they had bundles of money.

"It shows the kind of minds those"—Gwen cleared her throat, probably to show that she wasn't going to use the language that she had used before—"women have. It shows what conniving bitches they are. Maria gets herself legal, and then George is disposable. I wouldn't put it past her, or her sister."

"Her son is a really good soccer player." I had to say something positive.

"He'll probably get a nice fat offer from a college," Gwen said, curling her lip. "But don't you see they're users?"

"Look, Gwen, George is of the age of consent. It's his life. Or it was."

"Right, and Maria didn't need him anymore. But she will need his money. So, it's divorce, Italian style. Remember that movie?"

Her story was beginning to grate on me. "So I guess the police asked you where you were yesterday evening."

She smiled. "Tai chi class. All evening, seven to ten."

"When did you find out about George?" I said, trying to get businesslike and keep her from running off at the mouth again.

"At the Vat and Can. I went there after the class." The Vat and Can is a local bar and pickup place. "Everybody there used to talk about the Green Card girls. Laughed at the way they scouted out the single guys."

I almost asked her how come George was a target if he wasn't single. "Well, the cops are holding Maria."

"Good. But the sister wants to get me arrested. Probably figures that if I go to jail for the murder, Maria will get any money that's supposed to come to me."

"Well you're covered. Tai chi comes to the rescue."

"I told the cops something else, too, that maybe you want to know."

"What?"

"George called me a week or so ago. Said he wanted to talk to me about revising the divorce settlement. Well, right away I figured she's at him about the money."

She looked like her defenses were down, uneasy, fidgeting.

"George had plenty, didn't he?"

"Of course he did. It turned out he just wanted to talk to me, to complain about Maria and the boy."

"What? George?"

"Well, he always needed a mother and Maria has been too

busy being a mother to her son, so I was elected. I let him talk, but I didn't let it get too cozy if you know what I mean."

"Did he come here?"

"No. Do you think I'm crazy? I met him at a coffee shop at a mall in Queens."

"Can't be too careful," I said approvingly. "And did he say anything that the police were especially interested in?"

"He said that he and Maria weren't getting along very well. He said that maybe we should have tried harder. Then he went on to recite all the rotten things the kid had done. Maria doesn't discipline the kid apparently. He told Maria that he wanted the kid out of the house."

"No wonder the police are questioning her. But where was the kid supposed to go? He's only sixteen or so."

"Fifteen. George said the kid's father is living nearby. He's probably looking for an americano to make him legal." She laughed, regaining her poise. "I told George that I heard that Italian men were good lovers and that he should send the guy around to the Vat and Can."

"You were trying to torment poor George," I said.

"I did," she agreed. "I could almost see him writhe. But, you know, I'm sorry he's dead."

I believed her. Besides she did have an alibi. But I knew where she took tai chi, and intended to check up on her. She asked me then what I knew about what had happened to George, and I told her what Demi had told me.

She shook her head. "Did someone break in?"

"No sign of that."

"Then he let the killer in or the killer had a key."

"It would seem so."

"Are they doing an autopsy? Were there drugs or alcohol in his system? Did they find the murder weapon?"

"You'd make a good detective."

Her eyes narrowed. "Got any answers to those questions?"

"No alcohol. The other tests take a while. I haven't heard about the weapon. Mind if I check with you if there's anything about George that you can verify for me?"

An expression that looked like relief spread over her face. "Not at all. I'd be glad to help," she said. "You know if his second wife did him in, I might be able to claim what he owns."

"Don't say that too loud. Renata may be listening."

"You won't tell her that." It was a question.

"No, I won't tell her that. She doesn't need any information, she has her prejudices to rely on." And so do you, Gwen, I thought.

George's habits were ingrained. He was regular, predictable. Probably Gwen could have predicted his leaving if she had been paying attention. People stop listening to one another after a while. My own marriage started to clamor at the edge of my consciousness. I stuffed that, fast.

Demi's answering machine picked up when I called her. I wondered whether Mr. Standby was standing, sitting, or lying. Then I scolded myself for the thought.

The next stop would be George's place, where I had arranged to meet Renata.

The weather had warmed up, but she was still wearing the coyote coat. Her feet were now shod in brown leather boots that came up to her knees. Her skirt, woven in wool of the same shades as the coyote fur, stopped above her knees and showed black hose with gold stripes.

I longed for enough money to dress so badly.

She opened the front door with a key. "They took down the yellow tape," she said.

"He was right here." Her talonlike index finger pointed to

the floor in the front entry. Then she jerked her head, a gesture that meant I should follow her. "The pizza was here." The corner of the dining room table nearest to the doorway.

I was trying to get the feel of the place. Although I had visited and been to parties at George's place when he was married to Gwen, I had not been invited here. Nor had I been hired to do the catering at any party. Come to think of it, I hadn't heard about their doing much entertaining.

The decor was a lot busier than anything Gwen would have lived in. There were a lot of knickknacks and inexpensive pictures and statues that Gwen would call tacky. Frankly, so would I. The general feel of the place, though, was homey, a little cluttered, but tended-to—neat, clean. A house that showed the presence of someone who was keeping track of it. Not the house of a woman who was planning to kill her husband, I thought.

"Look, there's still blood. Those cops don't clean up anything." Renata tossed the coyote over a chair.

I watched her get a bucket and fill it with water and soap. She knew where everything was stowed in the house. I wasn't prepared for her next stunt, though. She got down on her knees, heedless of her expensive, ill-chosen hosiery and mandarin fingernails, and started to scrub away the blood.

"It would upset Maria to see that." Her hair was hanging down over her face and she was scrubbing with a vengeance. The thought of Lady Macbeth trying to wash the blood off her hands crossed my mind.

After she had scrubbed off the big spot, she changed the water in the bucket and scouted the tiled entry floor with her scrub brush poised. She pounced on a spot about ten feet from the site where George had been lying.

"Is that blood, too?"

"Yes. It's splattered all over."

I winced. Rage, I thought. Whoever killed George was enraged. Which didn't rule out a tidy wife in a temper.

"Did the police find any blood on Maria's clothes?"

"She had blood on her shoes and her knee."

"No splatters?"

Renata stopped scrubbing. "The splashes happened when he was killed. She wasn't here then."

I wondered whether she would aim the scrub brush at me. "I'm trying to figure out why the police are holding her. Did you ask her how her bloody fingerprints got on the pizza box? Was the pizza still hot? Did she tell you that?"

"No. What difference does that make?"

Defensive. *Renata knows something she's not telling me.* I spotted a few more specks of blood and pointed them out. This seemed to mollify her. I guess I was on her team again.

A tour of the house revealed nothing new, so I thanked Renata and got ready to leave. But the doorway was in use. Frankie Parma, the soccer star, was hauling in suitcases.

He looked at me and then at his aunt. "I guess I don't have to stay away now." His smile had a mean twist to it. "Papa should come here too. That dump he lives in is dirty and smelly."

"Your papa is not coming here," Renata said.

The boy uttered a four-letter word under his breath and stomped up the stairs with his bags.

"Has he been staying with his father? Where does the father live?"

"George told Frankie to get out. The father moved here a couple of months ago. I think that's when Frankie got to be more of a problem." Renata's jaw clenched and the little bump at the joint pulsed.

"Why didn't Maria tell the cops where he was?"

"She's stupid where the boy is concerned. Maria needs to sock him."

Never mind that the kid was a foot taller than Maria and looked like he had a mean streak a yard wide.

"The cops want to question him."

Renata's chin dropped to her chest. "I hope he didn't . . ." Sobs cut off her words.

I figured this was as good a time as any to tell her about Gwen. Since Renata was obviously entertaining the idea that someone other than Gwen might have killed George. "Gwendolyn Appleton has an alibi."

Renata kept sobbing. Finally she said, "You done here?"

Renata herded me out the door. She stayed. I wondered whether she was going to sock the kid around.

My house was on the way to the pizza parlor. I have a little house on a small lot overlooking Bull Neck Bay. The neighborhood is not fancy, but the view is terrific. I didn't have time to stay and enjoy it. A change of clothes and a call to Demi was what I came for.

"You again?"

"Did he go home?"

Pause. "Who?"

"Standby."

"Are you watching my house?"

I laughed. "I didn't call to talk about your love life. I need to know about how George was found when the cops got there."

Papers rustled. "I should tell you to take a flying . . ."

"Now, now. You know you love my pastries."

More rustling. "George was lying in a pool of blood near the front door of the house. He was fully clothed, trousers, shirt, underwear, socks, loafers, and cardigan sweater with a dollar in the pocket. No wallet. That was on the cabinet in the kitchen."

"I just watched Renata clean blood spatters from the

floor. Looked like the killer was angry. Did you tell me what the murder weapon was?"

"A wrench. A big monkey wrench. The officers found it on the workbench in the garage. It also had Maria's fingerprints on it."

"She doesn't look strong enough to wield a wrench like that."

"Don't say anything to anybody, but that's what the officers think. That and the angle at which the blows were delivered."

"Pretty good work the boys are doing."

"Did I ever say they did anything but good work." Her voice had a sly tone to it. I did not let the conversation go in that direction. What did I care about her love life?

"And the pizza box was on the dining-room table?"

"I did hear more about that," she said, all business once again.

"When? Tonight? From Standby?" I'm sure my voice was eager.

"I'd tell you what he said if you weren't such a smart-ass."

"Okay. What penance do I have to do?"

"Well, he likes apple pie."

"I've got one in the freezer."

"Bring it over."

"He's still there?"

"No, he's coming back."

"What did he say?"

"Maria told the officers that the pizza box was on the hall table when she found George. She knelt by the body thinking that he wasn't dead and that she could help him. When she realized he was dead, she got frustrated and picked up the pizza box and took it into the dining room.

She didn't know she had blood on her hands. She even got blood on the phone when she called her sister."

"How come she called her sister and not the cops?"

"They're tight, those two. If one lied, the other would swear to it."

"Someone else said that about them."

"Who?"

"Gwen."

"You saw her already?"

"Yeah. She has an alibi. Did anyone check it?"

"Yes," she said.

That would save me some time. "Anything more on the guy who delivered the pizza?"

The paper noises started up again. "Billy Watkins. Delivered at seven-thirty."

"You gave me that."

"There's nothing much more."

"I was on my way to see him anyway."

"Don't forget to deliver the apple pie."

"You're on my route. And Demi, one more thing. Did Maria say how her fingerprints got on the weapon?"

"Oh, I have that somewhere." Rustle, rustle. Thump. Rustle, crack. "Ouch."

"What are you doing?"

"Oh, damn. Stubbed my toe. Here it is. Mm. She didn't remember moving it."

"What do you know about the boy?"

"Maria said he left after an argument and she didn't know where he was."

I saw my chance to do my civic duty and give the kid something to think about. I told Demi that young Frankie Parma had just moved back into George's house with his suitcases. "If he ran out of the house after an argument, someone packed a lot of stuff for him. Renata said George threw him out. Did anyone check on his dad?"

"We don't know about the father. Where does he live?"

"Some place dirty and smelly, according to the soccer star."

"Looks like we'll have more questions for Maria. Standby will be even more delighted with our information than with the apple pie."

"Anytime I can help the Bull Neck PD, it's an honor." It occurred to me that I had just gotten Maria into more trouble. Not what I was hired to do.

The pizza parlor was in full swing. The parking lot was full and so were the booths inside. At the counter, a young man was hurriedly sliding pizzas into those insulating boxes. It didn't look like a great time to ask questions.

I followed the delivery boy to a car by the curb. He was juggling the boxes and they were sliding. I caught up with him and steadied the boxes.

"Thanks," he said. "You saved my life."

"You Billy Watkins?"

"Yeah, that's me." He smiled. A pleasant, freckled-face smile.

"I'm B.J. Jefferson, and I need to ask you some questions about the delivery you made to George Appleton yesterday."

"Are you a cop?"

"No. Private investigator."

"I already talked to the cops and I gotta deliver these pizzas while they're hot."

"Can I come along with you? Talk to you in the car?"

He set the boxes down on the roof of the car and they began to slide again. Again, I steadied them. "Yeah, maybe you oughta go along. I don't seem to be having much luck

with this bunch. If you leave, they'll all be on the ground."
He chuckled.

I helped him load the pizzas into the rack he had in the back of his car, and then I climbed into the front seat, which was so filthy I almost told him that I would catch him later.

"Too bad about Mr. Appleton," he said. "He was a good tipper, too."

"How much would he give you? I promise not to tell the IRS."

"Two bucks on a regular delivery. Bigger pie, bigger tip. He's a regular customer. Pepperoni pizza every Wednesday between seven-fifteen and seven-thirty."

"And the tip?"

"Two bucks."

"Anything unusual?"

"Nope. He came to the door, took the pie, gave me the tip. I had three more to deliver."

"Did he say anything?"

"Just hello, nice day, that sort of stuff. I don't remember exactly."

The pizzas in the back seat were giving me hunger pangs. Billy made his first delivery, two boxes. I was tempted to tear a piece of cheese off one of the remaining pies.

I thought about the people who might have killed George: Maria, Renata, Frankie, Gwendolyn. Would Maria and Renata have banded together? Where was Frankie the night before? How would Gwen have done it if she was at the tai chi class?

And Gwen wouldn't kill someone with a wrench. Probably Maria and Renata wouldn't either. Frankie might, though. He certainly was a strong-looking kid. It would take a lot of strength to kill someone with a wrench. Wouldn't it? But he was just a kid. Would he kill his stepfather?

Billy came back to the car then with a sour look on his

face. "Two large pizzas and a lousy dollar tip. I'm going to miss Mr. Appleton."

"Do you know his stepson, Frankie Parma?"

"Sure. Great soccer player. He'll be famous some day. He's so quick. And he's a smart player too, and, you know, sneaky. I love to watch him. His dad is real proud of him."

"You know his dad?"

"He works in the kitchen. He's fast, too, like Frankie."

"What kitchen?"

"Mama Mia's."

"Does he ever deliver?"

"Nah, he doesn't have a car."

"Is he legal? I mean does he have a green card?"

"I don't know."

"How long has he been working there?"

"Since the summer."

"Was he working last night?"

"He works every day. He only takes off for the soccer games. But they're in the afternoon."

I was wondering whether Mama Mia's was in the habit of hiring illegals. How else would they get somebody to work every day? "So he's in the kitchen all evening?"

"He's usually there when I leave."

"When's that?"

"Around eight. Sometimes earlier."

"What about last night?"

"I don't know. I didn't come back after my last delivery." He seemed uncomfortable.

"Why?"

"Look. It had nothing to do with Mr. Appleton."

I used the hard stare, which only works on the young and naive.

He twitched. "I can't tell you."

"Okay, okay. I'm not trying to be nosy."

"It's just that Frankie needed help."

Waiting for him to spill the rest seemed to take a year.

"He just moved in with Vince and he wanted to paint his room while his dad was gone. I only had about an hour and a half to help him. But we got it done." He smiled proudly.

"Why didn't you want to tell me that?"

He bit his lip. "I'm sort of on probation and I'm only allowed to work and then I have to go home. My folks could get in trouble. They're supposed to know where I am."

"I suppose you could get in trouble, too."

Alarm stretched his features. "You're not going to tell?"

"No. Where is Frankie's dad's place?"

"Around the corner from Mama Mia's."

"What are you on probation for?"

"Snorting. A bunch of us got caught. Somebody snitched."

"Who?"

"If I knew, I'd get him. And I'm not the only one."

"Who else got caught?"

He smiled. "We all did. But we hid Frankie."

"Frankie was snorting with you?"

"Yeah, but we didn't want him to get caught. He wouldn't be able to play."

Amazing that an unpleasant kid like that could inspire such loyalty. Must be that sports aura.

"Was Frankie with you all evening yesterday?"

"Aw, come on. You don't think Frankie would kill Mr. Appleton, do you?"

He stopped the car again. I thought he was going to argue with me, but he was delivering the rest of the pizzas.

When he came back, I repeated my question.

He tightened his lips. "He went out to get paint."

"When?"

"Right after I got there. He wasn't gone long. The store was still open."

"What time was it?"

"Maybe a quarter to eight."

"And he came back with the paint?"

"Right." His answer was short and his face was registering anger.

"Then what did you do?"

"We cranked up his boom box and painted. Got it done, too."

"And then?"

"I went home about nine forty-five. My dad was standing by the door. I really have to get there before ten, or else."

"How far away do you live?"

"Cove Road. Down at the end."

"You didn't leave yourself much time."

"It was enough. The clock hadn't struck ten and I was in the door." Self-satisfied grin.

I said a little prayer of thanks that I was neither a mother nor a teacher of teenagers.

When we got back to the pizzeria, I asked the owner if I could go in the kitchen and talk to Vincent Parma.

"He's busy," the owner said. "Come back later." He answered the phone.

I stood there wondering what to do next, when the cops came in. They didn't have any trouble getting into the kitchen to speak with Vince Parma. I stood by the kitchen door and strained to hear what was being said.

The cops asked the usual questions and they were finished in about ten minutes. Then they came out and arrested Billy Watkins.

Damn. I couldn't wait to talk to Demi. The cops wouldn't talk to me.

Demi's lights were out, and when I tried to call her, I got her machine. I was thinking the pie had been eaten.

I drove back to George's house, now Maria's house. Renata's car was still there.

Maria answered the door. Her pretty face was lined and sagging.

"Oh, you're home," I said, belaboring the obvious.

Renata came up behind her. "They arrested somebody."

"The pizza boy," I said. "Do you know why?"

"The man next door told them the pizza boy came here twice."

Billy Watkins is a good liar, I thought. "Is Frankie here?"

"Upstairs. Sleeping." Maria waved her arm toward the staircase.

"I'd like to speak to him," I said.

"What for? They arrested the pizza boy."

"The pizza boy told me he was with Frankie. And the police haven't talked to Frankie yet. Have they?"

Maria shook her head.

Frankie came down the stairs. He had been listening. "Why did they arrest Billy" He was talking to Renata and keeping an eye on me.

Renata told him what she had told me about the man next door seeing the pizza boy there twice.

Frankie frowned.

"Billy told me he was with you all evening," I said.

"He was." Frankie looked at his mother and then at Renata. "He helped me paint the room. I told you it was dirty and smelly."

"What time did your father get home?"

"Right after Billy left. I heard him come in. He went to the bathroom. Then I put on another CD." Frankie was twitching. There was something more he knew.

"How did Billy's car get here the second time?" I said.

Maria was twisting her hands. Renata looked like a bird watching out for a hawk.

"Dad only wanted the car to go see someone. It must have been another car that came here."

"Your father borrowed Billy's car?"

"No," Maria said.

Frankie frowned. "It's okay," he said to his mother. "Dad asked me to leave the keys in the car. He had to go someplace important. Billy didn't even know he had it." Then he smiled.

I was getting uncomfortable. It was apparent to me that the investigation by the BNPD wasn't over. It looked like Maria knew something about what happened.

My guess was that the anchovies were not a mistake. When George discovered the anchovies, he called the pizzeria. Vince was waiting for the call. George put the dollar in the pocket to meet the pizza boy.

I looked hard at Frankie. "Did your father know that George didn't like anchovies?"

The bluster was gone. The ego was gone. The big, celebrated star player was gone. A confused boy stood there with tears beginning to run down his cheeks.

Maria started to fidget. Then she, too, started to cry. "He wanted to marry me again. Now that I'm a citizen, he thought I should marry him."

"Was he still here when you got here?"

Maria didn't answer.

Renata looked at her sister. "Maria, what did you do?"

I dialed 911 on my cell phone before they had a chance to regroup and come up with a new strategy. I didn't know how far they would go to keep what they had.

The cops were there in minutes. Standby came in first. Even though I was a nervous wreck, I noticed that he had pie crust on his tie.

I gave the cops the information I had and went back to the office to write up my report and finish the apple filling.

Two days later, after a hugely successful rehearsal dinner, Demi called me.

"Maria told us her former husband was standing in the front hallway holding the wrench when she got home. She said she was afraid for herself and for Frankie, so she told him to go and she would call the police after he was gone."

"How come the neighbor didn't tell the cops that Maria got home before the pizza boy's car left?"

"He didn't see Billy Watkins's car leave. He only saw it arrive."

"What'll happen to Maria?"

"It doesn't look like she knew Vince's plan, but she'll probably have to answer for her part in trying to protect her ex-husband."

"What did you get out of Frankie?"

"Other than leaving the keys in Billy's car because his dad told him to, the kid doesn't seem to be involved."

"He'll have to go live with Aunt Renata," I said. "I think she has some ideas about his life. But I hope she doesn't pick out his clothes."

In a collection of stories that sport some unusual titles, maybe this one takes the cake. Barbara Collins now has a long line of short-story credits behind her, and was the co-editor of the original Lethal Ladies *anthology. Here she returns with another of her father-daughter, dual first-person-viewpoint tales, the first of which surprised us all in* Lethal Ladies.

EDDIE HASKELL IN A SHORT SKIRT
A SAM & REBECCA KNIGHT STORY

by Barbara Collins

THE POLK COUNTY Prison was located just north of Des Moines on four well-manicured acres. The newly constructed twenty-million dollar complex had no unsightly barbed wire fence surrounding its premises, nor a guard station at the front entry, or anything else that made it look like a prison. To the passer-by, the two-story red brick octagonal building might have been a clinic of some kind, a place you might go to have a skin tag lopped off, or an impacted molar extracted. Only the back of the building gave its purpose away: rows of small barred windows ran its length, windows so tiny that a man—or woman—couldn't possibly squeeze through.

I'd been to this prison just one other time, with my father, Sam Knight, to visit a client. He and I—my name is Rebecca—are partners in an investigations firm in the city. (You might have read about us in *People* magazine last year for cracking "The Cutthroat Cowgirl Case"—their title, not ours.)

Getting back to the prison, I was really impressed by this state-of-the-art facility, with its laser sensors, computer-operated doors, and prisoner-tracking bracelets. Even the cells were fairly comfortable, clean and new.

Anyway, mine was.

I was in for murdering my best friend, Vickie.

Footsteps echoed down the concrete hallway coming toward me, sounding like popguns going off, but I remained motionless on the little bed, my hands clenched tightly in my lap. Then a deputy sheriff, tall and gangly, was punching in numbers on a security pad, opening the barred door, informing me my father was here.

In the visitation room, which was small but not claustro-phobic, my father and I sat at a long table, the width of which was between us. He looked older than his sixty-four years, older than I'd ever seen him, his craggy face drawn, bronze tan faded from the long winter months. But his eyes were strong, determined. If he was at all frightened, those ol' blue eyes did not betray him.

I, too, must have looked a sight: no makeup, shoulder-length brown hair uncombed, and very unfashionable in the orange prison dress with orange slip-on tennies.

He cleared his throat. "Are they treating you okay, pumpkin?" He'd hardly called me that since grade school.

I nodded numbly.

"Got a call in to Walter Conlon," he told me. "He's a good criminal lawyer."

I nodded again. I would need the best.

Now my father stood up and came around the side of the table to stand before me, running the fingers of one hand on the tabletop, looking down at that hand. His voice was soft, even gentle. "You understand bail won't even be an issue until you've been arraigned."

"I understand," I said weakly.

I stood up and gave him the bravest smile I could muster, which wasn't much of one. "I'll be all right in here, really."

Then I fell into his arms, like I promised myself I wouldn't do, reduced from age thirty-four to four, and sobbed into his chest, leaving big, wet stains on his gray suit jacket, crying for me, crying for Vickie.

He smoothed my hair and said, "I could stay here longer if you want, but I'd like to get right to work on this."

"What is there you can do?"

He gave me a funny smile. "I might think of something. You hang in there, pumpkin."

Back in my cell, I returned to the bed, where I sat staring at the tan wall.

If only I hadn't gone to The Brew that night, our paths wouldn't have crossed . . . And I wouldn't be sitting here now with my life and business in shambles.

But then, our meeting again after so many years hadn't really been left to chance, had it? Because Vickie had come to town looking for me. I realized that now, too late.

We'd met in the seventh grade, Vickie and me, and soon became good friends. I had a cousin, Ann, a few years older, who'd had a number of best friends in school. One by one they betrayed her: Sue spread nasty, false rumors; Janice stole her boyfriend; and Liz got her kicked off the pom-pom squad when Ann gained a few pounds. I watched on the sidelines and made up my mind not ever to have a best friend.

But the more time I spent with Vickie, the more she seemed like the genuine thing: someone I could confide in and trust. She knew the value of keeping secrets. Hadn't she given me my first diary, for my thirteenth birthday?

And she was so confident, outgoing and fun. Qualities I felt I lacked. When I was around her, she made me feel like a different person, a person I liked much better.

I lost track of Vickie after high school, when we went on to different colleges, me to the University of Minnesota, her to Northwestern. She didn't come back for our tenth high-school reunion, but a photo of her (looking gorgeous behind a desk in a fancy high-rise office) was tacked on the bulletin board, along with those of other classmates who couldn't make it back. An accompanying letter said she and a partner named Kyle owned a very successful insurance company in Chicago. A P.S. on the note said, "A special hello to Rebecca!"

So you can imagine my surprise and delight when I turned around from the bar at The Brew six months ago, a glass of Chablis in one hand, to see my old friend Vickie. We squealed like little pigs, and hugged, and laughed and hugged some more, then found a booth in the back.

"You look terrific," I told Vickie. And she did: long blond hair, startlingly blue eyes, porcelain skin, perfect white teeth.

"Don't have a portrait of yourself, getting wrinkled in the attic, do you?" I asked.

She laughed and shook her head. "You look wonderful, too," she said.

Maybe. Maybe not. But it was nice of her to say it.

"What brings you back to town?" I asked.

"I'm going to open my own insurance agency here," she said happily.

"Really!" I was thrilled. I reached out and squeezed her hand, immediately visualizing us lunching at Noah's, shopping at Valley Junction, and spending Friday evenings at Billy Joe's Pitcher Show. Just like the good old days.

She ran one manicured fingernail around the rim of the glass of red wine she'd brought to the table, and looked down into the drink. "But before I can," she said, "I have to pass the Iowa exam, since I'm only licensed in Illinois. But that shouldn't be too hard."

Not for her. "What happened to your other insurance business?" I asked.

Her face clouded, and she stared off into the smoky, noisy room behind us. "My partner—Kyle was his name—and I had a rather bad falling out."

"I'm sorry."

She took a sip of her drink. "It's not what you think . . . We weren't lovers or anything. Just business partners who couldn't see eye to eye."

"I understand." I'd been there with my father, but never bad enough to call it quits.

"I couldn't take his unethical practices anymore," she explained sadly.

Curious, I asked, "What do you mean by 'unethical practices'?"

She paused a moment, wineglass to her lips. "Kyle would give customers more coverage than they needed, with outrageously high premiums, just so he could collect a big commission." She took a sip of wine, then added, "That's just one example, and believe me, there were plenty of others."

"Wow." I'd read about such scurrilous practices that were rampant in the 1980s, when suddenly, reputable insurance corporations found themselves in legal hot water because of some unethical agents. It cost the corporations millions and millions to settle all the claims.

"I just had to get out," Vickie said, pain showing on her pretty face, "so I left it all behind."

I smiled supportively at her. Leaving must have been hard. It had to have taken guts.

"Anyway," she went on, "the first thing I have to do is

find a temporary job, until I can move forward with my plans. Got any ideas?"

And a bolt of lightning struck me. Three weeks ago I let our office manager go because of poor performance, and I hadn't gotten around to finding a replacement, doing the work myself.

"Have I!" I said. "You can come and work for me, doing bookkeeping and such."

"Really?" she said, her face lighting up. Then she sat back in the booth, putting one hand to her forehead, as if she felt faint. "Oh, Reb, I'm soooo embarrassed. Here I've been talking about myself and my problems, never once asking you about yourself."

"That's all right," I said, warmed by how considerate she was. "I run an investigations firm here in the city. With my father."

"No kidding?" she said. "How exciting. With your father, you say."

"Uh-huh."

"How is he? Did he ever remarry after your mom died?"

"Nope. Too set in his ways."

She gave me a half-smile. "I always thought you were so lucky having him for a dad."

I smiled back; such a nice thing of her to say.

We fell silent for a few seconds; then Vickie raised her glass. "Here's to us," she said.

Our glasses clicked together. And I downed my drink.

Vickie would be perfect for the job, I had thought. After all, she had a business degree. She couldn't possibly do any worse than the previous manager had done.

You think you're way out in front of me, don't you?

Well, within a week Vickie had cleaned up the mess left by the other manager—straightening out the payroll, collecting delinquent accounts receivable, even cracking down on employee pilfering of company supplies. She ran one hell of a tight ship with, "Do we really need that?" and "Can't we buy it cheaper?"

Within the next few months, the coffers at Knight and Knight and Associates had never looked fuller. Which, in hindsight, made a lot of sense. Because there was just that much more money for her to steal.

Which she did.

Yesterday, Friday, the first day of spring, I stayed late at the office to finish some paper work, when I got a call from a West Coast electronics firm we'd purchased some surveillance gear from, saying their bill was ninety days overdue. I assured them there must be some kind of mistake because we always pay on time, but I'd look into it and call them back Monday morning.

I went into Vickie's office to scribble her a note about checking on the overdue bill, and I opened the right-hand desk drawer looking for a note pad. There was the company checkbook, so I flipped back through the register and found that the check to the L.A. firm had been written nearly a month ago. But there was no check mark by it, which meant that it hadn't cleared—as hadn't a great many of the checks written two, even three, months ago.

Some checks *had* cleared—ones written every week for thousands of dollars, payable to Vickie and marked "expenses."

Only we'd given Vickie no expense account privilege.

Ten minutes later, I found a large manila envelope stuffed in the back of the bottom drawer of a file cabinet; it contained the bills and checks that she'd never mailed.

It's hard to describe how I felt at that moment, but anyone who's ever been betrayed by someone they trust knows. The range of emotions was incredible: shock, disbelief, sadness.

Rage.

I don't remember getting my gun out of the safe in my office, but I must have, because I had it in my hand as I stood outside Vickie's apartment on Hickman Road, using the butt of it to bang on her door as I called her bad names.

I knew she was home because her car was in the lot. So when she didn't answer I shot wildly at the wooden door, the third bullet taking the knob off, then shouldered it open.

She was sprawled on the floor by the front door, face down, wearing the same blue suit she'd had on at work; a puddle of blood spread out from her chest like a red fan, soaking the beige carpet. She must have been coming to answer the door, I realized, when she was struck by one of my bullets.

Behind me, in the hallway, I heard alarmed voices. Someone yelled to call 911. My legs felt rubbery and I stepped into the apartment and eased myself into a chair by the front door to wait for the police to come. I felt detached, strangely cold—an out-of-body experience.

The room was in disarray, with papers and magazines strewn about and cardboard boxes sitting half-filled. On a coffee table lay Vickie's purse, open, its contents dumped out. And next to the table were two large black suitcases, ready to go.

I remember thinking that it wasn't very nice of Vickie to leave the apartment in such a mess.

It just wasn't nice at all.

The only thing harder than seeing my little girl sitting in that prison was leaving her there. But if I'd stayed any longer, she'd have got wind of how scared I was.

The chief of police had tracked me down the night before at Barney's Pub, where I was watching ESPN on a big screen, pretending an O'Doul's was a real beer (I'm a recovering alcoholic). At first I thought he was joking about the trouble Becky was in, because she's so straight, it's embarrassing, and the chief has a sense of humor like a rash. But there was too much sadness in those rheumy eyes.

I know my daughter's got a temper—you can blame my gene pool—because I've seen it once or twice, and it's not a pretty thing. But I never thought she'd get mad enough to kill somebody.

Especially her close friend Vickie.

I never liked that girl, from the first time she and Becky hooked up as kids; especially since that time I caught her reading Becky's diary. But I didn't let on. Becky seemed happy being around her, and as long as they weren't getting into trouble (none that I knew of, anyway), who was I to tell Becky who her friends should be. Most of mine, at the time, were fellow boozehounds.

But I'll tell you, I didn't like the way Becky behaved after spending time with Vickie, which was snotty and disrespectful.

So what was wrong with Vickie? She was smart, charming, and pretty. Usually a good combination. Yet there was something phony about her. When she came over to the house, I felt like I was Ward Cleaver and she was Eddie Haskell in a short skirt.

And she used Becky. Used her homework, her clothes, her meager allowance, all the while playing the grateful friend. Which kept Becky giving her more.

Then there was the time when Vickie stayed over when she was fourteen. In the middle of the night, I felt something soft and warm in my bed. She'd crawled under the covers and was crying about having a nightmare. I wasn't too sympathetic, though, thinking about another nightmare that might unfold if I didn't get her out of there. For years I believed it was just my dirty old man's mind that thought the worst of her . . . until three weeks ago.

She showed up on the stoop of my bungalow a little toasty, looking mighty fetching in a tight, low-cut red dress. She had a wicker basket and in it was a bottle of wine and two glasses.

"Well," I said as I stood in the doorway, in an undershirt and wrinkled trousers; I'd been watching a boxing match on the tube. "This is quite a surprise."

She smiled seductively, looking up at me through veiled blue eyes. "Aren't you going to ask me in?"

I smiled back a little. "I don't think that would be a good idea," I said.

"What's the matter?" she teased. "I won't bite."

She had the basket, so why did I feel like Little Red Riding Hood and she was the Big Bad Wolf?

She shifted the basket in front of herself, holding it with both hands, swinging it from side to side as she twisted her body back and forth like Baby Snooks in an old Warner Brothers picture. "Besides," she said slyly, "I'm a little older than fourteen now. You don't have to be afraid."

I dropped my smile, feeling heat spreading across my cheeks, which doesn't happen very often. "I don't sleep with employees," I told her. "Clients, maybe—but never employees."

The sweet, seductive look on her face turned savage. "You son of a bitch!" she spat. "Why I thought to waste a good bottle of wine on an old dinosaur like you, I'll never know."

I did. "Maybe I'm the one thing of Becky's you never got your mitts on," I said.

And I shut the door in her face.

It wasn't easy sending her packing. But nobody likes being had, even in the most pleasant of ways.

I could have been wrong. Maybe it *was* possible for a thirty-year-old woman with an angel's face and a hell of a body to be attracted to a man of sixty-four with a pot belly and a butch haircut.

And maybe one little drink wouldn't hurt, anyway. But I wasn't about to partake of either.

Night was setting in over the city as I wheeled my three-year-old Escort into the underground parking lot of 801 Grand, the deco marble tombstone of a building where we had our offices. I took the elevator up to the main lobby, which was deserted on this Saturday evening, and switched elevators up to the twenty-first floor.

A couple of things had been bothering me about the body and crime scene, which Chief Coderoni was kind enough to let me in to see. First, the blood left in Vickie's body, that which hadn't spilled out on the carpet, anyway, had just begun to discolor the skin and settle, which told me death was a little further along than it should be. I was willing to bet Ballistics would find that the bullet didn't come from Becky's gun.

Second, while it made sense Vickie was in a hurry to vacate the apartment, the place just didn't look right. Drawers and cabinets hung open, but nothing seemed to have been removed. And the only time I'd ever seen my wife (rest her soul) dump the contents of her purse out, was when she was frustratedly looking for something. Whoever killed Vickie hadn't found what he—or she—was looking for.

Maybe that person was now looking elsewhere.

The bronze elevator doors slid open and I stepped out into the hallway and followed the carpeted corridor around to the right, to the double glass doors of our office. I dug out my security card and used it to enter.

The reception area was dark, but the door leading into the back yawned open; I went quietly through it and into the bullpen area, which was awash in streetlight and neon.

Down a hallway to the right was my office, and Becky's. To the left was Vickie's, the door shut, but light streamed from under it.

And I doubted Vickie was in there.

I took my snubnose .38 from my jacket pocket, where I'd slipped it from the car's glove compartment. As I moved forward, I could hear the slamming of file drawers from behind the door.

Whoever was in there must have used Vickie's security card, from her purse, to get into our office.

I opened the door quickly, the snubnose ready.

"It's Pinkerton who never closes," I told the thin, middle-aged man in an expensive tan suit, who stood behind the desk, its top covered with files. The man's hair, which matched his suit, was cut conservatively, parted at the side, with bangs brushing the top of gold wire-framed glasses, behind which beady brown eyes went wide at the sight of me, his hands frozen inside a file he was going through.

"I just want my personal files," he said defensively.

I stepped inside the room, gun trained on him. "And what files might that be?" I asked.

His eyes narrowed to slits, and he dropped his hands down to his side.

"Vickie took *personal* papers of mine when she left Denver," he said. "I want them back."

Now I knew who he was: the unethical, untrustworthy Kyle I'd heard Becky mention.

And the person who killed Vickie.

"Put your hands in the air," I said, with a little gesture of the gun.

And he did, but one of his hands held a silenced automatic, which must have been lying on the desk, hidden behind the stacks of file folders.

There was a *snick* and a bullet missed me by inches. I

dove for the floor, firing back awkwardly, missing him. He was heading toward the office door before I could haul myself up, and I wasn't up to playing grab-ass with somebody, so I reached out and snatched a hefty stapler off the desk and flung it at him, smacking him in the back of the skull, and he went down like an arcade target. Lights out.

I stood up, breathing heavily. From the look of the blood that was oozing out of his head, he was going to need a few stitches.

He was coming around when I said, "Buddy, that's a nasty gash—I hope to hell you're insured."

As impressed as I was with the Polk County Prison, I was more impressed by the smell of the Iowa countryside outside its walls.

Ballistics proved what my father had suspected from the start: the bullet that killed Vickie did not come from my gun, but Kyle's, and the autopsy report showed the time of death to be earlier than when I arrived at her apartment in a red-hot rage.

Apparently, from statements made, and from what we were able to piece together, Kyle ran the shady insurance business with Vickie's full approval. In fact, Kyle taught her everything she needed to know about how to swindle a customer. You might say he taught her too well. Because later, perhaps when the partnership began to sour, she started keeping files of damaging evidence on him, to be used later for blackmail.

That cost Vickie her life. And nearly mine, and my father's.

Last week, I hired a new office manager. You can bet I did a comprehensive background check. As a matter of fact, during the interview I gave the poor bastard such a grilling, a big sweat stain formed around his neck. But he's working out fine. Just the same, every couple of weeks or so, I stay late at the office . . . and look through the checkbook and files.

The Des Moines *Register* ran an article on the embezzlement, and made me look like a sap, but Virginia Kafer from *People* (who wrote that terrific piece a year ago) did a follow-up story, focusing on the betrayal of a best friend, which I thought came out okay.

Anyway, a few days after that issue of *People* magazine appeared, I got a call at the office from Sheila, a woman I was friends with in college. She was in town from San Francisco on a business trip and wanted to get together for lunch and talk about old times.

I told her I was busy.

Maxine O'Callaghan's private investigator, Delilah West, has appeared in seven novels, the most recent Down for the Count *(St. Martin's Press, 1997). Maxine also has a series character named Anne Menlo, a psychiatrist who has appeared in two suspense novels, the most recent being* Only the Ashes *(Berkley, 1997).*

In this story Delilah deals with a diamond heist that has a twist ending.

DIAMONDS ARE FOR NEVER
A DELILAH WEST STORY

by Maxine O'Callaghan

I HAD NEVER been a diamond courier before, and by the time I got back to L.A. I'd decided I never would be again. There are too many people in this world who wouldn't think twice about hacking off a hand so they could take the briefcase manacled to a person's wrist, like about half the passengers milling around at Kennedy in New York as well as several on my plane. I even had my suspicions about the flight attendant who seemed overly attentive, constantly stopping by with coffee refills.

But then, of course, I have an overactive imagination. It comes with the P.I. territory. And I'd had a very long day, trying to get in and out of New York City before what would hereafter be referred to as the "Snowstorm of the Century" came blasting in. I'd even given up the convenience of flying from Orange County's John Wayne Airport and made the fifty-mile drive north to Los Angeles International so I

245

could get direct flights and make my round trip in less than twenty-four hours.

At 9 P.M. my big DC-10 glided down over the bright sweep of the L.A. basin, right on schedule. Since I had no luggage, I managed to make a quick exit, draping my jacket over my arm to hide the manacles and hoping I looked like any other harried businesswoman as I plowed through the crowds around the Jetway.

My assistant, Danny Thu, was supposed to be waiting out in the parking structure across from Terminal Four. I dug my cell phone from my purse and called him on the run. He answered on the second ring.

"On my way out," I said.

"Right," Danny said. "Uh, Delilah? There's been a slight change. Mr. Boudreau is with me. We're going up to Santa Monica from here."

I groaned at the prospect of my long day dragging on indefinitely and muttered, "Oh, great."

Well, that's not an exact quote. My words were a tad more colorful and delivered in a loud enough voice to earn me an approving grin from a skinny, denim-clad, pasty-faced Gen-Xer with a backpack slung over one shoulder. Male, I guessed—he looked like he posed for heroin-chic ads in *Vanity Fair* and *Cosmo*.

I vowed on the spot to clean up my language.

I also ended my call and walked faster to be sure I arrived at the curb outside baggage claim before Danny got chased off by some overly efficient cop. There was a million dollars worth of diamonds in the briefcase. That was wholesale value. Lord knows what the markup to retail would be. I didn't particularly relish the idea of hanging out curbside looking out for thieves with oversized pruning shears while Danny was forced to circle the huge U-shaped airport.

Just before we landed, the pilot had announced that it was

49 degrees at LAX. This was not exactly warm for Southern California, but as I stepped outside the terminal it felt downright balmy compared to the icy blasts of wind that had skirled down New York's concrete canyons. Even an outlander like me could smell the promise of wet, heavy snow, and I was more than happy to be back here inhaling that distinct L.A. odor of ozone and exhaust.

I spotted my blue Astrovan right away, double-parked with Danny at the wheel. Headlights from a continuous stream of cars, shuttle vans, and buses made up for the dim illumination. I could see Leo Boudreau's blocky silhouette just behind Danny.

I jumped into the passenger seat, slammed the door, and felt vast relief because basically my job was over. I was about to deliver the diamonds to my client, even if he happened to be sitting in my vehicle rather than waiting for me in his jewelry store in Newport Beach as planned.

"Any problems?" Boudreau asked.

I might have mentioned too little sleep, close encounters with New York cab drivers, and eleven hours of airline seats and airline food, not to mention my preoccupation with the prospect of being rudely detached from the briefcase.

Determined not to sound like a wuss, I shook my head and said, "Just the weather," while I fished a key from my purse, unlocked the manacles, and passed the briefcase back to him.

"You got out just in time," Danny said. "I heard on the radio that they closed Kennedy, must have been about two hours after you left."

Danny was already rolling. He left the inner lanes, swung out around a curb divider, and plunged into the dodge-ball traffic with the confidence of somebody whose main mode of transportation is a bicycle. He rides to UCI where he's completing a double major in business and computer science, through rush-hour traffic on the days he works in my office, and in biking marathons on weekends. This keeps my young assistant whip-thin and full of crackling energy. It also makes him absolutely fearless behind a wheel.

He flashed me a grin as I quickly fastened my seat belt.

Boudreau said impatiently, "Could I have some light back here?"

I had to undo the seat belt for a second so I could reach up and turn on the overhead light. Buckled back in, I turned to watch Boudreau unlock the briefcase.

He was in his late forties, good-looking in an overbearing sort of way, vain enough to keep his big hands carefully manicured and to be wearing a suit and a tie when something more casual would have done just as well. I wasn't quite sure all that thick, dark hair really belonged to him, but then, as we know, I have a suspicious mind.

"I assume we're going to the Gemological Institute," I said. "That wasn't part of the deal."

"I told you I wanted Moira to inspect the diamonds as soon as you arrived," he said testily. "I don't appreciate having to go all the way to Santa Monica either, but something came up. She's stuck at the lab."

So why not stash the diamonds in his safe at the store until his expert could come take a look? I didn't even bother to ask. If you didn't know the guy, you'd think his square-shouldered, square-jawed look suggested forthrightness. I'd quickly learned it just meant he was incredibly pigheaded.

Of course, his insistence on an immediate inspection suggested that he was more suspicious of me than of the diamond merchants back in New York. This bugged me, but, hey, if I had a cool million on the line, I'd be paranoid, too.

Inside the briefcase was a specially fitted insert, sectioned into little boxes and velvet-lined, covered by a plastic lid. Each cut, polished diamond was in its own tiny plastic Baggie labeled with a lot number. Then the diamonds appeared to be sorted by approximate weight, maybe seventy-five stones, most of them at least a carat.

In New York I'd had to wait while each stone was checked off an inventory sheet, thinking all the while that only a carefully controlled supply by a certain South African cartel made the sparkling rocks so valuable.

From the beginning I'd had my doubts about the courier bit. Myself, I think I would've put the gems in a sock and stuck them down in some dirty clothes in a carry-on. When I asked the wholesaler about the way they normally shipped diamonds, I was told the usual method was parcel post and not even insured. Boudreau was about the only retailer who wanted personal delivery. This last information was said politely enough but in such a way that there was no doubt Boudreau was considered a fool for this idiosyncrasy.

Now, behind me Boudreau took a long look to verify that I had indeed brought gemstones instead of some New York red-hots, his inspection taking much too long to suit my frayed nerves. I cast an anxious glance around at the bumper-to-bumper traffic on Century Boulevard. The side windows of the van were tinted. I doubted anybody could see in. Still, I felt better when Boudreau closed up the briefcase.

And a whole lot better when Danny murmured, "Glove box is unlocked," and I knew that if I had to I could get to the .38 I keep there.

Traffic was heavy but moving as we headed north on the 405. Boudreau wasn't much for small talk, thank goodness, because fatigue was fast catching up with me, and what energy I had left was spent on making sure nobody was tailing us. He sat with the case on his knees for the thirty-minute trip, silent except to give Danny directions on where to exit and how to find the institute.

The place didn't look like much from the outside, just a big nondescript building that could just as easily have housed a Wal-Mart. All the spaces out front said *reserved*. Probably not enforced this time of night but Danny said he'd wait in the van.

Boudreau carried the briefcase and rang a buzzer next to a door where the glass revealed an inner barrier of steel bars. A polite male voice over an intercom requested our names; then there was some silence while we got checked out. Waiting, I noticed a surveillance camera and a decal warning that security was provided by one of the best companies in the business. After a couple of minutes an armed guard came to let us in, a burly guy with a side arm only slightly smaller than a cannon. He was accompanied by a woman Boudreau introduced as Moira Sweeney.

After a distracted nod returned the guard to his post, Moira said, "Come on back to the lab."

She was shorter than my five-seven, one of those thin, fox-faced women that look as though they are being consumed by some inner fire. Her kinky red hair was brittle and dry, and her pale, freckled skin had unhealthy sallow undertones and looked stretched over the bones of her nose and cheeks.

She walked quickly, leading the way down a hall through a rabbit warren of darkened rooms with numbers on closed doors that gave no hint of their purposes. Boudreau was a step behind, grousing about having to come up from Orange County.

"I told you, Leo, it got hectic," Moira said, sounding edgy and stressed. "A large stone," she explained for my benefit as she stopped to unlock a door marked simply LAB. "Our policy is to process and return it the same day. Come on in."

Overhead lights were on in the bunkerlike room, and one of the big microscopes on the long bench was lit. There were maybe twenty microscopes in all, each with a high stool in front of it. Shelving beneath the bench was sectioned into cubbyholes, many of these spaces crowded with an assortment of binders and metal and plastic containers. Beside Moira's scope some kind of log book lay open.

There was a faint, oily smell in the room, but that was being quickly overpowered by the aroma of coffee brewing in a machine down on the end of the lab bench.

"I'm just finishing up here," Moira said. "Leo, why don't you and Ms. West help yourselves to a cup of coffee, give me a minute, and then I'll get to your stones."

She reached for the briefcase. This was Boudreau's expert and one we'd gone out of our way to see, but he hesitated for a second before he yielded the case.

I had assumed their relationship to be business, but now I was picking up on the kind of subtle tension that suggested more. He stood a little too close, invading her space. And there was a kind of tug of war going on, some sort of power thing. And maybe a flicker of triumph in her eyes as she took the case and put it on the bench.

Something else I noticed: Moira wasn't dressed the way a woman does for a lover. She wore a white blouse tucked into plain khaki slacks, an old, shapeless green cardigan, and some scuffed black leather flats. She hadn't bothered to put on any lipstick or powder her nose.

Well, maybe their intimacy was a thing of the past, but I'd bet there had been some. *And none of your business*, I told myself as I headed back to the coffee machine.

I kept glancing back at Moira, and so did Boudreau. She wrote something in the log book, closed it, and shoved it into the cubbyhole beneath the bench. Then she opened the briefcase containing the diamonds and snapped up the lid that covered the inner compartment.

I poured coffee into two of those waxed paper cups with the fold-out, pinch-together handles and handed one to Boudreau. There was a bowl with a sign that said, *twenty-five cents, please*, but he ignored it. He only took time to dump some sweetener into his cup, then went back to join Moira.

I threw in a couple of quarters, figuring it was worth it just to hear him holler when I put the contribution on my expense account.

Yeah, I admit it. I was not particularly fond of Leo Boudreau.

Meanwhile, Moira had taken out the inventory list. Boudreau quickly gulped his coffee, and the two began a careful count of the stones, Moira reading the lot numbers from the little plastic Baggies and Boudreau checking off each one.

I wondered if anybody would object to my moving one of the other stools over. Decided, what the hell, I didn't need to peer over their shoulders. I yawned and wished for a big comfortable couch, or at least a back to the stool next to Moira's where I sat, leaning against the hard edge of the counter, drinking the hot, strong coffee, and wondering why he needed a gemologist to check an inventory list.

Then, the count completed, Moira took a headpiece from the bench and put it on. The contraption had an eye loupe, and a big square light-housing that stuck out beyond that, a very bright light when she switched it on. She opened one of the Baggies, removed a diamond with a pair of oversized tweezers, held the stone in front of the loupe, and turned it back and forth for what seemed like a hell of a long time.

"What?" Boudreau said, reading something in her face, then hoarsely, "Jesus, is it—?"

"See for yourself." Moira took off the headpiece and gave it to him. Held the stone in front of the eye loupe so he could verify what she'd seen.

He pretty quickly ripped off the headpiece and handed it back, looking as though the coffee he'd drunk a few minutes earlier was on its way back up. I put my cup down carefully, knowing just how he felt.

"Fake?" I asked.

"Oh, it's real enough," Moira said. "Real cubic zirconia."

By the time Moira got through enough of the stones to figure they were all fakes, Boudreau was holding on to the bench, looking almost as green as her sweater. Good thing I was sitting down. My knees probably would have folded up on me. Just the velocity of the thoughts spinning in my head could have sent me falling on my face.

The stones had been placed in the inner compartment of the briefcase right in front of me in the diamond mart back in New York. The case had been closed and handcuffed to my wrist. I hadn't unlocked the manacles until I was in the van with Boudreau. I hadn't even unlocked the damn things when I used the lavatory on the airplane. Talk about awkward.

I had insisted that Boudreau buy the seat next to me on the flight to L.A., so it would remain empty. I had avoided conversations with strangers. Had drunk no alcohol. Had not fallen asleep—well, maybe I'd nodded off a couple of times, but never long enough for somebody to search me for the keys, unlock the cuffs, open the case, and substitute phonies for the real diamonds.

Assuming they were genuine to begin with. Could the

switch have taken place back in New York? Would an old,
established firm really do something like that?

I knew Boudreau would never believe it. There was only
one person he would hold responsible for the theft.

"You—" He wheeled around, teeth bared and ready to go
for my throat. "What the bloody hell have you done with my
diamonds?"

It turns out this was not a rhetorical question. As far as he
was concerned, I was a thief, no question about it. He
wouldn't for one second entertain the idea that the switch
took place in New York, and it certainly couldn't have
happened after I climbed into the van with him and Danny.
That left the time in-between, with me as the only culprit.

"Just a damn minute," I said, breaking into his tirade. "If
you really think I stole your diamonds, call the police. Make
a formal complaint. But you'd better be sure you want to do
that because when we find out what really happened, I'll sue
your ass for defamation of character."

Not that I could really afford a law suit. Not that I was
ready to risk wrangling with some cops who might look at
the situation just the way Boudreau did. But I was mad, and
my bluster seemed to make him hesitate.

"Leo, think," Moira said. "Are you sure you want the
police in on this right now? I know you'll need to file a
report for insurance purposes, but can't it wait? I can put the
case in the safe until morning. We'll all have clearer heads
then."

"And give her time to leave the country?" Boudreau shot
me another glare, but I could see the wheels turning, some
kind of frantic calculation going on.

Uncertain just how much ID the diamond wholesaler
would require, I had taken my passport along to New York.
Now I took it from my purse and handed it to Moira.

"Lock that up with the case," I said, adding to Boudreau, "For your information, the only place I'm going is home to bed." I was tempted to add that he could damn well find his own way south to Orange County, but I knew it wasn't smart to make him even madder. "If you want a lift, let's go."

"Moira can take me."

"You have to be kidding." There was enough ice in her voice to tell me she didn't expect to be asked to stay the night and she wasn't about to make a three-hour round-trip drive for him.

He didn't like it, but in the end, after the briefcase was locked in the lab safe along with my passport, we agreed to meet Moira back at the institute at ten o'clock the following morning, and Boudreau made the grim journey home with Danny and me.

To Danny's questioning look, I muttered, "Don't ask," and waited until we dropped off Boudreau at his store before I explained.

Looking as sick as I felt, Danny said, "I couldn't tell you earlier, but there's something else you ought to know. Boudreau's check—your retainer? It bounced."

Even though I was exhausted, I woke up before dawn and tossed and turned for a while, my anger growing by the minute. Bad enough to be accused of being a thief. Downright insulting to get stiffed out of my fee as well.

A shower and a jolt of caffeine cleared my head enough so I could do some thinking, and what I thought was that of the three people in that lab the night before, I was the only one who didn't know squat about diamonds.

Moira had said the stones were fake, Boudreau had agreed, and I had accepted what they said. But assume that everything that had occurred up to that point happened just the way I thought it had: I'd picked up real diamonds from a reliable dealer in New York and delivered them without incident to Boudreau in California. That being so, I could draw only one conclusion: The diamonds that Moira and Boudreau inspected had been the genuine articles.

Assuming *that*, than what did we have?

Insurance fraud was the first thing that came to mind. The two of them working the scam together was the second, quickly followed by the third, which was that exhaustion the night before was no excuse. It had been the worst kind of stupidity to let Moira keep the briefcase. If the diamonds had not been phonies when I delivered them, they surely would be by now.

Bloody hell, I thought and figured I might as well go stomp around my office rather than my apartment.

I went to join the rest of the crowd on the road in the chilly darkness with the fond hope of beating the rush hour. No big jams yet, but plenty of small ones and time to try and figure out what Moira and Boudreau would do next and to wonder at what point I should call a lawyer.

At the office, I found Danny's bike chained to a post in the parking lot and Danny upstairs in front of the computer.

"Couldn't sleep," Danny said. "I thought it wouldn't hurt to have some background on Boudreau."

What he had was pretty complete. Most of it had been obtained through perfectly legal research. As for the rest—I didn't want to know.

Scanning the reports, I saw that Boudreau had divorced his wife the year before and remarried. He lived in a pricey condo near Fashion Island, leased a Lexus and a Beemer, had been in the jewelry business for fifteen years. That was on the surface. Dig a little deeper and you found that, like a lot of people these days, the guy was skimming along on the edge of financial disaster: the condo mortgaged to the hilt, behind on child support for the two kids by his first wife, credit cards maxed out, his business close to going down the tubes, and checks bouncing all over the place. It was clear he didn't have the million to pay for the diamond shipment. He had a loan lined up, however, some bank ready to take a chance as long as there was collateral.

If the insurance company paid off on the diamonds, then he and Moira sold the stones, how much money would he wind up with? Not a fortune, but in his situation any infusion of cash would be a blessing.

It was a logical explanation, but I would have felt a lot better about buying into it completely if a couple of things hadn't been nagging at me. One was the look on Leo Boudreau's face when I mentioned calling the cops, even though he would have to make the report before he could file a claim. The other was the mention of all those rubber checks.

I remembered Boudreau's insurance carrier, the name having been on one of the forms I'd handed over in New York. I called them from the van while crawling through some serious rush-hour traffic on the way to Santa Monica.

A little bit of tap dancing and a few outright lies got me the information that threw my insurance fraud theory out the window. There was no coverage on the diamonds. The check for the premium, like my retainer, had bounced.

Leo Boudreau was already at the institute when I arrived, some ten minutes late. He was in the entry area arguing with a slender, tweedy man whose plastic nametag read *C. Goodykamp, Ph.D.*

Mostly Boudreau was doing the arguing, or rather the bellowing. The soft-spoken Dr. Goodykamp was holding his own, however, even though Boudreau kept cutting him off in mid-sentence.

"This is ridiculous," Boudreau said. "Moira wouldn't just take off."

"Mr. Boudreau, you're not listening," Dr. Goodykamp began. "She—"

"We had an appointment, dammit," Boudreau yelled. "Tell him, Delilah. Ten o'clock. We were meeting her here."

"That was the plan," I said. Since it was obvious Boudreau wasn't going to, I introduced myself and asked, "Where is she?"

"On vacation," Dr. Goodykamp said.

"She can't be," Boudreau said.

"Well, she is. She called first thing this morning and asked me to give you the briefcase you left here. If you'll excuse me, I'll go get it from the safe."

He hurried off, and I turned to Boudreau. "I think I owe you an apology. Guess you weren't in on it after all."

"What are you talking about?"

"Face it, Leo," I said. "Moira Sweeney stole your diamonds."

"No way." He glared at me, but the look on his face told me he was resisting an unwelcome reality check. "You don't understand. We were—close, for a while. *Intimate*."

Surprise, surprise.

"I know Moira," he went on. "For one thing, she wouldn't have the guts to do something like this. And even if she did, when could she have done it? There was no time to switch the stones."

I don't know which bothered him more, the fact that Moira would actually have the chutzpah to take such a chance or the possibility that he had been taken in by her guile.

"I think she did it while we were getting the coffee," I said. "And she didn't have to switch them all. How many did you look at? One? She knew you trusted her, figured after you saw a sample or two you'd take her word on the rest. If you didn't, well, you'd think somebody skimmed a couple of stones instead of stealing the whole lot."

"Jesus," he said, panic replacing his disbelief. "You have to find her before she sells my diamonds, before she leaves the country."

"I'd be happy to, but there's one little problem. I don't work without a retainer. Of course, you're so tapped out, you can't even cover my courier charges, so how about I take a finder's fee. Ten percent, that should do it."

"*What*?" His face seemed to swell up, and it turned a dull red. "I'm not paying you anything. You find her, or I'll call the police. I'll tell them you did it, that you and Moira were in it together."

"Go ahead," I said. "By the time the cops get up to speed, Moira could be in Rio. And here you'd be. No insurance, and you'll still owe your wholesalers back in New York. And think of all the free publicity I'm going to make sure you get. Bet the tabloids love it."

"You really are a heartless bitch," he said bitterly.

"Damn straight," I said. "Do we have a deal or not?"

Boudreau agreed to my terms, but he was not happy about it. I figured he was already hatching up a plan to make sure I didn't see even a *one*-percent recovery fee, let alone ten.

Except for a current address, he could supply little information about Moira's private life, which didn't surprise me much. I decided to start at the institute and hoped to find somebody who could provide a lead to Moira's whereabouts.

Covering all the bases, I suggested that we have another gemologist inspect the contents of the briefcase, and for once Boudreau didn't put up an argument. When Dr. Goodykamp returned with the case, I explained what was going on. He looked shaken by the news, but not exactly

overwhelmed by disbelief, even when we opened the
briefcase and found that it was empty.

After I convinced Boudreau to go back to Orange County,
not the easiest job, I asked Goodykamp if we could find
someplace to talk, alone.

"My office," he said without much enthusiasm.

We entered a small cubicle, sparsely furnished. A Shaker
desk held nothing except a telephone and a note pad with a
pen lined up beside it. These two items were placed squarely
in front of a black leather chair. Half of a bookcase was used
to display chunks of amethyst crystal, geodes sliced in half
to reveal their intricate structure, polished slabs of petrified
wood.

There was one straight-backed chair against the wall.
Without waiting for an invitation, I picked it up, planted it
in front of the desk, and sat down. Goodykamp sighed as he
took a seat across from me.

I said, "When Moira called this morning, you're sure she
didn't tell you where she was going?"

"This morning?" He considered briefly and seemed
happy to say, "No. She didn't mention it."

"How long have you known Moira?"

"Several years. Since she came to work here."

What can I say? Sometimes you get lucky.

"You're friends?" I asked, sure of the answer.

"Friends, yes. We certainly are." He frowned down at the
note pad, moved it a fraction of an inch to the left, a hair
toward me.

"She's in serious trouble," I said.

"Yes, I know. But I can't help you, Ms. West. So please
don't ask."

"You have it wrong," I said. "You'd be helping *her* by
telling me where she is. Let me talk to her and take a shot

at persuading her to give back the diamonds before Boudreau goes to the cops."

"He would, too," Goodykamp said. "Moira keeps things
to herself, but she's told me enough so I know what a rotten
man he is." He paused, clearly torn. "I'm really worried
about her, Ms. West. She's let her health go downhill. She
can't be thinking straight to do something this bizarre, this
desperate."

"Then, please," I said. "Where is she?"

"At my place." Relief was mixed with the guilt in the
admission. "I'll give you the address."

Goodykamp's small home was in an older section of Santa
Monica in what the social engineers like to say is a
neighborhood in transition. This meant the houses had been
mostly turned into run-down rentals where stucco was
crumbling, paint was peeling, and weeds and crabgrass were
taking back the yards.

Under a gray marine overcast, the area had a sad,
hunkered-down look—although, come to think of it, I
wasn't sure that sunshine would help much.

A fairly new Saturn sat in the driveway, and smoke curled
from a chimney, so Dr. Goodykamp must have kept his
promise not to call. Still, when Moira opened the door, she
didn't seem all that surprised to see me. She leaned against
the doorjamb, looking pale, gaunt, and exhausted, wearing
the same clothes she'd worn the night before.

"Poor Goody," she said. "I put him in such a spot asking
to stay here last night. I hope he's not too upset."

"He's worried about you. We need to talk, Moira."

"Okay." She stood aside to let me in. "He didn't know
about the diamonds. Please remember that."

Down here near the coast, there was a distinct chill in the
air, cool enough to make the blazer I wore over my slacks

feel good. The temperature was nothing like the bone-deep cold of that wind back in New York, nothing that warranted the bonfire that roared in the living room fireplace.

The place was so warm I immediately took off my jacket. I could feel the heat on my face and hung back, but Moira went to sit right in front of the fire on an old armchair. In contrast to his office, Dr. Goodykamp's home was comfortably cluttered, and I'd bet on a few dust bunnies over in the corners.

"Did Leo turn me in?" Moira asked.

"Not yet. There's still time to straighten this out."

"Time? No, you're wrong about that." She hugged herself, wrapping the green sweater tightly around her body. "Do you know how long I let Leo jerk me around? Ten years."

"We all do dumb things," I said. Sweat popped out along my hairline, but I was willing to sit on the couch as far from the fire as possible, drip a little perspiration, and listen to her story if it meant getting her to give up the diamonds.

"Well, I was dumber than most," she said. "He kept promising to divorce his wife, and I believed him until I just couldn't swallow his lies anymore. I was taking some courses at the institute while I worked at his store. When they offered me a job, I grabbed it. I thought I could break away from Leo, but I didn't, of course. He could always talk me into anything, like being his courier, back and forth to New York. I did that for a long time, even though I hated it." She stared into the fire where fierce blue flames consumed two huge hunks of oak that lay atop a bed of glowing embers. "When Leo got his divorce, he didn't say a word about it. A friend down in Orange County saw an announcement in the newspaper when he got married again."

"So you decided to pay him back," I said. "I can understand that, believe me. But this is not the way, Moira.

Walk away from him. Have a good life. That would be the best revenge."

She gave me a bleak smile, wintry in that tropical room. "We all think like that, don't we? We think we have forever. I did. Then, three weeks ago I found out I have pancreatic cancer."

"Ah, God," I said sadly, knowing as soon as she said it, she was telling the truth.

Moira said, "So you see, the time Leo stole from me is a lot more precious than it would be for most people."

"Yes, it would be."

I might have added how sorry I was for her, but the words seemed too trite, too knee-jerk to offer.

"So you planned to do what?" I asked. "Sell the diamonds to pay hospital bills? Leave the money to your family? To charity?"

"No, nothing like that. Nothing so noble." She gave me the ghost of a smile. "Did you ever see that James Bond movie where they hide the diamonds in a corpse, and recover them after the corpse is cremated? Pure Hollywood, Delilah. It could never happen. Because diamonds are carbon. Pure, and beautiful, but carbon all the same. Given a hot enough fire . . ."

"*Jesus*," I whispered, following her gaze to the fireplace and understanding only then the depth of her hatred for Leo Boudreau.

"You might as well call the police," she said.

I was too stunned to say anything for a few seconds, but then I asked, "What were your plans before I showed up?"

"I was going to stay here and make sure Goody's house didn't burn down," she said. "Then I thought I'd head south, go to the Baja. I know a place. It's cheap. There's a clinic. I don't think they're such sticklers about pain medication in Mexico. I wrote a couple of letters," she added. "Mailed

them this morning. One to Leo, explaining just how badly
I've screwed up his life. One to Goody to pass on to the
police so they'd know you were not involved."

What the hell, I thought. What would I have done with ten
percent of a million bucks anyway?

I said, "If you get going, you might make it through L.A.
before the rush hour."

She left quickly, pausing only to say thanks and give me
a quick hug. After she was gone, I opened a few windows
to cool off the place, and then I called Boudreau. I told him
I'd tracked her down, but, gee, wouldn't you know, she had
already flown the coop. And all the while I thought about
him reading that letter from Moira while I watched the oak
logs in the fireplace turn to ashes and those million-dollar
embers disintegrate in an eerie blue-white glow.

Deborah Morgan has previously published nonfiction, and Western short fiction, but this is her first foray into the mystery field.

"Freight" brings a fresh new voice to the genre, and a fine new female P.I. in Mary Shelley. Hopefully, this is only the first of many of Ms. Shelley's cases to see print, and starts a new—and additional—career direction for Ms. Morgan.

FREIGHT
A MARY SHELLEY STORY

by Deborah Morgan

K NOW YOUR GUN.

It can make the difference when the smoke clears, or the sun rises, or you're helping someone back through the door that separates humanity from the demons of the dark.

Mine's the latest Smith & Wesson Air Lite—a .22LR snub nose revolver with eight chambers on an aluminum alloy J-frame. It weighs less than a pound, loaded.

I didn't know all this shit a week ago. Now, ask me anything.

It was Friday afternoon and we were getting one of those heavy spring rains that throw most of the population of southeast Michigan into hysteria.

Since it's been known to snow here nine months out of twelve, those untouched three are prized, coveted, revered. When the threat of snow is past, half the lower peninsula

265

flies home at the end-of-the-week whistle and hauls boats and coolers stocked with microbrew and Perrier to its favorite shores. Rain is not on the list of preferred weekend beverages.

I'd shed my corporate costume and cookie-cutter Chevy for black Tony Lama's, faded jeans and my ginger metallic '56 GMC stepside, and was heading west on I-96, leaving Detroit in my proverbial dust.

I'd planned to be ahead of the rush—Vic was treating me to dinner and I needed to pick his brain concerning matters about which your general middle-aged female doesn't have a clue—but I got away from the office late after the computer ate my entire report on Mrs. VanPelt's missing poodle. Don't laugh. It's the best income I've had in two months. Paid for the computer, as a matter of fact.

Brake lights dominoed their way back to me. People are in a flaming hurry until there's something to gawk at, have you noticed?

We crawled along for fifteen minutes till I got near the commotion.

The tractor-trailer rig that hadn't quite made it to the shoulder was black, with large white letters on the side that said, simply, Museum Transport.

I'd never before seen a museum transport truck—or at least I didn't think so. It escaped me why they would advertise the transportation of priceless *objets d'art.*

Several feet in front of the semi was a hulk of a man in a yellow slicker, lumbering along the soggy shoulder.

Traffic was moving slow enough, so I figured I might as well stop as not. Locked in my pickup with a pistol at the ready, I felt safe. I cracked the passenger window a couple of inches and asked the man if I could call him a wrecker.

"I don't give a damn what you call me, just get me to the

next exit." His voice was deep, rough. He jerked on the handle before I answered, almost pulling it from the door.

When he looked at me again he found a .22 snub-nose where my helping hand used to be.

He assessed the gun, my outfit and the pickup. "Who you trying to be, Annie Oakley?"

"Don't have to. I can shoot better than her."

"You'd have to with that little thing." He retreated a step. "Look, lady, I'll ride in the back if you want. Just get me out of this damn rain."

I wondered if he had a partner waiting at the semi. Even if it was broken down, I couldn't imagine it being loaded with anything valuable and left abandoned on the highway.

"Why didn't you radio for help?"

He grabbed the window with one hand and the door handle with the other. "Open this son-of-a-bitchin' door," he barked, rocking my pickup.

I glanced over my right shoulder, out the back window, and saw an opening coming up in my lane. I floored it, fishtailing my way back into the congested traffic. When I checked the sideview mirror, Mr. Charm was picking himself up out of the rain-swollen ditch.

Quite different from the society wife I used to be, before the double wake-up call I got during my husband's trial: found out that Nicholas Shelley was the brains behind a lucrative white-collar crime operation and the true reason why our only child spent three years behind bars at the state penitentiary in Jackson.

Far less shattering but still a jangle was that hideous photo of me in the *New York Times* next to Nicky in his thousand-dollar suit. I had salt-and-pepper hair and an ass like a vat of cottage cheese. I looked more like Nicky's mother than his wife.

The trial was quick and quiet. Vic—that's my son—took the fall for his father without a peep.

The subsequent divorce was damn near a carbon copy, quick and quiet. Nicky said he'd had enough publicity, and all I wanted was *out* so I could concentrate on my son and myself.

I lost weight, cut the hair, then colored it "Teak" (or so the box said) and took out a lifetime membership at the local tanning bed. (It's the only place in the city where I can get away from a ringing phone.)

The name's Mary Shelley, by the way. Never thought much about it one way or another until someone asked if I was anything like the gal who dreamed up Frankenstein. That was twenty-four years and a dozen hells ago. I was pregnant at the time and the last thing on my mind was literature.

I grew up fast during the trials, and did a lot of soul-searching on those frequent trips to Jackson to see Vic. A night course in law finished up the requirements I needed for a private detective license. That done, I opened Prometheus Investigations.

The rain had eased up considerably when I arrived at Vic's apartment and he met me outside his front door.

"I've been keeping your dinner warm, Nancy Drew. What took you so long?" Vic liked to poke fun at my latest project, as he called it. I called it a living.

"Friday, rain, idiots. You do the math."

No one would guess Victor Shelley for a chef. He looks more like a rebellious teenager, complete with a large and varied array of silver loops piercing everything from his ears to his navel, his black hair in a buzz cut, clothes straight out of Catalog Grunge. Even has what they call a barbell through his tongue (thank you, *Body Piercing by Ned*). He's six-two, trim but muscular and his blue eyes are gorgeous if you can get past those rings hanging over them.

I figure since his real teen years were spent in crime under the heavy hand of his father, he's recapturing his youth. Could be doing a hell of a lot worse.

Vic took a long drag from his cigarette and planted the butt in a clay pot on the stoop. I vaguely remembered the philodendron that used to grow there. "I see you brought the buggy," he said, glancing toward the parking lot. "Can I take it for a test spin tomorrow?"

I nodded, smiling. Vic had completely renovated my pickup in exchange for a security deposit and first and last month's rent on his apartment. He looked for any opportunity to show off his handiwork. Great with sound systems, too. All I know about mine is that Travis Tritt kicks butt and takes names like never before.

During a pot roast dinner better than anything I'd ever created, I told Vic about the jerk on the expressway.

"Museum transport, huh? That's one I never heard of in Jackson." He set coffee and hot apple pie with ice cream in front of me. I wondered how he'd performed such magic in that coat-closet kitchen.

"Surprised me, too. He must have left someone guarding the truck. Looks like too much of a risk otherwise."

"Yeah. The risk would be getting his ass canned if his boss found out. That's all he's worried about." My son curtained himself around the pie and started shoveling. "Probably just pissed off 'cause he had to work on Friday night and he took it out on you."

I watched him for a moment. Here was a young man whose apple pie could win blue ribbons, yet prison life had taught him to eat it like a wild animal. As a mom, I beamed; as a member of humankind, I wanted to assure him that I wasn't going to steal his food.

What he said about the truck driver made sense. I pushed the incident from my mind and finished eating my dessert.

We cleared away the dishes, and after watching Mel Gibson and Danny Glover put away the bad guys in *Lethal Weapon*, I fought Vic for the couch and he won.

I was sucking down a cup of black coffee when Vic walked in with a bag of doughnuts and Saturday morning's *Detroit News and Free Press*.

"Check out the lead story," he said, freshening my coffee, then pouring a cup for himself. He tossed some napkins on the table beside breakfast.

The headlines read MUSEUM TRUCK LOCATED, DRIVER DEAD.

The victim's photograph was no larger than a postage stamp, but I could tell it wasn't the man I'd offered to help and I told Vic so.

"Listen to this: 'A Detroit Institute of Arts museum transport truck was found at an I-96 truck stop near Lansing last night. The driver, forty-seven-year-old Donald McAfferty of Dearborn, was fatally shot twice in the head at close range. He had been with the DIA eighteen years. Nothing was reported missing from the semi trailer, which contained Egyptian artifacts. The exhibit was being transported to the Art Institute of Chicago.'"

Vic looked over my shoulder. "You sure that's not the guy?"

"My roadie was three hundred pounds with jowls like a warthog. You could make a rug with his eyebrows. This McAfferty guy looks like a leprechaun." I studied the news photo. "I'll bet his murder was in the cards before that truck ever saw the loading dock."

"Maybe there's more than one truck like that." My son rummaged in the bag for another doughnut. "Anyway, I don't suppose the law says you can't be an asshole *and* a truck driver."

"Too bad it doesn't." I read the rest of the article, then looked at Vic and grinned. "How about we take that test drive you requested?"

Downtown Detroit's bouncing back from its near-ghost-town existence following the '67 riots, but there's still not much available in the way of decent office space. That's why you'll find me a few blocks off Woodward, up a musty-smelling flight of stairs in a grand old building rescued from the wrecking ball, first door on your left.

Two rooms make up the headquarters for Prometheus Investigations: a pillbox of a reception area for which I can't yet afford a secretary and my own cubbyhole which is only slightly larger.

I've got voice mail, E-mail, and the occasional blackmail. Oh, and the regular mail which hardly counts nowadays, it's so damned screwed up.

Vic lit a Camel as he stepped through the door, then drifted through the haze that quickly filled the tiny reception room.

I checked for phone messages (there weren't any), then booted up the computer on the ancient oak desk and peeked at my E-mail; nothing that couldn't wait. Next, I picked up the phone and hit the third button under quick dial.

"What happened to Saturday off, Harry?" I said when he choked off the first ring.

"Did you try me at home?" His voice was gravelly, worn out.

"And waste my time? I knew you couldn't go through with it."

"You've got this investigator game down pat, don't you?" he said with mock sarcasm.

Inspector Harold Bittenbinder—among the last of that tough old breed of cops that really does know it all and has lived long enough to prove it. We've only known one another for a couple of years, but it's one of those quick clicks where everyone who observes you together figures you for the family-of-the-year poster team. He's the nearest thing to a father I've ever had.

"Sounds like you need more coffee, Harry."

"Always." The *shink* of his cigarette lighter came across the line. After a short but successful coughing fit, he asked, "How's the boy?"

"Good. He's here with me." I tore off Friday's calendar and tossed it in the trash. "We're going to grab some lunch and thought you might like to come along."

"Can't. I'm working on a fresh homicide."

"Truck driver, right?"

"That's the one."

"Got anything yet?"

"Stay out of it, Mary. You know murder's for the cops."

"For the witnesses, too. I talked with your *driver* yesterday, and I don't mean the one on ice over at the morgue."

Silence, followed by a drawn-out sigh. "Where can we meet?"

The diner smelled like meat loaf, and I knew the rest of the day would be Wednesday.

Harry was in a corner booth with his back to the wall. I sat across from him and Vic pulled a chair up to the end of the table.

Bittenbinder's a large man, with thick white hair and shoulders stooped from thirty years' weight of Detroit crime. There's a twinkle in his squinty German eyes that he can shut off like beer on tap when the situation warrants—which is probably more often than not.

All policeman and procedure, he eyed me. "Let's have it, Mary. What have you fallen into this time?"

I told him what had happened the day before on I-96, then said, "Your turn, Harry. What does Detroit's finest know about the case?"

"Educated speculation, mostly. Nothing's missing from the load and, believe me, it was a pricey one. Looks like McAfferty's number came up, that's all."

"Seems pretty unlikely, doesn't it? According to the paper, McAfferty was as much a fixture of the DIA as the marble."

"Fixtures need upkeep, too. Maybe he was mixed up in something, got in over his head. At any rate, we've got a team checking him out."

The diner's owner, Betty, tall and big-boned and looking out of place in a ruffled pink broadcloth dress, showed up to flirt with Harry and, eventually, take our orders. She left and he said, "That gal sure knows how to cook." He tried to erase the grin from his face, but succeeded only in adding a tinge of red.

"I'm sure she does." I winked at Vic. "The newspaper article said there were four trucks. Are the drivers back in Detroit?"

"At Headquarters now. We've been questioning them all morning. None of them sound like your hitchhiker, but we'd better let you have a look-see."

Betty came back with lunch and a pot of coffee. She was so busy flirting with Harry, she might as well have been skidding the plates down a runway for all she noticed.

After lunch, I sent Vic to my house in the pickup and I went with the inspector to Police Headquarters.

My phony driver wasn't in the legitimate batch, so I gave a description of him to a young black female officer who quickly put together a computer composite.

Harry and I went to his office and worked on my incident report.

Two hours later, he said, "Mary, can't you give me more than this? The composite looks like half the white thugs in Detroit and we're not going to find a gorilla in a raincoat today. It's like the Fourth of July out there."

I got edgy. "There's nothing else to give you. He had the hood up on his slicker and it was raining like mad."

"Yeah, I got it. Big. Yellow." He called to the guy at the front desk. "Has Sesame Street reported a bird missing?"

"What?"

"Never mind." To me: "Sorry. Now, tell me about the hands again."

"Damn it, Harry. They were your typical, garden-variety, three-hundred-pound-roughneck hands. Beefy, coarse, grubby nails."

"Grubby nails? When did you actually see *nails*?"

"I told you, *Inspector*. When he was pulling on the handle, rocking my pickup like a cradle. He grabbed the window as I was spinning out."

I stopped. *He grabbed the window with his hand!* When I looked at Bittenbinder, I could see he was thinking the same thing.

"Hell, Harry, I blew it."

He rubbed his forehead. "Everybody's entitled to one, girl. Chalk it up to the first in a whole chain of lessons you'll learn in this damned business." He handed me the phone's receiver, punched in the numbers. "Tell Vic not to touch that pickup."

The phone took an hour between rings. Vic didn't answer.

Harry grabbed his hat. "Let's get over there."

We went west on Beaubien while I secured the flashing light on top of Harry's blue sedan. At Brush he peeled right, cornering on two wheels, then hopped the Fisher Freeway and took advantage of the straight shot to River Rouge.

My house, a two-story fixer-upper that belonged to a bootlegger in the twenties, is just a block off Jefferson. The sedan bounced when we hit the driveway, dragging a little before leveling off.

When I saw Vic, my heart fell to my stomach. He was cleaning the windshield with a chamois and a jug of blue liquid. My little pickup gleamed.

Harry leaned over the steering wheel. I thought he was going to cry. I beat him to it.

Vic walked toward us as I climbed from the car. "Mom? You guys okay?"

I ran past him toward my pickup. "God, son, please tell me you haven't cleaned the interior."

"You know I always do that first." He looked from me to Harry and back. "What's going on?"

I told him what I'd remembered.

Vic walked to the pickup, retrieved a small white envelope from the glove compartment, and handed it to me. "Is this what you're looking for?"

I slowly raised the flap. I couldn't even think what to ask.

Harry joined us. I gave him the envelope. He looked inside. "How in the *hell* did you get these?"

"Well, I figured Mom would have tape, but I have to admit I was pretty surprised to find flour in her kitchen." Vic went back to cleaning windows. "It was easy. My science teacher showed us how in sixth grade."

Harry took the makeshift fingerprints back to Headquarters. I changed into a navy pantsuit and headed for the Detroit Institute of Arts. I ran up the stairs just as a security guard pulled the accordioned steel bars over the doors. I flashed my license.

He frowned, but unlocked the door. "You're not here to visit Renoir, are you."

It wasn't a question. I stepped inside. "Could I talk to you about the truck driver who was killed?"

He frowned again. He was a tall lean black man with that ageless quality granted by opulent skin, a strong jaw line, and glittering eyes. A closer look showed laugh lines, a slight sag in the gullet, and wiry hair graying at the temples. I guessed him for mid-fifties, maybe older. "Donnie's family doesn't have the money to hire a gumshoe and if they did it wouldn't be a female. What gives?"

I told him I was working with the police and that I'd seen the driver of the stolen semi. "Call Inspector Bittenbinder at Headquarters if you don't believe me."

He gave me a tired, knowing look and held out his hand. I gave him the .22 from my purse.

"I've read about these. Kind of a stiff trigger pull for a little thing like you."

"Not if I remember to cock it."

He started walking. "Name's Terrence Ames."

I followed him to an office on the lower level. I accepted a cup of coffee and sat across the desk from him. "Do you work the evening shift, Mr. Ames?"

"Head of graveyard. But things are up in the air right now. Been working overtime, going over the past week's records—time cards, logs, any reports of unusual activity. You say you saw the driver?" He leaned forward.

I nodded, then gave him the story. It wasn't anything he wouldn't hear on tonight's news. "Have you found any discrepancies in the records?"

"Not yet. We did have a little incident Wednesday night, but nothing we couldn't handle. My son, Darius—he works graveyard with me—went out to pick up lunch. Leastwise, that's what we call it, even if it is at four in the morning.

"Everybody usually brings a packed lunch, but we had a couple of guards with the traveling exhibit here and Darius had left his lunch pail at home, so he made the run. An hour later they were in the emergency room with what looked like food poisoning. The restaurant's The Broken Rib. The cops are checking it out. Anyway, we had enough regulars on hand to cover things for the rest of the night."

"Darius was taken to the ER too?"

"Yes, ma'am." Ames grinned. "Pretty sharp, Miss Shelley. Father or not, I'd have thought the same thing if the exhibit guards were the only ones carted out of here on stretchers."

I thanked him, retrieved my gun, and left.

It took only a few minutes to hop from Woodward to Police Headquarters on Beaubien. Harry was hanging up the phone when I walked in. "We owe Vic a steak dinner. Your driver, a nickel-and-dimer who's now moved up to the big leagues, goes by the name of Jimmy Traina."

Traina. I watched Harry, who had already returned to deciphering scribbles on a yellow legal pad. I've got a damn good poker face, but I was glad he wasn't paying me any attention.

"It appears like he hooked up with the DIA truck at the museum. Probably not working alone." Harry looked up.

I chose my words carefully, trying to think what I'd say if I'd never before heard of Jimmy Traina. "Can they tell if McAfferty opened the trailer for this Traina guy?"

"No way of knowing, but like I said before, nothing's missing from the trailer, so it looks like a simple hit. Nothing was in McAfferty's log, so we figure Traina was in the cab when he climbed in.

"We've put out an APB. Soon as we nab him, our murder

case is a wrap." Harry slapped his palms on the desk and grinned.

I smiled back, but my heart wasn't in it. "Nothing's that simple, Harry." I told him I was going home to spend the evening with my son, but I pulled onto Beaubien and went toward Lake Shore Drive instead.

Salvatore Scabielli's basement office had stayed the same all these years, right down to the white dahlias he had delivered every week and placed in a crystal vase on the corner of his desk. Being there made me shiver. I'd never expected to return to the home I once shared with Nicholas Shelley.

Delores—her black hair and skin both faded with age since I'd lived there—offered to make some fresh coffee. I thanked her, but declined.

A few moments later Scabielli shuffled in. It had been only two years since I last saw him, but he'd aged thirty. His makeover was in no way similar to my own. I figured his for cancer.

He touched one of the dahlias, then lowered himself into the softened leather chair and stared at me across the desk. "Mary Shelley. I would not have recognized you without a warning."

"Salvatore." I kept my voice steady. "Or do you still prefer Sally Scabs?"

"As you can see"—he indicated his frail body—"it soon won't matter. Call me what you wish."

"Time isn't treating you well, is it?"

"I am afraid it is not." He breathed heavily. "How is Victor?"

"Immune to all of you now. I suppose we can credit the penitentiary for that, can't we?" *Keep a grip, Mary. Don't let him know he can still get to you.* "You never had any children, did you, Sally?"

"No, thank the Priest. Not because a son might have followed in his old man's footsteps. I would not have allowed it. But Nicky's footsteps? Your ex-husband is like the Pied Piper." He stared at me and for a moment I thought I detected compassion. "Of course, Mary, you know better than anyone the tune Nicky plays." He cleared his throat. "I do help my sister with her children, though. I believe family should be watched after, unlike your ex-husband."

Steady, girl. Hold your cards. Play out the hand. "I'm curious about the McAfferty hit that went down yesterday."

Scabielli steepled his slender hands, stared over them at me with a fiery intensity that could only come from the core of a burning soul. He grinned slightly. "I'd heard you were dabbling in private investigation. I think you need more practice."

"Getting it by the minute, Sally."

"Should I assume then that you're here officially?"

"Just following a string, seeing if it's tied to anything."

"You should realize that there are no strings connected to this place."

I let that one slide. "Where's Nicky keeping himself?"

"Chicago. He should be back in a few days."

I paused. "Your sister's children are almost grown by now, aren't they?"

"Yes. As a matter of fact, I'm expecting my nephew any moment." Scabielli poured water from a pitcher into a rocks glass and drank. "Shall I have him call you? Nicky, that is. Tie a knot in that so-called string you're following?"

He was biting. Fine, give him something to swallow. Let him choke on it. "The string, Sally, is fingerprints. Jimmy Traina's fingerprints."

Scabielli's face, already paled by disease, turned as white as the dahlias. His burning eyes fought for control.

I smiled. "Like you said, Sally, it soon won't matter."

After showing myself out, I sat in my car across the street for the better part of thirty minutes, working the angles, tying the strings together.

I had started to drive away from the curb when a new Mustang pulled into Nicky's driveway. A young man jumped out and hurried toward the house, walking in the beam of his vehicle's headlights. I could see the Scabielli family resemblance. On the arm of his shirt was a sleeve patch I recognized. It was the uniform of a DIA security guard.

I glanced at my watch. It was almost eight o'clock. I stopped at a drive-through burger place, then pulled up to their pay phone and called Vic.

It didn't even ring on my end, he grabbed it so fast. "Where in the hell are you? Harry's here. He said you left for home over an hour ago."

"Are you girls sitting there waiting for your dates to call? Loosen your hair curlers and stop worrying so much." I wolfed down a wad of fries.

"Not funny, Mom. I tried your cell phone, but you weren't in your bedroom to answer it."

I could tell he was upset, so I apologized. "Listen, son, I've got a lead that should close some gaps in this case, but I might require a little backtracking. I'll be there in an hour or two."

"Wait. Harry wants to talk to you. Be careful, Mom," he added.

"What's new, Inspector?" I tried to sound casual. It only set him off.

"Don't give me that crap. You're on to something, aren't you?"

"Just working on a hunch."

"I should've had you tailed when you left the station." He coughed. "What have you found out?"

We made a swap we both could live with, and I made another call.

Terrence Ames met me at the main entrance of the DIA. He didn't bother with my revolver this time. It almost hurt my feelings. We walked through the maze of corridors, our shadows climbing ahead of us, footsteps bouncing off the old marble and stone of the building.

Ames must have sensed it, too. He said, "Turns a little spooky around here when it gets dark."

"Doesn't everything?"

"You got that right."

He didn't speak again until we were seated in the security office. "Have you already solved Donnie's murder?"

"I wish I could tell you I have. Actually, I need to speak with your son. Is he on duty?"

"Yeah, he's filling in tonight, but I don't see how he can give you any more than I did earlier."

"I have to touch every base, Mr. Ames. You know how it works."

He paged his son twice over the intercom before the boy showed. Darius Ames had that ageless quality just like his father, except this one's youth held up to a second glance.

Ames introduced us and I asked Darius to tell me what had happened Wednesday night. He looked annoyed, but gave me a brief version of what his father had relayed earlier.

I stared him down. "The police have been investigating

The Broken Rib. Did you know there's never been a case of food poisoning there?"

He snorted. "First time for everything."

"Darius, I like to play cat and mouse as much as the next person, but it's Saturday night and frankly I'd rather be somewhere else. So let's cut to it.

"The police played sanitation crew this morning and gathered the trash from the dumpsters out back. Your so-called food poisoning can be picked up at the local pharmacy. It's called syrup of ipecac."

Terrence looked at his son.

"Who paid you to get the exhibit's guards out of the way?" I asked.

"You got nothin' and I got work to do." Darius stood up, started toward the door. His father blocked his path.

"You're forgetting who you work *for*. Put your butt in that chair and tell us what's going on."

Darius hesitated, then sat back down.

I continued. "If you think your part in this is no more than a stunt, you're wrong. Especially if you knew they were going to kill the driver."

"Huh?"

I told him about McAfferty. The glitter left his eyes.

"You really should read the paper, kid," I said.

He finished unraveling. "I didn't know! I swear I didn't! He told me nobody was gonna get hurt."

Terrence Ames slumped at his desk. "God, son. I really believed you had changed."

"All he said was that he needed to get something to Chicago and he had this great way figured out to do it. It sounded so easy. A thousand bucks for a bellyache."

"Who, Darius? Who gave you a thousand dollars?"

"I haven't got paid yet." He looked sullen. "I shoulda just taken it out of the shipment."

"Was there money in the shipment?"

"Not *just* money." He grinned perversely. "Twelve million dollars stuffed in one of those fancy Egyptian mummy cases."

Twelve million. Ames and I stared at each other.

"We need a name," I said.

He looked away. Finally, he spoke. "It was Jared Wright."

"Let me get him in here." Terrence Ames turned toward the door.

"He's gone, Dad."

His father turned back.

"He said something went wrong with the deal and he had to find his boss."

"Did he tell you who his boss is?" I asked.

"No. He just said his uncle wouldn't help him make the big bucks, so he went to his uncle's boss."

After the police came to question his son, I gave Terrence Ames my card. "Mine spent three years in prison. If you ever need to talk . . ."

He nodded. The ageless illusion was gone.

I had almost everything I needed. Only one thing remained.

Nicholas Shelley still considered himself untouchable. I found the extra house-key hidden where it had always been, in the mouth of a cast-iron jockey's horse in the garden just beyond the pool.

I'd parked one street over and poked the .22 in the pocket of my suit jacket before picking my way to the back of the house.

Slowly, quietly, I let myself in the door of the home in Grosse Point Shores where I used to live. In a fair world, I would have owned the place.

There was no light, but it didn't matter. I could have found my way with both eyes tied behind my back.

To my relief, the basement door didn't creak when I opened it. I passed through and pulled it closed behind me. The metal railing chilled my fingers as I descended the staircase, one step at a time. It took hours to reach bottom.

A long corridor split the large basement into two banks of rooms. I'd been in most of them. Only one was guarded with a high-tech alarm system, its contents kept secret from everyone but my ex-husband and his long-time accomplice, Sally Scabs.

Pressed against the clammy wall, I made my way toward the far end where a splinter of light shone around the dark door to Scabielli's suite of rooms. The blackness pulled at the light, coaxing voices from within the office. I reached the door and steadied myself against its facing.

Scabielli was speaking. "I've gone to great lengths to protect you from this business, Jared. You should be grateful."

"Grateful? My mother barely scrapes by on the small allowance you dole out. Don't ask me for gratitude."

"I'm not asking, son. I expect it."

"I'm not your son." Jared spoke evenly.

"Nicholas told me of his plans to invite you in."

A pause. "You knew?"

"Of course I knew. You forget that Nicholas and I are partners, have been since before you were born."

"He promised me you'd never find out."

"I believed you would turn him down."

"Turn down more money than I can make in a *year* at the DIA? Nicky gave me a chance to take care of my mother the way you should have."

"You call being a thug for Nicholas Shelley a *chance*? It will only get you killed, Jared. Let me help you get away

from here, away from this business so you *can* take care of
your mother."

"What do you care? You don't know how she feels,
watching you live here while we fight to survive in the old
neighborhood. 'I take care of my family,' you always say.
'Nothing comes before my family.' Your *family* can make it
without you, you son of a bitch."

Glass shattered. I flinched. "You ungrateful little bastard.
Not another cent from me, you understand?"

"I don't need your stinking help. I wanted to work with
you, but you wouldn't let me. Well, I made my own way in.
Nicky will take care of me now."

"Nicholas Shelley let his own son go to prison, for God's
sake. What makes you think he'll do any better by you?"

Needles pricked the nape of my neck seconds before a
beefy hand clutched my shoulder. Something cold and hard
pressed against my back.

"Let's go," said Jimmy Traina.

We burst through the door. Jared pulled his gun. He would
never look more like his uncle than he did at that moment.

Scabielli rose from his chair behind the desk. "What in
hell is she doing here?"

"I found her in the hall." Traina groped me, found the .22
and laid it on the desk.

Flustered, I jerked away. He laughed, then grabbed my
arms and shoved me into the chair opposite Scabielli. The
dahlias lay on the floor in a litter of broken glass.

"How much did she hear?"

I answered, rubbing my biceps. "Enough to know you're
lying, Sally. Traina's the one who told you about the deal,
not Nicky. You were furious, figured you were getting
squeezed out, so you decided to take the loot from the

mummy case for yourself. That was before you knew Nicky had brought in your nephew."

Jared said, "You expect me to believe Jimmy would turn against Nicky? No way." He looked at Traina. "Tell 'em, Jimmy."

Scabielli shrugged. "All it takes is money, son. I was willing to pay more for loyalty than Nicholas. You want in? Fine. Even your mother knows where I hid the cash."

No one spoke. He continued.

"After you helped Traina get safely into the transport truck, he persuaded McAfferty to drive to one of our warehouses on the river. I gave Traina his cut from the twelve million and he loaded the rest in my vehicle.

"You see, Traina realized my power. Nicholas underestimated me. That's where he went wrong."

"Nicky won't walk again, Sally," I said. "And neither will you. I'll see to that."

Scabielli shook his head. "Won't be easy, Mary. Nicholas has a foolproof alibi on this one, and I'm beyond it all now."

I looked at Jared. "When the boys in Chicago can't find Nicky, they'll come after you."

"Then I'll send them to Traina. Look at me in this uniform, then look at him. Who would you believe?" Jared drew a bead on Traina.

Traina leveled his gun at Jared. "Don't mess with me, you little punk. I'll wrap rags around you and stash you right under their noses at the museum. Make 'em their own little mummy. What do you think of that?"

"That's enough, Traina," Scabielli warned.

Jared said, "You double-crossed Nicky, didn't you, Jimmy?"

"I don't have to tell you a damn thing."

The sound of Traina's nine millimeter deafened me. Jared dropped his .38 and grabbed his stomach with both hands.

Blood seeped through his fingers as he fell to his knees. Traina kicked the .38 across the room, then aimed at Scabielli.

I lunged for the desk, snared my .22 and swung on Traina. I forgot to cock it and the stiff trigger-pull threw off my aim. The bullet struck the wall. Traina turned from Scabielli to me.

I cocked, squeezed, and put a slug in his heart. My ears were ringing. I didn't hear his body hit the floor.

Then Bittenbinder was in the room, filling it with those shoulders that carry all the weight of Detroit's crime. Following him were uniformed cops, paramedics, my son, and Delores, the housekeeper.

"Good timing, Inspector."

He let my sarcasm pass. "You okay?"

Vic wrapped his arms around me. I nodded.

I gave Harry the story while the paramedics tended to Jared. They didn't even bother with Traina.

The inspector cuffed Scabielli, started toward the door.

I stopped them. "You said Nicky has an alibi. What is it?"

Scabielli's eyes burned. The rest of his face was dead white. "Ask him yourself. He's in the case."

Jan Grape is the Vice-President of PWA, and the editor of the organization's newsletter, Reflections in a Private Eye. *She also has a long list of short-story credits which includes the original* Lethal Ladies *anthology, as well as* Deadly Allies *I & II and several* Cat Crimes *anthologies. She is the co-editor of the forthcoming* Deadly Women *(Carrol & Graf, 1997).*

FUNNY HOW DECEIVING LOOKS CAN BE
A JENNY GORDON & C.J. GUNN STORY

by Jan Grape

S PRING FLOUNCED HERSELF all over central Texas. The March showers and 80-degree temperatures caused the wildflowers to pop along the Interstate, along state and county roadways, in open fields and in people's yards. Not only the world-renowned Texas bluebonnets but Indian paintbrush, black-eyed Susan, verbena, lantana, bluebells, pink evening primrose and wine cups. Lady Bird Johnson's highway beautification showed up with more splendor than we'd seen in recent drought years. The riotous colors were magnificent.

I walked into the LaGrange Building, where my office is located, a few minutes before eight A.M. with plans to finalize some paperwork and then take my own version of a spring break; driving out into the hill country with a picnic basket and an intriguing male companion. Brian was a Dallas television news reporter who wanted me to go to Switzerland with him on a ski trip. Since my idea of winter sports leaned toward roaring fireplaces and mugs of hot buttered rum, I wasn't making it too easy for him.

My partner, C.J., looked up as I pushed open the door that read G & G Investigations, and I could immediately see from that haughty Nefertiti look on her face someone was in trouble. I searched my mind quickly and thoroughly and didn't think it was me.

"What's up, girl?" I asked.

"Did you see today's paper?"

"No, sorry." I only subscribed for weekend delivery because there never seemed to be time enough to read the news daily. Mentally, I sighed with relief, glad to know I hadn't messed up the checkbook or something equally drastic to get her riled at me. A good six feet tall in her stocking feet, Cinnamon J. Gunn (only her nearest and dearest know her full name) was not someone to ever make angry. I didn't take any guff off her, mind you, but I did hate it when she got teed-off at me. "What did I miss?"

"Some scumbags'll doctor a young girl's drinks with this drug rohypnol. They call it ropies or roofies on the street," C.J. said. "The girl drinks her drink not aware the drug is in it and boom. The next thing she knows, she wakes up someplace knowing she's been sexually assaulted but doesn't remember who did her or much else for that matter. The cops call it the date-rape drug."

"Damn Sam. They're doing it right here in Austin?"

"'fraid so. Problem is my nieces go bar-hopping on Sixth Street every weekend, listening to live music, and I sure as hell don't want to see one of them into trouble like that."

"Do we know anyone official we can call to see what's being done? Or how we can help?"

She nodded. "You remember Doug Vance? I met him at a seminar last fall. He's been a Department of Public Safety narc for 'bout a hundred years. I'll call Dougie. If he doesn't know who's working the case, he can find out for me."

"Do I know him?"

"You've met him. Tall silent type. Pretty blond wife, Barbara, who likes horses."

"Oh, yes. Down at Sam's Wholesale Club one afternoon. You introduced us. She's got personality plus."

"That's the one." C.J. picked up the telephone and that look came back to her cola-nut-colored face. "I'm calling him right now. Some of those guys need an attitude adjustment."

"You got that right."

I could tell she hadn't heard me, and hastened into my inner office to get started on my paperwork. Not that I'm so crazy about paperwork but I was looking forward to finding out if a certain news guy's perfect hair could be mussed up easily.

Foster Kinney looked like a killer. I know that is a stupid assumption. Many killers are the baby-faced all-American boy-next-door-types. My mother always said to look beneath the façade and find the real person inside. But this time I succumbed to the stereotypical idea of a killer looking mean and ugly. Sometimes your mind only works one way in spite of everything you do to try and change direction.

The man's wide-set but tiny black eyes bulged in his bullet-shaped head. His black brows came together in the center of his forehead and gave him a permanent scowl. His middle-aged body grew rounder in the middle and ended in thick thighs. One single feature drew your eyes like a magnet and pinned them there: a wart with black hairs grew near his nose. You couldn't call him plain or even homely;

only one word fit—ugly. Just look up "scary monster" in your dictionary; you might find this man's photograph.

Mr. Kinney had walked into G & G Investigations less than an hour ago and said he needed a private eye as he was about to be arrested for murder.

"How do you know?" I asked, waving for him to be seated in one of the client chairs in my office. "And who did you allegedly murder?"

"My wife was murdered but not by me," he said. "And the reason I know a warrant has been issued is because I have a police scanner in my car."

"Perhaps you need a lawyer and not a private investigator."

"I don't know any lawyers, Ms. Gordon."

"Call me Jenny," I said.

"And I'm Foster or Fos." He shrugged. He tried to smile but it looked more like a grimace.

"I know several lawyers in Austin," he said. "But they're wheeler-dealer types in the corporate jungle. I live in Pflugerville."

I nodded. Pflugerville is an older town, a settlement started by a German named Henry Pfluger in 1849 who moved there with his eight sons. Now the area was one of the fastest-growing bedroom communities in the state and lay just north of the capital city. The pangs of growth recently surfaced as the local news reported on gang-related activities. The very idea of gang-style graffiti in suburbia sent parents and schools into a tailspin.

"I need a criminal attorney," he continued. "I thought a good private eye might know who to call."

"There are several legal minds I could put you in touch with."

He shook his head. "Who's the best? Money is no object."

"In my opinion, Bulldog Porter is the top man in this state."

It would be worth a week's pay just to see Bulldog's face animated and excited over a good case again.

"Could you see if he's available?" The man's shoulders slumped and he looked about as low as a rattlesnake's belly. "I'm completely innocent, Jenny Gordon. Someone could be trying to frame me."

I pushed the intercom button to call C.J. in. After she joined us and I filled her in on Foster's problem, she had a couple of questions for him.

"Who hates you enough to kill your wife and to frame you?" she asked, cutting to the bottom line.

"Nelda's first husband comes to mind right off." Hopelessness appeared in his eyes when he lifted his head in the brief moment it took to look at her. "Next, if pressed I'd guess my business partner."

"Your business partner hates you that much?" C.J. asked.

"I caught him embezzling six months ago."

"Did you turn him in?"

"No. I felt sorry for his wife. I've been letting him pay the money back but he resents me for it."

"Why don't one of you just buy out the other?" asked C.J.

This line of questioning could take all day and I thought Bulldog might want to handle it himself. "Mr. Kinney, uh, Foster, I think we should call Mr. Porter before any more discussion takes place," I said.

C.J. reached out and patted his arm. "Why don't you make yourself comfortable here while Ms. Gordon goes out to reception and sees if Mr. Porter is available?"

He took only a moment to think about it, then said, "It doesn't make much difference. I'm screwed anyway you look at it."

"I'll keep you company," C.J. told him and her dark eyes showed concern, but I wasn't sure why. She's the cynic in our partnership. I'm usually the one who gets "sentimental or emotional," as she calls it, about our clients.

As I walked out I heard her say, "Fos, you obviously didn't take the crash course on how to win friends."

C.J. attempting humor? Now I was surprised, but when I looked back at her, Mr. Kinney was not smiling. In fact he looked as if he was asleep.

Fifteen seconds later C.J. confirmed it, walking up beside me as I dialed Bulldog's office.

"He's gone to sleep. Sitting straight upright there in your overstuffed customer chair, the man has gone to sleep."

"It's hard work being a wanted man."

C.J.'s voice sounded compassionate. "Just remember— he's only a suspect . . ."

A refined feminine voice spoke softly in my ear, a distinct contrast to my partner. "Law office."

"Martha May? It's Jenny Gordon."

"Jenny. My goodness, honey. Haven't talked to you in a month of Sundays. How are you? and how's C.J.?"

"We're both fine, Martha May. And you?"

"I'm here, Jenny. More than I can say about Bulldog. He's here, but he ain't with it, if you get my drift."

I hated to hear Bulldog was giving up on life. We'd helped him on a case a few months ago in which he had a personal connection and the end results had taken a lot out of the man who would turn eighty this year.

"Well, put the old curmudgeon on the horn, Martha May. My news might knock his socks off."

"To what do I owe this pleasure?" the deep voice intoned with only a hint of the oratory.

I could see his pale blue eyes behind his new wire-rim spectacles. It had been months since those eyes had twinkled, but I remembered. "You'll never guess who just walked into my office?"

"A knight in shining armor who wants to marry you and take you away from all this."

"No. This man would never qualify as a knight."

"Why? Is he too good-looking?"

"Not exactly. Looks a little like a toad if you must know. He's got pots of gold, he says . . ."

"Don't waste any time, you fool, kiss him."

"Right. But in the meantime he needs a lawyer and since you're the bestest of the best, the cream of the crop, the top of the line . . ."

"Flattery will get you a no, my dear. But I do not want any new clients. Even one sent by such a charming lady as yourself. I do not have the time. My dance card is full, so to speak."

The quiet voice of Martha May broke in. "Bulldog, I know good and well you're not doing a darn thing right at this moment, so there."

A brief silence ensued; then her whispered "sorry" came.

"Martha May?" he said in an aside to his secretary. "You're fired. You have just opened your big mouth one time too many." To me, he said, "I may have the time but not the enthusiasm for clients. I am seriously thinking of retiring."

"Sit around on your duff all day? No way. Sorry. Can't let you do that," I said.

He grunted.

"Look, pal," I said. "For once in our relationship, let me send *you* a client. He's about to be arrested, he says. For the murder of his wife."

"Not interested. I will have Martha May give . . . you a referral— Wait just a gosh-darn minute. Is this client's name, uh . . . Foster Kinney?"

"And just how do you know Mr. Kinney?"

Bulldog remained silent for so long I thought maybe he'd dropped the phone and I hadn't heard it. When he did speak, I heard a tenuous vigor and vitality coming into his voice again.

C.J. and I thought we might not ever hear him being excited about anything ever again.

"I don't. Keep him there. Do not let him out of your sight unless the police come inside your office to arrest him." He covered the phone with his hand, obviously telling Martha May something.

"I think he'll stay," I said. "He's gone to sleep in the client chair in front of my desk."

"Do the cops know where he is?"

"Not to my knowledge."

"Good," Bulldog said. "I shall be there in thirty minutes."

"What got his knickers in a twist?" asked C.J. when I told her Bulldog's reaction.

"I can't imagine."

"Wonder how he knows Kinney? Business or something?"

"Maybe. But I heard something in his voice . . . like . . . I don't actually know what it was like. Something akin to rejuvenation."

"Guess we'll find out when he gets here."

"Or maybe we'll find out when Foster Kinney wakes up."

"Nelda Kinney came to see me a few months ago," said Bulldog.

"What?" asked Foster. "Why was she there?"

"Said she thought someone was trying to kill her."

"Did she say who?" I asked.

"She mentioned being afraid of her ex-husband, Stoney Lykes."

"And did she mention Foster, here?" I asked.

"No. But she also mentioned that Foster's adopted sister, Deana, had always hated her."

Foster Kinney stood up. "See? Like I said earlier, Stoney Lykes couldn't stand it because Nelda married me."

"And what about your sister?" I asked.

"Oh, that Deana. My sister's a bitch kitty who resented the hell out of Nelda—but kill her? I don't think so."

"But did your sister hate you enough to frame you?" asked C.J. "Maybe she didn't do the actual deed herself."

He hung his head. "I think Deana would do almost anything she could short of murder to get back at me . . ."

"Okay, what does she have against you?" asked C.J.

Foster didn't answer; instead he looked over at Bulldog Porter. "Did you go to the police, Mr. Porter? Did you tell them how my wife came to see you? And that I'm not guilty?"

"Call me Bulldog, son. No. I haven't talked to the police yet. When I heard of your wife's death this morning I didn't know if you had a lawyer or—"

"Maybe your information can get the ball rolling to clear Foster," I interrupted.

Bulldog scratched his head and looked at Foster Kinney. "Do you want me to represent you, son?"

"Hell yes. Especially now when you'll even be able to clear this all up."

"There's still the matter of the arrest warrant that's been issued," said C.J.

Bulldog said, "I'll call and tell APD I'm bringing you in on your own."

"Well, shit," said Foster Kinney, visibly upset. "You want me to give myself up? I thought your job was to keep me out of jail."

"If a warrant hadn't already been issued, I might have

kept you out, but not now. Turning yourself in will help you in the long run."

I could tell Foster wasn't too happy at the prospect of going to jail, but after a few more minutes of conversation, he was finally convinced of Bulldog's wisdom.

Foster made out a retainer check to pay Bulldog's fee.

"You want to pay for their services through my office or do you want to write a separate check to them?" Bulldog indicated C.J. and myself.

"I'd just as soon it goes through your office, Bulldog," C.J. said. "If that's acceptable to you, Mr. Kinney. That's so we'll have an official standing with the cops. Easier to deal with some of those guys when we have an official status."

C.J. must be sick, I thought. Or she'd lost her caustic tongue. In fact she kept acting strangely about Mr. Foster, too. What was going on with her?

I placed a phone call to Lt. Larry Hays, homicide division of the Austin Police Department, to report that Mr. Porter and Mr. Foster were on their way to police headquarters, at I-35 and Eighth Street.

"And just how did you get involved here, Miz Gordon?" asked Larry Hays. His tone was not friendly. "We just pulled her body out of Town Lake yesterday."

Larry and Tommy, my late husband, had partnered at APD for ten years until Tommy, tired of law-enforcement politics, quit and opened a detective agency. The men had remained close friends and when Tommy had been killed working a case and I reopened his office to find his killer, Larry appointed himself my "big brother."

Neither of us was totally comfortable with that role, but in recent months we'd both become more accepting of the situation. Occasionally Larry even admitted I could make it on my own.

In actual fact, C.J. and I were doing quite well—we paid

the rent, pulled a salary draw each week and managed to have money left over to keep up with the office expenses. We did a lot of insurance- and employee-investigating which paid the weekly bills, but we mostly had Bulldog Porter to thank for our success. The jobs he'd thrown our way paid well and brought us favorable publicity which in turn brought us more business. It was nice feeling successful after so many lean months.

"What evidence do you have against Foster Kinney?"

"This one is cut and dried, Jenny. I can't say any more than that. It's an active case."

"Nothing like thinking someone is innocent until proven guilty in a court of law."

"We don't try them, we just put them in jail so the lawyers can let them out to kill again," he said.

I could tell his skivvies were all in a knot about something and he would be no more help at this point, so I told him thanks and hung up the phone.

Bulldog asked if we'd check on the whereabouts of Stoney Lykes and called Martha May at his office to have her get in touch with some legal clerks he'd need for research.

"What about checking out Deana Kinney?" I asked.

"Her married name is Haggen," said Foster. "You can check but you're wasting time there. Deana might shoot me in a New York minute, but she wouldn't hurt Nelda."

"Foster, we need to check anyway," I said. "What is it about you that—" I stopped when I saw his face. Obvious pain, and also obvious he'd fought battles over his looks— probably all his life. "What does Deana have against you? She's adopted. Is that why she hates you?"

"She thinks I was Mother's favorite and that's reason enough."

"Being a son, you probably were your mom's favorite," I

said. "Mothers do that, you know. Maybe because you're her natural child."

"I've heard all that psychobabble stuff, but I don't believe it. Deana was Mom's favorite. She's the oldest and Mother wanted her for such a long time that when she got her she doted on her. But Deana is jealous-hearted. She never saw how Mother cared. And she doesn't hate me—deep down she loves her little brother."

He sounded wistful, and for the first time since he'd walked into G & G Investigations I felt a pang of sympathy for this ugly man. Could anyone except a mother have ever loved him? Obviously someone had—Nelda Kinney cared enough to marry him. But did she marry him for love or for his money?

"Didn't you say Deana resented Nelda?"

"But not enough to kill her," said Foster. "Nelda and I have been married nearly two years. Deana hated it because I'd found happiness and she hadn't."

"Okay, your sister was jealous, but is that a strong enough motive to frame you?" C.J. asked, interrupting my train of thought.

"Deana had a new reason to despise me, and Nelda, too. Mother died a month ago and I was her sole beneficiary.

"My father made a fortune in the oil business back during the boom times. He pulled his money out before the first energy crash in 1973 and when the eighties hit he got into real estate and made another huge fortune."

"Maybe you *were* your mother's favorite child," I said.

"No, that's not true."

"Okay. I know it's impolite to ask, Mr. Kinney, but it's only to discover where the money trail might lead. Are we talking thousands of dollars here or what?"

"Millions."

"And you don't think losing out on millions would

make your sister angry enough to hurt you in the most hateful way she could?" C.J. asked.

"Deana knows I'll give her half the money as soon as she divorces Paul Haggen. That was the clause in Mother's will."

I was all set to ask about that new factor—Deana's husband—when Bulldog walked back into my office.

He'd reported circumstances to Martha May, and said they'd better leave at once for police headquarters. "We don't want them to send anyone after you, son."

After they left, C.J. began her background checks on Stoney Lykes, Deana Haggen, and her husband, Paul.

I was curious to get C.J.'s reactions on Bulldog Porter and Foster Kinney but knew she wouldn't say anything while she had business on her mind. I kept myself busy by calling my reporter friend to cancel our picnic.

"Cancel," he said. "I can't believe this. I made reservations for us and I made arrangements and I . . ." His voice had a funny tone that I finally decided sounded like a whine. "Couldn't your partner handle it?"

"I'm sorry," I said. "That's not the way we work. We generally work as a team. You and I can picnic next weekend."

"Next weekend? Do you realize how much trouble I had trying to get these reservations for us? I booked us at the Old Settler's Inn. Now what am I going to do? I don't understand how you could do this to me."

Funny, I'd not noticed before how his conversation centered on himself. "I'm sure you'll think of something, and frankly, my dear, I really don't give a big rat's ass." I hung up before he could respond.

"That asinine, self-centered egotist," I muttered. A pretty face solely in love with himself. Funny how deceiving looks can be.

People wonder why I seldom date. The majority of men

I meet don't understand the hours I keep and don't understand how my job comes first. Only someone in law enforcement themselves could comprehend plans changing in the blink of an eye. Or needing to stay on a stakeout fourteen hours straight.

Many female P.I.'s I'd met through the years at seminars were single or divorced. Two who had married since I'd known them divorced after less than a year.

Even a somewhat enlightened man could get bent all out of shape when you called to say you were tailing a suspect to Phoenix and had no idea when you were coming home.

A couple of hours later C.J. came into my inner office. "Paul and Deana Haggen are deeply in debt. Getting their hands on the Kinneys' money could be a strong motive."

"What about Stoney?"

"He also has a strong motive. He owns a failed computer games company and Nelda was his partner. He still holds a business insurance policy whereby he inherits over five hundred thousand if she dies first."

It sounded so familiar and so sad. Big money changing nice people into something even greedy didn't describe.

"You know what I'd like to do, C.J.? I'd really like to leave here now. Let's go see where they found Mrs. Kinney's body. Let's talk to people who might have seen her that night and try to—"

"That sounds an awful lot like messing in an active homicide investigation."

I grinned at C.J. "Don't it, though? Oh, okay. We won't start messing, but there's nothing wrong with going out to Town Lake and taking a look at the crime scene, is there? Anyone can go looking around on public property, can't they?"

"True, and besides we'll need sustenance soon. The Hyatt is right there on Town Lake and I can smell fajitas already."

We shot out of the office so quick, you could have heard the front door slamming clear out to Pflugerville.

"Yes, it's true my ex-wife is still on my insurance policy," said Stoney Lykes. "She was my business partner."

He wasn't what I expected, because he was movie-star-handsome. In white Levi's and a black knit open-collared shirt, his thick auburn hair and dark mustache accented the green eyes above a strong jaw. Nicely chiseled body from regular gym work, but not musclebound. A man as completely opposite from Foster Kinney as day is from night. If this was her ex, and Foster was her current husband, what did that say about Nelda's choices? Did I hear a little gold-digging somewhere in the background?

"How long had you been divorced?" I asked.

"Two years. Well, the divorce has been final for two years."

"And during that time you didn't think to drop her from your policy?"

A taller, younger version of Stoney Lykes, but without the mustache, walked into the room. "Nelda and Dad were still business partners until three months ago." The kid didn't look a day over twenty.

"This is my son, Geoffrey," Lykes said as the younger man held out his hand to shake. He was dressed in denim cutoffs, sandals, and a faded T-shirt with a deck of cards logo on it—a typical Austin-style grunge.

"Oh, I didn't realize the business termination was such a short time ago."

"It's probably a good idea to check all your facts first," said Geoffrey.

"Spoken like a true law student," said Stoney Lykes. "Geoff's at the University of Texas Law School."

"Congratulations," I said. "I understand they are pretty tough over there."

"One prof is tough as cowhide." He turned on a 100-watt smile. "Foster Kinney is being represented by Bulldog Porter?"

"Yes."

"Fantastic. Even if Fos is guilty, Bulldog is the main man and will get him off."

"Have you ever met Mr. Porter?" I asked.

"Never had that honor. One day, I hope," Geoff said. "In fact I've thought of calling to see if he'll need an extra researcher if old Fos goes to trial."

"That's out of my territory, but I can tell you one fact about Bulldog you can always count on."

Geoff and Stoney Lykes both looked at me. I almost staggered with all that handsome testosterone washing over me. "Bulldog doesn't take clients who are guilty."

"I'd heard that. But you wonder how true it can be."

"It's true. If a man is guilty or if Bulldog has a suspicion of guilt, he finds someone else to represent that person."

"A man of principles. I like that," said Stoney.

"It sounds as if you two and the Kinneys had a somewhat unusual relationship. No animosity? No fighting over lost loves or anything like that?"

"Absolutely not. She and I were like oil and water and never should have tried marriage. Friends is how we should have stayed. Nelda wanted more out of life than I could give her. She was never satisfied with the simple life."

"So the major problem was money," I said.

"You make her sound mercenary, Dad," said Geoff. "She wasn't like that." There was a sparkle in the young man's eyes when he mentioned Nelda's name.

"You were still living at home while Nelda and your dad were married?"

"I was in high school and living with my mother when they first married. But when Mom remarried she didn't want me around, so Dad took me in."

"And Nelda doted on him. He blames me for the breakup and will never let me say anything against her," said Lykes.

"A far cry from the days of wicked old stepmothers, huh, Geoff?"

"Right. She was never anything but wonderful to me," said Geoff with a voice that cracked. "And I'll miss her."

"Okay," I said to Lykes. "So you severed the business arrangement amicably. Do you know why she would say to someone that you wanted her dead?"

"I . . . have no idea."

He had some thoughts, but was not about to share. Maybe he threatened her over the insurance money. I decided another line of questioning might be in order. "So how did Foster Kinney feel about his new wife working with her ex-husband?"

"You have to know him to understand Foster," Geoffrey broke in. "I don't think there's a jealous bone in his body, do you, Dad?"

"No. Foster's very sure of himself," said Stoney. "And for what it's worth, I don't think Foster is capable of killing anyone.

"You might want to talk to that weird sister of his," Stoney continued. "She and her husband are just kooky enough to want to get back at Foster and at old Mrs. Kinney. He was furious over the will and Deana being disinherited."

"One more question . . . out of curiosity . . . where were you the night Nelda died?"

"You sure you want to answer, Dad?" Geoffrey grinned at his father.

"Mrs. Gordon's not the police, Geoff. But I told them the same thing I'll tell her," said Stoney. "I was at the airport in

Dallas waiting for the thunderstorm to slacken enough for my plane to get airborne."

"Thank you," I said and headed to the front door. "I appreciate your input on this. If you think of anything that might help, please give me a call." I walked slowly back to my car.

At the office, C.J. was still digging for the paper trails of the Haggens—both Paul and Deana. She's a computer genius. I'll admit horned toads and myself are highly allergic to computers and thereby we stay technology-challenged.

I filled C.J. in on my interviews with the Lykes duo. "Stoney reminds me a little of that television reporter. A slick, smooth operator. I wouldn't trust him as far as I could throw him."

"Whatever happened to him?"

"Who, Stoney Lykes?"

"No, silly. That reporter guy."

"I have no idea. My guess is he's still hanging around up in Big D. looking at himself on screen."

"Oh, I see. You don't want to discuss it?"

"Nothing to discuss. He turned out to be a jerk and I mentioned he might want to stay lost."

She laughed.

"Back to business, C.J. What more have you found out?"

"Stoney Lykes needs that insurance money badly. He'll have to file bankruptcy if he doesn't get it. Personal and business."

"Wait . . . how is the son able to afford going to law school?"

"His mother pays. She's married to a stockbroker and will never have money worries again," C.J. said.

"Interesting how both of Stoney's previous wives left him and fell into a golden lake while he's left clutching at a straw raft. I think he might begin to feel a bit resentful after a while."

"I checked his alibi," she said. "It's unshakable."

"Wonder if he could have paid someone to kill her? He still tops my list."

"Have you talked to Lieutenant Hays? Do we have a cause of death?"

"No. I haven't spoken with him. He's a bit angry with me because we're investigating."

"Why?" C.J. asked. "We do work for Bulldog and he represents Foster Kinney. We have every right to try and help our client."

"You know how blockheaded Larry can get at times; it's that Swedish blood in him," I said. "Bulldog says Nelda was asphyxiated."

"Any drugs?"

"The tox screens aren't complete yet. The crime-scene investigator had some suspicions and ordered a more detailed screening than usual."

"Okay. So who's next on our list?" C.J. said. "Deana and Paul Haggen?"

"Foster says Deana has filed for divorce, so we'll have to find out where Mr. Haggen went. She's living in her mother's house as is Foster."

C.J.'s voice changed when she mentioned Foster Kinney. "When are you going to tell me what's going on with you and Foster?" I asked.

C.J. snapped her head around and looked at me. "You think I got something going with the beast from the bayou?"

"No, and he's not so bad once you get over your initial shock. I got to where I don't even think about how he looks anymore."

"I agree."

"But you usually don't have so much sympathy for clients."

"Well, for one thing he reminds me of my grandpa. My grandpa was the biggest, ugliest old guy you ever saw," she said. "Black as a chunk of anthracite coal and a mean-looking dude. When Foster Kinney walked in, it was like my grandpa walked over my grave.

"And when he went to sleep in your office it was exactly like Grandpa. Grandpa would sit down anywhere anytime and drop off, sound asleep. In fifteen or twenty minutes he'd wake up and be ready to go full speed again for about three or four more hours. Guess seeing Foster sleeping got me all sentimental."

"I don't remember you ever talking about him, C.J." But she didn't answer because she'd slipped out of the room. I didn't bring it up when she returned.

We got two for the price of one at the Kinneys' house. Foster and Deana were both there. Without any plans or saying so, we split them up. C.J. and Deana Haggen went out into the rose garden, where I knew C.J. would get Deana talking about the roses and ask her questions in a most unobtrusive manner.

Foster and I sat in the front parlor of the old-fashioned house. The dark antique furniture and heavy brocade drapes felt oppressive.

"Stoney Lykes says you and he and Nelda all got along like one big happy family."

"He would imply that," said Foster. "It's mostly true but the two of them could get into each other's faces sometimes."

"What about?"

"Nelda still had the hots for him. They went to bed every chance they got."

"My gosh, you didn't try to stop it?" I asked.

"What could I do? Look at me. Would you want to crawl into bed with someone who looks like this?"

"Are you saying she never slept with you?"

"She had sex with me but only once every three or four months." Tears welled up in his eyes and rolled down his face. "I loved her and if I'd called her out about Stoney she would have left me forever."

"You've just given me a strong motive, Foster."

"I didn't do it. I don't know how I can live day after day without her. If my mother hadn't made me promise to get Deana straightened out and away from Paul Haggen, I don't know what I might do. But I've got to help my sister."

C.J. and Deana chose that moment to return, and soon afterwards we left, heading to the LaGrange Building and our office.

"I don't think she did it," said C.J.

"I don't think Foster did it either."

"Okay, so who have we got left?"

"No one really." I thought about it for a moment. "What about Foster's business partner. What was his name?"

"Osborne, wasn't it? Larry Hays has cleared him," C.J. said. "He was in the drunk tank the night she was killed. No way could he have murdered her."

"And the evidence against Foster is only circumstantial, so how will Bulldog create doubts?"

"I don't know. The woman is dead and nothing we've found yet leads to anyone who could have done it."

"Let's get the file out again," I said. "Surely we're missing something somewhere."

We spread the file out on C.J.'s desk. Notes and interviews and all the printed-up material on finances. We pored over it all for two solid hours and came up empty.

"Don't we have notes from Larry on how they retraced

Nelda's steps that night?" I asked and began reading papers C.J. handed to me. "This says she went to a club. The next morning her car's pulled from Town Lake with her in it. One report says she might have been drugged and mentions that date drug—rohypnol."

"And exactly where was she seen?"

I scanned the police duplicates. "The King of Hearts," I said, wondering why it sounded familiar. I checked some of my earlier notes but nothing rang any bells.

"Something's in my skull and I can't bring it up."

"Let's go have a beer and some barbecue and relax. The more you try to think the worse it gets—we both know that."

About an hour and two beers later I touched C.J.'s arm. "Geoffrey Lykes. That day I talked to him and his dad he had on a faded T-shirt but I remember some playing cards on it—maybe the King of Hearts."

"Any reason to suspect him?"

"Not really. Nothing ever pointed us in that direction."

"Let's go to the King of Hearts and see what we can find out," said C.J.

"We should call Larry and have him meet us. He's always happier when we let him in on things."

"Good idea."

It only took a few minutes for the bartender to confirm Geoff Lykes was a regular. The young man often met and left with pretty women.

"Did he ever meet and leave with this one?" Larry Hayes asked and handed over a photo of Nelda Kinney.

The man looked at it for only moments. "I remember that redheaded beauty. She was a little older than Geoff's usual pickup but a real looker."

Larry had put three steaks on the grill in my back yard when the telephone rang.

"Come on over," I said after listening briefly. "But you'll have to stop and buy three more steaks."

Larry and C.J. looked up expectantly. "Bulldog, Martha May, and Foster Kinney."

Thirty minutes later Larry put the final touches on the steaks and I finished tossing the expanded salad. While we ate, Larry told us about Geoffrey Lykes's confession.

"He'd always had a crush on Nelda. That night at the King of Hearts she walked in because she and Foster had had an argument. She was surprised to see him and more than pleased, he thought. He made a pass at her, which she rebuffed. He left for a few minutes and when he came back in he brought her a drink. He took her to the motel where he raped her. We suspect he didn't give her a strong enough dosage and she began struggling with him. Somehow he wound up smothering her with a pillow."

"I don't think he meant to do it," said Foster.

"I don't either," said Larry. "Geoff said he loved her and couldn't believe she didn't feel the same. Said she always rebuffed him but he knew she didn't mean it. He felt that she really wanted him.

"He told her that night, 'How can you refuse me? Your husband's a joke.' And he felt sure if she had him just once she'd fall madly in love."

I looked to see what effect those words had on Foster, but he'd gone to sleep. "Probably the best thing for him," I said.

After everyone except C.J. had gone I asked, "You going to tell me what else's going on with you?"

"What do you mean?"

"You've been so laid-back—you're driving me nuts."

"Guess I have been Miss Goody Two-Shoes lately, haven't I?"

"Yes and it scares me. Are you sick or something?"

"Well, when you were dating the TV news guy, I was

afraid you were going to fall for him and move up to Dallas."

"So? Even if I did get married and move to Dallas, things wouldn't change. We'd either move our office to Dallas or we'd keep an office here and open a second one up there."

"Are you serious?"

"You're stuck with me," I said. "Even if I were married, I wouldn't give up our partnership or my job. I like what I'm doing too much. Now, it's a moot point anyway because the dumb jerk is out of my life. Now if you were just trying to be nice to butter me up, it won't work."

C.J. laughed. "You ain't never lied, girl."

Marcia Muller has won the Anthony and American Mystery Awards, as well as the Shamus Award and the Life Achievement Award from the Private Eye Writers of America. The publication of each new McCone novel has become an anticipated event. The most recent was Both Ends of the Night *(Mysterious Press, 1997). Marcia shares her character's love of flying, and the basis of this story is a conversation she heard one day between two pilots.*

This story first appeared in the premier issue of Mary Higgins Clark *Mystery magazine. Marcia's husband is legendary P.I. writer Bill Pronzini.*

IF YOU CAN'T TAKE THE HEAT
A SHARON MCCONE STORY

by Marcia Muller

THE PRIVATE INVESTIGATION business has been glamorized to death by writers and filmmakers, but I can tell you firsthand that more often than not it's downright tedious. Even though I own a small agency and have three operatives to take on the scut work, I still conduct a fair number of surveillances while twisted into unnatural positions in the front seat of my car, or standing in the rain when any fool would go inside. Last month I leaped at the chance to take on a job with a little more pizzazz—and even then ended up to my neck in mud. Quite literally.

The job came to me from a contact at a small air-charter company—Wide Horizons—located at Oakland Airport's north field. I fly in and out of there frequently, both in the passenger's and the pilot's seat of my friend Hy Ripinsky's Citabria, and when you're around an airport a lot, you get to know people. When Wide Horizons' owner, Gordon Tillis, became nervous about a pair of regular customers, he called me into his office.

"Here's the problem," he told me. "For three months now, Sam Delaney's been flying what he calls 'a couple of babes' to Calistoga, in the Napa Valley. Always on the same day—the last Wednesday. On the flight there they're tense, clutch at their briefcases, don't talk much. A limo picks them up, they're gone a few hours. And when they come back, it's a whole different story."

"How so?"

"Well, I heard this from the airport manager up there, and Sam confirms it. They're excited, giddy with relief. Once it was obvious they'd been drinking too much; another time they had new hairdos and new clothes. They call a lot of attention to themselves."

"Sounds to me like a couple of rich women who like to fly, shop and do some wine tasting—and who don't hold their alcohol too well."

"It would sound that way to me too except for two things: the initial nervousness and the fact that they come back flush with cash."

"How do you know?"

"They pay cash for the charter, and one time I got a look into their briefcases. Even after the plane rental and a big tip for Sam, there was plenty left."

The cash did put a different spin on it. "I assume you think they may be carrying some kind of illegal substance?"

Gordon nodded.

"So why don't you tell Sam to search their cases? The FAA gives him the authority to, as pilot in command."

Gordon got up and went to the window, opened the blinds

and motioned at the field. "You see all those aircraft sitting idle? There're pilots sitting idle, too. Sam doesn't get paid when he doesn't fly; my overhead doesn't get paid while those planes are tied down. In this economy, neither of us can afford to lose paying customers."

"Security at the main terminal X-rays bags—"

"That's the main terminal; people expect it there. If Sam suddenly demands to go through those women's personal effects and word gets out, people might take their business elsewhere. If he does it in a way that embarrasses them—and, face it, Sam's not your most tactful guy—we're opening the door for a lawsuit."

"But you also don't want your planes used for illegal purposes. I see your problem."

In the end, Gordon and I worked out a plan where I would ride in the fourth seat of the Cessna that Sam would fly to Calistoga the next Wednesday. My cover story was that I was a new hire learning the ropes. I found myself looking forward to the job; it sounded a whole lot more interesting than the stakeout at a deadbeat dad's apartment that I had planned for the evening.

"They're babes, all right," Sam Delaney said, "but I'll let you judge for yourself." He grunted as he stowed his bag of takeout cartons in the back of the plane—his lunch, he'd informed me earlier. Business had been so bad recently that he couldn't even afford the relatively inexpensive airport diners.

Eating bad takeout food, I thought, probably accounted for the weight Sam had gained in the year or so that I'd known him. He'd always had a round face under his mop of brown curls, but now it resembled a chipmunk's, and his body was growing round to match. Poor guy had probably hired on with Wide Horizons thinking to build up enough hours for a lucrative job with the airlines; now he wasn't flying enough to go to a decent restaurant.

"Here they come," he whispered to me. "Look at them— they make heads turn, especially when they've had a few pops of that Napa Valley vino."

The women were attractive, and a number of heads did turn as they crossed from the charter service. But people take notice of any woman tripping across the tarmac in high heels, her brightly colored silk dress blowing in the breeze. We women pilots are pretty much confined to athletic shoes, shirts and pants in cotton and denim—and the darker the color, the less the gas and oil and grease stains will show.

The woman Sam introduced as Melissa Wells had shoulder-length red hair and looked as though she could have used a few more hours' sleep; Angie Holbrook wore her dark hair close-cropped and spoke in a clipped manner that betrayed her tension. Neither had more to say than basic greetings, and they settled into the back seats quickly, refusing headsets. During the thirty-minute flight, Melissa sipped at a large container of coffee she'd brought along and Angie tapped her manicured fingernails against her expensive leather briefcase. Sam insisted on keeping up the fiction that I was a new Wide Horizons pilot by chattering at me—even though over the noise of the engine the women couldn't hear a word we said through our linked earphones.

"Gordon's real strict about the paperwork. Plan's got to be on file, and complete. Weight-and-balance calculations, too. It's not difficult, though; each of us has got his own routes. Mine're the Napa and Sonoma Valleys. I'd like to get some of the longer trips, build up more hours that way, but I don't have enough seniority with the company. At least I get to look at some pretty scenery."

He certainly did. It was springtime, and the length of

California's prime wine-growing valley was in its splendor. Gentle hills looking as if someone had shaped bolt after bolt of green velvet to their contours; brilliant slashes of yellow where the wild mustard bloomed; orchards in pink and white flower. It made me want to snatch Sam's takeout and go on a picnic.

We touched down at Calistoga shortly before ten. The limo was there for Melissa and Angie, as was the rental car Wide Horizons had arranged for me. I waited till the limo cleared the parking lot, then jumped into the rental and followed, noting the other car's license number. It took the main road south for several miles, past wineries offering tours and tasting, then turned off onto a secondary road and drove into the hills to the west. I held back, allowing a sports car to get between us; the sports car put on its brakes abruptly as it whipped around a curve, and by the time I'd avoided a collision, the limo had turned through a pair of stone pillars flanking a steep driveway. The security gates closed, and the car snaked uphill and disappeared into the trees.

I pulled my rental into the shade of a scrub oak on the far side of the road and got out. It was very quiet there; I could hear only birds in a grove of acacia trees on the other side of the high stone wall. I walked its length, looking for something that would identify the owner of the heavily wooded property, but saw nothing and no way to gain access. Finally I went back to the car to wait it out.

Why did everything always seem to boil down to another stakeout?

And three hours later was when I found myself up to my neck in mud.

The limo had departed the estate in the hills and, after a few wine-tasting stops, deposited Melissa and Angie at Serenata

Spa in Calistoga. Calistoga is famed for its hot springs, and initially I'd fancied myself eavesdropping on the pair while floating in a tub of mineral water. But Calistoga is also famed for its mud baths, and in order to get close enough, I'd had to opt for my own private wallow. As I sank into the gritty stuff—stifling a cry of disgust—I could clearly hear Angie's voice through the flimsy pink partition. In spite of the wine they'd sampled, she sounded as tense as before.

"Well, what do you think? Honestly?"

"They're high on it."

"But are they high enough?"

"They paid us, didn't they?"

"Yes, but . . ."

"Angie, it was the best we could come up with. And I thought it was damn good."

"It's getting more difficult to come up with the stuff without making it too obvious what we're doing. And this idea of yours about image—the charter flight cuts into our profits."

"So I'll pay for it out of my share from now on. I love to fly. Besides, it's good for Carlos's people to see us getting off a private plane. It establishes us as a cut above the competition."

Silence from Angie.

I couldn't believe what I was hearing—people getting high; difficulty coming up with the stuff; Carlos . . . In the eighties, nine out of ten fictional arch villains dealing in terrorism and drugs had been named Carlos. Was I to assume that one had materialized in the Napa Valley?

"Angie," Melissa said impatiently, "what is with you this week?"

"I don't know. I'm really spooked about getting caught. Maybe it was the way Sarge looked at me last night when I told him we wouldn't be in to HQ today."

"He can't possibly suspect. He thinks we're out in the field, that's all."

"But all day, every fourth Wednesday? We're going to have to shift the deliveries around among our clients. If Sarge finds out we've been stealing—"

"Stop, already!"

Now what I couldn't believe was that they'd discuss such things in a public place. A sergeant, headquarters, being out in the field, deliveries, stealing . . . Was it possible that Angie and Melissa were a couple of undercover narcs who were selling the drugs they confiscated?

After a while one of them sighed. Melissa's voice said, "It's time."

"Yeah. Back to the ghetto."

"Listen, if you can't take the heat . . ."

"Funny. Very funny."

When we got back to Oakland I hung around Wide Horizons while Melissa paid for the flight in cash and gave Sam a two-hundred-dollar tip. Then I went to Gordon's office and made a verbal report, asking him to keep the information confidential until I'd collected concrete evidence. I'd have that for him, I said, before the women's next scheduled flight.

As I drove across the Bay Bridge to my offices at Pier 24½, one of the renovated structures along San Francisco's Embarcadero, I thought over what I'd heard at the mud baths. Something was wrong with the picture I'd formed. No specific detail, just the nagging sense that I'd overlooked an item of importance. I wanted to get my computer researcher, Mick Savage, started on the case as soon as possible.

The next morning, Mick began by accessing the Napa County property-tax assessor's records; he found that the estate in the hills belonged to Carlos Robles, a prominent vintner, whose wines even I—whose budget had only recently expanded to accommodate varieties with corks—had heard of. While Mick began tracking information on Robles in the periodicals indexes, I asked a contact on the SFPD to check with the National Crime Information Center for criminal histories on the vintner, Angie Holbrook and Melissa Wells. They all came up clean.

Mick began downloading news stories and magazine articles on Robles and his winery, and soon they formed an imposing stack on my desk. I had other work to do, so I called in Rae Kelleher, my field investigator, and asked her to check with our contacts at Bay Area police departments for detectives answering to the women's names or matching their descriptions. At six o'clock I hauled the stack of information on Robles's home to my brown-shingled cottage near the Glen Park district, curled up on the couch with my cats, and spent the evening reading.

If you believed Robles's press, he was a pillar of the Napa Valley community. His wines were considered excellent and frequently took gold medals at the various national competitions. Robles Vineyards hosted an elegant monthly wine, food and music event at their St. Helena Cellars, which was attended by prominent social and political figures, many of whom Carlos Robles counted among his close friends. I couldn't detect the slightest breath of scandal about his personal life; he'd been married to the same woman for thirty-five years, had four children and six grandchildren, and by all accounts was devoted to his family.

A paragon, if you believed his press . . .

As the next week passed, I dug deeper into the winemaker's life, but uncovered nothing significant, and I finally concluded that to get at the truth of the matter, I'd have to concentrate on the two women. Rae had turned up nothing through our PD contacts, so I asked Mick to do an area-wide search for their addresses—a lengthy and tedious process, as far as I was concerned, but he didn't seem to mind. Mick, who is also my nephew, has a relationship with his PowerBook that I, no fan of the infernal devices, sometimes find unnatural.

The search paid off, however: He turned up two Melissa Wellses and three Angela Holbrooks in various East Bay locations, from Berkeley to Danville. I narrowed it down by the usual method—surveillance.

The building I tailed Angie Holbrook to from her Berkeley apartment was vine-covered brick, set well back from the sidewalk on Shattuck Avenue, only two blocks from the famous Chez Panisse restaurant in the heart of what's come to be known as the Gourmet Ghetto. Polished brass lettering beside the front door said *HQ* Magazine. By the time I went inside and asked for Angie, I was putting it all together. And when she started to cry at the sight of my ID, I knew I had it right.

But even after Angie, Melissa Wells and I sat down over a cappuccino at Chez Panisse and discussed the situation, something still nagged at me. It wasn't till the Monday before their next flight to Calistoga that I figured out what it was, and then I had to scramble fast to come up with the evidence.

"Open their briefcases," I said to Sam Delaney. We were gathered in the office at Wide Horizons—Sam, Gordon Tillis, Melissa, Angie and me.

Sam hesitated, glancing at Gordon.

"Go ahead," he prompted. "You're pilot in command; you've got the FAA in your corner."

He hesitated some more, then flipped the catch of Melissa's case and raised its lid. Staring down into it, he said to me, "But . . . you told Gordon we had big trouble. This is . . . just papers."

"Right. Recipes and pictures of food."

"I don't get it. I thought the babes were into drugs."

Unfortunate word choice; the "babes" and I glared at him.

"Ms. Wells and Ms. Holbrook," I said, "are chefs and food writers for a very prestigious magazine, *HQ*—short for *Home Quarterly*. Unfortunately, like many prestigious publications, it doesn't pay very well. About a year ago Melissa and Angie started moonlighting—which is strictly against the policy set by the publisher, Sarge Greenfield."

"What's this got to do with—"

"I'm getting to that. For the past six months Melissa and Angie have been creating the menus for Robles Vineyards' wine, food and music events, using recipes they originally developed for *HQ*. Recipes that Sarge Greenfield would consider stolen. Since they didn't want to risk their jobs by leaving a paper trail, they arranged for Robles and their other clients to pay them in cash, upon acceptance of the proposed menus. Naturally they're always somewhat tense before their presentations to the clients, but afterward they're relieved. Relieved enough to indulge in wine tasting and spending."

Sam's eyes narrowed. "You say these recipes are stolen?"

"I suppose Greenfield could make a case for that."

"Then why don't you have them arrested?"

"Actually, the matter's already been settled." Angie and Melissa had decided to admit what they'd been doing to their employer, who had promptly fired them. They had now established their own catering firm and, in my opinion, would eventually be better off.

Gordon Tillis cleared his throat. "This strikes me as a good example of how we all rely too heavily on appearances in forming our opinions of people. Not a good practice; it's too easy to jump to the wrong conclusion."

Sam looked down, shuffling his feet. "Uh, I hope you ladies won't hold this against me," he said after a moment. "I'd still like to fly you up to the Valley."

"Fine with us," Angie replied.

"Speaking of that"—I glanced at my watch—"isn't it time you got going?"

Gordon and I walked out onto the field with them. The two men preflighting the Piper next to Sam's plane cast admiring glances at Angie and Melissa, and I was surprised when one of them winked at me. When we got to the Cessna, I snapped my fingers and said, "Oh, there's something I want to check, just out of curiosity. May I see the paperwork Sam gave you for this flight, Gordon?"

Sam frowned, but Gordon, as prearranged, handed the folder to me. I opened it to the weight-and-balance calculation that a pilot always works up in order to know the best way to arrange the passengers and their baggage.

"Uh-huh," I said. "Fuel, pilot . . . Sam, you've really got to stop eating that junk food! Passengers one and two, plus purses and briefcases. Additional baggage stowed aft. Hmmm."

"Just get to the point," Sam said, glancing around nervously.

"In a minute." I slipped inside the Cessna and checked the rear compartment. One bag of takeout. One large bag of takeout.

Sam was leaning in, reaching for my arm.

"Golden Arches?" I asked.

"KFC. Leave it!"

I picked it up. Heavy KFC.

"Sam," I said, "you really ought to go on a diet."

After the DEA agents who had been hanging around the
Piper with their warrant had opened the takeout containers
full of cocaine and placed Sam under arrest, Gordon, Angie,
Melissa and I slowly walked back to Wide Horizons in
subdued silence.

"What I don't understand," Gordon finally said, "is why
he always entered the stuff he was carrying on the weight-
and-balance."

"To cover himself. He knew if you caught him stowing
any package he hadn't entered, you'd start watching him.
But why he put down the accurate weight for the bag is
beyond me. Nobody would believe he could eat that much
for lunch—even with his weight problem."

Gordon sighed. "And here I thought Sam was just getting
fat because of bad eating habits, when all the while he was
eating too well on his profits from drug running."

I grinned at him. "Widening his horizons at the expense
of Wide Horizons," I said.